William Sloane Kennedy

Henry W. Longfellow

Biography, Anecdotes, Letters, Criticism

William Sloane Kennedy

Henry W. Longfellow
Biography, Anecdotes, Letters, Criticism

ISBN/EAN: 9783744687317

Printed in Europe, USA, Canada, Australia, Japan

Cover: Foto ©Raphael Reischuk / pixelio.de

More available books at **www.hansebooks.com**

HENRY W. LONGFELLOW

BIOGRAPHY ANECDOTE, LETTERS, CRITICISM

BY

W. SLOANE KENNEDY

AUTHOR OF "POEMS OF THE WEIRD AND THE MYSTICAL," ETC.

A Student of old books and days,
To whom all tongues and lands were known,
And yet a lover of his own;
With many a social virtue graced,
And yet a friend of solitude;
A man of such a genial mood
The heart of all things he embraced,
And yet of such fastidious taste,
He never found the best too good.
Tales of a Wayside Inn.

PORTRAIT AND ILLUSTRATIONS

CAMBRIDGE, MASS.

MOSES KING, PUBLISHER

HARVARD SQUARE

1882

Franklin Press:
RAND, AVERY, AND COMPANY,
BOSTON.

PREFACE.

IT is the part of a host who is entertaining a distinguished company to keep himself in the background, and see that his guests are properly introduced and grouped. What is true of a social gathering is true of such a work as the present: it is eclectic in character, a mosaic of the choicest thoughts of many minds, — for the most part digested and incorporated into a continuous narrative by one whose own personality is kept as much as possible out of view, — thus fully justifying the pleasant and characteristic remark of Oliver Wendell Holmes : " Your book," he said, " is like a huckleberry-pie, containing a great many good huckleberries and very little batter."

Materials for a biography of Longfellow were abundant and rich. Much had been written about him previous to his death ; and, after that event, reminiscences, anecdotes, and reviews appeared in profusion, both at home and abroad. Whatever was of permanent value and interest in this published material has been culled for the present work, due credit being given to the authors in every case. But scattered throughout the volume are very many anecdotes and reminiscences now for the first time published. They were obtained

by personal conversation and correspondence with friends of
the poet. Authorities have been consulted at first hand
whenever it was possible. Proof-slips were sent to those
whose writings are quoted in the volume, and many corrections and improvements have been made by them. Proof-
sheets of the entire volume have been carefully read in
detail by several eminent men of letters who were intimate
friends of the poet. To these gentlemen, and to all who have
given their generous aid and advice, the writer renders most
sincere thanks. Yet, after all, such work as this is its own
reward. It is impossible to study so pure a life as this volume commemorates, without receiving some of its lustre and
perfume into one's own nature.

Besides the full biographical, anecdotical, and critical information furnished in the following pages, there are also
given Mr. Longfellow's juvenile poems hitherto unpublished in America in book form, his letters to various
persons, a selection of poetical tributes, and a Longfellow
bibliography. It is believed that all readers of the juvenile
poems will find in their quiet beauty and tender purity of
sentiment abundant justification for their presentation here,
although they were not considered by their author to be
worthy of preservation in permanent form. It is interesting
to see, that, from the first note to the last of our poet's
songs, hardly one discord, or one instance of bad taste, can
be found.

CAMBRIDGE, MASS., May 15, 1882.

CONTENTS.

LIST OF ILLUSTRATIONS.

LONGFELLOW'S EARLY HOME.

HENRY WADSWORTH LONGFELLOW.

BIOGRAPHY.

INFLUENCES THAT MOULDED HIS CHARACTER.

IT is no accident that the (writings of the six chief New England poets — Emerson, Longfellow, Whittier, Bryant, Holmes, and Lowell — should be characterized by exquisite moral purity. All of these poets, except Whittier, are of Puritan stock; and their poems are nearly all suffused with a subtle moral atmosphere,) — as are also the romances and stories of Hawthorne.

The (town of Portland, Me., where on the 27th of February, 1807, Henry Wadsworth Longfellow was born, and the town of Brunswick, where, as a student in Bowdoin College, he passed some years of his youth, are, like the towns of Connecticut, pervaded by a spirit of the most austere Puritanism. In the days of Longfellow's boyhood, this stern religious spirit was all-dominant. Each community, in those days, was a little theocracy. Tocqueville rightly says that the New England town-meeting was the germinal unit of American democracy; but the town-meeting was ruled by the pulpit and the pew. William Willis, in his history of Portland, tells us that as late as the first quarter of the present century public dancing in that town was prohibited by law, and cases of actual arrest for the violation of the law are noted. The inhabitants fought with tireless persistency all attempts to introduce theatres and theatrical performances into the town. It was not until 1831 that a theatre was built in Free Street. It was a small affair, and never flourished, and in 1836 was sold to a Baptist society for a church.

There were very few public amusements in the Portland of that day, and such as were in vogue were of a very homespun character. Mr. Willis says (p. 783) that "it was common for clubs and social parties to meet at the tavern in those days; and Mrs. Greele's, in Congress Street, was a place of most fashionable resort for both old and young wags before, as well as after, the Revolution. It was the *Eastcheap* of Portland, and was as famous for baked beans as the 'Boar's Head' was for sack." In an old number of The Cumberland Gazette we read of a "spinning-bee," given at the house of the Rev. Samuel Deane. Sixty fair hands made music with the humming of sixty wheels, and near the close of the day the company presented to Mrs. Deane two hundred and twenty-four skeins of cotton and linen yarn spun that day. Homely amusements enough, these!

The Wheelers, in their history of Brunswick, Me., say (p. 214) that "about 1821 an attempt was made to introduce a bass-viol into the church of the First Parish; but the project was thwarted by Mr. William Randall, an influential member of the society, who declared that he 'wouldn't hear a fiddle in God's house.'"

Wagons were not introduced into Brunswick until 1816 or 1817, and there had been but two or three carts in the town previous to that date. The first carpet ever made in Topsham (a neighboring village) was made in 1799 by Miss Margaret Rogers, the late Mrs. Nathaniel Greene. The first theatrical performance in Brunswick was given in 1828, for one week, at Nichols Hall, by a company of comedians from the Tremont Theatre, Boston.[1] In 1826 a man named John Cleaves Symmes gave a course of three lectures on an interior world which he maintained was open to voyagers in the southern hemisphere. "*His lectures were well attended, and were listened to with respect and interest*"!

Such were some of the surroundings of Longfellow's boyhood. The kind of society described in the local histories above quoted is similar to that depicted in books on Connecticut history and antiquities; such, for instance, as the pleasant little book entitled "New Connecticut," recently published by Mr. A. Bronson Alcott; or in such works as the Life of Horace Bushnell.

THE POET'S PATERNAL ANCESTORS.

Let us now turn our attention first to the paternal, and then to the maternal ancestry of the poet. The American ancestor of the Longfellow family was William Longfellow of Newbury, Mass., who came to this country from Yorkshire, Eng., about the year 1651. He was the great-great-great-grandfather of the poet, and the lineal succession is as follows : —

William, merchant.	Stephen (3), judge.
Stephen (1), blacksmith.	Stephen (4), lawyer and legislator.
Stephen (2), teacher, etc.	Henry Wadsworth, the poet.

[1] The entertainment of the evening consisted of Tobin's comedy of "The Honeymoon," and the farce of "The Young Widow."

Of William Longfellow this much is known, that he was a merchant in the parish of Byfield, Newbury; that he married Anne Sewall; and that in 1690, as ensign of a Newbury company, he took part in the ill-fated expedition of Sir William Phips against Quebec. The fleet, on its return, was overtaken by a violent storm in the Gulf of St. Lawrence, and the vessel containing the Newbury company went ashore at the desolate island of Anticosti. William Longfellow and nine others were drowned.

Of Stephen (1) the blacksmith, little is known. He married Abigail Thompson of Marshfield.

His son, Stephen (2), graduated at Harvard in 1742. Stephen (2) was the first of the Portland Longfellows, coming to the town, April 11, 1745, by invitation of Parson Thomas Smith, to act as teacher. Portland was then called the Neck. Stephen was schoolmaster of the town for fifteen years (1745–60). His father, dying in 1764, left him a small legacy. The son sent the silver coin to Boston for the purpose of having it converted into a memorial silver-service. Unfortunately the vessel by which it was sent was lost, and the coin with it. But Stephen immediately made up the amount, and sent it to Boston, this time successfully, where it was manufactured, by the silversmith John Butler, into a tankard, a can, and two porringers, each piece bearing the initials S. L., and the words *ex dono patris.* "The tankard has been preserved; and one of the porringers, after a somewhat eventful history, has found its way back into the family, and is one of the treasures of the poet's brother, Alexander W. Longfellow." Stephen (2) held many important town offices. It is interesting to find that his handwriting,

like that of his great-grandson the poet, was beautiful
and clear, "symbolical of the purity and excellence of
his own moral character." He married Tabitha Brag-
don of York in 1749, and died at Gorham in 1790.

Stephen (3), son of Stephen (2), was born in 1750,
married Patience Young of York, and died at his home
in Gorham in 1824. He represented Gorham in the
Massachusetts General Court for eight years; was for
several years senator from Cumberland County, and
judge of the Court of Common Pleas from 1797 to 1811.
" He was a fine-looking gentleman, with the bearing of
the old school ; was erect, portly, rather taller than the
average, had a strongly marked face, and his hair was
tied behind in a 'club' with black ribbon. To the
close of his life he wore the old-style dress, — knee-
breeches, a long waistcoat, and white top-boots. He
was a man of sterling qualities of mind and heart, great
integrity, and sound common-sense."

Stephen (4), son of Stephen (3), was born in Gorham
in 1776, and was the father of Henry Wadsworth Longfellow, the poet. Stephen (4) entered Harvard College
in 1794, and graduated in 1798. Daniel Appleton
White, a college friend, said of him, that "he was evidently a well-bred gentleman when he left the paternal
mansion for the university. He seemed to breathe the
atmosphere of purity as his native element; while his
bright intelligence, buoyant spirits, and social warmth
diffused a sunshine of joy that made his presence always
gladsome." He graduated with rank and honors. Returning to Portland, he entered the law-office of Salmon
Chase (an uncle of Chief Justice Salmon P. Chase), and
in 1804 married Zilpah, eldest daughter of Gen. Peleg
Wadsworth. Stephen's sister, Abigail Longfellow, had

married Samuel Stephenson, a rich merchant of Portland. In the winter of 1806–7, Mr. Stephenson having
gone to the West Indies on business, his wife invited
her brother Stephen and his wife to spend the winter at
her house, which they did ; and there Henry Wadsworth
Longfellow was born, Feb. 27, 1807.[1] He was named
from his uncle, Lieut. Henry Wadsworth of the United
States navy, who lost his life at Tripoli on the night
of Sept. 4, 1804, in a gallant attempt to destroy the
enemy's flotilla by a fire-ship.

In the spring of 1807 Gen. Peleg Wadsworth, the
maternal grandfather of the future poet, removed to
Hiram on the Saco River in order to occupy and improve seventy-five hundred acres of wild land granted
him in consideration of his military services. Accordingly Stephen Longfellow took up his residence
in the Wadsworth house at Portland, and made it
thenceforth his home. This venerable brick building is
still standing, and, together with the Stephenson house
where the poet was born, attracts the attention of most
visitors to the city. Henry Wadsworth Longfellow
was the second son, the first being named Stephen.
Besides these there were afterwards born two other
sons, Alexander Wadsworth and Samuel, and four
daughters, Elizabeth, Anne, Mary, and Ellen. The old
Wadsworth (or Longfellow) house on Congress Street
is now occupied by the poet's sister, Mrs. Anne L.
Pierce, and contains many interesting relics of the
Longfellow family. The Stephenson house (the poet's
birthplace) is also still standing on its original site, corner of Fore and Hancock Streets. It is now used as
a tenement-house.

[1] It is a fact not generally known, that the poet Nathaniel Parker
Willis was also born in Portland in this same year.

Before passing on to speak of Gen. Peleg Wadsworth and the other maternal ancestors of the poet, let us return for a moment to speak of the Byfield Longfellows in Newbury, Mass. Byfield is the original "home-nest" of the family. It is an interesting fact that the families of the two poets, Whittier and Longfellow, should have originated in the same neighborhood. The Longfellow homestead in Byfield is only about five miles distant from the old Whittier homestead in East Haverhill. Near Byfield were born Cornelius Conway Felton, president of Harvard University; Professor Parker Cleaveland, Judge Tenney of Maine, the poet Albert Pike, and Chief Justice Parsons. The Byfield Longfellows are prominent in local politics. One of them, Joseph, who is quite a wit, says that when he was a young man he was ashamed of his name, as he was literally a Long-fellow. But when Henry Wadsworth became famous, and people asked him if he were a kinsman of his, he became proud of the name.

In February, 1882, Mr. Horace F. Longfellow of Byfield wrote to Mr. S. T. Pickard, one of the editors of "The Portland Transcript," the following letter, descriptive of the old homestead: —

DEAR SIR, — At the request of my father, Joseph Longfellow, I answer yours of the 14th in regard to the old Longfellow house at Byfield, Mass. It was probably built by William Longfellow, about 1676, at or about the time of his marriage with Anne Sewall. The location of the house is unsurpassed. It is situated on a sightly eminence at the very head of tide-water on the river Parker, the sparkle of whose waters, as they go tumbling over the falls, adds a picturesqueness to the natural beauty of the scenery that lies spread out on either hand, — hill and dale, forest and field, the outgoing or incoming tide.   Nature was lavish here; and young Longfellow, appreciating it all, erected the old house to which he took his young bride.   It still stands, although two centuries and more have passed since its oaken frame was put together.   It has not been occupied for twenty-odd years, and, of course, is in a dilapidated condition.   I was born under the old roof-tree myself; and so were my father, grandfather, great-grandfather, and great-great-grandfather (son of William) before me.   The large chimney was taken down years ago; a part of the house itself has been removed; but

"The scenes of my childhood are brought fresh to my mind,"

and I can see the old weather-beaten house, with its rear roof descending nearly to the ground, the long kitchen with its low ceiling and wide fireplace, the big brick oven in which were baked the Thanksgiving pies and puddings (I can taste them now), the big "best room," the winding stairs, the old spinning-wheel in the attic, the well-curb and its long sweep at the end of the house, in front the granite horse-block, and the large elm spreading over all.   The old elm still lives, but is feeling the effects of age.   The old elm and the house will end their existence together, and soon.

Very truly,

HORACE F. LONGFELLOW.

HIS MATERNAL ANCESTORS.

Gen. Peleg Wadsworth, the maternal grandfather of the poet, was the son of Deacon Peleg Wadsworth of Duxbury, Mass., and was fifth in descent from Christopher Wadsworth, who came from England and settled in Duxbury previous to 1632.   Peleg Wadsworth, jun., was born at Duxbury in 1748, and graduated at Harvard College in 1769.   In 1772 he married Elizabeth Bartlett of Plymouth, Mass.   They had ten children,

THE BIRTHPLACE OF LONGFELLOW,

CORNER OF FORE AND HANCOCK STREETS, PORTLAND, MAINE.

one of whom was Zilpah, the mother of the poet. Zilpah inherited the blood of four or five of the "May-flower" Pilgrims, including Elder Brewster and Capt. John Alden, immortalized in the "Courtship of Miles Standish." Gen. Peleg Wadsworth served with great distinction in the Revolutionary war. He was second in command in the ill-fated expedition of 1779 against the British at Castine, Me., on Penobscot Bay; and the next year, while in command on the coast, with headquarters at Camden, a town situated on the same bay, he was captured by the British, and imprisoned in the fort at Castine. After four months' imprisonment he made his escape in the following manner: —

"Major Burton," says the Hon. William Gould, "a resident of St. George's River, who had served the previous summer under Gen. Wadsworth, was a prisoner in the same room with him. After a long preparation, and after obtaining a gimlet from the fort barber, they made their escape on the night of the 18th of June, 1781, by passing through an opening previously and laboriously made in the board ceiling with the gimlet, the marks of which were filled with bread. They adroitly evaded the sentinels, but got separated in the darkness, both, however, getting off safely. They kept much in the shoal-water of the shores, to prevent being tracked by the bloodhounds which were kept at the fort for that purpose. The two friends came accidentally together on the next day. Major Burton dropped a glove in the darkness, which pointed out to their pursuers the route they had taken on leaving the fort. They, however, found a canoe, got across the river, and pursued their course through the woods by a pocket-compass to the settlements, and were assisted to Thomaston, after much suffering."

The appearance of Gen. Wadsworth after the close of the Revolutionary war is thus described by the mother of the poet Longfellow: —

"Perhaps you would like to see my father's picture as it was when we came to this town after the war of the Revolution, in 1784. Imagine to yourself a man of middle size, well proportioned, with a military air, and who carried himself so truly that many thought him tall. His dress, a bright scarlet coat, buff small-clothes and vest, full ruffled bosom, ruffles over the hands, white stockings, shoes with silver buckles, white cravat bow in front; hair well powdered, and tied behind in a club, so called. . . . Of his character others may speak; but I cannot forbear to claim for him an uncommon share of benevolence and kind feeling.

"Z. W. L.

"JANUARY, 1848."

It was the son of the Gen. Wadsworth described in this letter who perished at Tripoli, and from whom the poet Longfellow received his baptismal name.

From such noble ancestors descended, and in such sternly religious communities educated, the poet Longfellow grew up. From such a stem sprang the beautiful blossom of his song.

THE PORTLAND OF THE POET'S BOYHOOD.

But an account of the boyhood of Longfellow would be incomplete without a few more picturesque details of the Portland of that time. It has had its eras of great commercial prosperity, as, for instance, during the last decade of the preceding century. At present it is a flourishing seaport city, beautifully situated on the broad Casco Bay, with its quiet waters and numerous beautiful islands. Landward the landscape stretches away for eighty miles to the White Mountains, with

Mount Washington indistinctly visible on the far horizon. The town, as it was in Longfellow's boyhood, is thus described by Mr. Edward Henry Elwell: "It lay on the narrow peninsula, or Neck, in the depression between the two hills which mark its extremities, — Munjoy and Bramhall. In a square house, standing on the one hand within a stone's throw of the spot where the first settler landed and built his cabin in 1632, and on the other not much farther from the site of old Fort Loyal, our poet was born. . . . It was a pleasant site, not then, as now, hemmed in by new-made land encroaching on the sea. It looked out on the waters of our beautiful bay, commanding a view of those

> — ' islands that were the Hesperides
> Of all my boyish dreams.'

Near by was the beach, the scene of many a baptism on ' the Lord's day.' "

"On Indian Point, where the Grand Trunk bridge leaves the hill, stood seven or eight lofty ancient pine-trees, and in the high branches the fish-hawks were wont to build their nests. The boys went a-gunning ' back of the Neck,' and shot plovers and curlews and sand-birds, which visited the shore in great numbers."

"With the revival of commerce, after the war, trade with the West India Islands sprang up, and low-decked brigs carried out cargoes of lumber and dried fish, bringing back sugar, rum, and molasses. This trade made lively scenes on Long Wharf and Portland Pier. From lack of system, and the appliances of steam, every thing was then done with great noise and bustle, and by main strength. The discharging of a cargo of molasses set the town in an uproar. The wharves resounded with the songs of the negro stevedores hoisting the hogsheads from the hold without the aid of a winch; the long trucks, with heavy loads, were tugged by straining horses, under the whips and loud cries of the truckmen. Liquor was lavishly supplied to laboring men, and it made them turbulent and uproarious. Adding to the busy tumult were the teams coming into town by the two principal avenues, — over Deering's Bridge and up Green Street, or over Bramhall's Hill by way of Horse Tavern, — bringing charcoal from Waterborough, shooks from Fryeburg, Hiram, and Baldwin, hoop-poles, heading, cord-wood, and screwed hay; and the Vermonters, in their blue woollen frocks, bringing in their red pungs round hogs, butter, and cheese."

Rev. Elijah Kellogg, jun., gives a lively picture of Portland at this time, on a winter morning: "Then you might have seen lively times. A string of board-teams from George Libby's to Portland Pier; sleds growling; surveyors running about like madmen, a shingle in one hand and a rule-staff in the other; cattle white with frost, and their nostrils hung with icicles; teamsters screaming and hallooing; Herrick's tavern, and all the shops in Huckler's Row, lighted up, and the loggerheads hot to give customers their morning dram."

It is with such scenes as these rising in his memory that Longfellow sings, in his poem entitled

MY LOST YOUTH.

I remember the black wharves and the slips,
  And the sea-tides tossing free;
And Spanish sailors with bearded lips,
And the beauty and mystery of the ships,
  And the magic of the sea.

> And the voice of that wayward song
>   Is singing and saying still :
> " A boy's will is the wind's will,
> And the thoughts of youth are long, long thoughts."
>
> I remember the bulwarks by the shore,
>   And the fort upon the hill ;
> The sunrise gun, with its hollow roar,
> The drum-beat, repeated o'er and o'er,
>   And the bugle wild and shrill.
>   And the music of that old song
>   Throbs in my memory still :
>   " A boy's will is the wind's will,
> And the thoughts of youth are long, long thoughts."
>
> I remember the sea-fight far away,
>   How it thundered o'er the tide !
> And the dead captains, as they lay
> In their graves, o'erlooking the tranquil bay,
>   Where they in battle died.
>   And the sound of that mournful song
>   Goes through me with a thrill :
>   " A boy's will is the wind's will,
> And the thoughts of youth are long, long thoughts."

" Portland was a lumber-port, driving a brisk little trade with more tumult and hurrah than now accompanies the transaction of ten times the amount of business then done. In addition to its lumber-trade it had its distilleries, its tanneries, its rope-walks, and its pottery, — the latter two of which so impressed themselves upon the memory of the boy Longfellow that in after-years they suggested his poems, ' The Ropewalk ' and ' Kéramos,' the song of the potter.[1] Men now living,

---

[1] Mr. H. H. Clark, who, as the proof-reader at the University Press, read the proof of "Kéramos," says that Mr. Longfellow spoke to him of having visited the old potter at his wheel under the hill, and of seeing him go to and fro under the branches of the trees, as described in the first stanza of the poem.

going back in memory to those bustling days, will tell you those were the times when business was lively, and think it but a dull town now, though with five times the population and many times the amount of business."

There was a good deal of intellectual life in the town. In 1790 the Rev. Dr. Samuel Deane published his New-England Farmer, or Georgical Dictionary, which was for a long time a standard work on matters of agriculture. In 1816 Enoch Lincoln of Portland published his poem, The Village, containing over two thousand lines, and "remarkable for its advanced moral sentiment, anticipating many of the reforms of our day, as well as for its erudition and its evenly sustained poetical merit."

Of the social life of the period, Mr. Elwell thus speaks : —

"In social life the marked distinctions of the ante-Revolutionary period are giving way under the influence of our democratic institutions. Cocked hats, bush wigs, and knee-breeches are passing out, and pantaloons have come in. Old men still wear queues and spencers, and disport their shrunken shanks in silk stockings. A homely style of speech prevails among the common people. Old men are 'Daddies,' old ladies are 'Marms,' ship-masters are 'Skippers,' and school-teachers are 'Masters.' There are no stoves, and open fires and brick ovens are in universal use. The fire is raked up at night, and rekindled in the morning by the use of flint, steel, and tinder-box. Nearly every house has its barn, in which is kept the cow, pastured during the day on Munjoy. The boys go after the cows at nightfall, driving them home through the streets. There are few private carriages kept in town, and fewer public vehicles. When, in 1824, Gen. Lafayette visits the town, and Gov. Parris gives a ball in his honor, at his residence on Bridge Street, — the site of which is now covered by the beautiful lawn attached to the residence of H. P. Storer, Esq., — a storm coming up prevents the attendance of a great part of the company invited, because of the distance out of town and the scarcity of carriages. The coin in circulation is chiefly Spanish dollars, halves, quarters, pistareens, eighths, and sixteenths, the last two of which are known as ninepence and fourpence 'alfpennies. Federal money is so little recognized that prices are still reckoned in shillings and pence, — two-and-six, three-and-ninepence, seven-and-sixpence. It is a journey of two days, by the accommodation stage, to Boston, costing eight to ten dollars. If you go by the mail-stage you may be bounced through, with aching bones, in the hours between two o'clock in the morning and ten at night. Or you may take a coaster, and perhaps be a week on the passage. The old Portland Gazette and The Eastern Argus come out once a week, and the town-crier supplies the place of the daily newspaper. There are few amusements. Theatrical performances have been voted down in town-meeting, and prohibited under heavy penalties; but by 1820 the poor players venture to make an occasional appearance, and set up their scenery in Union Hall. It is not until 1830 that a theatre is built, and it is soon converted into a church. In the summer there are excursions by sailing-boats to the islands, with an occasional capsize and loss of life. In the winter, merry sleighing parties drive out to 'Broad's' for a dance and a supper. These are merry times, especially if the party is snowed up, and compelled to remain over night.

Flip and punch flow freely, and sobriety is the exception rather than the rule."

THE POET'S BOYHOOD.

Of Mr. Longfellow's early boyhood not many details are known. He manifested a turn for poetry and poetical composition at a very early age. It has been several times stated that the first poem of his, known to be preserved in manuscript, is. that called " Venice, an Italian Song," and dated Portland Academy, March 17, 1820, when he was hardly thirteen. But the writer is informed by Col. Thomas Wentworth Higginson that this is a mistake. The poem is by Samuel Rogers, and may be found in his printed works. The poem had only been copied by the boy-poet as an exercise in penmanship. His first published poem was entitled " Lovell's Fight,"[1] printed in the Poet's Corner of a Portland paper previous to his entering college. Other poems of his also appeared in the local papers at about the same time.

The first school that young Longfellow attended was kept by " Marm Fellows," in a small brick schoolhouse on Spring Street. Later he went to the town school on Love Lane, now Center Street; and soon after, to the private school of Nathaniel H. Carter, in a little one-story house on the west side of Preble Street, now Congress. Afterward he attended the Portland Academy, under the same master, and also under the mastership of Bezaleel Cushman, who had Jacob Abbott as one of

---

[1] The scene of Lovell's fight (or " Lovewell " as it used to be called) was but a few miles from Hiram. Here, at the Wadsworth homestead, the boy Longfellow spent many of his summers. It is known that the few of Lovell's men who escaped returned down the road to Ossipee past the old Wadsworth house.

his assistants. Here he fitted for college; and at the age of fourteen, in the year 1821, he entered Bowdoin College at Brunswick, Me., in company with his elder brother Stephen.

AT BOWDOIN COLLEGE.

The poet once told Mr. John Langdon Sibley, librarian *emeritus* of Harvard College, that, if his father had not been a trustee of Bowdoin, he would have been sent to Harvard College, and that he would have then been in Mr. Sibley's class.

The Bowdoin class contained sons of some of the first families of New England. Among Longfellow's classmates were such young men as Nathaniel Hawthorne, George B. Cheever, John S. C. Abbott, and others. One of his classmates, the Rev. David Shepley, D.D., says of him, "He gave diligent heed to all departments of study in the prescribed course, and excelled in all, while his enthusiasm moved in the direction it has taken in subsequent life. His themes, felicitous translations of Horace, and occasional contributions to the press, drew marked attention to him, and led to the expectation that his would be an honorable career." The Hon. J. W. Bradbury, another classmate, describes him as having a "slight, erect figure, delicate complexion, and an intelligent expression of countenance. He was always a gentleman in his deportment, and a model in his character and habits." Professor A. S. Packard, D.D., of Bowdoin College, remembers Longfellow as "an attractive youth, with auburn locks, clear, fresh, blooming complexion, and, as might be expected, of well-bred manners and bearing."

While in college he wrote a number of poems, many

of which were first published in The United-States
Literary Gazette, and thence found their way into the
daily and weekly papers of the country. This periodical,
published at New York and Boston simultaneously, was
much in favor with the poets of that day. It was
founded by the late Theophilus Parsons; but at the
time Longfellow sent in his poems it was edited by
James Gordon Carter of Boston (Harvard, 1820), well
known from his relation to the public schools. Longfellow's poems were probably anonymous; for once,
when Professor Packard was spending an evening with
Mr. Carter in Boston, the latter asked him who that
young man was at Bowdoin who sent him such fine
poetry. Professor Packard thinks Longfellow was at
this time a junior in college.

Longfellow graduated second in a class of thirty-seven,
Joseph S. Little of Portland being first. Professor
Packard says: "Of his standing as a scholar in college,
one may judge from his assignment at Commencement
of an English oration, when fewer parts of that rank
were given than of late years. His was the first claim
to the poem; but, as the poem had no definite rank, it
was thought due to him, since his scholarship bore a
high mark, that he should receive an appointment
which placed his scholarship beyond question." His
English oration had for its subject, "Our Native
Writers." "Chatterton and his Poems" had been assigned him as a subject, but was afterwards changed,
and the change noted in ink on the programmes. The
class poem was read by Frederic Mellen. During the
first half of his senior year, Longfellow read the poem
before the Peucinian Literary Society of the college.
Hawthorne embodied some features of Bowdoin College life in his suppressed novel, "Fanshawe."

It is now known that Longfellow received one dollar each for his poems contributed to The Literary Gazette, while William Cullen Bryant received two dollars a poem, a sum fixed by himself.[1] For Sandalp on, the poet received by way of payment a year's subscription to the paper in which it was published.

In 1826, the year after Longfellow graduated, there was published a little volume entitled Miscellaneous Poems, selected from the United-States Literary Gazette. The contributors to it were Bryant, Longfellow, Mellen, Percival, Dawes, and Jones. A writer in the New-York Evening Post, understood to be Col. Higginson, remarks that this volume "offered a curious contrast to that equally characteristic volume of 1794, The Columbian Muse, whose poets were Barlow, Trumbull, Freneau, Dwight, Humphreys, and a few others; not a single poem or poet being held in common by the two collections." In the Gazette collection were fourteen of Longfellow's poems, all written before he was nineteen. Among them were The Hymn of the Moravian Nuns, and The Rivulet: these and four others are retained in the collected works of the poet to this day.[2]

Longfellow at first began the study of law in his father's office in Portland, but took little interest in his studies. In 1826 he received an invitation to fill, at Bowdoin College, a chair which had been almost created for him; namely, a professorship of modern languages and literature. The establishment of such a

---

[1] See the Reminiscences of Gen. James Grant Wilson, p. 215 of this volume.

[2] For Mr. Longfellow's juvenile poems never published in this country in book form, see p. 335, where all of them will be found in full, with interesting details concerning them.

chair as this was considered at that time to be quite
an innovation ; the languages and literatures of Greece
and Rome having been considered, from time imme-
morial, as entirely sufficient for the culture and discipline of the young mind. Mrs. Bowdoin had, however,
some years before, given one thousand dollars as the
beginning of a fund for such a chair. Mr. Longfellow,
when appointed, was only nineteen years of age ; and he
at once set off for Europe, visiting and studying for
nearly four years in Spain, France, Italy, and Germany,
in order to prepare himself for his duties. In Pierce's
Memoir and Letters of Charles Sumner is recorded
the fact that Longfellow met Sumner at Marseilles in
1827, and they journeyed together to Rome. Sumner
afterwards became distantly connected with Longfellow
through Harriet Coffin Sumner, the second wife of
Nathan Appleton of Boston, Mr. Longfellow's second
wife being a daughter of Nathan Appleton by his first
wife.

In 1829 he returned to America, and entered upon
his duties at Bowdoin College. Such a rare opportunity for future success must have been appreciated
by him. The tradition is, that this appointment was
given to Longfellow as a result of the impression made
upon a member of the college examining committee by
his translation of one of Horace's odes. He entered
upon his professional duties with zeal and fidelity. The
department was a new one, and there was a lack of
suitable text-books. Accordingly he prepared "Elements of French Grammar. Translated from the
French of C. F. L'Homond." (Boston: 1830.) "Syllabus de la Grammaire Italienne." (Boston: 1832.)
"Cours de la Langue Française" (Boston: 1832), in-

cluding (1) "Le Ministre de Wakefield" and (2) "Proverbes Dramatiques." "Saggi de' Novellieri Italiani d' Ogni Secolo: Tratti da' più celebri scrittori, con brevi notizie intorno alla vità di ciascheduno." (Boston: 1832.) He also published "Coplas de Manrique. A Translation from the Spanish." (Boston: Allen & Ticknor, 1833.) Included in this volume are translations by Mr. Longfellow of sonnets of Lope de Vega and others. The poem was prefaced by an essay on Spanish Moral and Devotional Poetry, which had previously appeared in The North-American Review, xxxiv. 277. (For a complete list of Mr. Longfellow's contributions to The North-American Review, see the bibliography appended to this volume.) George Ticknor, in his History of Spanish Literature, speaks of the translation of "Coplas" as "a beautiful one." This edition is now very rare. Mr. Thomas Niles (of the firm of Roberts Brothers), the Boston publisher, says that when he first went into the book-trade, many years ago, he found in his stock one hundred and fifty copies of "Coplas de Manrique." He does not remember what became of these books, but thinks they went to the paper-mill, being then unsalable. They would now, probably, be worth their weight in gold. The book was a thin duodecimo, with Longfellow's name as Bowdoin professor on the title-page. The translation was afterwards slightly altered by the poet. The historian Prescott said of it, "Mr. Longfellow's version is well calculated to give the English reader a correct notion of the Castilian bard, and, of course, a very exaggerated one of the literary culture of the age." There was a previous version of the "Coplas" by Bowring, but Longfellow's was considered its superior.

At the Bowdoin College commencement, in 1832, Mr. Longfellow delivered the poem before the Phi Beta Kappa Society. In 1833 also appeared the first two numbers of Outre-Mer; or, A Pilgrimage to the Old World by an American (Hilliard, Gray, & Co., Boston), and two years later the whole work was published by Harper & Brothers of New-York City; Mr. Longfellow selling it to them for five hundred dollars. It is written in a most charming vein. The light and lambent humor is like that of Irving or Lamb or Sterne. There is a buoyancy in the style like that of the blue sky, and a freshness as of clover or dew. The work is picturesque, antiquarian; golden and mellow as the shield of its *Lion d'Or*, full of quiet *causerie* about mediæval legends, trouvères, and old chansons. Quaint characters are depicted; and the beautiful scenes of classic Italy, sunburnt Spain, and vine-covered France are lovingly portrayed. There is a chapter on "Old Spanish Ballads," and in the second volume appears the translation of the stanzas of Don Jorge Manrique on the death of his father Don Rodrigo.

The title of the book was probably suggested by Thibaut, who in his "Roi de Navarre" says, —

> "Si j'ai long tems été en Romanie,
> Et *outre-mer* fait mon pèlerinage."

On the title-page appears this quotation from old Sir John Maundeville : —

"I have passed manye landes and manye yles and contrees, and cherched manye fulle straunge places, and have ben in manye a fulle gode honourable companye. Now I am comen home to reste. And thus recordynge the tyme passed, I have fulfilled these thynges and putte hem wryten in this boke, as it woulde come into my mynde."

To the Epistle Dedicatory is prefixed this stanza from Hurdis : —

> " The cheerful breeze sets fair : we fill our sail,
> And scud before it. When the critic starts,
> And angrily unties his bags of wind,
> Then we lay to, and let the blast go by."

In the course of his remarks in the Epistle Dedicatory the author says : —

" Besides, what perils await the adventurous author who launches forth into the uncertain current of public favor in so frail a bark as this! The very rocking of the tide may overset him; or peradventure some freebooting critic, prowling about the great ocean of letters, may descry his strange colors, hail him through a gray goose-quill, and perhaps sink him without more ado."

The book is conceived (in a playful and merry vein) to be a series of tales told by a pilgrim, — like those told by palmers in baronial castles of old. The first chapter begins thus : —

" ' Lystenyth, ye godely gentylmen, and all that ben hereyn ! ' I am a pilgrim benighted on my way, and crave a shelter till the storm is over, and a seat by the fireside in this honorable company. As a stranger I claim this courtesy at your hands; and will repay your hospitable welcome with tales of the countries I have passed through in my pilgrimage. . . . I have traversed France from Normandy to Navarre; smoked my pipe in a Flemish inn; floated through Holland in a Trekschuit; trimmed my midnight lamp in a Ger-

man university ; wandered and mused amid the classic
scenes of Italy ; and listened to the gay guitar and
merry castanet on the borders of the blue Guadal-
quivir."

As a specimen of the book, take this description of
the old Norman diligence : —

" It was one of those ponderous vehicles which totter
slowly along the paved roads of France, laboring beneath a mountain of trunks and bales of all descriptions, and, like the Trojan horse, bearing a groaning
multitude within it. It was a curious and cumbersome
machine, resembling the bodies of three coaches placed
upon one carriage, with a cabriolet on top for outside
passengers. On the panels of each door were painted
the fleurs-de-lis of France ; and upon the side of the
coach, emblazoned in gold characters, ' *Exploitation
Générale des Messageries Royales des Diligences pour le
Havre, Rouen, et Paris.*' "

In an article on Longfellow in The Atlantic Monthly
for December. 1863, George William Curtis said of
Outre-Mer : " It is the romance of the Continent, and
not that of England, which inspires him. It is the
ruddy light upon the vines, and the scraps of old chansons, which enliven and decorate his pilgrimage ; and
through all his literary life they have not lost their
fascination. While Irving sketches ' Rural Life in England,' Longfellow paints ' The Village of Auteuil ; '
Irving gives us ' The Boar's Head Tavern,' and Longfellow ' The Golden Lion Inn ; ' Irving draws a ' Royal
Poet,' Longfellow discusses ' The Trouvères ' or ' The
Devotional Poetry of Spain.' . . . Geoffrey Crayon is
a humorist, while the Pilgrim beyond the Sea is a poet.
The one looks at the broad aspects of English life with

the shrewd twinkling eye of the man of the world: the other haunts the valley of the Loire, the German street, the Spanish inn, with the kindling fancy of the scholar and poet." During the twenty years following the publication of Outre-Mer, seventy-five hundred copies were sold.

Under the title, The Schoolmaster, Mr. Longfellow began, in Buckingham's New-England Magazine, the sketches and studies which he afterwards published with the title Outre-Mer.

To the Longfellow number of The Literary World (Feb. 26, 1881) Mr. Horace E. Scudder contributed a pleasant paper in which he compared the two productions. Mr. Scudder's paper shall here be given entire, and will speak for itself: —

" There were kings before Agamemnon; and the reader of 'The Atlantic' to-day will find that his fathers had also their literary magazines — of somewhat precarious existence, to be sure, but containing often papers and poems which have passed into the accepted literature of the country. The New-England Magazine, published and conducted by J. T. Buckingham and his son until the son's death, and after that by the father alone, was for a time a fair representative of the culture of Boston. The contributions were rarely signed, and the publisher could offer only very diminutive golden bait; but, besides the work of aspirants who never came to fame, one may find here articles, sketches, and poems, by Everett, Story, Hillard, Hildreth, Withington, Dr. Howe, Dr. Peabody, Epes Sargent, Holmes, and Longfellow. It was in this magazine, the reader will remember, that Dr. Holmes published a trial chapter of 'The Autocrat;' but so completely had the title disappeared that nobody remembered it when he resumed it twenty-five years afterward, in the more mature wit and wisdom which made the early numbers of The Atlantic famous. Many of his bright young poems appeared here; and a curious experiment, headed 'Report of the Editorial Department,' and signed O. W. H., will be found in the number for January, 1833.

"Mr. Longfellow's contributions, so far as we know, are confined to a series of sketches, appearing at irregular intervals, which interest us from their relation to his subsequent acknowledged work. In the first number of the magazine, that for July, 1831, will be found among the original papers one entitled 'The Schoolmaster,' Chapter I., and having all the air of being the first of a series. A motto from Franklin stands at the head: —

"'My character, indeed, I would favor you with, but that I am cautious of praising myself, lest I should be told my trumpeter's dead; and I cannot find in my heart at present to say any thing to my own disadvantage.'

"The Schoolmaster opens with a half-confidential disclosure to the reader. It is written in the first person: —

"'I am a schoolmaster [it begins] in the little village of Sharon. A son of New England, I have been educated in all her feelings and prejudices. To her maternal care I owe the little that is good within me; and upon her bosom I hope to repose hereafter when my worldly task is done, and my soul, like a rejoicing schoolboy, shall close its weary book, and burst forth from this earthly schoolhouse. My childhood was passed at my native village, in the usual amusements and occupations of that age ; but as I grew up I became satiated with the monotony of my life. A restless spirit prompted me to visit foreign countries. I said, with the cosmopolite, " The world is a kind of book in which he who has seen his own country only has read but one page." Guided by this feeling, I became a traveller. I have traversed France on foot, smoked my pipe in a Flemish inn ' —

" And the reader who has read thus far finds the words beginning to be familiar. He turns to Outre-Mer, and discovers the same passage in the chapter headed ' The Pilgrim of Outre-Mer.' The Schoolmaster, however, immediately recovers its own separate character, and for a page or two more one reads of the return of the narrator to his native village, and thenceforth of his travels by memory.

" In September, 1831, appeared the second chapter of The Schoolmaster, which proves to be substantially the same as The Norman Diligence in ' Outre-Mer.' The motto, indeed, is that which in the book precedes the ' Journey into Spain,' and the chapter in The Schoolmaster is longer. The slight mention of the cabaret in Outre-Mer is an abbreviation of a fuller and more detailed sketch in The Schoolmaster, where an old soldier and some wagoners have a half-operatic scene, and sing an apology for cider, an old French song of the fifteenth century. Both the French and an English version of the song are given; and it is a little curious, that, in the revised edition of Poets and Poetry of Europe, Mr. Longfellow has given Oliver Basselin's modernized version of the song as translated by Oxenford, but says nothing of his own earlier rendering.

"The third chapter of The Schoolmaster, published April, 1832, is 'The Village of Auteuil;' and one or two variations are interesting. The introductory paragraphs in Outre-Mer are new; and a happy little improvement is made, when, in place of the words in The Schoolmaster, —

"'I took up my abode at a *maison de santé ;* not that I was a valetudinarian, but because I there found society and good accommodations,' —

"Outre-Mer has, —

"'Not that I was a valetudinarian; but because I there found some one to whom I could whisper, How sweet is solitude!'

"Dr. Dardonville in The Schoolmaster becomes Dentdelion in Outre-Mer, and some details are given in the first form which do not appear in the second. In the 'Outre-Mer' chapter, on the other hand, the account of the *fête patronale* is new. It would seem as if the author, in revising his chapters, removed them a little from a too literal transcript of his note-book, and threw over them a further air of refinement and imagination.

"In July, 1832, the fourth chapter was printed, headed 'Recollections of the Metropolis,' and consisting of a stroll through Paris with reference to certain historical sights. The fifth chapter, in October of the same year, continues this imaginary walk, but is occupied chiefly with a romantic story from a chronicle of the time of Charles VI. The sixth chapter, in February, 1833, resumes the walk, interrupted by the story, and brings the reader finally to the gates of Père la Chaise. The reader turns over the numbers afterward, expecting to find the chapter so headed which he remembers in Outre-Mer; but he discovers that The Schoolmaster

has come to an abrupt close. The reason appears in
the publication, this year, of the first part of Outre-
Mer, containing, as we have shown, material used in
the first three chapters of The Schoolmaster. Outre-
Mer appeared at first with no name attached, but it
was probably tolerably well known who wrote it; and
when the second part appeared, shortly afterward, Professor Longfellow's name was openly mentioned with
it. It is a little odd, however, that, in the book-notices
of the September number, 1833, there is a very good-
natured notice of the first part of Outre-Mer, which
closed with Père la Chaise, but without a word that
indicates a knowledge of the authorship, and several quotations from pages which had already formed part of
The Schoolmaster. However, this innocence may have
been assumed, though one would not have predicated
it from an acquaintance with more modern magazine
editors. The last three chapters of The Schoolmaster
were not reprinted, and the serial was not resumed,
perhaps because the author preferred the more satisfactory and more dignified appearance in book-form. A
prior publication in a magazine was more likely to obscure a book then than now. It is not impossible that
the slight conception of a schoolmaster was reserved
also for future use in the tale of Kavanagh."

The publication of the Outre-Mer of Professor Longfellow, together with a number of articles by him
in The North-American Review, served to call attention to him in a marked degree. In 1835 Mr. George
Ticknor, professor of modern languages at Harvard,
having resigned his position, Mr. Longfellow was appointed his successor.

But we must return to Bowdoin for the purpose

ot recording several things that took place previous to the removal of the young and popular professor to Cambridge. One of these events was his marriage, in September, 1831, to Mary Storer Potter, daughter of Judge Barrett Potter and Anne Storer Potter of Portland. Those who saw him at this time describe him as somewhat of an exquisite in appearance, always swinging a slender little cane as he walked about. This custom he continued for a time in Cambridge also. He became very popular as an instructor. President Hamlin of Middlebury College, who entered Bowdoin in 1830, says: "Longfellow had occupied the chair about one year. Our class numbered fifty-two, the largest freshman class that had up to that time entered college ; and many of its members were attracted by Longfellow's reputation. His intercourse with the students was perfectly simple, frank, and gentlemanly. He neither flattered nor repelled : he neither sought popularity, nor avoided it. He was a close and ardent student in all Spanish and French literature. He had no time to fritter away ; but he always and evidently enjoyed having students come to him with any reasonable question about languages, authors, literature, mediæval or modern history, more especially the former. They always left him, not only with admiration, but guided and helped and inspired."

During his residence in Brunswick Mr. Longfellow became a member of the Maine Historical Society ; and in 1834 he held the office of librarian and cabinet-keeper. It was therefore peculiarly fitting, that, on the recent occasion of Mr. Longfellow's seventy-fifth birthday, the Maine Historical Society should celebrate the occasion by having a series of careful and elaborate historical

and biographical articles prepared on the poet's anc v-
try and birthplace, etc. These articles have been of
great use in the preparation of this volume.

AT HARVARD COLLEGE.

As Mr. Longfellow went abroad to prepare himself
for his Bowdoin College duties, so did he when he was
called to Harvard College, this time for the purpose
of studying the languages of Northern Europe, Danish,
Swedish, etc. He took with him his young wife, whom
he had the misfortune to lose at Rotterdam. She died,
Nov. 29, 1835, from an illness contracted after confine-
ment.

In an admirable and pains-taking article in The New-
York Evening Post for March 25, 1882,[1] the writer,
who is understood to be Col. Higginson, says, —

"How profound was the impression produced upon
him, is evident from The Footsteps of Angels, and
from the allusions in the early part of Hyperion.
Mrs. Longfellow was, by the testimony of all who
knew her, a person of rare loveliness of person and
mind. Her father, Hon. Barrett Potter of Portland,
was a judge of probate, and a man of strong character, holding very decided views as to the education
of his children, of whom only the daughters lived to
maturity. Although himself an old-fashioned classical
scholar, he believed the study of Greek and Latin to
be unsuitable for girls: all else was open to them, —
modern languages, literature, and mathematics. For
all these, especially the last, his daughter Mary had a

[1] The above-mentioned article, by reason of its fulness of detail, has
been of more use in the compilation of this volume than any other
newspaper memoir of the poet thus far published. It will be frequently
quoted in the following pages.

strong taste. Her note-books preserved by her family give, for instance, ample and accurate reports, recorded as being 'from memory,' of a series of astronomical lectures; and she learned to calculate eclipses, which must have been quite beyond the average attainments of young ladies of her day. She was for several years a pupil at the excellent school of Miss Cushing, at Hingham; and all her school papers, abstracts and compositions, show a thoughtful and well-trained mind. Some exhibit a metaphysical turn, others are girlish studies in history and geography; but the love of literature is visible everywhere, in copious extracts from the favorite authors of that day, — Cowper, Young, Mrs. Hemans, Bernard Barton, and even Coleridge and Shelley. Farther on in the series of note-books the handwriting becomes firmer' and maturer; and notes and translations appear upon the pages in the unmis-takable autograph of Longfellow, almost precisely the same at twenty-four as at seventy-four."

The spring and summer subsequent to the death of his wife were spent in Switzerland and the Tyrol; he having previously travelled in Denmark, Sweden, Germany, and Holland. In November, 1836, he returned to Harvard, and entered upon the duties of his professorship, which he discharged for eighteen years. At the end of this period (1854) he resigned, to devote himself to literature wholly, and was succeeded by James Russell Lowell. Of his popularity and faithfulness during his service with the university, there are many testimonials. Says one, —

"His professional service at Cambridge contributed in no small degree to his own fame and to that of the university. During eighteen years he was the valued and ever popular head in the department of modern literatures. His intellectual gifts and already great acquirements were fortified and constantly refreshed by new studies and explorations among the original sources of information; and herein lay the recognized value of his services, while the great charm of his presence and manner, which made him the light of every social circle which he entered, were an accompaniment of what might otherwise in some particulars have been a dull process of instruction. Thus he was ever a favorite professor with the college youth. These instructions were chiefly in Italian and Spanish literature, and largely from the writings of Dante and Cervantes, and were given in the form of lectures. During the period named, he usually lectured three times a week during the college term; and his method was mostly in the form of a translation from the original. So perfect was his familiarity with the theme, and ready his speech, that he would read Don Quixote in this way almost into verse. The translation of Dante, which was afterwards prepared for publication, was made in its original form as incidental to this method of class instruction."

Rev. Edward Everett Hale gives this account of Mr. Longfellow's method with his students while professor of modern literature at Harvard: "As it happened, the regular recitation-rooms of the college were all in use; and we met him in a sort of parlor, carpeted, hung with pictures, and otherwise handsomely furnished, which was, I believe, called 'the Corporation Room.' We sat round a mahogany table, which was reported to be meant for the dinners of the trustees; and the whole affair had the aspect of a friendly gathering in a private

house, in which the study of German was the amuse-
ment of the occasion. He began with familiar ballads,
read them to us, and made us read them to him. Of
course we soon committed them to memory without
meaning to, and I think this was probably part of his
theory. At the same time, we were learning the para-
digms by rote. His regular duty was the oversight of
five or more instructors who were teaching French,
German, Italian, Spanish, and Portuguese to two or
three hundred undergraduates. We never knew when
he might look in on a recitation, and virtually conduct
it. We were delighted to have him come. We all
knew he was a poet, and were proud to have him in
the college, but at the same time we respected him as
a man of affairs."

He was always careful to address the students as
"Mr.,"—a rare thing in those days. This attitude
won the respect of the students. Once when there
were very threatening indications of a rebellion among
the students, and the other professors were unable to
get a hearing from the angry and excited mob, Mr.
Longfellow began to speak, and instantly the students
became quiet, saying, "Let's hear Longfellow, for he
always treats us as gentlemen."

The writer in The New-York Evening Post says
that "as an instructor he was clear, suggestive, and
encouraging; his lectures on the great French writers
were admirable, and his facility in equivalent phrases
was of great use to his pupils, and elevated their standard of translation. He was scrupulously faithful to
his duties, and even went through the exhausting
process of marking French exercises with exemplary
patience. . . . There was probably no college in the

United States which had so large a corps of instructors in the modern languages as had Harvard at that time."

At a memorial service held in East Boston, the Sunday succeeding Mr. Longfellow's death, the Rev. N. H. Chamberlain said: "He laid the stress of his refinement upon all the members of his class." The Rev. Mr. Cudworth said: "His nature was so broad, that, while he was ready to welcome the quickest and most acute intellect in the class, he was so patient and considerate that he waited for the natural development of the intellect of the slowest."

One who was a pupil of Professor Longfellow at Harvard says, in The Springfield Republican: "The old New Englanders praise a man by calling him 'communicative;' and the word describes Longfellow in its finest shades of meaning. He did not talk, or read, or lecture for display, but to put his hearers in possession of what he knew. No man had less of the schoolmaster, or of that dry and technical wisdom which the title of 'professor' too often implies. . . . He had a weakness in dress which provoked the college satirist to doggerel wit; but this only brought him nearer to the graceless young scamps who satirized him, for they would all have been dandies if they could, even while laughing at the professor as a dandy. The gibe of Margaret Fuller about 'a dandy Pindar' took its sting from the slight youthful fondness of Longfellow for display in cravats and waistcoats."

It should have been mentioned that Mr. Longfellow's new title was Smith Professor of the French and Spanish Languages and Literature, and Professor of Belles Lettres. On coming to Cambridge, in 1836, he was attracted by the appearance of

THE CRAIGIE HOUSE, THE HOME OF LONGFELLOW,

BRATTLE STREET IN CAMBRIDGE.

THE CRAIGIE HOUSE

on Brattle Street, and applied there for rooms. The house was occupied by Mrs. Craigie, widow of Andrew Craigie. When Professor Longfellow made known his errand, the quaint old turbaned lady drew herself up with dignity, and replied, " I lodge students no longer." But when he told her he was a professor, her manner changed, and she showed him over the house. As she closed the door of each room she said, " But you can't have that." At last she led him to the north-east chamber, told him that it had been Washington's room, and said, " This you can have."

" The room," says George William Curtis, "was upon the front of the house, and looked over the meadows to the river. It had an atmosphere of fascinating repose in which the young man was at once domesticated. as in an old home. The elms of the avenue shaded his windows, and, as he glanced from them, the summer lay asleep upon the landscape in the windless day. ' This,' said the old lady, with a slight sadness in her voice, as if speaking of times forever past, and to which she herself properly belonged, — ' this was Gen. Washington's chamber.' " The room was then, and still is, adorned by the gayly-painted Dutch tiles, characteristic of houses built a century ago. It was afterwards the nursery of the poet's children. He makes allusion to it in his poem To a Child.

The lexicographer Joseph E. Worcester once lived with the poet in this house; also Miss Sally Lowell, an aunt of James Russell Lowell. In 1843, after Mrs. Craigie's death, the estate was bought for Mr. Longfellow by his father-in-law, Nathan Appleton, who also presented to him a deed of the lot opposite the house, which assured him an unobstructed view of the broad rich meadows of the Charles River and the steeples of Brighton in the distance. It has always heretofore been erroneously stated that Mr. Longfellow purchased this lot. He did purchase some adjoining lots, on one of which stands the house now occupied by his son Ernest. He also bought a lot connecting his lawn with Berkeley Street in the rear, and on this lot Mr. Ernest Longfellow has erected a cottage in the Queen Anne style. Mr. Longfellow's estate comprised about ten acres. The old house, which continued to be Mr. Longfellow's home for the rest of his life, is rich in association. It was built midway in the last century, by a gentleman of family and distinction, named Col. John Vassal, whose gravestone in the Cambridge churchyard bears upon it, by way of inscription, figures of a goblet and a sun (*Vas-sol*), a pun upon the family name. In the same churchyard reposes a lady of the same family, with a slave buried at her feet and another at her head. This is the lady of whom Longfellow wrote in his poem entitled In The Churchyard at Cambridge : —

> " In the village churchyard she lies,
>   Dust is in her beautiful eyes,
>   No more she breathes, nor feels, nor stirs;
>   At her feet and at her head
>   Lies a slave to attend the dead,
>   But their dust is white as hers.

> " Was she a lady of high degree,
>   So much in love with the vanity
>   And foolish pomp of this world of ours?

> Or was it Christian charity,
> And lowliness and humility,
>   The richest and rarest of all dowers?
>
> "Who shall tell us?   No one speaks;
> No color shoots into those cheeks,
>   Either of anger or of pride,
> At the rude question we have asked;
> Nor will the mystery be unmasked
>   By those who are sleeping at her side."

After the death of Col. Vassal the house was inherited by his son, who, being a Tory, forfeited all his property. Washington, as everybody knows, made it his headquarters for a time, his reception-room being the front right-hand apartment used by the poet as a study, while the opposite room was used by Mrs. Washington for receptions.

"After the Revolutionary war the house was sold to one Thomas Tracy, who appears to have been a sort of American Vathek, emulating as far as possible in an uncongenial clime the magnificent doings of the Eastern prince. Some of his wealth he got by privateering. With the passing of his wealth, clouds gathered about the old house. We hear of it no more until it came into the hands of the last owner save one, Andrew Craigie." Craigie was a wealthy commissary or apothecary-general in the Revolutionary army. He was interested in land speculations in East Cambridge, and built the bridge between Cambridge and Boston, which was named for him, and still bears his name.

"The expenses it entailed ruined him: he became so embarrassed with debt that it is said he was afraid to come out of his house except on Sundays. Necessity obliged him to part with all save eight of the two hundred or a hundred and fifty acres, originally included in the estate; and after his death Mrs. Craigie was forced to let lodgings to the youth of Harvard, pygmies all to her, though to us such intellectual giants as Everett, Sparks, and Longfellow were among them. Of the reduced gentlewoman some curious stories are told. On one occasion her young poet-lodger, entering her parlor in the morning, found her sitting by the open window, through which innumerable canker-worms had crawled from the trees they were devouring outside. They had fastened themselves to her dress, and hung in little writhing festoons from the white turban on her head. Her visitor, surprised and shocked. asked if she could do nothing to destroy the worms. Raising her eyes from the book which she sat calmly reading, like Indifference on a monument, she said, in tones of solemn rebuke, 'Young man, have not our fellow-worms as good a right to live as we?'—an answer which throws 'Uncle Toby's' 'Go, little fly,' quite into the shade."

/ The house came into Mr. Longfellow's possession in 1843. It was built in the Georgian style of architecture, a capacious and imposing mansion, square in front, the color buff, with window-framings, antique pilasters, and balustrade on the roof, all in white. It stands some fifty yards back from winding Brattle Street, on a slight rise in the ground, which is broken by two grassy terraces. The wall along the sidewalk has inside of it a high hedge of purple and white lilac-bushes. The grounds immediately surrounding the house. are adorned with not too many tall trees, and with shrubs. In the rear is a stable, also buff in color.

Along each side of the house extends a wide veranda. In front, the view stretches away to the Brighton meadows and• hills, often suffused with dim gray and violet tints.

"The house," says The New-York Evening Post, "had its stately halls, its cavernous recesses, its secret crypts; from one of which hiding-places came forth mysteriously, dropping **night** by night upon the stairs, those letters yellow with age, and recording some dim secret, which have been made the theme of one of Saxe Holm's best stories, i.e., ‘Esther Wynn's Love-Letters.'" The Craigie House letters were addressed to the husband of the picturesque old lady just referred to, who sat with her fellow-worms by the parlor window. Mr. Longfellow had intended to write a poem about these letters, but Saxe Holm anticipated him. The age of Craigie House is attested by an iron in the back of one of the chimneys, which bears the date 1759. There is a tradition that the house is connected with the Batchelder house on the opposite side of the street by a subterranean passage. The poet took the greatest pride in his house and in its traditions. He was fond of telling how, in the room used by him as a study, Gen. Washington had received with the most freezing politeness the gentleman sent from Boston by Gov. Hancock, with the request that Gen. Washington would call upon him. The governor conceived that in his own State he was the superior of Washington. The general, on learning this, slipped out of Boston, and, returning to Cambridge, staid there until the governor avaled the flag of his pride, and came to see him at Craigie House.

A writer in The Boston Book Bulletin has given

LONGFELLOW'S HOME.

WEST SIDE OF THE CRAIGIE HOUSE, CAMBRIDGE.

a complete and charming picture of the interior of the Longfellow mansion : —

"Passing through the hall we enter 'Lady Washington's Drawing Room.' The furniture is white satin covered with gay flowers in vines and clusters ; armchairs and sofas are heaped with soft cushions covered with the same material. The carpet is a bed of flowers.

"The effect is greatly heightened by a large mirror opening another gay vista, and a picture in gorgeous colors extending from wall to ceiling. It is one of Copley's, 'The Grandchildren of Sir William Pepperell.' A quaint little maiden, in a high cap and stiff bodice, a youth with flowing curls, and a wooden-looking poodle, compose the group. The picture is set in a massive burnished frame, and the effect would be oppressive in another room, but is in admirable harmony with this state apartment.

"On an *étagère*, laden with treasures, is an agate cup from the hand of no less a master than Benvenuto Cellini, — clear, exquisitely carved, graceful in shape, and guarded by two tiny open-mouthed dragons. It was sent to Longfellow from the collection of the poet Rogers, and had therefore a double value in his eyes. As he held it in his hand, and pointed out its beauties, one could but think what a crowd of associations were gathering in its delicate cup.

"In the dining-room we see rare old china, a modern picture of a cardinal in red, walking in the Borghese Gardens, and several family portraits. Among them is Buchanan Read's picture of 'Longfellow's Daughters,' that has been photographed so often, — the 'blue-eyed banditti' that the poet-father has so charmingly apostrophized in The Children's Hour : —

> ' Grave Alice, and laughing Allegra,
>   And Edith with golden hair.'

" From this room we pass into a long, narrow hall, running the length of the house. At its head great Jove looks before him with big, unseeing eyes ; while on either side are those lovely marble women, who, in spite of Lord Byron's couplet, —

> ' I've seen more beauty, ripe and real,
>   Than all the nonsense of their stone ideal,'

still hold their own — as embodied ideas in human shape — against their living sisters.

" The library is the most beautiful room in the house, — dark and rich in tone, with a look of spacious elegance and home-like comfort. On three sides the walls are lined with books. The bronzes and Japanese screens are studies.

" Here hangs a portrait of Liszt. The background is dark, and he is dressed in the long black convent robe. High above his head he holds a lighted candle. The rays shape themselves like a halo round his head, and throw into fine relief the thin, spirited face.

" Mr. Longfellow saw him thus for the first time as he stood in the convent-door peering out into the night. The vision impressed itself upon the poet, and he persuaded Liszt to have his picture painted.

" From the library a passage leads to the billiard-room, now fallen into disuse, and converted into an æsthetic lumber-room, where one would delight to dream away a rainy day.

" The rooms up-stairs are as full of interest as those below.

" One suite has been fitted up by Mr. Longfellow's

son (Charles Appleton) in Japanese style. The wall-paper is of neutral tint, ornamented with Japanese fans in groups of twos and threes. The heathen gods frown at you, national arms are collected, tables are heaped with Japanese books made on the principle of cat-stairs, and photographs of Japanese beauties, with button-hole mouths and long bright eyes, abound.

" This article would become a catalogue of description should I try to enumerate half the curiosities to be seen in this grand old house. One cabinet alone, with its medley of treasures, is worth an afternoon's study. Here is a bit of Dante's coffin ; there an agate cylinder, and some brilliant African beetles. Two canes attract you: one is made from the spar of the ship on which ' The Star-spangled Banner' was written; the other comes from Acadie, and is surmounted by a hideous head, which, Mr. Longfellow used to say, with a twinkle in his eye, was the poet's idea of Evangeline."

HYPERION.

In 1839 appeared " Hyperion : a Romance," the first of the poet's works written in Craigie House. It was published in New York. It was the only one of his works ever published outside of Boston and Cambridge, with the exception of Poets and Poetry of Europe, a compilation made for Philadelphia publishers, and Outre-Mer (Harpers, 1835).[1] It may be noted that the only one of Hawthorne's works published outside of Boston was his " Mosses from an Old Manse," published in New York.

[1] Reference is made here to the first publication of his works. All his works have been republished in England, and an illustrated edition was published in Philadelphia.

The origin of Hyperion was as follows. Being in Switzerland in 1839, some considerable time after the death of his wife, Mr. Longfellow chanced to meet the family of Mr. Nathan Appleton of Boston. They were travelling in style through the country, with foot-men and postilions.[1] Miss Fanny Elizabeth Appleton, the daughter of Mr. Nathan Appleton, and sister of Mr. Thomas Gold Appleton, the well-known Boston author, was at that time a most beautiful girl of eighteen or twenty, and she completely captivated the heart of the poet. The suit was not well received by her at first, the disparity of age probably seeming disagreeable to her. But the suitor was not to be put off, and deliber-ately set to work to win her by writing his Hyperion, in which Miss Appleton was introduced under the name Mary Ashburton.

THE POET'S SECOND MARRIAGE.

It is well known that the heroine of the romance was not wholly pleased at being the recognized subject of so much sentiment. The marriage, however, took place at last, in July, 1843; and for nearly twenty years their married life was one of unmingled happiness. Five

---

[1] A pleasant little incident is related in this connection. Mr. Long-fellow had joined the Appleton party; and "at Zürich the innkeeper, as innkeepers often do, thought he could charge heavily for what he gave. Mr. Appleton had written his name in the travellers' book, with compliments to the hotel, which he regretted when the bill was brought to him. 'But I have not written my name,' said Mr. Longfellow; 'and if you will allow me, I will treat the innkeeper as he deserves.' The name of the inn was 'The Raven.' Mr. Longfellow withdrew with the book, and in five minutes returned with these witty lines written under his name: —

'Beware of the Raven of Zürich!
'Tis a bird of omen ill;
With a noisy and an unclean nest,
And a very, very long bill.'"

children blessed their household, — two sons, Charles Appleton and Ernest Wadsworth; and three daughters, Alice M., Edith (now wife of Richard Henry Dana), and Annie Allegra. Mrs. Longfellow was a lady of rare beauty and great dignity of bearing: her "deep, unutterable eyes" have been sung by her husband. On July 9, 1861, Mrs. Longfellow was burned to death by her clothing catching fire from a wax taper with which she was sealing a letter enclosing a lock of hair of one of her children. She wore a light summer dress of inflammable material, which made the extinguishing of the flames more difficult. Mr. Longfellow ran out from an adjoining room, clasped his wife in his arms, and succeeded in partially subduing the fire on one side of her face and person; but the envious flames had done their work, and she presently expired in great suffering. Mr. Longfellow was himself severely burned. He was nearly crazed with grief: he shut himself up in his room, walking to and fro, wringing his hands, and crying out, "Oh, my beautiful wife, my beautiful wife!" The writer of these lines was told by a friend of the Longfellow family, that, when Mrs. Longfellow was placed in the coffin, the side of her face which had been protected by the effort of her husband to extinguish the flames was placed uppermost, and was so fresh and beautiful that it seemed as if she lay there asleep. Mr. Longfellow never fully recovered from this shock, and ever afterwards seemed an old man.

Of this grief Mr. R. H. Stoddard in "Poets' Homes" (D. Lothrop & Co.) writes: —

"He has known poignant sorrow. Death has entered his home, and taken from it his dearest. That this, a sorrow ever abiding, is one from which, in a sense, he will never recover, the years have proved. His melancholy is but dimly seen, like a smoke curling upward from a blazing fire. Yet it is present always, veiling his cheerfulness and saddening his smiles."

" I never heard him make but one allusion to the great grief of his life," said an intimate friend. " We were speaking of Schiller's fine poem, The Ring of Polycrates. He said, ' It was just so with me. I was too happy. I might fancy the gods envied, if I could fancy heathen gods.'"

NATHAN APPLETON, — MRS. LONGFELLOW'S FATHER.

The father of the lamented Mrs. Longfellow, Mr. Nathan Appleton of Boston, was in many respects a remarkable man. He was born in New Ipswich, N.H., Oct. 6, 1779, and was descended from respectable and knightly ancestry. He married Miss Maria Theresa, daughter of Thomas Gold, Esq., a Pittsfield lawyer. The reader will peruse with much interest the following sketch of Nathan Appleton, written by the Hon. Robert C. Winthrop: —

" At early dusk on some October or November evening, in the year 1794, a fresh, vigorous, bright-eyed lad, just turned of fifteen, might have been seen alighting from a stage-coach near Quaker Lane,[1] as it was then called, in the town of Boston. He had been two days on the road from his home in the town of New Ipswich, in the State of New Hampshire. On the last of the two days the stage-coach had brought him all the way from Groton in Massachusetts; starting for that purpose early in the morning, stopping at Concord for the passengers to dine, trundling them through Charlestown about the time the evening lamps were lighted, and

<hr>

[1] Now Congress Street.

finishing the whole distance of rather more than thirty miles in season for supper. The Boston stage-coach in those days went no farther than Groton in that direction. His father's farm-horse, or perhaps that of one of the neighbors, had served his turn for the first six or seven miles; his little brother of ten years old having followed him as far as Townsend, to ride the horse home again. But from there he had trudged along to Groton on foot, with a bundle-handkerchief in his hand, which contained all the wearing-apparel he had, except what was on his back.

.   .   .   .   .   .

" At early dawn on the morning of Sunday, July 14, 1861, there died, at his beautiful residence in Beacon Street, adorned within by many choice works of luxury and art, and commanding without the lovely scenery of the Mall, the Common, and the rural environs of Boston, a venerable person of more than fourscore years; a merchant of large enterprise and unsullied integrity; a member of many learned societies; a writer of many able essays on commerce and currency; a wise and prudent counsellor in all private and public affairs; who had served with marked distinction in the legislative halls both of the State and of the Nation, and who had enjoyed through life the esteem, respect, and confidence of the community in which he lived."

HYPERION.

To return to Hyperion. The work became extremely popular, and remained so for many years. Up to 1857 upwards of 14,550 copies had been sold. On March 18, 1840, Charles Sumner writes from London to his friend, George S. Hillard: "I have just found

Longfellow's Hyperion, and shall sit up all night to read it. I have bought up all the copies of Voices of the Night in London to give to my friends." The book has a sweet and mellow tone, like Outre-Mer. What reader of books does not remember how it charmed him with its subdued humor, its fresh pictures of German life, and its solemn pathos? What young man that read after Flemming these words on the tablet in the church, did not carry them away forever impressed on the tablets of his heart?—"Look not mournfully into the Past. It comes not back again. Wisely improve the Present. It is thine. Go forth to meet the shadowy Future, without fear, and with a manly heart." How beautiful, too, the following!—"In ancient times there stood in the citadel of Athens three statues of Minerva. The first was of olive-wood, and, according to tradition, had fallen from heaven; the second was of bronze, commemorating the victory of Marathon; and the third of gold and ivory, a great miracle of art in the age of Pericles. And thus in the citadel of Time stands Man himself. In childhood, shaped of soft and delicate wood, just fallen from heaven; in manhood, a statue of bronze, commemorating struggle and victory; and lastly, in the maturity of age, perfectly shaped in gold and ivory,—a miracle of art!" Or this often-quoted passage about the Rhine: "By heavens, if I were a German I would be proud of it too, and of the clustering grapes that hang about its temples, as it reels onward through vineyards in triumphal march, like Bacchus crowned and drunken!" The book is written in a style more verbose and rhetorical than now prevails, and therefore is apt to be "skimmed" by readers of to-day; but it is still the best guide-book to the Rhine and Heidelberg. Professor Felton said of it on its appearance, " It is a book for minds attuned to sentiments of tenderness, — minds of an imaginative turn, and willing and ready to interest themselves in reveries as gorgeous as morning dreams, and in the delicate perceptions of art and poetry, — minds tried by suffering, and sensitively alive to the influence of the beautiful. . . . In tender and profound feeling, and in brilliancy of imagery, the work will bear a comparison with the best productions of romantic fiction which English literature can boast."

In the Longfellow number of The Literary World Col. Higginson said, —

" The travelling American will find himself an object of interest to every Englishman so soon as he claims personal acquaintance with Mark Twain ; and to every English woman, after she discovers that he has the honor of a personal acquaintance with Professor Longfellow.' We heard a lady of that section say to her companions, on a Rhine steamer, that it was all nonsense to carry guide-books, since nothing was really essential on that river except the writings of Longfellow. On the lofty heights of the Gorner Grat, above Zermatt, we met a party of English school-girls, who declared that Hyperion was their favorite book ; and we encountered an elderly Englishman at Chamonix, who sighed over the memory of Emma of Ilmenau, and murmured solemnly, ' That night there fell a star from heaven.' This is fame, — a fame almost as substantial as to have written Robinson Crusoe or Don Quixote.

" Emerson tells us to hitch our wagons to a star ; and it is a good thing when a romance has a permanent place among the guide-books. No traveller can fully enjoy

Quebec without Howells's Wedding Journey, or Heidelberg without Hyperion. Our copy—the cheap German imprint—gained a new charm from being carried as a pocket treasure among the ruined halls of the beautiful castle, and to the summit of the 'Rent Tower.' It produced a momentary doubt when we failed to find on that eminence any 'great linden trees;' but it was easy to convince one's self that forty years might have removed them from their airy perch, and that even Paul Flemming and his Baron would now have to content themselves with second-growth trees. But the glory of the castle is still there, and the throng of people; and the American visitor enjoys it all the more from the knowledge that his own fellow-countryman has embalmed it in literature.

"Yet, while reading Hyperion at Heidelberg, and while passing maturer judgment on a book which we almost knew by heart at sixteen, we were compelled to recognize a certain crudeness of quality and a turgidness of style which were singularly absent from Mr. Longfellow's poetry at the same period. Hyperion did great service in its day, and certainly shared with Carlyle's essays the merit of directing the attention of English-speaking people to the wealth of German literature. When we now read what the author says of Goethe and Jean Paul, and the wild thoughts he has gleaned from Fichte and Schubert, we judge them in the light of forty years of later literature; but at the first publication this book brought Germany to us almost as Madame de Staël had brought it to French readers; and was our guide into a new world of delight. Moreover, the blossoming period of German poetry was then less remote, by nearly half a century,

than now; and the bards whom Longfellow translated
seemed contemporaries.   Now we know that, for whatever reason, their reign is over, and that Germany no
longer produces even Rückerts and Freiligraths.   But
it is none the less true that Hyperion will represent,
so long as it is read, the freshness of German romance
as it was transmitted to the still fresher apprehension
of newly-awakened America.

"An enthusiastic young Dane, a Harvard student,
who in those days beguiled a summer vacation by
translating the Heinrich von Ofterdingen of Novalis, closed his preface to that charming and incompre-
hensible tale by saying solemnly: 'Novalis died young.
The translator is also young.'   Probably much of the
power of Hyperion lay in the fact that the interpreter of all this romance was 'also young.'   He was but
thirty-two when it appeared, and was indeed but twenty-
nine when he returned from Europe, where most of the
book was probably written.   All that could be fairly
asked of a romance produced at that age and under
such circumstances was that it should have superabun-
dant wealth, and this Hyperion certainly had.   With
fewer faults it would have had less promise.   Professor
Channing used to say that it was a bad sign for a young
man to write too well : there must be something to be
pruned down."

VOICES OF THE NIGHT.

Since the publication of Coplas de Manrique, Mr.
Longfellow had at various times been contributing
poems to the magazines, and particularly to The
Knickerbocker.   In 1839 these, together with some
of his earlier poems and translations, were published

at Cambridge, Mass., by John Owen, who was then
conducting the University Bookstore, corner of Harvard
and Holyoke Streets. The volume was a pretty little
16mo, in light cream-colored binding, the covers having
elaborate colored designs, — the front one showing a
curtain half-drawn back upon a night landscape. " It
is remembered as if it were yesterday," says one, " when
a printer's devil invaded the peaceful recitation-room
of Harvard, where the students sat in the pleasant
fashion of those days around a table, and laid upon it
the proof-sheet of a title-page, Voices of the Night."

The success of the book was striking and immediate.
Up to 1857 more copies of it had been sold than of any
other work of the poet except Hiawatha (namely, forty-
three thousand of the " Voices," against fifty thousand
of Hiawatha). The Psalm of Life appeared here, as
well as The Reaper and the Flowers, and Footsteps
of Angels, The Beleaguered City, and Midnight Mass
for the Dying Year.

In Pierce's Memoir and Letters of Charles Sumner
(ii., 227), there is a letter from Sumner to Longfellow,
in which he says, " A few days ago an old classmate,
upon whom the world has not smiled, came to my office
to prove some debts in bankruptcy. While writing the
formal parts of the paper, I inquired about his reading
and the books which interested him now (I believe he
has been a great reader). He said that he read very
little ; that he hardly found any thing which was written
from the heart and was really true. 'Have you read
Longfellow's Hyperion?' I said. 'Yes,' he replied,
'and I admire it very much : I think it a very great
book.' He then added in a very solemn manner, 'I
think I may say that Longfellow's Psalm of Life saved

me from suicide. I first found it on a scrap of newspaper, in the hands of two Irishwomen, soiled and worn ; and I was at once touched by it.' "

The Chinese translator and noted scholar, Tung Tajen, a great admirer of Mr. Longfellow, sent the poet a Chinese fan, upon which was inscribed in Chinese characters a translation of the Psalm of Life. The fan is one of the folding kind, and the characters are inscribed on it in vertical columns.

A still greater curiosity is a re-translation of the Psalm of Life into English out of the Chinese. It was made by an Englishman serving on the staff of the Hon. Anson Burlingame, then American minister to China. The first stanza of the " Psalm " is given below, accompanied by the re-translation : —

> Tell me not in mournful numbers
>   Life is but an empty dream ;
> For the soul is dead that slumbers,
>   And things are not what they seem.

RE-TRANSLATION.

Do not manifest your discontent in a piece of verse :

A hundred years [of life] are, in truth, as one sleep [so soon are they gone];

The short dream [early death], the long dream [death after long life], alike are dreams [so far as the body is concerned; after death]

There still remains the spirit [which is able to] fill the universe.

Mr. Longfellow used to tell the following incident: "I was once riding in London, when a laborer approached the carriage, and asked, ' Are you the writer of the Psalm of Life?'—'I am.'—'Will you allow me to shake hands with you?' We clasped hands warmly. The carriage passed on, and I saw him no more; but I remember that as one of the most gratifying compliments I ever received, because it was so sincere."

Mr. Longfellow's next published work was

BALLADS AND OTHER POEMS.

This contained Excelsior, The Village Blacksmith, The Wreck of the Hesperus, The Skeleton in Armor, etc., and was published at Cambridge in 1841. All of the pieces mentioned have been extremely popular, and are among his best minor poems. It is said that Oliver Wendell Holmes, when once riding by Mr. Longfellow's residence, was asked by a friend which of Mr. Longfellow's poems he considered to be the finest. " Excelsior," he replied; and when asked which of his own he thought the best, he said, " The Chambered Nautilus." The critical and the uncritical alike have almost universally admired the ballads in this collection. Even Poe could not withhold his meed of praise, although he objected to the salt tears in the eyes of the skipper's daughter, in the poem called The Wreck of the Hesperus; and Mr. John Burroughs has, with characteristic devotion to truth, revealed the inaccuracy of Mr. Longfellow's statement about the cormorant sailing with wings aslant, when bearing off his prey : such birds always flap their wings heavily when they rise from the water with a fish, or are carrying off any prey in their talons.

In 1842 appeared a thin volume entitled

POEMS ON SLAVERY,

composed during a return voyage from Europe in 1842 (the summer of this year having been passed by Mr.

Longfellow at Boppard on the Rhine). At a meeting of the Cambridge Sunday Club, shortly after Mr. Longfellow's death, a gentleman who had had access to unpublished letters of Charles Sumner during the editing of Mr. Sumner's complete works remarked that in these unpublished letters were many urgent appeals from Mr. Sumner to Mr. Longfellow that he would write some stirring anti-slavery poems. Longfellow, like Sumner, was by nature (it is needless to say) a peace-man; and it was late before he responded to his friend's requests.   The letters, however, show that Sumner was highly gratified with the Poems on Slavery when they did appear. Longfellow's poems, while spirited, are not considered equal to the war-poems of Whittier, or the Drum-Taps of Whitman, which won so much praise in Europe. But his views on slavery were far in advance of the prevalent thought and sentiment of the day. When the poet's works were reprinted in Philadelphia, the Poems on Slavery were omitted by the publishers, without any authorization, and for political reasons.

THE SPANISH STUDENT.

In 1843 appeared The Spanish Student, a play in three acts (Cambridge). The popular song entitled Serenade, and more familiarly known by its first line, Stars of the Summer Night, appears in this play, or poem as it should more properly be called. The following are some of its stanzas : —

> Stars of the summer night!
> Far in yon azure deeps,
> Hide, hide your golden light!
> She sleeps!
> My lady sleeps!
> Sleeps!

> Moon of the summer night!
> Far down yon western steeps,
> Sink, sink in silver light!
> She sleeps!
> My lady sleeps!
> Sleeps!
>
> Wind of the summer night!
> Where yonder woodbine creeps,
> Fold, fold thy pinions light!
> She sleeps!
> My lady sleeps!
> Sleeps!

Of The Spanish Student, the critic Edwin Percy Whipple said, "In this poem the affluence of his imagination in images of grace, grandeur, and beauty is most strikingly manifest. The objection to it as a play is its lack of skill or power in the dramatic exhibition of character; but read merely as a poem, cast in the form of a dialogue, it is one of the most beautiful in American literature. None of his other pieces so well illustrate all his poetical faculties, — his imagination, his fancy, his sentiment, and his manner. It seems to comprehend the whole extent of his genius." This was written, it must be remembered, almost in the infancy of our literature.

The verdict of other critics has by no means been so favorable. Poe, in one of his terrible pieces of ratiocination and steel-cold logic, asserts that The Spanish Student has originality neither in thesis, incidents, nor manner of treatment. The theme is taken from La Gitanilla of Cervantes. Of the incidents Poe says that there is not one, from the first page to the last, which he would not "undertake to find boldly at ten minutes' notice in some one of the thousand and one comedies of intrigue attributed to Calderon and Lope de Vega;" that in treating his subject he "has jumbled together the quaint and stilted tone of the old English dramatists with the *dégagée* air of Cervantes," and that his "Chispa discourses pure Sancho Panza."

Poe shows the dramatic inconsistencies and improbabilities of the plot, points out a few instances of tautology and bad grammar, and concludes as follows: "Upon the whole, we regret that Professor Longfellow has written this work, and feel especially vexed that he has committed himself by its publication. Only when regarded as a mere poem can it be said to have merit of any kind. For, in fact, it is only when we separate the poem from the drama, that the passages we have commended as beautiful can be understood to have beauty. We are not too sure, indeed, that a 'dramatic poem' is not a flat contradiction in terms. At all events, a man of true genius (and such Mr. Longfellow unquestionably is) has no business with these hybrid and paradoxical compositions. Let a poem be a poem only; let a play be a play, and nothing more. As for The Spanish Student, its thesis is unoriginal; its incidents are antique; its plot is no plot; its characters have no character: in short, it is little better than a play upon words to style it 'A Play' at all."

It is a noteworthy fact, in view of such criticisms as these, that in fourteen years thirty-eight thousand copies of The Spanish Student were sold.

In 1844 Mr. Longfellow edited "The Waif: a Collection of Poems." It was published at Cambridge by John Owen. It is a very slight volume. It was reprinted in England in 1849. In 1845 also appeared

THE POETS AND POETRY OF EUROPE,

edited, with a preface, by Mr. Longfellow, and published in Philadelphia. It contained selections from three hundred and sixty authors, translated from ten different languages; Mr. Longfellow himself gave translations from eight languages. Professor Francis Bowen said of it, " In this great crowd of translations by different hands, certainly very few appear equal to Professor Longfellow's in point of fidelity, elegance, and finish." The Irish Quarterly Review said, "Longfellow's translations from the German, Swedish, Spanish, French, Danish, Italian, and Anglo-Saxon possess in a very high degree that elegance of diction and thoroughly classical coloring for which all his other poems are remarkable." The preface to The Poets and Poetry of Europe begins with this quaint extract from the writings of the old Spanish Jew, Alfonso de Baena: " The art of poetry, the gay science, is a most subtle and most delightful sort of writing or composition. It is sweet and pleasurable to those who propound and to those who reply, to utterers and to hearers. This science, or the wisdom or knowledge dependent on it, can only be possessed, received, and acquired by the inspired spirit of the Lord God; who communicates it, sends it, and influences by it those alone who well and wisely, and discreetly and correctly, can create and arrange, and compose and polish, and scan and measure feet, and pauses, and rhymes, and syllables, and accents, by dextrous art, by varied and by novel arrangement of words. And even then, so sublime is the understanding of this art, and so difficult its attainment, that it can only be learned, possessed, reached, and known to the man who is of noble and of ready invention, elevated and pure discretion, sound and steady judgment; who has seen, and heard, and read many and divers books and writings; who understands all languages; who has, moreover, dwelt in the courts of kings and nobles; and who has witnessed and practised many heroic feats. Finally, he must be of high birth, courteous, calm, chivalric, gracious; he must be polite and graceful; he must possess honey, and sugar, and salt, and facility and gayety in his discourse."

THE BELFRY OF BRUGES, AND OTHER POEMS,

was the title of a volume published in Boston in 1846 (the first of his books to be published there). It contained the poem To a Child: —

> O child! O new-born denizen
> Of life's great city! on thy head
> The glory of the morn is shed,
> Like a celestial benison!
> Here at the portal thou dost stand,
> And with thy little hand
> Thou openest the mysterious gate
> Into the future's undiscovered land.
>
> By what astrology of fear or hope
> Dare I to cast thy horoscope!
> Like the new moon thy life appears;
> A little strip of silver light,
> And widening outward into night,
> The shadowy disk of future years.

Here also appeared Seaweed, doubtless inspired by some scene at Nahant, the poet's seaside residence: —

> When descends on the Atlantic
> The gigantic
> Storm-wind of the equinox,

> Landward in his wrath he scourges
> The toiling surges,
> Laden with seaweed from the rocks.

Other songs in the collection are The Day is Done, and The Old Clock on the Stairs : —

> Somewhat back from the village street
> Stands the old-fashioned country-seat.
> Across its antique portico
> Tall poplar-trees their shadows throw ;
> And from its station in the hall
> An ancient timepiece says to all, —
>> " Forever — never !
>> Never — forever ! "
>
> .   .   .   .
>
> By day its voice is low and light;
> But in the silent dead of night,
> Distinct as a passing footstep's fall,
> It echoes along the vacant hall,
> Along the ceiling, along the floor,
> And seems to say, at each chamber-door, —
>> " Forever — never !
>> Never — forever ! "
>
> .   .   .   .
>
> From that chamber, clothed in white,
> The bride came forth on her wedding night ;
> There, in that silent room below,
> The dead lay in his shroud of snow ;
> And in the hush that followed the prayer
> Was heard the old clock on the stair, —
>> " Forever — never !
>> Never — forever ! "

It is generally believed that the old clock referred to is the one which now stands on the landing half-way up the stairs in the old Craigie House at Cambridge, and which has been gazed upon with wonder and veneration by so many visitors. This, however, is a mistake. "The original clock, which served as the inspiration of the poem, is an heirloom in the Appleton family, and stands at present at the head of the staircase in the home of Mr. Thomas G. Appleton, No. 10 Commonwealth Avenue, in Boston. Mrs. Longfellow's mother was a Miss Gold of Pittsfield; and the clock originally stood in the family mansion at that place, where the Appletons resided for some thirty years. When Mr. Appleton decided to remove to the seaside in 1853, he sold the old home, the purchaser being a Mr. Plunkett. At this time Mr. Thomas G. Appleton insisted that the clock should not be sold with the house; and his wishes were complied with, although Mrs. Plunkett was very unwilling to give it up." This clock is in an excellent state of preservation, and its appearance would hardly indicate its age. Mr. Longfellow bought a handsome old-fashioned clock at an auction-sale in Boston several years ago, and this is the one now standing on the staircase in the Craigie House. Visitors naturally associated the clock with the poem, and it was not always possible or convenient to correct the error. Another clock of similar appearance, which now stands in the old family mansion in Pittsfield, has also been erroneously taken for the clock mentioned in the poem. The poem refers entirely to incidents in the history of the Appleton family, and was written by Mr. Longfellow while spending a summer in Pittsfield. One of his friends asked the poet one day if he would not write a poem upon some subject which he had in mind. Mr. Longfellow replied that he thought he had an idea, and the next day produced the poem as it now stands.

In 1847 Mr. Longfellow edited another small collection of poems called "The Estray," and in the same year also appeared

EVANGELINE, A TALE OF ACADIE.

Of this poem upwards of thirty-seven thousand copies were sold in ten years: the whole reading world was full of enthusiasm over it. It was reviewed by The North-American Review, The American Whig Review (in which Poe had published his Raven a few years previous), The New-Englander, The Southern Literary Messenger, Brownson's Quarterly, and The Eclectic. In England it was favorably reviewed in Fraser's, The Irish Quarterly, Blackwood's, The Athenæum, and The Examiner. The picture of Evangeline, which, not long after the publication of the poem, was designed by Faed, is universally known and admired, and gave Mr. Longfellow himself much pleasure.

The origin of the poem is this: Hawthorne one day came to dine with Mr. Longfellow, bringing with him a friend from Salem. While at dinner the friend of Hawthorne said that he had been trying to persuade him to write a story about the banishment of the Acadians, founded upon the life of a young Acadian girl who got separated from her lover, and spent the rest of her life in searching for him. Hawthorne thought that it would hardly do for a story, and gave it to Longfellow for a poem. The poet, when in Philadelphia, had his fancy touched by the hospital on Spruce Street, with its high-walled grounds and antique appearance; and he decided to locate there the final scene of the poem, namely, the meeting between Gabriel and Evangeline.

There is a passage in Hawthorne's "American Note-

Books" which gives the kernel of the story as Hawthorne had it: "H. L. C—— heard from a French Canadian a story of a young couple in Acadia. On their marriage-day all the men of the province were summoned to assemble in the church to hear a proclamation. When assembled, they were all seized and shipped off to be distributed through New England, among them the new bridegroom. His bride set off in search of him, wandered about New England all her lifetime, and at last, when she was old, she found her bridegroom on his death-bed. The shock was so great that it killed her likewise."

One who is familiar with the place, in a private note to the writer, speaks of the scenery which probably inspired the opening stanzas of Evangeline. He says: —

"Longfellow often visited, when a boy, the old Wadsworth mansion in Hiram, which is still standing, and loved to ramble over it and look out from the balcony on the roof upon the woods and hills in the midst of which it is situated, and especially upon the river winding through the beautiful valley. Near by the Great Falls of the Saco tumble over the steep ledges, and in spring present a grand spectacle with the logs leaping furiously over each other and plunging into the foaming abyss below. As I have sat watching this tumult of waters, how often have I thought of Longfellow drinking in the scene with all a boy's enthusiasm; and the prelude to the Evangeline came forcibly to mind:

'This is the forest primeval. The murmuring pines and the hemlocks,
Bearded with moss, and in garments green, indistinct in the twilight,
Stand like Druids of eld.'

And as I listened to the roar of the falls and the murmur of the forest, I could but think it was here Longfellow took in the scene that in after-years he so beautifully wrought into his imperishable song."

The Scotch author Gilfillan has said, " Next to Excelsior, and the Psalm of Life, we are disposed to rank Evangeline. Indeed, as a work of art it is superior to both, and to all that Longfellow has written in verse. . . . Nothing can be more truly conceived or more tenderly expressed than the picture of that primitive Nova Scotia, and its warm-hearted, hospitable, happy, and pious inhabitants. We feel the air of the fore-world around us. The light of the golden age — its joy, music, and poetry — is shining above. There are evenings of summer or autumn-tide so exquisitely beautiful, so complete in their own charms, that the entrance of the moon is felt almost as a painful and superfluous addition. It is like a candle dispelling the weird darkness of a twilight room. So we feel at first as if Evangeline when introduced were an excess of loveliness, an amiable eclipse of the surrounding beauties. But even as the moon by and by vindicates her entrance, and creates her own holier day, so with the delicate and lovely heroine of this simple story: she becomes the centre of the entire scene."

Fraser's Magazine said, " This is an American poem; and we hail its appearance with the greater satisfaction, inasmuch as it is the first genuine Castalian fount which has burst from the soil of America." The Metropolitan said, " No one with any pretensions to poetic feeling can read its delicious portraiture of rustic scenery, and of a mode of life long since defunct, without the most intense delight." President Charles King, of Columbia

College, said: " The Evangeline is the most perfect specimen extant of the rhythm and melody of the English hexameter." But The [London] Athenæum thought that "with the sorrows of Evangeline a simpler rhythm would have been more in harmony," and suggested that the "real charm of the tale lay in its insulated pictures of scenery." Speaking in a recent issue of the metre of Evangeline, The London Daily News thought it a failure, but said: " Evangeline contains one line, —

' Chanting the Hundredth Psalm — that grand old Puritan anthem,'

which is metrically perfect; but this is an isolated instance, and may be fairly confronted with another verse from the same poem, —

'Children's children sat on his knee, and heard his great watch
    tick,'

which is almost as bad as it can be."

Oliver Wendell Holmes has said of Evangeline: " Of the longer poems of our chief singer I should not hesitate to select ' Evangeline ' as the masterpiece, and I think the general verdict of opinion would confirm my choice. The German model which it follows in its measure and the character of its story was itself suggested by an earlier idyl. If Dorothea was the mother of Evangeline, Louise was the mother of Dorothea. And what a beautiful creation is the Acadian maiden ! From the first line of the poem, — from its first words, — we read as we would float down a broad and placid river, murmuring softly against its banks, heaven over it, and the glory of the unspoiled wilderness all around.

' This is the forest primeval.'

The words are already as familiar as

'Μῆνιν ἄειδε, θεά,'

or

'Arma virumque cano.'

The hexameter has been often criticised; but I do not believe any other measure could have told that lovely story with such effect as we feel when carried along the tranquil current of these brimming, slow-moving, soul-satisfying lines. Imagine for one moment a story like this minced into octosyllabics. The poet knows better than his critics the length of step which best befits his music." A Blackwood critic said, "It is a peculiarity of this sweet singer, that his best strains are always wistful, longing, true voices of the night."

Mr. F. Blake Crofton of Nova Scotia has in The Literary World an article on Evangeline, from which the following extracts are made: —

"A Nova Scotian doctor, with a practice involving frequent long drives, observed to the writer that he seldom passed through a forest of native firs without thinking of the '*murmuring* pines and the hemlocks' in the first line of Evangeline. He held that the epithet suited these particular trees better than any others. Whether his idea was objectively true, or only fanciful, our senses are not fine enough to decide. In the latter case, however, the tribute to the poet's art is quite as great as in the former. The physician's fancy then becomes another of the many instances that prove how much the coloring of Evangeline tinges the feelings and views of Nova Scotians about Nova Scotia.

"The first appearance of Evangeline gave rise to sundry warm efforts to vindicate Gov. Lawrence's treatment of the Acadians. We have now before us three histories of this Province published within the last decade ; and they unite in condemning the manner of the expulsion, — 'at which,' says one historian, 'the moral instincts of mankind shudder.' Evangeline has proved, in fact, one of the decisive poems of the world. The most sanguine partisans, we think, have realized the impossibility of stemming the flood of pity it has created for the Acadians, by pleading the political expediency of removing them somewhere. The people of the Province, albeit prosaic in the main, glory in the soft poetic halo Mr. Longfellow has thrown round their rugged coasts. And they have no inclination to depreciate the Acadians. They have their lands, and think they see some distant prospect of inheriting their enviable reputation too!

"The tragedy of *le grand dérangement*, as the Acadians termed their expatriation, is, in truth, thrown into more striking relief by the great dissimilarity of the men who occupy their fields. A genial population has been replaced by an austere one (we use the epithets comparatively, and admit thousands of exceptions) ; a chaste by a squeamish, a temperate by a 'temperance' people ; a people that preferred practising virtues, by a people that prefers professing them. Raynal and Longfellow represent the Acadians as singularly peaceful among themselves. Governors Armstrong and Lawrence, writing before the expulsion, called them 'litigious.' There is no dispute about the litigiousness of their successors. Stern Scotch Presbyterianism and New England Puritanism, unmellowed by the transplanting, are foils to the gentle, undictatorial religion of Father Felician. There is, indeed, a little Roman Catholic chapel in the valley of Grand-Pré ; but the

picturesque superstitions of Rome are scowlingly toler-
ated in the surrounding country. 'The common drink
of the Acadians,' says the Abbé Raynal, 'was beer and
cider, to which they sometimes added rum.' Nova
Scotians warm their colder temperaments almost exclusively with strong spirits, and do so unconvivially
and furtively. A modern maiden who bore

> 'flagons of home-brewed ale

to the reapers, or filled for her father's guests

> 'the pewter tankard with home-brewed
> Nut-brown ale, that was famed for its strength in the village,'

would be charged with every sin the ingenuity of the
scandal-mongers could invent.

> 'Only along the shore of the mournful and misty Atlantic
> Linger a few Acadian peasants.'

"Small communities of these returned exiles still
exist at Clare, at Minudie, at Chezzelcook, at Tracadie,
at Arichat, in parts of Prince Edward Island, and on
the north coast of New Brunswick, speaking a corrupt
French *patois* in most cases, and preserving some of the
traits depicted by Raynal. If their maidens still

> 'by the evening fire repeat Evangeline's story,'

they repeat Mr. Longfellow's own version of it now.
His tale was gracefully translated into French alexan-
drines in 1865 by a Canadian, M. Le May. 'The
great poet of America,' says a writer in the Canadian
Monthly, 'occupies a warm corner in the French
Canadian heart'; and Fréchette, the first foreign poet
crowned by the French Academy, has paid him more
than one liberal tribute of song."

KAVANAGH,

a prose tale of New-England life and manners, appeared in 1849. It was written by the poet during a summer that he passed at the old Melville House in Pittsfield, Mass. The house was situated half a mile from the village, on the road to Lenox, and very near Dr. Holmes's house. Kavanagh is replete with descriptions of the mountainous scenery of that part of Massachusetts.

Of this book James Russell Lowell said (North-American Review, July, 1849), " Kavanagh is, as far as it goes, an exact daguerrotype of New-England life. We say *daguerrotype*, because we are conscious of a certain absence of motion and color, which detract somewhat from the vivacity, though not from the truth, of the representation. From Mr. Pendexter with his horse and chaise, to Miss Manchester painting the door of her house, the figures are faithfully after nature."

" The story, too, is remarkably sweet and touching. The two friends with their carrier-dove correspondence give us a pretty glimpse into the trans-boarding-school disposition of the maiden mind, which will contrive to carry every-day life to romance, since romance will not come to it."

Lowell further says, " If we hold Kavanagh strictly to its responsibility as a ' tale,' we shall be obliged to condemn in it a disproportion of parts to the whole, and an elaboration of particulars at the expense of unity.

" It is a story told to us, as it were, while we lie under a tree, and the ear is willing at the same time to take in other sounds. The gurgle of the brook, the rustle of the leaves, even noises of life and toil (if they be distant) such as the rattle of the white-topped wagon and the regular pulse of the thresher's flail, reconcile themselves to the main theme, and re-enforce it with a harmonious accompaniment."

THE SEASIDE AND THE FIRESIDE.

In 1850 appeared The Seaside and the Fireside, a further collection of his poems, among which was The Building of the Ship, a remarkably powerful work, equal to Schiller's Song of the Bell.

THE GOLDEN LEGEND

was published in 1851. In Homes of American Poets, George William Curtis speaks thus of the work: "In this poem he has obeyed the highest human-ity of the poet's calling by revealing — what alone the poet can — not coldly, but with the glowing and affluent reality of life, this truth: that the same human heart has throbbed in all ages, and under all circum-stances, with the same pulse, and that the devotion of love is for ever and ever, and from the beginning, the salvation of man."

From Blackwood's Magazine for February, 1852, the following is extracted: "We have no hesitation in expressing our opinion that there is nearly as much fine poetry in Mr. Longfellow's Golden Legend as in the celebrated drama of Goethe. . . . We have already, at the commencement of this paper, expressed our de-cided objection to the machinery employed by Mr. Longfellow. It is the reverse of original, being now very hackneyed; and it is absurdly disproportionate to the object for which it is introduced. . . . Occasionally, whilst retaining rhyme and the semblance of metre, Mr. Longfellow is betrayed into great extravagance."

Ruskin said, "Longfellow in The Golden Legend has entered more closely into the temper of the monk, for good and for evil, than ever yet theological writer or historian, though they may have given their life's labor to the analysis."

The following is from an article by Mr. N. H. Chamberlain of Cambridge, in The Literary World: —

"Longfellow is undoubtedly our American Minnesinger, with no rival on either side the Atlantic. He belongs to the morning, the summer, and the sunshine; and shuns, in his authorship, the Dantesque, the gloom, and the flame. If ever forced to paint the gates of the grave, he would be sure to plant some spring violet or anemone by the grim portals, and scatter along the path to it some tender mementos of a weak, clinging, undying human affection. The roots of his nature, saturate with mercy, good-will, and beauty, choke out from his song the lower and coarser qualities of our human life. That sister of Beauty, Purity, dwells everywhere in his song; and the landscapes of his poetry, even to their flora and grasses, in a purity approaching to austerity, remind one of the vestal chasteness of Alpine flowers. Only the sunshine of his gracious nature drives away the Alpine gloom.

"The Golden Legend is in point. It is a brief song of mediæval life in its aspects of religion and monasticism. It is only after due inspection that we find it to be a singularly inclusive story of that life in its dominant features. Undoubtedly, in his plan he excludes some characteristics; and if, with his mediæval lore, more profound, perhaps, than that of any other American, Longfellow had been led to write a mediæval story in prose, after the manner of Hyperion, he would have given us a more encyclopædic narrative of the æsthetics and ethics of that singular age. The Golden Legend introduces us to the monasteries and churches when they had now been long established, and were ripe towards decay.

"He has not told us of the wandering monks, hutted by the river-side among German or Celtic savages, tilling land with their own toil, and preaching under the great oaks to the painted and fair-haired barbarians in those better days of

> ' Crosier of wood
> And bishop of gold,'

but rather of the comfortable monk, with his stately cloister and well-filled cellars, fed by the largess of dead generations of the pious, when

> ' We have changed
> That law so good
> To crosier of gold
> And bishop of wood.'

"The Golden Legend, which is neither comedy nor tragedy, but an historic melodrama, has a very simple plot, elastic almost to looseness. It serves as a thread for the stringing of pearls, only the thread itself leads the thoughtful into the presence of profound problems of life and duty, pointed at but not dissected, as Mr. Longfellow's habit is. The three chief characters are a prince, a peasant-girl, and Lucifer, whom the poet in charity has painted hardly as black as he is. The story opens around the spire of Strasburg Cathedral, with devils raging in the night and storm to destroy that house of God. Here, as everywhere, Longfellow shows that exquisite discernment of the spiritual in material things, as where he notes that the apostles are in stone over the great portal to show the way in — angels inside, and devils and brutes outside, all in stone — as is ever the church and the world ; and even when in his note of explanation he makes the choir sing a Gregorian chant, which of all music, as running to monotones, has most the sense of eternity in it, he shows his insight and craft."

THE SONG OF HIAWATHA

followed The Golden Legend, appearing in 1855. Its success was phenomenal, ten thousand copies having been sold at the end of the fourth week after publication, and thirty thousand at the end of half a year. The author called it "an Indian Edda." The scene was laid among the Ojibways, on the southern shore of Lake Superior, between the Grand Sable and the Pictured Rocks. Four months after its appearance it was translated into German by Adolph Böttger, and was soon hailed with acclamations by the entire European world as it already had been by the New World. Two months after the appearance of Böttger's translation, another was published by Ferdinand Freiligrath. It had been printed in the original English at Leipzig before the translations appeared. Hiawatha was written in unalliterative rhymeless trochaics, a novelty which the poet's readers accepted with some wincing and shrugging of shoulders. Sir John Bowring, in reviewing Hiawatha, said, "Most of the poetry of the Finns is written in that peculiar metre to which Longfellow has given a certain popularity in his Hiawatha; but I believe I may take credit to myself for having been the first to introduce it into our language in an article which appeared in The Westminster Review of April, 1827."

Perhaps no poem in the English language was ever so immediately popular. It furnished topics to the sculptor, the painter, the *littérateur*, the ethnologist, and the philologist. In The Literary World, Edward Everett Hale has spoken of the origin of Hiawatha as follows : —

" A floating anecdote gives this history of the origin of Hiawatha. It is said that one of Mr. Longfellow's Harvard pupils, of one of those early classes which were favored with much of his personal care, returned to Cambridge a few years after graduating, fresh from a summer on the plains among the Indians. Meeting Professor Longfellow at dinner one day, he eagerly told his kind friend some of the legends of lodge and camp-fire, and begged him to rescue them from the extinction which seemed almost certain, by making them the subject of a poem. Now, Mr. Longfellow has the historic instinct as strong as any other of the poetical instincts. To put yourself in another's place is the business of a poet; to be able to do it is the warrant of success in poetry. Whoever gave the hint, Mr. Longfellow entered thoroughly into Indian life; and Hiawatha is now a handbook, which may be relied on, of the best Algonkin legends.

" Hundreds, not to say thousands, of people had said this very thing ought to be done. Every Phi Beta Kappa oration dwelt on the resources of 'boundless prairies and untrodden forests' for poetry. Campbell tried his hand in 'Wyoming;' Goldsmith even put an accent on the penult of ' Niagára ; ' Southey made a failure in ' Madoc ' so far as presenting Indian life was concerned ; and as for ' Yamoydens ' and similar forgotten Indian poems, there is no end to the catalogue. Hiawatha is wholly different. Mr. Longfellow took the simplest and most entertaining of the Indian legends, did not think it his business to improve upon them, nor even to adapt them to each other. He sang the song as an Indian singer would sing it.

" He had the resource of Schoolcraft's collections in the line of Algonkin legends. Schoolcraft had the advantage of marrying a half-breed wife, — herself an accomplished lady, — and of living most of his life among the tribes of the North-west. . As early as 1839 he published, from her dictation, two volumes called ' Algic Researches,' which are to this moment the mine where one finds the most charming of these stories. No nursery library is complete without the book, for children cry for the stories when they have once tasted. And the scholar who has selected the best editions of the Arabian Nights, of Grimm, and other Aryan folk-lore, puts on his shelf by the side of them Schoolcraft's Algic Researches. The name, of course, ruined the circulation of the book. The public does not know up to this hour that under this cumbrous name is buried the most charming collection of pure American stories.

" Afterwards somebody persuaded Congress to publish some immense ornamented quartos, with all Mr. Schoolcraft's lore about the Indians. It was none too soon ; and in those great picture-books, as in an ark of safety, will be found preserved all manner of learning and speculation, the bad and the good, about the Indian tribes and their history. Like specks of gold in these great pans of gravel may be found the glistening grains of the stories in the Algic Researches.

"All these pans of gravel has Mr. Longfellow rocked and rocked, pouring on fresh water and cold and clear all the while, and has washed out the pure gold. Not once has he introduced the Harvard professor into the lodges or on the prairies. Always it is the Indian girl or the Indian boy who sings. You have, pure and unalloyed, the Indian legend.

"It is said that he has never yet seen the Falls of Minnehaha, as he never saw the 'coast' of the Mississippi, where Evangeline lost her lover. All the more wonderful is the insight which paints for us the one and the other better than those do who have seen."

In dedicating his work called "Algic Researches" to Mr. Longfellow, Dr. Henry R. Schoolcraft expressed his admiration of Hiawatha in respect of its fidelity to local coloring and to Indian manners and customs. No living man was a better judge of these things than Dr. Schoolcraft.

A few weeks after the appearance of Hiawatha, a writer in The National Intelligencer, Washington, D.C., published an article charging the poet with having "borrowed the entire form, spirit, and many of the most striking incidents, of Kalevala, the great epic of the Finns." A great storm of controversy thereupon broke forth. A writer in The [London] Athenæum said, "Rhymeless trochaic dimeter is commonly used throughout Europe; and Mr. Longfellow, in his unalliterative trochaics, may with as little reason be said to imitate the metre of the Kalevala as Philalethes, in his rhymeless iambic trimeter catalectic version of The Divine Comedy, can be asserted to represent the music of

Dante." Ferdinand Freiligrath said, in The Athenæ um, that Hiawatha "is written in *a modified Finnish metre,* — modified by the exquisite feeling of the American poet according to the genius of the English language and to the wants of modern taste. I feel perfectly convinced, that, when Mr. Longfellow wrote Hiawatha, the sweet monotony of the trochees of Finland, and not the mellow and melodious fall of those of Spain, vibrated in his soul." It is thought with justice that Herr Freiligrath's intimate acquaintance with the Finnish runes and with the Kalevala made him entirely competent to detect any close imitation of the Finnish work, if any such existed. That such imitation did not exist has now for a long time been thoroughly established.

There was some adverse criticism, — much of it true. Blackwood's Magazine said, "This song is a quaint chant, a happy illustration of manners; but it lacks all the important elements which go to the making of a poem. We are interested, pleased, attracted, yet perfectly indifferent. The measure haunts the ear, but not the matter; and we care no more for Hiawatha, and are as little concerned for the land of the Ojibways, as if America's best minstrel had never made a song."

"Das Ausland" said, "Anybody who has read the five thousand and odd verses of 'Hiawatha' has certainly had enough of the epic metre, which very soon becomes as tiresome to the ear as the tune of a barrel-organ."

On the other hand, The Oxford and Cambridge Magazine thus expressed itself: "Henceforth the Ojibway and the Dacotah are to us realities, — men of like passions with ourselves. In our own dear mother-tongue, their sweet singer, Nawadaha, has spoken to us; and the voice has gone directly from his heart to ours." A writer in The Revue des Deux Mondes said, " The melody of the verse, rapid and monotonous, is like the voice of nature, which never fatigues us though repeating the same sound. Two or three notes comprise the whole music of the poem, melodious and limited as the song of a bird. . . . The feeling for nature that pervades the poem is at once most refined and most familiar. The poet knows how to give, as a modern, voices to all the inanimate objects of nature; he knows the language of birds, he understands the murmur of the wind amongst the leaves, he interprets the voices of the running streams; and yet, notwithstanding this poetic subtlety, he never turns aside to minute description, nor attempts to prolong by reflection the emotion excited. His poem, made with exquisite art, has thus a double characteristic: it is Homeric from the precision, simplicity, and familiarity of its images, and modern from the vivacity of its impressions and from the lyric spirit that breathes in every page."

Dr. Oliver Wendell Holmes has thus expressed himself concerning Hiawatha: " Suddenly and immensely popular in this country, greatly admired by many foreign critics, imitated with perfect ease by any clever schoolboy, serving as a model for metrical advertisements, made fun of, sneered at, admired, abused, but at any rate a picture full of pleasing fancies and melodious cadences. The very names are jewels which the most fastidious muse might be proud to wear. Coming from the realm of the Androscoggin and of Moosetukmaguntuk, how could he have found two such delicious names as Hiawatha and Minnehaha? The eight-syllable trochaic verse of Hiawatha, like the eight-syllable iambic verse of The Lady of the Lake and others of Scott's poems, has a fatal facility, which I have elsewhere endeavored to explain on physiological principles. The recital of each line uses up the air of one natural expiration, so that we read, as we naturally do, eighteen or twenty lines in a minute without disturbing the normal rhythm of breathing, which is also eighteen or twenty breaths to the minute. The standing objection to this is, that it makes the octosyllabic verse too easy writing and too slipshod reading. Yet in this most frequently criticised piece of verse-work, the poet has shown a subtle sense of the requirements of his simple story of a primitive race, in choosing the most fluid of measures that lets the thought run through it in easy sing-song, such as oral tradition would be sure to find on the lips of the story-tellers of the wigwam."

THE COURTSHIP OF MILES STANDISH

is another of the poet's purely American productions, published at Boston, in 1858. It touched the New England heart, and became at once a favorite. Like Evangeline, it is written in hexameters.

TALES OF A WAYSIDE INN.

In 1863 was published the first instalment of this, which was eventually to become the poet's longest work.

These poems first appeared singly in the magazines, and were afterwards collected and published in book form, with interludes. The idea and plan of the series were taken from Chaucer, and in the treatment we are continually reminded of the Canterbury Tales. But what of that? What lover of sweet and quaint stories

can object to another Dan Chaucer, "on fame's eternal
bead-roll," as "worthy to be filed," as was his English
brother? Longfellow's forte lay in power of translating, adapting, re-stating quaint and picturesque legends
in melodious verse; and this gift of his flames out in
all its sunset splendor and gorgeousness in the Tales
of a Wayside Inn. They are capital reading for a
rainy day, or for the winter fireside. They correspond
in length and in antiquarian character with Tennyson's
Idyls of the King. The diction is rich and varied,
and the handling of the metres shows the mature poet.
In short, in these tales the poet felt himself in his
element: the music rolls true and perfect, and with the
power of all the pedals and stops at the musician's command. Story succeeds story, — from the old Scandina-
vian Eddas, from Spanish legends, and from Italian
sources. In The Theologian's Tale, the poet tries his
hand once more at the familiar task of writing hexameters. The following very discriminating and delicate criticism of this work is taken from The London
Spectator for 1863: "Even in *subjects* there is a greater
and a less capacity for what we may call the crystal
treatment; and Longfellow always selects those in
which a clear, still, pale beauty may be seen by a
swift, delicate vision, playing almost on the surface.
Sometimes he is tempted by the imaginative purity
of a subject (as was Matthew Arnold, in his poem of
Balder Dead) to forget that he has not adequate
vigor for its grasp, as in the series in this volume
on King Olaf, which is, in his hands, only classical,
while by its essence it ought to be forceful. . . . Longfellow's reputation was acquired by a kind of rhetorical,
sentimental class of poem, which has, we are happy to

say, disappeared from his more recent volumes, — the
'life is real, life is earnest' sort of thing, and all the
platitudes of feverish youth. Experience always sooner
or later filters a genuine poet clear of that class of sentiments, teaching him that, true as they are, they should
be kept back, like steam, for working the mill, and not
let off by the safety-valve of imaginative expression.
In this volume such beauty as there is, is pure beauty,
though it is not of a very powerful kind. . . . Longfellow does not catch the deepest beauty of the deepest
passions which human life presents to us. . . . But he
catches the surface bubbles, — the imprisoned air which
rises from the stratum next beneath the commonplace,
the beauty that a mild and serene intellect can see
issuing everywhere, both from nature and from life, —
with exceedingly delicate discrimination ; and his poetry
affects us with the same sense of beauty as the blue
wood-smoke curling up from a cottage chimney into an
evening sky." In speaking of The Falcon of Ser
Federigo, the critic quotes with admiration the lines
describing —

> "The sudden, scythe-like sweep of wings, that dare
> The headlong plunge thro' eddying gulfs of air."

When the volume containing King Robert of Sicily
appeared, a graduate of Brown University carried
a copy of it to the Emperor of Brazil, Dom Pedro
II.   It was the year in which the two princes, the
Count Gaston d'Orleans, and the Prince August
Saxe-Coburg-Gotha, grandsons of Louis Philippe, had
come to Brazil to marry the two princesses.   The
young men were living in the city of Rio de Janeiro,
but went every day into the emperor's palace of Boa

THE OLD HOWE TAVERN AT SOUTH SUDBURY, MASS.,

NOW FAMOUS AS THE WAYSIDE INN.

Vista, where, after the emperor had devoured the Tales of a Wayside Inn, they also read them with avidity. They were all especially charmed with King Robert of Sicily; and, before the departure of the American gentleman, the emperor gave him his autograph manuscript of a translation of the poem into Portuguese, which he was to deliver to Mr. Longfellow. Mr. Longfellow told the bearer of the manuscript, when he came to Cambridge, that several Portuguese poets had translated the poem, but that the one made by the Emperor of Brazil was the best.

The interest of the reader in these beautiful poems never flags, and his only regret is that the series should end at all. One echoes heartily the words of George W. Curtis when he says, "So ends this ripe and mellow work, leaving the reader like one who listens still for pleasant music i' the air which sounds no more."

> "'Farewell!' the portly Landlord cried;
> 'Farewell!' the parting guests replied,
> But little thought that nevermore
> Their feet would pass that threshold o'er;
> That nevermore together there
> Would they assemble, free from care,
> To hear the oaks' mysterious roar,
> And breathe the wholesome country air." [1]

The first series of Tales of a Wayside Inn came out during the progress of the civil conflict. The war

[1] From what is known of Mr. Longfellow's character, many of his readers have been led to suppose that the picture of the student, drawn in these tales, was but a description of himself. The wayside inn is an old house in Sudbury, Mass., the story-tellers are guests who used to gather there. The names given to the story-tellers are as follows: the Sicilian, Professor Luigi Monti; the student, Henry Wales; the musician, Ole Bull; the poet, Thomas William Parsons; the merchant, Edulci, a Boston Oriental dealer; the theologian, Professor Treadwell; the innkeeper, Lyman Howe.

made a great impression upon Mr. Longfellow, from the fact that his oldest son, Charles Appleton, was then a lieutenant in the First Massachusetts Cavalry, in which he served with credit for two years. Lieut. Longfellow was very severely wounded in the Mine Run campaign in Virginia, in the autumn of 1863, and Mr. Longfellow went down to meet him at Washington. It is very likely that his beautiful poem, Killed at the Ford, was inspired by this event. While in the city the poet suffered from an attack of malaria. Lieut. Longfellow inherited the bravery and daring energy of his great-grandfather, Gen. Wadsworth, and the manliness and generosity of his father. Gen. Horace Binney Sargent used often to speak of him with admiration. It was the custom of Lieut. Longfellow to give all his salary to be divided between two of his comrades; but it was only after urgent solicitation on the part of Gen. Sargent[1] that he consented to have it made known to the soldiers that the money came from him. He has travelled extensively in the East, and has brought home from China

[1] Gen. Sargent writes from Salem, under date of April 20, 1882, that the facts were as follows: "Two lieutenants of the First Massachusetts Cavalry were captured, and dropped from the rolls as lost. We thought them dead. Meanwhile Professor Longfellow's son, afterwards Major C. A. Longfellow, was assigned to this regiment, and had, I think, served six months when the missing officers came back. The United States paymaster had no authority to pay two extra lieutenants *dropped from the roster*, and properly enough paid Lieut. Longfellow his deserved pay, leaving the officers who had been captured to whistle for their money. When Lieut. Longfellow heard their case, he instantly determined to surrender the whole of his merited salary, and asked me to give it to one or both of them, '*as from an unknown friend, without letting (him) be known in the matter.*' It was with great difficulty that I persuaded him that a knowledge of his generous and manly act would conduce to discipline and good order, by letting the command know how worthy he was of every soldier's affectionate respect. You are right in saying I admired this young officer."

and Japan large quantities of bric-à-brac. Once when a lad he made a trip to England, — he and two other young friends making the passage in a small sloop in eighteen days.

In the year 1864 Hawthorne died (May 24); and Longfellow, who attended the funeral in Concord, soon afterwards wrote his beautiful poem on his dear friend.

FLOWER-DE-LUCE.

In 1866 Flower-de-Luce appeared. It contained among other pieces that marvellous poem on the Divina Commedia, part of which shall here be quoted : —

I.

Oft have I seen at some cathedral door
A laborer, pausing in the dust and heat,
Lay down his burden, and with reverent feet
Enter, and cross himself, and on the floor
Kneel to repeat his Paternoster o'er;
Far off the noises of the world retreat;
The loud vociferations of the street
Become an undistinguishable roar.
So, as I enter here from day to day,
And leave my burden at this minster gate,
Kneeling in prayer, and not ashamed to pray,
The tumult of the time disconsolate
To inarticulate murmurs dies away,
While the eternal ages watch and wait.

DANTE'S DIVINE COMEDY.

In 1867 Longfellow finished his translation of the Divina Commedia of Dante. In 1863 Mr. George William Curtis said, in The Atlantic Monthly (December, p. 772), " Would not a translation of Dante's great poem be a crowning work of Longfellow's literary life?" This was said in ignorance of the fact that Mr. Longfellow had already been engaged upon such a task for more than twenty-one years.[1] The revival of interest in Dantesque literature began in England about 1840. As early as 1831 Mr. George Ticknor used to expound Dante to his scholars at Harvard College, and to him belongs the credit of introducing the study of the Tuscan poet into America. Almost at the beginning of his career as professor at Harvard, Longfellow must have begun his translation of Dante's Divine Comedy. One of his earliest courses of lectures was on Dante. In The Poets and Poetry of Europe, published in 1845, appeared his translation of his own selections from the Purgatorio; he also wrote the essay prefixed to these selections. He had published a few translations from the Purgatorio as early as 1839. In 1867 the complete work appeared in three volumes royal octavo (Boston: Ticknor & Fields). It was in the same year that Professor Charles Eliot Norton published his fine translation of Dante's Vita Nuova. In the same memorable year, also, Mr. Thomas William Parsons published his admirable version of the Inferno.

Mr. Longfellow's version was hailed with delight at home and abroad. Professor Norton, in reviewing the work (North-American Review, July, 1867), said, " His translation is the most faithful version of Dante that has ever been made. . . . His work is the work of a scholar who is also a poet. Desirous to give the

---

[1] Mr. George Ticknor wrote to Prince John of Saxony, in 1867, that Mr. Longfellow had then been engaged upon his translation of Dante for twenty-five years at least.

reader unacquainted with the Italian the means of knowing precisely *what* Dante wrote, he has followed the track of his master step by step, foot by foot, and has tried, so far as the genius of translation allowed, to show also *how* Dante wrote."

It may be remarked here that Mr. Longfellow did not attempt to reproduce the rhymes of the original, but he has reproduced its deep interior music or rhythm. Schopenhauer remarks in his Die Welt als Wille und Vorstellung, that rhythm is intuitive, has its origin in the deeps of the soul, in *pure sensibility;* while rhyme is "a mere matter of sensation in the organ of hearing, and belongs only to *empirical sensibility.* Hence rhythm is a far nobler and worthier aid than rhyme."

To return to Professor Norton's review. He says that the version is characterized by naturalness, simplicity, and directness. "Mr. Longfellow has proved that an almost literal rendering is not incompatible with an exquisite poetic charm; and, although he may in some instances have followed the exact order of the Italian phrase too closely for the best effect, his diction is in the main graceful and idiomatic." He has given "the spirit of Dante's poem." His translation "will take rank among the great English poems."

Undoubtedly the version of Mr. Longfellow is disappointing to many, especially to those who have not read Dante in the original. And those who have must miss in the translation the deep glow and passionate intensity of the Inferno. The sharp lines of the fresh-minted gold are often (but inevitably) blurred in the version. The *alti guai* that rise from Dante's pit of woe, passing through the alembic of Mr. Longfellow's gentle soul, are somehow changed into milder plaints,

— as the wailings of the damned in Poe's Duc de l'Omelette are transmuted into sweet music when passed through the medium of the enchanted panes. Thomas Carlyle should have translated Dante's Inferno. It seems to the writer, that, for the general reader, the prose version of the Inferno by John A. Carlyle (brother of Thomas Carlyle) still gives the best idea of the intensity of Dante's soul.

Professor C. L. Speranza of Yale College has published in The Literary World the following remarks on the translation, in which he compares Longfellow's version with Cary's, as Mr. Norton, in the article just quoted, compares it with that of Rossetti: —

"The difficulty of Longfellow's undertaking did not lie, perhaps, so much in the actual rendering of the 'Commedia,' as in that industrious and conscientious preparatory process which rewarded him with the absolute mastery over the poem. This once attained, a poet and a man like Longfellow must needs have done what he has done with not only unqualified success, but even comparative ease. This is not our opinion merely, but so strong a conviction on our part, that, when we imagine him set about the work of translating, we see in him not a writer who is toiling over a literary task, but a messenger of Dante, who repeats his master's message — that poem which he has made a sacred part of himself — with the natural flow and faithfulness of an ardent disciple. The reader will not, however, be content with these generalities; and we proceed to such illustrations as the limits of our space allow, only premising that our standpoint is that of persons who, while familiar with the Commedia in its original, that is written in their own native tongue, have but a recent and very imperfect knowledge of English; so that any inquiry relative to the value of the translation from a literary point of view exclusively English is wide of our purpose.

"We will take Canto XIII. of the Inferno, since it is quite popular. Its first part describes the punishment of suicides; they are changed into trees, on the leaves of which the harpies feed, causing ceaseless torment. We quote here Longfellow's version of the description of the forest formed by these trees, as it appeared to Dante when he entered it with Virgil : —

> 'We had put ourselves within a wood,
> That was not marked by any path whatever.
> Not foliage green, but of a dusky color;
> Not branches smooth, but gnarled and intertangled;
> Not apple-trees were there, but thorns with poison.'

"In four lines not only is the fantastic forest powerfully sketched, but the real one which forms its antithesis. Each line gives one of the contrasting features, and is complete in itself. By means simply of this arrangement and fewness of appropriate words, the reader, while beholding the forest in all its mysterious sullenness, is forced to stop and think. Then he is reminded of Dante, sees the amazement which at each step deters him from proceeding and examining more minutely. This continued pausing at the very entrance of the awful wilderness, marked by no path whatever, enables us to hear the breath of the poet, the rapid pulsations of his frightened heart, and we feel his horror stealing over us. Longfellow felt it; consequently, aware that any slightest change in the arrangement or words of the original would spoil the scene, by a sorcerous power of his own has transported it from hell to America. There it stands untouched, as arid and dismal, as infernally natural, as Dante saw it. Let us read now Cary's version of this same passage : —

> 'We enter'd on a forest, where no track
> Of steps had worn a way. Not verdant there
> The foliage, but of dusky hue; not light
> The boughs and tapering, but with knares deform'd
> And matted thick; fruits there were none,
> But thorns instead, with venom fill'd.'

" This is not Dante's forest, it is Cary's: the outline is different, different the movement. The very redundance of the words, their polish, breaks the spell. We lose sight of the wood to wonder at the task of the translator: we see him busy deforming his trees with knares, 'matting' them 'thick' together, and filling them up with poison. Alas! could he, at least, have found upon them some fruits to refresh his lips! But 'fruits there were none.' "

As early as sixteen years ago, Mr. Longfellow, while engaged on his translation of Dante, used to gather Dante scholars together, and read to them portions of his translation, for the sake of criticism and discussion. At a meeting held at his house on Feb. 11, 1881, and at a later meeting at the house of Professor Norton, March 17, 1881, a Dante Society was organized, — the first in America. The writer is indebted to Professor Norton, and to Mr. John Woodbury, secretary of the society, for details of its organization and work. Some young gentlemen of Harvard College proposed such a society to Professor Norton, who said at once, "There is one man in Cambridge who should be its president, and that is Mr. Longfellow." When the matter was proposed to him, he consented, on condition that no duties should be laid upon him. At the third meeting of the society, May 21, 1881, at the house of Mr. Justin Winsor, Mr. Longfellow was present, and made some remarks on a translation of Dante's poem into the Catalan dialect of Spain. One object of the Dante Society is to establish at Harvard University a library of Dantesque literature, and another object is to translate such works of Dante as have not yet appeared in English. The vice-president is James Russell Lowell, and the membership now numbers about fifty.

CHRISTUS.

The New England Tragedies (1868), and The Divine Tragedy (1872), were not successful as poems. They fell flat on the market, the books remaining largely unsold. In 1872 they were published with The Golden Legend in one volume, under the title Christus, a Mystery, and thus formed a consecutive series. They were not included in Osgood & Co.'s popular centennial (1876) " complete " edition of Longfellow's poems.

The New England Tragedies are in two parts: I. John Endicott; and II. Giles Corey of the Salem Farms.

John Endicott describes the persecution of the Quakers. Both poems deal with scenes in early colonial times, and show deep study. The following passage has the accustomed ring of Mr. Longfellow's poetry : —

> " As the earth rolls round,
> It seems to me a huge Ixion's wheel,
> Upon whose whirling spokes we are bound fast,
> And must go with it! Ah, how bright the sun

> Strikes on the sea, and on the masts of vessels,
> That are uplifted in the morning air,
> Like crosses of some peaceable crusade!"

Mr. Henry H. Clark, who for more than thirty years was either a compositor or proof-reader of Mr. Longfellow's works, has kindly furnished the writer with the following reminiscences and remarks concerning The Divine Tragedy: —

"I thought he had a consciousness that this book had not taken the place it ought, as if somehow the public did not comprehend it or appreciate it according to the time and pains he had taken in its production. But this is the experience of authors. The work thrown off in a moment of impulse is often caught up as the most precious gem. But perhaps the prime cause of its failure is not so much in the poet as in the impossibility of any one, however gifted, improving upon the simple beauty of the Bible narrative.

"One day Mr. Longfellow came in with a sort of triumphant air, and handed me a copy of The Divine Tragedy, brought out in London (as if it were worth reprinting, anyhow, on the other side of the water), and said he had received two copies from the publishers, and he thought perhaps I would like one of them. Upon opening it I found it inscribed, ' With the compliments of the author.' "

VISIT TO EUROPE.

In 1868–69 Mr. Longfellow revisited Europe, where he was received with marked honors, which naturally reached their climax in England, where it was said by The Westminster Review that not one of his English contemporaries had had a wider or longer supremacy.

The London Times published a poetical welcome signed
"C. K.," generally attributed to Charles Kingsley, of
which the following are the opening lines : —

> Welcome to England, thou whose strains prolong
> The glorious bead-roll of our Saxon song :
> Ambassador and Pilgrim-Bard in one,
> Fresh from thy home,— the home of WASHINGTON.
> On hearths as sacred as thine own, here stands
> The loving welcome that thy name commands;
> Hearths swept for thee and garnished as a shrine
> By trailing garments of thy Muse divine.
> Poet of Nature and of Nations, know
> Thy fair fame spans the ocean like a bow,
> Born from the rain that falls into each life,
> Kindled by dreams with loveliest fancies rife ;
> A radiant arch that with prismatic dyes
> Links the two worlds, its keystone in the skies.

Among the numerous festive occasions that were
made in his honor was one at which Mr. Gladstone was
present.   Although it had been decided that no speeches
should be delivered, Mr. Gladstone was compelled to
respond to the inexorable demands of the company,
saying, among other graceful things, that, "after all, it
was impossible to sit at the social board with a man
of Mr. Longfellow's world-wide fame without offering
him some tribute of their admiration.   Let them, therefore, simply but cordially assure him that they were
conscious of the honor which they did themselves in
receiving this great poet among them."   The University
of Cambridge conferred upon him the degree of LL. D.,
which he had previously received at Harvard in 1859.

An English reporter thus describes him as he appeared, arrayed in the scarlet robes of an academic
dignitary : "The face was one which, I think, would

have caught the spectator's glance, even if his attention had not been called to it by the cheers which greeted Longfellow's appearance in the robes of a LL. D. Long, white, silken hair, and a beard of patriarchal length and whiteness, enclosed a young, fresh-colored countenance, with fine-cut features and deep-sunken eyes overshadowed by massive black eyebrows. Looking at him, you had the feeling that the white head of hair and beard were a mask put on to conceal a young man's face; and that if the poet chose he could throw off the disguise, and appear as a man in the prime and bloom of life." This was the patriarchal appearance of the poet: of what he was in his early prime we have the following mere glimpse, furnished by one who met him on his first trip to Europe. He was just from college, says this gentleman, and "full of the ardor excited by classical pursuits. He had sunny locks, a fresh complexion, and clear blue eyes, with all the indications of a joyous temperament."

In 1828 Mr. Longfellow received the degree of A.M. from Bowdoin College, which also conferred upon him in 1874 the degree of LL.D. In 1868 Mr. Longfellow was also elected a member of the Reform Club. In July, 1869, he received the degree of J.C.D. at Oxford; and he returned to this country in the "China" on the 31st of August, 1869. In 1874 Mr. Longfellow was nominated Lord Rector of the University of Edinburgh, and received a large complimentary vote. He was a member of the Historical and Geographical Society of Brazil, of the Scientific Academy of St. Petersburg, of the Royal Academy of Spain, of the Massachusetts Historical Society, and of the Mexican Academy of Arts and Sciences.

THE MASQUE OF PANDORA, AND OTHER POEMS.

In 1874 the volume entitled "Aftermath" was published. In 1875 appeared The Masque of Pandora, and other Poems. This latter contained the beautiful poem, The Hanging of the Crane, a little domestic idyl, which was made the subject of a beautiful series of tableaux represented on the stage of the Fifth-avenue Theatre in New York. It is said that the subject of the poem was suggested by a visit Mr. Longfellow made at the rooms of Thomas Bailey Aldrich and his newly married wife. The book formed one of the most popular holiday works ever issued.

It may be mentioned here, that Mr. Longfellow's poetic dramas have seldom been put upon the stage. Two years ago Miss Blanche Roosevelt proposed the production of The Masque of Pandora, and Mr. Longfellow was much interested in the matter. He recast the poem, and added a few verses for stage purposes. The score for The Masque was written by Mr. Alfred Cellier, the composer of Prince Toto; and a company including Miss Blanche Roosevelt, Mr. Hugh Talbot, and others, was engaged for its representation. The play was creditably brought out in Boston (January, 1880), but was a complete failure. It was utterly lacking in attractive power. It is said that the poet himself was considerably out of pocket by the transaction. Another attempt will be made to bring out The Masque on the stage in New York.

Mr. Longfellow was very fond of the theatre and the opera. The first night of Rossi's engagement at the Globe Theatre, in Boston, he occupied a box with his friend Luigi Monti, and applauded very heartily.

In the volume entitled The Masque of Pandora was published

MORITURI SALUTAMUS,

a poem read at Bowdoin College in 1875, on the occasion of the semi-centennial celebration of his class. It is a poem pitched in a lofty and solemn key, and ranks with Bryant's Thanatopsis, and excels Wordsworth's Intimations of Immortality. The Rev. Dr. Charles Carroll Everett of Harvard University said, in his funeral address upon Longfellow, that the "marvellous poem, Morituri Salutamus, is perhaps, to-day, the grandest hymn to age that was ever written."

Mr. Henry H. Clark says, in a private note to the writer, that the poet took the most elaborate pains in the perfecting of the poem. "Months before he was to deliver it at Bowdoin, he had it put in type, his pencilled copy bearing evidence of many erasures, and looking like some old palimpsest which had been written over and over again. Then in proof he revised it and revised it, and finally had it printed in large, clear type, as if for preservation or presentation to his friends.

"I knew how fearful he was that what he was writing would be noised abroad, and I never felt so great anxiety for any thing intrusted to my care. He charged me to keep it quiet; and it was not known at the time that he was preparing it for any especial occasion, and no unusual curiosity was excited in regard to it among those through whose hands it necessarily had to pass in the process of correction. But I have always observed that printers as a class have a nice sense of honor in such matters, and no oath could bind them to greater secrecy than the simple request that what they have in hand should not be mentioned. With every new proof taken of this poem, Longfellow would require the old one returned, that by no possibility it should be left about where it could be seen or taken away; and we were as careful as those employed in the Printing Bureau of the United-States Treasury, to return every scrap of proof. In the intervals of waiting, I would sometimes look to see that the dust on the type-form had not been disturbed; for I felt more than ever before that it would not only be doing him a great wrong to allow it to get out, but would rob him of the pleasure he had so long contemplated, of coming before his old classmates fresh with the richest treasures of his heart."

Says one (speaking of the reading of the poem by Mr. Longfellow), " Of those who were present on that memorable day, none will ever forget the scene in the church, when the now venerable poet, surrounded by his classmates, saluted the familiar places of his youth; beloved instructors, of whom all but one had passed into the land of shadows; the students who filled the seats he and his companions had once occupied; and, finally, his classmates, —

> ' against whose familiar names not yet
> The fatal asterisk of death is set.'

" One of these classmates, Rev. David Shepley, D.D., referring to the poet, says, ' How did we exult in his pure character and his splendid reputation! with what delight gaze upon his intelligent and benignant countenance! with what moistening eye listen to his words! And what limit was there to the blessing we desired for him from the Infinite Author of mind!' And he adds, ' Just before leaving for our respective homes, we gathered in a retired college-room for the last time; talked together a half-hour, as of old; agreed to exchange photographs, and prayed together. Then, going forth and standing for a moment once more under the branches of the old tree, in silence we took each other by the hand and separated, knowing well that Brunswick would not again witness a gathering of the class of 1825.'

"But the poet had not indulged in any vain regrets. Manifestly he revealed somewhat his own purpose when, in closing his poem on that occasion, he said, —

> ' Something remains for us to do or dare;
> Even the oldest tree some fruit may bear.
>
> .   .   .   .
>
> For age is opportunity no less
> Than youth itself, though in another dress;
> And as the evening twilight fades away,
> The sky is filled with stars, invisible by day.' "

In 1876 Mr. Longfellow published a centennial poem in The Atlantic Monthly. Some time during the year 1877 a Parker Cleaveland memorial tablet was placed on the walls of the entrance stairway in Massachusetts Hall, Bowdoin College. It was done at the instance of Peleg W. Chandler of Boston. One morning there was quietly placed on the opposite side another tablet bearing photographic likenesses of Mr. Cleaveland and the poet Longfellow, between which likenesses was placed the following epitaph, written by Mr. Longfellow during his visit to Brunswick in 1875:

PARKER CLEAVELAND.

> Among the many lives that I have known,
> None I remember more serene and sweet,
> More rounded in itself and more complete,

Than his who lies beneath this funeral stone.
These pines that murmur in low monotone,
These walks frequented by scholastic feet,
Were all his world; but in this calm retreat
For him the teacher's chair became a throne.
With fond affection memory loves to dwell
On the old dark days when his example made
A pastime of the toil of tongue and pen.
And now amid the groves he loved so well
That nought could bear him from their grateful shade,
He sleeps, but wakes elsewhere, for God has said, Amen!

KÉRAMOS, AND OTHER POEMS.

In 1877 Kéramos, and other Poems, was published. It included the beautiful tribute to James Russell Lowell, entitled The Herons of Elmwood, and the poem of The White Czar.

The poem to Lowell is pitched in a high heroic strain, and breathes a most noble spirit. Elmwood is a great haunt for birds, a perfect medley of bird-voices often saluting the ear of the passer-by. Mr. John Holmes, in an article in The Harvard Register, gives a pleasant sketch of rural Elmwood, with its trees and birds and whispering pines, showing that others besides Longfellow have heard and enjoyed —

"The cry of the herons winging their way
O'er the poet's house in the Elmwood thickets."

Those familiar with the Portland of Longfellow's boyhood have thought that the imagery of Kéramos, or the potter, must have been suggested to the poet by the old Portland pottery, with which he was familiar in his youth. The truth of this surmise is now established by the following note communicated to the writer by

ELMWOOD, THE HOME OF LOWELL,

LOWELL STREET IN CAMBRIDGE.

Mr. Henry H. Clark, to whom the reader is already indebted for pleasant reminiscences: —

"He went over the poem many times in proof, elaborating and perfecting it, and making the verse smoother and sweeter each time. There was one little halt in the measure, I thought. The expression 'quilted sunshine and leaf-shade' jarred slightly on the ear. I told him if he would remove this there would not be one imperfect line in it. He said he would consider it; but in the morning he came down saying it must stand; for it expressed just what he wished to say, and any other arrangement of words would fail to do it. And he related how when a boy he had watched the old potter at his work under the hill, going back and forth under the branches of a great tree; and it was the light and shade falling on him that he wished to picture in the verse. And how beautifully he has done it in the opening stanzas of the poem!"

> *Turn, turn, my wheel!   Turn round and round*
> *Without a pause, without a sound:*
> *So spins the flying world away!*
> *This clay, well mixed with marl and sand,*
> *Follows the motion of my hand;*
> *For some must follow, and some command,*
> *Though all are made of clay!*

> 'Thus sang the Potter at his task
> Beneath the blossoming hawthorn-tree,
> While o'er his features, like a mask,
> The quilted sunshine and leaf-shade
> Moved, as the boughs above him swayed,
> And clothed him, till he seemed to be
> A figure woven in tapestry.'"

The year 1879 saw the completion of

POEMS OF PLACES,

edited by Mr. Longfellow with the assistance of his friend John Owen. These thirty-seven dainty volumes certainly form a most enticing and valuable thesaurus of poems. But because the sale of the books was not pushed, or for some other reason, they never obtained much circulation, and the 'publishers lost many thousand dollars by the undertaking. Mr. Owen's work was chiefly in verifying and ascertaining the authorship of the poems. In order readily to distinguish the volumes devoted to the different countries, Mr. Owen has had his set of Poems of Places bound in a unique and fanciful style, in cloth of many colors. The volumes devoted to English poetry are bound in smoke-tinted cloth, Ireland rejoices in a green binding, Spain appears in a wine-color, Greece in olive, Africa in black, etc.

The following from the charming preface to the series will be read with interest: —

"Madame de Staël has somewhere said, that 'travelling is the saddest of all pleasures.' But we all have the longing of Rasselas in our hearts. We are ready to leave the Happy Valley of home, and eager to see something of the world beyond the streets and steeples of our native town. To the young, travelling is a boundless delight; to the old, a pleasant memory and a tender regret.

"I have often observed that among travellers there exists a kind of free-masonry. To have visited the same scenes is a bond of sympathy between those who have no other point of contact. A vague interest surrounds the man whom we have met in a foreign land; and even reserved and silent people can become communicative when the conversation turns upon the countries they have seen.

"I have always found the Poets my best travelling companions. They see many things that are invisible to common eyes. Like Orlando in the forest of Arden, they 'hang odes on hawthorns and elegies on thistles.' They invest the landscape with a human feeling, and cast upon it

> 'The light that never was on sea or land,
> The consecration and the poet's dream.'

Even scenes unlovely in themselves become clothed in beauty when illuminated by the imagination, as faces in themselves not beautiful become so by the expression of thought and feeling.

"This collection of Poems of Places has been made partly for the pleasure of making it, and partly for the pleasure I hope to give to those who shall read its pages. It is the voice of the Poets expressing their delight in the scenes of nature, and, like the song of birds, surrounding the earth with music. For myself, I confess that these poems have an indescribable charm, as showing how the affections of men have gone forth to their favorite haunts, and consecrated them forever.

"Great is the love of English poets for rural and secluded places. Greater still their love of rivers. In Drayton's Poly-Olbion the roar of rivers is almost deafening; and if more of them do not flow through the pages of this work, it is from fear of changing it into a morass, which, however beautiful with flowers and flags, might be an unsafe footing for the wayfarer."

To Mr. Clark the reader is again indebted for the following charming account of the compilation of the poems : —

"These selections were made at a time when he was confined to his house by illness that would not permit him to go out or engage in more serious labors; and it was his delight to take down the 'treasured volumes of his choice,' and mark the passages appropriate for the collection. This was more truly a selection, and an original selection by himself, than any other collection of verse heretofore published; for the pieces are culled largely from long poems, now little read, and from a wide range of authors, and would seem to include all of interest that has been written about places of note by the best poets. The volumes on England are fitting companions to Hawthorne's Note-Books; and if brought out together, accompanied by illustrations, the two would form a delightful guide-book to the traveller.

"Longfellow was choice in his selections. He did not take every thing that came to hand, and was criticised for having omitted some familiar pieces; but he would not include any he felt were unfit in language or unworthy in merit, and, even after the pieces were in type, many at first selected were cut out for some passage he could not approve, or to make room for some better choice. And in this he showed the same purity of taste and discriminating judgment as in his own works. But sometimes, in consequence of these changes when the forms were made up, he was compelled to write a poem to fill the place when no other was available; and scattered through the volumes are many original poems of his that had never appeared before and do not appear elsewhere. But, having been written for this purpose, and with more haste than usual, he at first credited them to 'Anonymous,' that prolific writer, as if he did not feel they were fully up to his standard; but he was persuaded at last to give them his name, and they stand as worthy of his muse as any other work of his pen.

"It was singular to note, in reprinting from 'best editions,' how errors had crept in ; and sometimes I came upon a passage I thought incorrect or obscure, or a piece too commonplace, when he would say, 'Let us read it ;' and he would at once discover the defect, while I had the benefit of his fine reading (for it may not be generally known that he was a fine reader, the melody of his voice giving a sweetness to his expression that was charming, and his eyes glowing with the rapture of the thought. He would sometimes brace himself up, and throw back his shoulders, and read with all the impression of the professional actor). It was such a treat to hear him read, that I fear I was tempted to find difficulties to be decided by so pleasant an ordeal.

"However coldly the public received this work, I enjoyed it intensely. Mr. Emerson coming in one day, and finding him looking over his proof, asked what he was doing. When told he was making a compilation, the old sage shook his head doubtfully, and said, 'The world is expecting better things of you than this. You are wasting time that should be bestowed upon original production.' But Longfellow explained that he was not feeling well enough for other work, and this diverted and interested him. And inasmuch as Emerson himself had but a short time before made a collection of verse (Parnassus), they grew jolly over the incident, and shook hands heartily as they parted, — perhaps never to meet again, I thought; for Emerson was very feeble, and it seemed as if he would be the first to be called to realize the glories of the better land.

"What a picture for memory — these two authors

grasping hands, as it were, on the verge of eternity! so dissimilar in appearance, so unlike in their work, but the foremost men of the time in all that ennobles and enriches literature, and elevates the heart, and sanctifies the home.

" What a delight it was to have all the great poet's library to go over! for the books were brought to the office, and the type set directly from them. These were the ' grand old masters ' whose ' footsteps echo through the corridors of time ; ' these were the friends with whom he took counsel, but not from whom he drew his inspiration ; for Nature was his master, and these but his servants. He drank of the living fountain, and was refreshed himself, and gave refreshment to others."

We approach now the last years of the poet's life, every one of which, from 1879 to 1882, was signalized by some public ovation in his honor. How unspeakably precious now is the thought that these tributes of love were made before it should be forever too late !

THE CHILDREN'S ARM-CHAIR.

The year 1879 was the children's year, when, on the occasion of his seventy-second birthday (Feb. 27), they presented Mr. Longfellow with the now famous arm-chair, made from the wood of the old horse-chestnut tree, that stood at the corner of Brattle and Story Streets, by the " village smithy,"[1] celebrated by Longfellow in his poem of The Village Blacksmith.

Says a writer in The New York Evening Post: " In the half rural city where Longfellow spent his maturer life, — that which he himself described in

[1] The house in which the village smith lived is still standing at No. 54 Brattle Street.

Hyperion as 'this leafy, blossoming, and beautiful Cambridge,' — he held a position of as unquestionable honor and supremacy as that of Goethe at Weimar or Jean Paul at Baireuth. He was the First Citizen, — the man whose name had weight beyond all others not only in social but in civic affairs. This was the more remarkable as he rarely attended public meetings, seldom volunteered counsel or action, and was not seen very much in public. But his weight was always thrown on the right side; he took an unfeigned interest in public matters, always faithful to the traditions of his friend Sumner; and his purse was always easily opened for all good works. On one occasion there was something like a collision of opinion between him and the city government, when it was thought necessary for the widening of Brattle Street to remove the 'spreading chestnut-tree' that once stood before the smithy of the village blacksmith, Dexter Pratt. The poet earnestly expostulated: the tree fell, nevertheless; but, by one of those happy thoughts which sometimes break the monotony of municipal annals, it was proposed to the city fathers that the children of the public schools should be invited to build out of its wood, by their small subscriptions, a great arm-chair for the poet's study. The unexpected gift, from such a source, salved the offence, but it brought with it a sore penalty to Mr. Longfellow's household: for the kindly bard gave orders that no child who wished to see the chair should be excluded; and the tramp of dirty little feet through the hall was for many months the despair of housemaids." The chair was set in a place of honor by the study fireside. Its design is very pretty, and in perfect taste. The color is a dead black, an effect produced by eboniz-

THE CHESTNUT ARM-CHAIR.

THE GIFT OF THE CHILDREN OF CAMBRIDGE.

ing the wood. The upholstering of the arms and the
cushion is in green leather, and the casters are glass
balls set in sockets. In the back of the chair is a cir-
cular piece of exquisite carving, representing horse-
chestnut leaves and blossoms. Horse-chestnut leaves
and burrs are presented in varied combinations at other
points. Around the seat, in raised German text, are
the following lines from the poem : —

> " And children coming home from school
>   Look in at the open door :
>   They love to see the flaming forge,
>   And hear the bellows roar,
>   And catch the burning sparks that fly
>   Like chaff from a threshing-floor."

Underneath the cushion is a brass plate on which is
the following inscription : —

To

THE AUTHOR

of

THE VILLAGE BLACKSMITH,

This chair, made from the wood of the spreading

Chestnut Tree,

is presented as

an expression of grateful regard and veneration

by

The Children of Cambridge,

who with their friends join in the best wishes and

congratulations

on

This Anniversary,

February 27, 1879.

Mr. Longfellow conveyed his thanks to the children
in a beautiful little poem, entitled "From my Arm

Chair," first published, very appropriately, in The Cambridge Tribune : —

> " Am I a king, that I should call my own
>   This splendid ebon throne?
> Or by what reason, or what right divine,
>   Can I proclaim it mine ?
>
> .   .   .   .
>
> " And thus, dear children, have ye made for me
>   This day a jubilee,
> And to my more than threescore years and ten
>   Brought back my youth again."

SPEECH AT SANDERS THEATRE.

On Dec. 28, 1880, at the celebration of the two hundred and fiftieth anniversary of the founding of Cambridge, Mr. Longfellow appeared with his friend Oliver Wendell Holmes on the platform at Sanders Theatre. It was his last public appearance. He and his brother poet Holmes stood up to receive the storm of applause that greeted them from the audience, among which were a thousand grammar-school children. The pleasantest feature of the occasion was this ovation of the children to their poet. Contrary to all expectation, and against his own uniform custom, he made a speech to the children by way of response : —

" My dear young friends, I do not rise to make an address to you, but to excuse myself from making one. I know the proverb says that he who excuses himself accuses himself; and I am willing on this occasion to accuse myself, for I feel very much as I suppose some of you do when you are suddenly called upon in your class-room, and are obliged to say that you are not prepared. I am glad to see your faces and to hear your voices. I am glad to have this opportunity of thanking you in prose, as I have already done in verse, for the beautiful present you made me some two years ago. Perhaps some of you have forgotten it, but I have not; and I am afraid, — yes, I am afraid that fifty years hence, when you celebrate the three hundredth anniversary of this occasion, this day and all that belongs to it will have passed from your memory: for an English philosopher has said that the ideas as well as children of our youth often die before us, and our minds represent to us those tombs to which we are approaching, where, though the brass and marble remain, yet the inscriptions are effaced by time, and the imagery moulders away."

At the close of the exercises the children pressed around their dear friend in crowds, — little boys and girls with albums, begging for his signature. His patience and good nature were inexhaustible; and, when the dinner hour came, he told all who had not got the signature to come to his house, every one, and he would give them the autograph there. When a gentleman present made some pleasant remark to him about his speech, he said, "My best speech to the Cambridge children is my poem on the arm-chair."

LOVE OF CHILDREN.

This seems a fit place to give a few anecdotes of his rare love of children. Probably no other poet ever had so many lovers and friends among " the little people of God." One day, during his last sickness, some little children were passing his gate; and, when told that their dear friend was soon to die, they began to speak in whispers, and one little boy said to his companion, "Let's walk softly by, and not make a noise." A company of little five-year-old soldiers, marching by the house the day after the passing away of the poet, lowered their flag out of respect. On the occasion of Mr. Longfellow's last birthday (Feb. 27, 1882) the children of the schools all through the country, to a large extent, gave up the day, or a part of it, to the honoring of their poet, — the exercises consisting of studies and readings of his poems, and essays and addresses upon his character and genius.

"His native city of Portland desired to honor him with a public reception upon the same occasion, but failing health and his aversion to public displays compelled him to decline the honor. The members of the Maine Historical Society, however, kept the day with eulogies, critical and personal essays, and a poem. At the Blind Asylum in South Boston there was a pleasing celebration, in which the pupils participated, and in preparation for which a volume in raised letters had been printed, containing tributes to Mr. Longfellow and some passages from his poems."

Among his many poems expressing his love and tenderness for children, Weariness is one of the best : —

> O little feet ! that such long years
> Must wander on through hopes and fears,
>   Must ache and bleed beneath your load ;
> I, nearer to the wayside inn
> Where toil shall cease and rest begin,
>   Am weary, thinking of your road !

The following story has been widely copied by the newspapers. For many years Mr. Luigi Monti was in the habit of dining at Longfellow's house on Saturdays, and then playing on the piano for the entertainment of Mr. Longfellow, who was very fond of music. On Christmas Day, while walking briskly toward the old historic house, he was accosted by two ladies and a girl about twelve years old, who inquired the way to Longfellow's home. He told them it was some distance down the street, but if they would walk along with him he would show them. When they reached the gate, the girl said, " Do you think we can go into the yard? " — " Oh, yes ! " said Signor Monti. " There are no dogs barking at anybody." As they entered the lawn the little girl exclaimed : " Oh, I should like to see Mr. Longfellow so much ! " To which Mr. Monti replied : " Do you see the room on the left ? That's where Martha Washington held her receptions a hundred years ago. If you look at the windows on the right, you will probably see a white-haired gentleman reading a paper. Well, that will be Mr. Longfellow." She looked gratified and happy at the unexpected pleasure of really seeing the man whose poems she said she loved. As Signor Monti drew near the house, he saw Mr. Longfellow standing with his back against the window, his head of course out of sight. When he went in, the kind-hearted Italian said, " Do look out of the window, and bow to that little girl, who wants to see you very much." — " A little girl wants to see me very much, — where is she? " He hastened to the door, and, beckoning with his hand, called out, " Come here, little girl, come here, if you want to see me." She needed no second invitation ; and, after shaking her hand and asking her name, he kindly took her into the house, showed her the " old clock on the stairs," the chair made from the village smithy's chestnut-tree, and the curious pictures and souvenirs gathered in many years of foreign residence.

Not many months before the poet's death, he called on Rev. Minot J. Savage of Boston. Mr. Savage's little boy and he struck up quite an acquaintanceship; and when Mr. Longfellow was leaving, and had got quite to the bottom of the stairs, the little fellow called out, " Mr. Longfellow, 'oo must come back, and tiss me once more!" And back he went to the top of the stairs to kiss the little fellow.

A gentleman relates, that once, when he was a small boy, he was present with a large company of ladies and gentlemen whom Longfellow had, with accustomed kindness, consented to show over the old historical mansion. All the rest had been introduced save himself (the small boy), and the company evidently considered him too insignificant to deserve notice. The host noticed the omission, " and, grasping his hand, gave him a more cordial greeting even than he had given to the rest of the company."

Mr. J. Q. A. Johnson of Cambridge is the authority for the statement that a gentleman of that city preserves a pleasant memento of the poet in the shape of a little boat, whittled out of a shingle, with places for three masts. It was made several years ago by Mr. Longfellow, for a little girl. The noticeable feature of it, says Mr. Johnson, is that —

> " With nicest skill and art,
> Perfect and finished in every part,
> A little model the master wrought."

ULTIMA THULE.

It was during 1880 that Ultima Thule, the last published volume of the poet, appeared. The title was, alas! prophetic and true. He was nearing the end of those songs that he had so long and so sweetly sung to cheer his own pathway, and that of others, through the world of sense.

Ultima Thule contained the graceful poem on the pen presented by "beautiful Helen of Maine."[1] The following lines are from the poem which gives its title to the book : —

> " With favoring winds, o'er sunlit seas,
>   We sailed for the Hesperides,
>   The land where golden apples grow ;
>   But that — ah ! that was long ago.
>
>   .   .   .   .
>
> " *Ultima Thule !*   Utmost isle !
>   Here in thy harbors for a while
>   We lower our sails ; a while we rest
>   From the unending, endless quest."

. In 1881 The Literary World published a Longfellow Number, a beautiful tribute to the poet. Extracts from its careful papers have been embodied in this book. In this year was published The Longfellow Birthday Book, edited by Miss Charlotte Fiske Bates. Of this book nineteen thousand copies were sold during the first year after its publication. It is a handsome little volume, with quotations from Longfellow's writings sprinkled through a calendar containing blank spaces for autographs and dates of birth. On Feb. 27, 1882, the school-children of the country, as has been said, devoted the day to honoring the name of Longfellow.

LAST SICKNESS.

The last two summers of his life were spent at Nahant, his daughter and her children being there. He found the sea air very cold, however ; and it was his custom to

---

[1] The pen was made from a fetter of Bonnivard, the prisoner of Chillon; the handle, of wood from the frigate "Constitution," bound with a circlet of gold, inset with three precious stones, from Siberia, Ceylon, and Maine.

wear a heavy overcoat to protect him from the chill breezes. At Nahant Mr. Longfellow wrote very little. He took only a few volumes with him, but received impressions which he later expressed in verse.

His health remained tolerably good until within about three months of his death, although his digestive powers were considerably impaired, and he was obliged to live at times almost exclusively on bread and milk. His health had received a shock on the occasion of the death of his friend Louis Agassiz, and he perhaps never fully recovered from that blow. During the last three months he scarcely walked outside of his private grounds. He now wrote very few letters, using a printed form for the acknowledgment of such communications as he received from others. On Saturday morning, the 18th of March, he walked for a while on the piazza, and on going into the house complained of being chilled. At dinner he expressed a fear that he should have a return of vertigo. On retiring to his chamber, he was taken violently ill with vomiting and diarrhœa. Dr. Morrill Wyman was summoned, and later Dr. Francis Minot. Sunday morning he was so dizzy as to be unable to rise. His sufferings were severe, and opiates were administered. On Monday the symptoms were alarming and dangerous in character, and peritonitis had plainly developed. On Tuesday the lungs became affected, and bronchitis set in, the patient suffering extremely from coughing fits. Wednesday and Thursday he suffered less pain; and, recovering during the latter day from a sleepiness that was upon him the day before, he became as bright and genial in conversation as was his wont. An increase of inflammation, Thursday night, induced partial unconsciousness, which recurred at intervals.

His talk was often incoherent and rambling. As the morning of Friday wore on, there was a return of complete consciousness, and the sick man knew his end was near. Pain was now nearly absent, but there was a disposition to dulness. He talked very little, and for an hour before death became unconscious. He died easily and peacefully, at ten minutes after three o'clock on Friday afternoon, March 24, 1882, surrounded by the complete circle of his family. By the bedside were the three daughters, Edith (wife of Richard Henry Dana), Alice M., and Annie Allegra (unmarried); the two sons, Ernest and Charles Appleton; his brother, Alexander W. Longfellow of Portland; his sisters, Mrs. James Greenleaf of Cambridge and Mrs. Annie L. Pierce of Portland: his brothers-in-law Thomas Gold Appleton and Nathan Appleton of Boston; Mrs. Ernest Longfellow; and Wadsworth and William P. P. Longfellow, nephews, of Portland. The poet's brother, Rev. Samuel Longfellow of Germantown, Penn., arrived too late at Craigie House: its owner had passed into the silent land.

The people of Cambridge were most of them well informed of the dangerous character of his sickness, so that, when the solemn bells slowly tolled seventy-five strokes, they knew what had occurred; and deep and genuine was the sorrow, as if each had suffered a severe personal bereavement. It was touching to witness the grief of the servants of the house. Soon after the death became known, tokens of mourning were exhibited on many houses, and the poet's portrait draped in black was seen in many shop-windows.

Among those who sent letters of inquiry, or called personally, during the sickness, were Dr. Oliver Wendell Holmes, President Charles William Eliot and many Harvard professors, William D. Howells, John G. Whittier, Mayor Samuel A. Green of Boston, Hon. Robert C. Winthrop, Walt Whitman, James Russell Lowell, and George W. Childs.

THE FUNERAL.

The funeral was held on Sunday, March 26, and was both private and public. To the service at the house none were admitted but the members of the family and a very few of the poet's most intimate friends who had cards of invitation. The services at the house began at three o'clock. At that time the sky was heavily overcast; and soon the snowflakes began to fall, recalling Longfellow's beautiful poem : —

> Out of the bosom of the Air,
>   Out of the cloud-folds of her garments shaken,
> Over the woodlands brown and bare,
>   Over the harvest-fields forsaken,
>   Silent, and soft, and slow
>   Descends the snow.
>
> Even as our cloudy fancies take
>   Suddenly shape in some divine expression,
> Even as the troubled heart doth make
>   In the white countenance confession,
>   The troubled sky reveals
>   The grief it feels.

Throughout the city, flags were displayed at half-mast. Before the gate of the Longfellow mansion were a few hundred people braving the snow and the cold. A reverential stillness characterized the company; and, when the remains were brought out to the hearse, nearly all stood with uncovered heads. Many eyes were moistened with tears.

Among those present in the house, besides the relatives above mentioned, were Alexander Agassiz and Mrs. Louis Agassiz; Peter Thacher; Mr. and Mrs. Frank I. Eustis; Mr. and Mrs. I. M. Spellman; Ralph Waldo Emerson, and his daughter Ellen Emerson; Oliver Wendell Holmes; George William Curtis; Professor Charles Eliot Norton; Miss Grace Norton; Rev. Cyrus A. Bartol, D.D.; Dr. Morrill Wyman; Miss Charlotte Fiske Bates; Samuel Ward of New York; Luigi Monti; Mrs. James Ticknor Fields; Mrs. Ole Bull; Mrs. Beane (Helen Marr); Mr. and Mrs. Eben N. Horsford and daughters; John Owen; the Misses Palfrey; Mr. William Dean Howells; Mr. James Myers; Professor Louis Dyer; Mr. and Mrs. John Brooks; Mr. and Mrs. Joseph Warner; Mr. and Mrs. Benjamin Vaughan.

The remains were laid in a plain casket covered with broadcloth embossed with black ornaments. On the top were placed two long palm-leaves crossed; and the casket was encircled with a rim of the passion-flower vine, bearing one beautiful blossom. The silver plate bore the inscription: —

> *Henry W. Longfellow.*
> **Born February 27, 1807.**
> **Died March 24, 1882.**

The brother, the Rev. Samuel Longfellow, conducted the services, making a short prayer, and reading selections from Mr. Longfellow's poems, one of which was the exquisite poem entitled Suspiria: —

Take them, O Death! and bear away
  Whatever thou canst call thine own!
Thine image, stamped upon this clay,
  Doth give thee that, but that alone!

Take them, O Grave! and let them lie
  Folded upon thy narrow shelves,
As garments by the soul laid by,
  And precious only to ourselves!

Take them, O great Eternity!
  Our little life is but a gust
That bends the branches of thy tree,
  And trails its blossoms in the dust!

During the services the aged poet Ralph Waldo Emerson was observed to come forward several times to the coffin to take one more long look at the face of his dead brother-singer and friend.

The remains were deposited in the family vault in Mount Auburn Cemetery, the only ceremony there being the repeating of the following words by the Rev. Mr. Longfellow: "O Death, where is thy sting? O Grave, where is thy victory? Dust thou art, and unto dust shalt thou return. The Lord gave, and the Lord taketh away. Blessed be the name of the Lord."

The company were then driven to Appleton Chapel, Harvard College, where impressive public services were held. On a table in front of the altar was a beautiful floral harp, nearly three feet in height, made of smilax and white and yellow flowers, with one broken string. The harp was the gift of the Bohemian Club of San Francisco, and had been ordered by telegraph. The exercises were conducted by the Rev. Dr. Charles Carroll

Everett, who, it is interesting to remember, was in his
youth an instructor at Bowdoin College. He was assisted by the·Rev. Francis Greenwood Peabody, who
was formerly the pastor of the First Parish Church.
Among selections read at this service was one from
Hiawatha, beginning,—

> "He is dead, the sweet musician!
> He the sweetest of all singers!
> He has gone from us forever,
> He has moved a little nearer
> To the Master of all music,
> To the Master of all singing!"

From the remarks of Professor Everett the following
beautiful passages are extracted:—

"I said he poured his life into his work. It is singular that the phase of life and of experience which forms
so large a portion of most poetry, which many sing if
they sing nothing else, he was content to utter in prose,
if prose we must call the language of his romances. He
seems content to have scattered unbound the flowers of
romantic love at the door of the temple of his song.
There is something strange, too, in the fascination
which the thought of death has for so many generous
youth. You remember that Bryant first won his fame
by a hymn to death; and so, I think, the first poem of
Longfellow's which won recognition for him was that
translation of those sounding Spanish lines which exalt
the majesty of death, and sing the shortness of human
life. But the first song that rang with his own natural
voice, which won the recognition of the world, was not
a song of death, it was a Psalm of Life. That little
volume of the Voices of the Night formed an epoch
in our literary history. It breathed his whole spirit,

his energy, his courage, his tenderness, his faith: it formed the prelude of all that should come after.

.   .   .   .

"That marvellous poem Morituri Salutamus is perhaps to-day the grandest hymn to age that was ever written. It is no distant dream, as it was when those sounding Spanish lines flowed from his pen. He feels its shadows, he feels that the night is drawing nigh, and yet he stands strong and calm and bold as at first. He greets the present as he greeted in old times the future. He gathers from the coming on of age, the approaching night, no signal for rest, but a new summons to activity. He cries, —

> ' It is too late ! Ah, nothing is too late
> Till the tired heart shall cease to palpitate.'

. .   .   .

"He had breathed himself into his songs: in them, he is with us still. Wherever they go, as they wander over the world, he will be with them, a minister of love. He will be by the side of the youth, pointing to heights as yet unscaled, and bidding him have faith and courage. He will be with the wanderer in foreign lands, making the beauty he sees more fair. He will be with the mariner upon the sea, he will be with the explorer in the woods, he will be in the quiet beauty of home; he will be by the side of the sorrowing heart, pointing to a higher faith; and, as old age is gathering about the human soul, he will be there to whisper courage, still to cry, —

> ' For age is opportunity no less
> Than youth itself.'

"Thus will he inspire in all faith and courage, and point us all to those two sources of strength that alone can never fail, 'heart within, and God o'erhead.'"

TRIBUTES.

When the death of Longfellow was made known in England, there was not a single paper of repute in Great Britain that did not contain a long editorial on the poet's life and writings, with reminiscences of his visits to England. The Daily Telegraph said, "It is for a singer and for a friend for whom America and England are mourning alike." The general sentiment of the whole nation was that a dear friend had gone.

Among the many American tributes to Longfellow's memory and name, the following by George William Curtis bears the stamp of great tenderness and beauty: —

"No American could have died who would have been more universally mourned than Longfellow. He had come into all homes, and was beloved of all hearts. His sweet and pure and tender genius has hallowed all domestic relations and events, and there is no emotion which does not readily and fitly express itself in his verse. He was the most famous of Americans, and his fame had become a personal affection and a national pride. This was from no misconception of his position in literature, or of his peculiar power; but it is the most significant tribute to the man.

"A more symmetrical and satisfactory character it is not easy to conceive. Rectitude and simplicity, exquisite courtesy and gentleness, infinite patience and sympathy and tact, blended in a manner which was as gracious as a poem, and benignant as a benediction. His accomplishment in letters, his elegant scholarship, were extraordinary. The felicity of citation, the aptness of allusion, were delightful; and with all his wealth of resource he never tipped a sneer, or permitted an innuendo. His perfect humanity instinctively apprehended every fellow-man; and, known to everybody, not one who knew him personally can have had any unkindness of feeling for one who could not be unkind. His home, if deeply saddened in recent years, was always the House Beautiful; and its noble, urbane, and beloved master welcomed guests from every land, and, greeting them in their own language, revealed to them an America which they had not suspected, and which they could never forget.

" Although for many months his friends have watched him wistfully, and waited for news with half-foreboding hearts, the old, old sorrow comes at last with the old pang and unappeasable sense of loss. He was old, but still his sweet song was heard with all the familiar music and the inexpressible charm. Age touched his silvering head, but not his heart nor his mind. His place among us, in our busy life, was that of the bard in the fond old golden legends that he loved, the honored and cherished singer whose hand the youth and maidens kiss, and in whose lofty and tender melody the older men and women hear once more the accents of their early aspiration, and own a consolation for long-baffled hopes.

> ' And though at times, impetuous with emotion
> And anguish long suppressed,
> The swelling heart heaves moaning like the ocean,
> That cannot be at rest, —
>
> We will be patient, and assuage the feeling
> We may not wholly stay;
> By silence sanctifying, not concealing,
> The grief that must have way.' "

The Christian Register had these sentences: " ' It

often happens,' said Thomas à Kempis, 'that a stranger, whom the voice of fame had made illustrious, loses all the brightness of his character the moment he is seen and known.' Such was not the case with Henry Wadsworth Longfellow. To know him as a man was to add to the impression he had made as a poet. The sweetness, the refinement, the gentle and lovable qualities of his character, strongly endeared him to those who came within the circle of his personal influence. It was this underlying richness of his nature which bloomed into fragrance and color in his poetry."

At a memorial service in the Unitarian Church of East Boston, Sunday, April 2, 1882, Gov. John Davis Long spoke as follows: —

" It was a delightful thought to devote the happiness and April softness of this Sunday afternoon, this best day of our cheerful and sunny religion, to Longfellow, — to the companionship of an exquisite, uplifting poet, and to the influence of a gentle, refining spirit, which now, and for time to come, will mellow our sadnesses with tender hymns of resignation, will inspire us far up the heights with his soul-stirring songs, and will fill our lives, though we grow to be bent and gray, with children's hours. We are here to sing with him, not to mourn him. Why is it that we used to shudder at this death, which now we find only strings the chords of a more comprehending love, and opens full to view the rarer sweetness and the pure gold which the dust of life half hid before? Have you not looked at a picture, and only been blinded by the sunbeam that shot across it? It was not till the sunbeam went out and died, that the lineaments stood forth relieved, distinct, and perfect. What a poor and meagre chain of little-meaning links is this narrative of dates and events, which we sometimes call a man's life! It is of little consequence, except for the dear association's sake, what was the name or residence or birthplace or age of the poet. Of what interest to us is even the great globe of the sun in itself, compared with the radiance which is its soul and which fills the universe with light? Do not tell me that Longfellow was born, and had honors and degrees and a professorship, and crossed the seas; for these things come and go, and now flash, now faint. But tell me that his mind was full of gentle and ennobling thoughts; for these live forever, and are now in your hearts and speaking in you. Tell me that he loved children, and wrote songs for them and of them; and let me hear my little girl, as she comes down the stairs in the morning, repeat untaught the verses which he made, and which are a bridge from his soul to hers, and from all human souls to one another. The material is nothing, and dies; but the soul sings on, and in these tributes which we and many another assembly are paying it, we are acknowledging, we are asserting, we are proving its immortality. When some poor creature with nothing but a throne and a crown is dead, his subjects hail his successor, and shout, *The king is dead, long live the king!* When our king, the poet, is laid to rest, we may well cry, *The poet is dead, long live the poet!* For he succeeds himself, and is dead only to live, even on earth, a larger and more present life in his verse, and in the songs and hearts of the people.

"It is a poor commonplace to say that Longfellow is the poet of the people, for no poet is a great or true poet who is not that. And what a tribute is this to our common humanity! Lives of great men all remind us

not so much that we can make our lives sublime, as that
our lives *are* sublime, if only we will not cumber or
debase them. Not by putting into melody something
that is beyond and above you and me, not by breathing
a music so exquisite that it never trembles in our fancies
and prayers, does the poet rise to excellence; but by
voicing the affections, the finer purpose, the noblenesses,
that are in the great common nature, — in the sailor up
the shrouds, in the maiden lashed to the floating mast,
in the mother laying away her child, in the schoolboy
at his task or play or counting the sparks that fly
from the blacksmith's forge, in the youth whose heart
beats Excelsior, in the man at his work or, when he
rests from it, raided by blue-eyed banditti from the stairway and the hall. So the poet teaches us not our disparity from him, but our level with him; not our mean-
ness, but our loftiness. Let us not forget that he owes
as much to those who inspire him to sing their thoughts,
as they to him for singing them. Or, rather, not trying
to strike the balance of credit, let this name and memory
and life of Longfellow, this recognition of the poet and
the poet's work, in which we are all sharers in common,
lift us all, as he would have wished, to higher consecration, to the sweet, angelic community of finer feeling
and thinking, and to that moral elevation, like a dewy
hill in the morning sunrise, where we all wake to the
divinity of our natures and the glory of these souls that
come from God's own harmony. At such a lofty and
serene height, we find there has been and can be no
death. For here is Dickens, and the children are laughing and crying by turns at his humor or his tears. Here
are the rounded character of Washington, the eloquent
loyalty of Webster, the patient faith of Lincoln, all up-

holding, far more than before, the idea of a nation of liberty and union. Here are the serene illumination of Channing and the chivalrous enthusiasm of Bellows. We do not see them, but they live and breathe and are of the very air in which we live and move. Something is indeed gone from them, but it is only the dross. And so Longfellow was never more present with you than here and now. It is for us to tune our hearts and voices in harmony with his. Remember that his fame and effluence came not so much from the long poems, — these are in most poets often buoyed by the shorter songs, — but from these utterances of the heart which, like the Psalm of Life, Resignation, The Day is done, The Children's Hour, The Footsteps of Angels, seem like the spoken language of our own souls. The music he wrote is all lying unwritten in us. Let us sing it in our lives, which we can, as he sung it from his pen, which we cannot.

"It was a beautiful life. It was felicitous beyond ordinary lot, and yet not so far beyond. The birds sang in its branches. The pleasant streams ran through it. The sun shone and the April showers fell softly down upon it. The winds hushed it to sleep. And, while now he falls asleep, let us read his verse anew; and through the lines let us read him, and draw into our lives something of these serenities and upliftings. So for ourselves and one another, remembering this Sunday afternoon, remembering the poet's life, living hereafter with the poet's hymns in our ears, may we, like him, leave behind us footprints in the sands of time; may our sadness resemble sorrow only as the mist resembles the rain; may we know how sublime a thing it is to suffer and be strong; may we wake the better soul that slumbered to a holy, calm delight; may we never mistake heaven's distant lamps for sad funereal tapers; and may we ever hear the voice from the sky like a falling star,—Excelsior!"

On Sunday, April 2, Dr. Cyrus A. Bartol delivered a eulogy upon Longfellow. It was filled with the sweet fragrance and mellow maturity of thought and diction which make Dr. Bartol's sermons such enduring gems of Christian oratory. He said: —

"I knew the early haunts in Portland of his fledgling muse, spreading its wing to the woods on the bay and the observatory on the hill, hovering over the wharf and the ropewalk, looking into the sky and the creek, listening to the wind and the brook and the sea. How little he thought some of his lines would come to be translated into ten languages, to have popularity without precedent, — one of his pieces, 'The Hanging of the Crane,' not a very long poem, having been sold for four thousand dollars, a price beyond all parallel in this country! I have some personal cause to speak of him. Almost fifty-four years ago Mr. Longfellow, at the age of twenty-three, taught in Bowdoin College, Brunswick, Me., the Spanish language and French to me, a boy of sixteen.

"I had listened with him to the same instruction from that man of genius, Dr. Nichols, in Portland, his native town. He was the same gentleman then, instinctively treating every student as such, that sat in the Bowdoin or afterwards the Harvard recitation-rooms. Just so, too, he walked Boston streets, or at home yonder answered every letter, received every caller, wrote his name in every album, gave his autograph to boys and girls without number, won the love and praise of school-children throughout the land, and was so large and free in his hospitality that I, for one, felt it a duty rather to stay away from his frequented house, in the doubtless vain fear that even his abundant courtesy might be overtasked or strained.

" From his father, whom I well remember, this most fortunate of our poets, resembling him in feature, also inherited a singular modest and winsome mood of temper, only barely stirred as by American slavery into burning heat, as though a beam of the moon became one of the sun. Never did imagination have happier blending with love. His fancy transfigured the details of common life. Nothing to his eye was stiff and stark and straight. All danced and sang, revolved or swung. Every thing and everybody, like the person in the nursery-ballad with rings and bells, to his ear made music wherever it went. With no other bard had the measure such freedom and ease. He could not hear of Acadia but Evangeline started up, nor think of Indian story without Hiawatha, nor see the word ' Excelsior ' on a bit of paper but the youth scaled the mountain. The ocean-cable that brought to our breakfast-boards laudations of the London press the next morning after his decease showed what universal esteem he was held in, how broad and cosmopolite the web of sympathy that drew his fellows to him by millions of threads, and how mankind are woven together and telegraph to each other by every tone of harmony and syllable of truth. Beyond any other writer of our time, he made the music, the ' folk-songs ' of the English race. The Scottish Burns says of a projected piece of his own, —

> ' Perhaps it may turn out a sang,
> Perhaps turn out a sermon.'

" Dewey, the impressive preacher, and Longfellow, the melodious rhymer, had the very same word of God to say or sing, as if the eloquent periods of the former had but been raised to a higher power in the rhythmical accords of the latter, the identical truth in verse reaching a thousand to one that would peruse or had listened to the homiletic prose. Indeed, this singer has become part of the atmosphere with his song, in which sorrow is more musical than joy. He is in the air we breathe, he is part of the light we see by, he breaks part of the bread we eat: and the marvel of the phenomenon is that by no peculiar or sublime originality he so becomes. He ranks not with the grander bards of the nations — Greek, Roman, Italian, German, English — in every age. He must be placed among the minor, secondary ones, if we compare him with Homer, Dante, Shakspeare, Milton, and Wordsworth, not to speak of others nearer than those to us in time or space, who have hewn out of the living rock their shrines or voiced at first hand the Holy Ghost. Because he is so familiar and home-like, he is so welcome. He does not soar like Emerson, or dive like Browning. He does not quarry or mine. He is the ground swallow, dear among us and in the mother land ; not admired and wondered at, as the eagle is, but more cherished and oftener distinctly in our view. If he is not a virile guide through the grand and dreadful passes, he is a womanly comforter.

" A poet may be too high or deep for immediate effect or common esteem, and so may have to wait, like Kepler in science and Plato in philosophy, for a far-off future to appreciate the work which only a select and sifted class feels or suspects the beauty of now. He did not have to winnow his audience. What Longfellow surpasses all his contemporaries in, overmatches the comrades and fellow-artists who join to love and generously delight in him and his success, is his broad, present, and instant influence, his sure striking of the common chord vibrating and resounding through two hemispheres in the human breast, his revealing to the meanest capacity the poetry hid in the human soul, putting into his picture-gallery blacksmith and duke, sailor and king, translating not only the Coplas of Don Manrique, but out of invisible ink on the heart's tables bringing out the lines written in the general image of God, rendering ordinary experience of pleasure or toil into strains so simple as to be commonplace, yet as sweet as they are clear; composing, not seldom, a symphony, without profundity, of delicious words, a combination of concords to the ear, if not always an interior creation of melody created by thought, holding up a mirror for everybody to see his own face in, idealizing nature and human nature, legend and history, and making, to our pride and joy and gratitude, poets of us all, placing his poetry on the level of actual life.

"Every stroke told. His arrows hit. With conscious aim or unawares, he never missed his mark. Young men and maidens he poetized, psychologized, with his verse. Every latent bit of romance in all minds he touched and stirred into life. Dirge or serenade, his music was for the million, the people. This, like the old harper, has gone, not in bodily form, but ghost-like, from door to door through the land, for two continents, stringing and striking his lyre.

"The modest man, devoid of boasting, lowly, while wide as the prairie, the Acadian wood, or the watery main, understood his especial function and singular

strength.   In that charming poem, The Day is done,
he calls for one to read to him, —

> 'Not from the grand old masters,
>   Not from the bards sublime,
> Whose distant footsteps echo
>   Through the corridors of Time.
>
> .   .   .   .
>
> ' Read from some humbler poet,
>   Whose songs gushed from his heart,
> As showers from the clouds of summer,
>   Or tears from the eyelids start.
>
> .   .   .   .
>
> ' And the night shall be filled with music,
>   And the cares that infest the day
> Shall fold their tents, like the Arabs,
>   And as silently steal away.'

He is just that.   His marvellous acceptance is especially
due to his being, among poets, the consoler.   Mr. Longfellow's instrument is not the trumpet, but the flute.
He does not so much stir as assure and soothe, more
lullaby than appeal. He croons a cradle-song to this
great humanity, still a child, tired and worn, on its way.
He gives the peace it implores.   A religious trust
breathes through all his books, the spirit of faith.   He
flouts no one's convictions.   In a doubting or half-
believing age, there is no query of the primal truths of
God and heaven on his page.   He sings to the last as
his childhood learned.

   "Mr. Longfellow is dead: but, as he himself has
written, 'The artist never dies;' and, like Benvenuto
Cellini in gems and metals, he was a worker in words.
The Latin poet Horace writes, 'I shall not wholly die;'
and Shakspeare in his Sonnets betrays his sense of im-

mortality; and Milton avers, in one of his, he can confer fame on the 'Captain, Colonel, or Knight at Arms,' who spares his dwelling. This American songster shall survive, like the song-birds in the forest he loved to hear. He tells us of the hour-glass on his desk, —

> ' A handful of red sand, from the hot clime
>   Of Arab deserts brought,
>   Within this glass becomes the spy of Time,
>   The minister of Thought.'

While the sand shall run or flow may the verses last, — clean as the drift on the shore, pure as pearls, polished and unspecked as the coated grains in the deep, decoration and delight of the world, from whose crowding he did not, like Goethe's lonely youth, turn aside to muse deeply, but mixed with so humanely to give his own gifts broadcast and gather his themes from every scene and sight. As a rosy cloud, so his mortal presence melts away; but all his genius, which was his spirit, is left in colors that are now fine and fast. His excellence, his moral elevation, is large part of his fame. Faith, Hope, Love abiding, — was not such not so much the burden as the flying pinion of Longfellow and Dewey, as of Paul? They mount on wings, as do the eagles."

Rev. Minot J. Savage, in his pulpit in Boston, spoke thus of the poet (the words are given in abstract): —

"Singularly fortunate was the poet. He achieved his reputation early, and kept it to the last. As a robin in spring he was welcomed. He was heard and given the freedom of every home in Christendom. Unlike many unfortunate and unappreciated poets, he flew on free pinions through a clear sky, and only ceased at the declining of the sun. He went through

life loving and loved, till the light faded into the
sunrise of another life.   He made himself the best-loved
poet of the nineteenth century.   Probably more homes
in England and America are familiar with his poetry
than with that of any other poet in the world.   He was
on a level with the people.   Hardly a line he wrote is
not clear to every one.   Browning, perhaps the greatest
poet of the century, is a poet of scholars, and needs to
be interpreted to the people.   Tennyson's poetry is
frequently a sinewy grappling with great problems.
Longfellow wrote but little on transitory themes.   Lowell's and Whittier's poetry sprang like men full armed to
engage in the conflict of the times.   But reforms achieved
become history, and most men are too busy for any thing
but the present duty.   Longfellow came into every home
in the country."

On the Sunday following Longfellow's death, the Rev.
Dr. Franklin Johnson of Cambridge preached a sermon
in his memory.   He said :

" His writings are distinguished for their beauty,
but they are distinguished not less for their purity.   As
he lay dying, there was no line which he would wish to
blot.   His songs have gone into all the world, a help
to the struggling, an inspiration to the weak, a consolation to the sorrowing, a benediction to childhood, a stay
and staff to age.   The pulpit will learn more and more
to prize the aid he has given it, and to use his words as
the Apostle to the Gentiles used those of the Greek
poets who had caught some glimpses of divine truth,
and had uttered their thought in language made charming with the genius of song.

" Longfellow may be called pre-eminently the poet of
humanity.   No other poet has so fully entered into our

various struggles and trials, and brought to our struggles and trials so much of hope and cheer. Miss Bates has collected those portions of his writings which are most helpful, under the title of 'Seven Voices of Sympathy,' and they make a large volume. From no other poet that ever wrote could so many things of this kind be culled. We find in the writings of all great singers utterances which go to our hearts, and aid us in the pain and sadness of life; though usually they are few and far between. But they constitute the very substance of all that our poet has produced."

TRIBUTES FROM ENGLAND.

There were many tributes of respect from England. The Times said, "The purity of Mr. Longfellow's thoughts, his affinity with all that is noblest in human nature, his unfailing command of refined, harmonious language, will continue to draw readers notwithstanding the judgment of critics that he is not a poet of the very first rank. It will seem to many that his death marks the close of a distinct era of American literature. One cannot readily point to worthy successors of the brilliant group to which he belonged."

Said The Globe, "It is not yielding to the supposed prevailing tendency indiscriminately to extol Americans to say that the death of Mr. Longfellow is a national loss to England. A general and true appreciation was accorded him here, even at a time when America was anything but popular."

The Telegraph said, "The place Longfellow occupies in English literature is decidedly bright. He is almost as well known and widely read in England as in America. His influence has been wholly good. As long as the English language lasts, his works will be quoted as models of simplicity of style, and purity of thought. Death has taken America's greatest literary son."

PERSONAL APPEARANCE AND HABITS.

Among the recent friends of Mr. Longfellow was Madam A. Machetta, better known by her maiden name, Miss Blanche Roosevelt, the young cantatrice who took the part of Pandora when his Masque was put upon the stage in New York and Boston. She often visited him at Cambridge and at Nahant, and is now preparing a book about him to be called "Reminiscences of a Poet's Life." From the manuscript of this volume the following description of Mr. Longfellow's personal appearance has been furnished to the public: "His face, filled with rugged lines, presents a contour of great firmness and intelligence. The nose is Roman rather than Greek, with the very slightest aquiline tendency. His eyes are clear, straightforward, almost proud, yet re-assuring. They are rather deeply set, and shaded by overhanging brows. In moments of lofty and inspired speech they have an eagle-like look; the orbs deepen and scintillate and flash; like the great bird of prey, they seem to soar off into endless space, grasping in the talons of the mental vision things unattainable to less ambitious flight. With his moods they vary, and when calm nothing could exceed the quietness of their expression. If sad, an infinite tenderness reposes in their depths; and, if merry, they sparkle and bubble over with fun. In fact, before the poet speaks, these traitorous eyes have already betrayed his humor. I must not forget the greatest of all expressions, humility. To one whose soul

HENRY W. LONGFELLOW,
AND HIS EARLY HOME IN PORTLAND.

and mind are given to divine thought, it is in the eye that this sentiment finds its natural outcome; and the world knows that Longfellow's faith is the crowning gem in a diadem of virtues. His face is not a mask, but an open book, — a positive index to his character. The forehead is high, prominent, and square at the temples; numberless fine lines are engraved on its surface, and on either side a slender serpentine vein starts from the eyes, and, mounting upwards, loses itself beneath a mass of silvery white hair. I should scarcely call them the work of time, but rather the marks of an over-active intelligence. They may have appeared to others at thirty as plainly as they do to me to-day. The cheek-bones are high, and near the jaw the cheeks are slightly sunken. The mouth is the most sensitive feature in the face: its character is mobile, even yielding, absolutely belying the outspoken firmness of the other features. The lips are rather full, sharply outlined, and faintly tinged with color. They close softly, and are sometimes tremulous with emotional speech. Longfellow might be coaxed, but never driven. The whole of the face glows with a beautiful carnation, more suggestive of youth than old age. The lower part is completely hidden by a wavy beard of snowy whiteness, which also half conceals the slender throat. The chest is broad, not deep. With a supple and graceful carriage, he is as straight as an arrow, and has a nature of extraordinary vigor. The hair mingling with the beard sets the rosy face in an aureole of snow. The charm of a well-bred manner asserts itself over every other personal attribute."

To this description may be added an account of his daily life at seventy. He rose early, took a rather light breakfast, and, if the day were pleasant, generally set out for a walk, either in his own grounds or elsewhere, varying his route each day, if possible. It was always his custom to carry his overcoat on his arm if there was the slightest indication of a change in the weather, i.e., a fall of the thermometer. Whenever he was preparing any work or poem for publication, he would often call on his printers at the University Press, not far from his residence, and receive and return proofs of his works. He studied his matter carefully after it was in type. He kept his productions by him, and used the file with patient industry. The Divine Tragedy is said to have been entirely re-written after it was in type. Perhaps the recasting of it spoiled it, for it is unpopular. He sometimes (not, as has been stated, always) sent his copy to the publishers in a printed form. His manuscripts were written with a lead pencil, in a clear, round, back hand, and he has preserved them all bound in handsome volumes. In writing he made many erasures with a rubber, writing neatly over the erased spaces, so that the manuscript presented a perfectly neat appearance. It was his custom to have every scrap of his manuscripts sent back to him from the printers.

He was accustomed to alter more or less the poems published in magazines and papers before putting them into book-form. He was never discovered writing a poem. Mr. Longfellow could not write " poems to order " for anniversaries, re-unions, and other occasions. *Apropos* of this fact, a little incident is in point. At the time of the death of President Garfield, Mr. Moses King of Cambridge called on the poet, at the request of the managers of The Boston Daily Globe, for the purpose of securing, if possible, a poem for that journal.

He was authorized to offer as much as one thousand dollars, if necessary, to secure the coveted prize. But Longfellow, although he was known at the time to have in his pocket the sonnet which later appeared in The Independent, and was subsequently reprinted in The Poets' Tributes to Garfield, could not be influenced by any means to part with it, because he had not yet satisfied himself that it was perfect enough to give to the world; this, too, in spite of the fact that Joaquin Miller had read it previously, and had congratulated Longfellow on its production. As illustrating this positive reluctance to write for occasions, one who was witness to the colloquy says, "I remember with what earnestness Gilmore tried to persuade him to write an ode for the opening of the great Peace Jubilee, picturing with all his own enthusiasm the greatness of the occasion, and the glory it would give the poet. But no. He never sought popularity: it came to him. He could not do any thing for the sake of applause."

A word should be said of his humor. It was of so quiet and furtive a nature that it was only discovered by personal intercourse. One who knew him, speaking of the tender glance of his eye, says: "It had a peculiar brightness. There was a sharpness, yet softness, in it that was fascinating, — a lurking wit that seemed to peep out from behind his wisdom." His glance was penetrating and keen, and seemed to read one through and through. Professor Charles Eliot Norton has thus alluded to his friend's humor: "One day I ventured to remonstrate with him on his endurance of the persecutions of one of the worst of the class of mendicants, who to lack of modesty added lack of honesty, — a wretched creature; and when I had done, he looked at me with a pleasant, reproving, humorous glance, and said: 'Charles, who would be kind to him if I were not?' It was enough. He was helped by a gift of humor, which, though seldom displayed in his poems, lighted up his talk, and added a charm to his intercourse."

It is unnecessary to say that Mr. Longfellow spoke several European languages fluently. A French gentleman well known in Boston told a friend that Mr. Longfellow was the only American he knew who spoke French quite like a Parisian.

His study at Craigie House has been thus described by a foreigner: —

" A door opens, and you are in the study of the great poet of the New World. The walls are panelled to the ceiling with dark polished oak; and you see from the circular-headed windows with their heavy wooden mullions and the tall oak chimney-piece with its classic ornamentation, that the architect has but reproduced some mansion of the early Georgian era with which he was familiar, across the sea. At one end of the room stand lofty oaken bookcases, framed in drapery of dark red cloth. Here and there on ornamental brackets are some marble busts, among them a fine effigy of Washington. Easy chairs and reading stands are scattered around.

" In the centre of the room, which is covered with a well-worn Persian carpet, there sits, writing at a round table littered with books and papers, a medium-sized, bony man, apparently about seventy. His hair and beard are white as snow; but from beneath an ample forehead, indicating considerable intellectual power, there gleam a pair of dark lustrous eyes, from which the fire of youth seems not yet to have fled. He rises with a grave sweetness to salute you. Some chance remark or some tone of your voice, that recalled to him the wild fells and moors of distant Yorkshire, makes you at once something more than a mere passing stranger. He tells you with pride of the remote Yorkshire ancestry to which perhaps his poetry owes something of its. manliness and vigor. And, if you happen to be familiar with many of the scenes which he visited nearly half a century ago in Europe, he listens with strange interest as you tell of the changes which time has wrought in some of the spots on which his muse has bestowed an undying fame."

Mr. Longfellow's study generally contained flowers. Upon the walls are crayon likenesses of Emerson, Hawthorne, and Sumner. The bookcases completely cover the sides of the room. Among other precious relics are Coleridge's inkstand, Tom Moore's waste-paper basket, a fragment of Dante's coffin, the children's arm-chair, and the pen presented by " Helen of Maine."

He was the most modest of men. His gentle, unassuming manner charmed his friends very much. Mr. Thomas J. Kiernan of the Harvard Library says that Mr. Longfellow used the College library very little, his own private library being very complete; but when he did come in to consult a work he was extremely modest, seeming to be afraid of making trouble. He would work away between the two cases of the card-catalogue for a long time before the assistants noticed his presence, or could render him any help. What could be more charming than such utter freedom from pride and assumption? Only the personal, and very intimately personal, friends of Mr.

LONGFELLOW'S STUDY IN THE VASSAL-CRAIGIE-LONGFELLOW HOUSE

Longfellow will ever be able to tell the story of his inner life. Some, even of his own townsmen, considered him aloof and unsocial. They did not know that what seemed so in him was only the result of his shrinking sensitiveness and exquisitely tuned susceptibility.

He has been charged with lack of sympathy with the great common humanity, — with the broad national life of his own country. The truth of the matter is, that he was sensitive, he was a scholar, he had a scholar's fastidiousness, and he was the gentlest of poets. Being so, he was not born to enter into the stormy life of the rude and comparatively coarse-fibred masses: he did not sympathize with them in the 'full range of their existence to such an extent, for instance, as Walt Whitman does; he only entered sympathetically into their spiritual natures; he interpreted their gentler and holier moods, and sympathized with them in their joys, their sufferings, and their bereavements. Yes, he did sympathize with our common humanity, but as a poet, as a scholar. We may blame him, if we choose, for a certain aloofness; but this was the source of his strength. We are always quarrelling over the great poets; but there is not one of them that the world could spare, — all different, all imperfect, but all the delight and solace of mankind. Different impressions as to his sociability exist, especially in his own Cambridge. A neighbor of his, writing anonymously to The New York Independent, says that " he became closely identified with all classes of the community in which he lived," and that there was " apparently absolute unconsciousness of distinction " in the " intercourse of Mr. Longfellow and his family with Cambridge society." This is undoubtedly true. But one must remember the position in which a world-famous man is placed: he cannot, if he is sensitive, endure to be stared at incessantly by everybody, and especially if he lives in a village, such as Old Cambridge essentially is, and always has been. The world knows Mr. Longfellow as the most cordial of hosts. He loved all gentle people. He could love children without feeling any jar or disturbance: hence his frequent exhibitions of fondness for them. His phenomenal kindness to strangers is proverbial. Let us not complain, then, of his aloofness, but take him as he was, and thankfully.

> "According to his virtue let us use him."

He was a man who had suffered deeply, and more deeply than others on account of his sensibility. His first wife died in the bloom of womanhood; and his second idolized wife was burned to death before his eyes, while friend after friend went away into the silent land, leaving him behind. Suffering gave a sweet and pensive sadness of tone to his poetry. And yet his essential cheerfulness never left him for any long period of time. He was religious, a believer in God and in immortality; and his life was blameless, and sweet with love and good deeds. One who knew him says, —

"To the poorer classes Mr. Longfellow was endeared by his discriminating and unostentatious benevolence. I happened to be often brought in contact with a very intelligent but cynical and discontented laboring-man, who never lost an opportunity of railing against the rich. To such men, wealth and poverty are the only distinctions in life. In one of his denunciations I heard him say, ' I will make an exception of one rich man, and that is Mr. Longfellow. You have no idea how much the laboring-men of Cambridge think of him. There is many and many a family that gets a load of coal from Mr. Longfellow, without anybody knowing where it comes from.' "

The writer of this volume, although having access to some details of the inner life of the poet, has studiously refrained from making use of them, agreeing therein with his friend Professor Charles Eliot Norton, that these " sweet privacies of life " should be scrupulously respected. If others have not this feeling, the world will some day know in how many cases of distress the purse of the great-hearted singer was opened to relieve suffering and want.

After the above paragraph had been written, there appeared in The New York Independent an interesting letter from an anonymous lady writer, who had been encouraged and financially assisted by the Cambridge poet. She had come to Boston from a distant part of the country, and was eking out a living by teaching music and writing for the press. " One day," she says, " I visited an editor, with some verses of greater length than usual. He said, ' This is too long for a newspaper or magazine. Finish it, and then I want you to take it to Mr. Longfellow.' I opened my eyes in wonder. ' I go to Mr. Longfellow!' " She thought the editor was speaking ironically. It was three months later that she one day impulsively decided to write to the poet. She received an answer inviting her to visit him. She went, and found a life friend. She went abroad, and the poet's constant care and watchfulness followed her. She says : —

"At one time his letters before me show him taking charge of a production of my pen, to place it in the hands of the editor; at another, visiting the dusty office of the paper for which I was writing letters, to subscribe for it with his own hand, and the editor, who never expected such an honor to be paid his poor paper, immediately begs me to consider myself engaged to write the following year. Finally, when I chose an operatic career, and made my *début* in Italy, where temptations are no longer temptations, but deliberately set nets of the most intricate description to waylay and trip the footsteps of the most clear-headed, he gave his warnings and suggestions very wisely and kindly. This friend of friends taught me to confide my trials to him, until I wrote as freely as if to the pages of my journal.

"Again and again would he give some little commission to do for him, as if it were granting him a great favor, while it is only his delicate way of presenting me to persons who might be interested in my struggles and prove themselves friends.

"Too proud to reply to his oft-repeated question of whether he might aid me, he finally visited some of my friends, to learn my exact needs; and then one New Year's morning I remember myself seated on the side of my bed, where letters have been brought to me, the tears rolling down my cheeks, for I feared I must yield to the inevitable and go home. 'Only a little New Year's gift that will serve to buy gloves,' said his letter. Did he know that it was bread, not gloves, I feared I should need, and which his generous gift supplied?

"But I copy from these letters, my choicest treasure, a few paragraphs which will give an idea of his thoughtfulness and kindness. In one of his earlier letters he writes: —

"'Your last letter in Italian showed your great progress in the language. But now I think it would be well to come back to the English again; for one's pen gallops and gossips more easily in one's native language, and perhaps you would write oftener if you wrote in English. You can keep your diary in Italian; and do not forget to put down everybody's name whom you care to remember. . . . Do not mind what I say about writing in Italian. Only write; and, whether in English or not, your letters will always be welcome.'

.   .   .   .

"His criticisms of a young author's work were tenderness itself, and full of appreciating encouragement. When he made a criticism, it was so delicate as to be hardly felt. There was not a bit of severity intended in the following mention of a very immature and perhaps ambitious poetical venture : —

"'Your poem I read in The ——. It is a little bit mystical, but I had no great difficulty in understanding it. Now that you tell we where it was written, it has a double interest for me.

"'This brief note is another of my poor returns for your longer and better ones; but, if you saw the pile of unanswered letters heaped up around me, you would pardon and pity me.'

.   .   .   .

"The following was in response to some confidences, such as I have referred to above : —

"'I feel now, more than ever before, the dangers that surround you; but I am sure you will be strong and valiant. Instead of giving you good advice, I send you a song I wrote the other day. It has already been set to music two or three times; but that is no reason why you should not set it again, if you feel inclined to do so.'

" The song is that beginning 'Stay, stay at home, my heart, and rest,' the last verse of which is, —

> 'Then stay at home, my heart, and rest,
>   The bird is safest in its nest:
>   O'er all that flutter their wings and fly,
>   A hawk is hovering in the sky;
>   To stay at home is best.'

" Again he writes, speaking of an attempted injury : —

" ' Alas! an artist's life is never without its thorns; but it has its roses also.   Above all, it has —

> *La procellosa e trepida,*
> *Gioja d'un gran disegno*
> *. . . La gloria*
> *Maggior dopo il periglio*
> *La fuga e la vittoria.' "*

Another instance of the poet's benevolence is furnished by a young lady who tells her story in The Congregationalist.   In the year 1867 there was, in a well-known New England academy, a young girl who was trying to complete her academic course with very slender resources.   At length the time came when she must leave her studies, and teach, unless she could obtain funds.   The interruption of her studies would have been a serious injury.   She thought of her pen as a means of livelihood, wrote some poems, and sent them to Mr. Longfellow, hoping that his influence might procure their publication.   He took them to Mr. James T. Fields of The Atlantic Monthly, and then wrote to her that while the poems were not exactly available for that periodical, and neither he nor Mr. Fields knew any way of disposing of them, yet they both felt a great interest in her, and were so desirous that she should continue her studies that they begged her to accept an enclosed check for a generous amount of money. She did accept it, finished her studies, became a clergyman's wife, and is leading an influential and successful life.

LONGFELLOW'S RELIGION.

Mr. Longfellow was not, as has been stated, a regular attendant at the First Parish Unitarian Church in Cambridge. He was not a regular attendant at any church, but had a family pew in Appleton Chapel of Harvard College. He was not a member of the college church, his name not appearing in the record book; nor was he a member of any church. The Rev. Minot J. Savage, from whose address on the poet a quotation has already been given, speaks thus of his personal relations to the churches : —

" Longfellow's grave is hardly closed ; and already, as I hear, he is beginning to be claimed as an 'evangelical.' If it be indeed so, it is only because evangelicalism has been converted. You may study his complete works from one end to the other, and find no single trace of belief in any one of the distinctive and peculiar doctrines of the so-called evangelical churches. It is no wonder they would like to claim him ; for if flowers like him can grow out of doors, in the common air and sunshine of the world, then it is conclusively proved that their walled hot-houses have no monopoly of the sweet blossoms of the religious life. As matter of fact, his Christ ideal is only the traditional one of Unitarianism. And if sweet and loving words about him of Nazareth make one evangelical, then, behold, the Church has suddenly become wide enough to enfold

Theodore Parker and John Stuart Mill. Mr. Long-fellow's own brother, who spoke the last loving words at his house, hardly clings to the name of Christian even, but loves the wider fellowship of all true souls of whatever name."

Quite another view is given by the Rev. Franklin Johnson, D.D., of Cambridge, a life-long student of Longfellow: —

"But 'sweet and loving words about him of Naza-reth' do not constitute the sum of his religious teaching. He belonged to no school of dogmatic theology; and it is idle for a sect to claim one who did not identify himself with any particular denomination; yet it is remarkable that there is scarcely a single important doctrine of our holy religion which may not be expressed in his exquisite language. The excellence of the Scriptures; the existence, the justice, and the love of God; the divinity, the miracles, the atoning death, and the glorious resurrection of Christ; the efficacy of prayer, the necessity of the new birth, the forgiveness of sins, the salutary influence of the Church, and a thousand other verities akin to these, — may be found upon his pages. Sometimes they occur in translations from foreign authors, sometimes they are put into the mouths of historic characters, and sometimes they are the utterances of his own thought; but they form one of the most prominent features of all his writings. This great man, who was sincerity itself, could not have veined his poems so deeply and so uniformly with the truths of revelation, had he not believed them. It is equally remarkable that he wrote no syllable of doubt or denial; that scepticism cannot discover, from the beginning to the end of his works, a line in which to

clothe itself. His position was as far as possible from
that of Theodore Parker and John Stuart Mill."

RELIGIOUS LIFE.

The Rev. Dr. Ray Palmer speaks thus beautifully of
the poet's religious life : —

"Most of the poetical writings of Mr. Longfellow
reveal his genuine sympathy with the Christian reli-
ligion ; not only with its æsthetic aspects, but with the
grand spiritual truths which give it power to awaken
the best affections and the highest aspirations of the
soul. Even his choice of pieces for translation and his
legendary renderings, in many cases, indicate the religious habit of his mind ; as, for example, the Coplas
de Manrique, The Image of God, The Children of the
Lord's Supper, and The Legend Beautiful. Many
poems, not in form directly religious, bear about them
the aroma of myrrh, spikenard, and frankincense, as
offered on God's altars, and the fragrance of the rose
of Sharon and the lily of the valley. One cannot but
recognize the genuineness of the Christian tone, or,
where not positively this, the elevated moral tone,
which everywhere pervades them. The style of treatment is not such as might have been assumed by a
writer, who, in deference to public opinion, has wrought
into his compositions some conventional expressions
of respect for Christianity. It is such as fitly and
unequivocally expresses the honest conviction and feeling of one whose mind and heart have been so entirely
possessed by a healthful religious spirit, that, spontaneously and half-unconsciously, this spirit habitually
suffuses the whole substance of his thought, and becomes an element of his best inspirations. A religious

style may easily be borrowed. Genuine religious feeling, it is nearly or quite impossible successfully to counterfeit."

In the Revue Politique et Littéraire for April 1, 1882, M. Léo Quesnel has some important remarks bearing upon the development of Longfellow's genius. He says (after speaking of the death of his second wife), "From this time onward, as he approaches the evening of his life, his tone becomes modified. He had always been a moralist: he becomes a Christian moralist. He approaches nearer and nearer to those doctrines of Christianity, the intimate affinity of which with human nature is only brought out by suffering. Still the change in the case of Mr. Longfellow was an evolution, and not a revolution. He had always been too much of a poet, and too spiritual, to permit the change which was taking place within him to be abruptly perceived. It was at first only from certain secret signs that a penetrating eye could discover it: there was more sweetness, and more benevolence still towards all men, more true humility of soul. But little by little the ideas that took possession of him made themselves apparent in his works, and religious morality became the very marrow of his writings."

IMMORTALITY.

The Rev. H. R. Haweis of England, in a work entitled Poets in the Pulpit, thus speaks of Longfellow's belief in immortality: —

" And whether he touches on the passing away of a little child in the first dawn of life, or a young woman taken in the glowing bloom of youth, or the more mature companion of our later years, there is the same undefinable glow of hope and aspiration, and the same recurrent feeling that they are not dead, but gone before, — the very message which every one who has lost a dear friend longs to receive. Ah! we often hear it from lips which pronounce it apparently without feeling it, and are not able to convey to those who want to feel it, the precious faith in the existence, perchance the presence, of the dear, the forever-remembered dead! Then are the words of the true and faithful poet helpful. He never sounds the note of despair: doubt never sweeps darkly across his soul. But the spirit world itself becomes visible to him : he is looking out from the loneliness of his life with the eyes of an inspired seer; and we sit at his feet and listen whilst he pours forth, without constraint or effort, such a flood of spiritual emotion that our drooping souls are indeed lifted up with the hope that is full of immortality."

ANECDOTES AND LETTERS.

THE heading of this portion of the volume should not lead the reader to suppose that all the anecdotes about Mr. Longfellow are collected here. The biographical portion of the work is rich in anecdotes, and only those are grouped here which could not be conveniently woven into the narrative.

INTERVIEW WITH A FRENCHMAN.

The writer is indebted to Professor Charles Eliot Norton for the following little incident: A certain Frenchman called on Mr. Longfellow for the purpose of getting an account of his life to send to some journal in France. Mr. Longfellow, with his usual patient good-nature, submitted to be interviewed on all points connected with his public and objective life. At length the Frenchman said, "*Maintenant, monsieur, quelques anecdotes, s'il vous plait, de la vie intime?*" — "That," said Mr. Longfellow, "is just what I cannot tell you." His inner life he never revealed to the public, and let us hope that these sacred privacies never will be revealed.

FAVORITE PIECES OF SCULPTURE.

When Mr. Longfellow returned from Europe in 1869, he was enthusiastic in his praise of two pieces of sculpture which had been exhibited, — one at the World's Fair of 1862, in London, and the other at that of 1867, in Paris. They were " The Reading Girl " by P. Magni, and " The Last Hours of Napoleon," often called " The Sitting Napoleon," by Vela. One understands at once why he should be captivated by the Reading Girl, such a deep, almost unutterable calm, and unconscious purity and intellectual earnestness breathe from the face ; but one is unable to account for his admiration of the Napoleon.

JOHN OWEN AND LONGFELLOW.

John Owen published Longfellow's first volume of poems, "Voices of the Night," and was for many years his publisher in Cambridge. He occupies a quaint suite of rooms on the third floor of a Cambridge house. The rooms are pervaded by an antiquarian aura, and are stuffed and crowded with bric-à-brac and books. One of the curiosities of the rooms is the manner in which the owner admits visitors. He has a speaking-tube, a bell, and a wire connecting his room with the street-door below. When the bell is rung the visitor receives the query, " Who is it ? " through the tube, and, if invited to ascend, finds the door-catch pulled back by the wire ; and, thus invisibly ushered in, he mounts the stairs. Mr. Longfellow frequently called on his friend in these rooms. They called each other by their initials, — " My dear J. O.," and " My dear H. W. L." Pleased indeed was the amiable solitaire, when, in familiar tones, he heard the magic letters " H. W. L." gently spoken through the tube. Mr. Owen and Mr. Longfellow were accustomed to sip a little spirits or wine together

of an evening while they chatted ; Mr. Longfellow
sometimes not retiring till eleven o'clock on these occasions, although his usual hour was ten. Mr. Longfellow, being one of the literary executors of Charles
Sumner, superintended the publication of his complete
works ; the bulk of the editorial work being performed
with admirable thoroughness by Mr. George Nichols,
who had previously assisted Little, Brown, & Co. to
bring out an edition of the works of Edmund Burke.
Mr. Owen had suggested to Sumner the publishing of
his works, and he says Sumner waited several years
for him to get ready to do the editing. In the end
he was employed to oversee the phraseology, and suggest rhetorical emendations. During the progress of
the work he had one of the longest and most curious
hunts after a quotation that was ever heard of. It is
worth telling, to show the exhaustive accuracy with
which the works of Sumner (Boston : Lee & Shepard)
have been edited. The writer got the anecdote from
Mr. Owen. Sumner, in his " Prophetic Voices," had
quoted from Daniel Webster these lines : —

> " In other lands another Britain see,
> And as thou art, America shall be."

The question was, who wrote them? Where did
Webster get them? Webster quoted from any thing
and every thing, and was just as likely to embellish a
speech with a sentence from a spelling-book as from
any other source. The quotation *could* not be found.
It was published in all the literary journals : it was
given out at dinner-parties. Holmes and Emerson, and
about every other author of note, were enlisted in behalf
of the quotation. No one could find it. One day Mr.

Owen, in verifying another reference, read through by accident the preface to an old edition of Griswold's "Poets and Poetry of America." At the very close what should he see but the long-sought lines! But alas! the author's name was not given. The next thing to do was to hunt up the library of the deceased Griswold ("sea-green" Rev. Griswold, the defamer of poor Poe). The library was discovered in Philadelphia, where Griswold lived when he died. But in the mean time Mr. Owen had written to the librarian of the Lenox Library in New York. This gentleman solved the riddle: the lines *had never been published in a book*, so far as could be determined, but *had been written with a diamond on a window-pane in London by Gulian C. Verplanck of New York*. Some one had sent them to a newspaper, and it was probably in a newspaper that Webster saw them. But the indefatigable editors of Sumner's works were still unsatisfied. Perhaps Verplanck had at some time written them in a book: if so, perhaps the newspaper lines were not absolutely as he had written them. Webster had made one mistake, substituting "lands" for "worlds;" there might be others. So the search through Griswold's library was renewed. But the lines have never as yet been found in book form.

READING BY TWILIGHT.

Longfellow told Mr. George Nichols of Cambridge that in 1845 his eyes were so much injured by his habit of reading too late into the twilight, that, when he was applied to by a Philadelphia firm to edit "The Poets and Poetry of Europe," he had to get the assistance of Professor Felton, at whose house he was a constant caller. He also drew on his college lectures for the introductions to the selections in the book.

THE FIVE OF CLUBS.

In the "Memoir and Letters of Charles Sumner," by Edward L. Pierce (2 vols., Boston: 1877. Roberts Brothers), is found the following (vol. i., p. 161) : —

"In the early part of the year 1837, an intimate friendship was formed between Cornelius C. Felton, Henry W. Longfellow, George S. Hillard, Henry R. Cleveland, and Charles Sumner: they called themselves the 'Five of Clubs.' They were near to each other in age; Longfellow being thirty, Felton twenty-nine, Hillard and Cleveland twenty-eight, and Sumner twenty-six. Of the five Hillard only was married. All achieved an honorable place in literature. Cleveland was a teacher by profession, refined and delicate in character, but poor in health. He died at the age of thirty-four. The Five came together almost weekly, generally on Saturday afternoons. They met simply as friends with common tastes, and the fullest sympathy with each other, talking of society, the week's experiences, new books, their individual studies, plans, and hopes, and of Europe, — which Longfellow and Cleveland had seen, and which the others longed to see. They loved good cheer, but observed moderation in their festivities. A table simply spread became a symposium when Felton, with his joyous nature, took his seat among his friends; and the other four were not less genial and hearty. There was hardly a field of literature which one or the other had not traversed, and they took a constant interest in each other's studies. Each sought the criticism of the rest upon his own book, essay, or

poem, before it was given to the public. Their mutual
confidence seemed to know no limitation of distrust,
or fear of possible alienation ; and they revealed, as
friends do not often reveal, their inner life to each
other. Rarely in history has there been a fellowship so
beautiful as that of these gifted young men."

JULIA WARD HOWE'S REMINISCENCES.

In The Critic for April 8, 1882, Mrs. Julia Ward
Howe says, Mr. Longfellow "once told me that he disliked the study of history; . . . I will mention in this
connection that he told me one day of a very dispara-
ging criticism of his works which had just appeared, and
of which Miss Margaret Fuller was the author. I asked
him what she had said; and he replied that he had not
read the article, and that he usually thought it best not
to read what would be likely to cause him useless irri-
tation."

HIS KINDNESS TO STRANGERS.

Madam A. Machetta thus describes the poet's manner of receiving visitors: "In a general conversation
an unerring instinct guides his questions and replies.
He is so quick a reader of character, that not one word
fell on an unappreciative person. Betrayed into some
warmth of feeling at a casual remark, he commenced
what would have been a glowing description of something that he had seen ; but, glancing a second time at
his visitor, he quietly dropped the thread of his remark.
He knows instantaneously, by the questions put to him,
the mental calibre of each and every interlocutor. Of
course, as many epistolary tramps visit him out of curiosity, as well as well-intentioned *littérateurs* who worship at the shrine of poetic art, it was really delicious to

see him quietly put down the former without their ever
being aware of it, and to remark with what astuteness
he divined the tastes of the latter. Evidently the old
adage of casting pearls before swine is not unknown
to him. A bright little lad was shown into the room.
He was very young, perhaps seven years of age, and
held in his hand a newly bound volume. His manner
suggested foreign breeding, as he bowed with marion-
ette gravity to every one in the room, and then stood
still as if at a loss how to proceed. Longfellow looked
up smilingly, and his great love of children was evident in the mildness of his speech.

"'Good-morning, my lad,' said he amiably. 'Did you
wish to see me?'

"The boy said hesitatingly, 'Professor Longfellow?'

"'Yes,' responded the poet kindly. 'What is it?
Come here.'

"'This is my birthday,' he said excitedly, 'and I
have come to ask you to put your autograph in my new
album. Mother just gave it to me, and she thought I
might ask you.'

"'What is your name?' asked the poet.

"The boy looked up shyly. 'I am named for you,'
he said simply; 'and my father works in the college.'"

AN AFTERNOON AT HIS HOME.

A correspondent of The Chicago Times writes of a
visit to the poet Longfellow as follows: —

"In contrast with this day my thoughts revert to a
bright day in last September, when, with a friend, I
passed the morning and the greater part of the afternoon in Longfellow's home with the poet and his daughters, Misses Alice and Annie Longfellow. Over the

door of the old-fashioned and very interesting house
hung the American flag, half furled, and draped in
mourning fot President Garfield, who had died but two
days before. I lifted the brass knocker with nervous-
ness, thinking of the many distinguished people who
had sought admittance there; and at once it was answered by a neat maid-servant, who ushered us into the
quaint old drawing-room, the walls of which were hung
with light-colored paper with vines of roses trailing over
it, a style of many years ago. We had no time for
further observation; for almost immediately Mr. Longfellow came in, greeting us most kindly, saying, 'Come
into my room, where we shall be more at ease: I cannot
make strangers of you!' How gladly we followed him,
but without a word of reply; for, to acknowledge the
truth, my heart at least was beating too painfully with
the realization that I was in the presence of the poet
beloved from my childhood. In person he was smaller
than I had fancied him, — only of medium height, —
but his face, made familiar by his portraits, seemed that
of an old friend. His silvery hair was carelessly thrown
back from his forehead, the full beard and mustache
partially concealed the pleasant mouth, but his mild
blue eyes expressed the kindliness of his heart and his
quick reading of the hearts of others. He wore a Prince
Albert coat of very dark brown cloth, with trousers of
a much lighter shade, having an invisible plaid running
through them. A dark-blue necktie and spotless linen
completed his costume. In his study we sat some hours,
listening to his low, musical voice as he talked on many
interesting topics; read aloud to us from his own beautiful 'Evangeline,' or selections from other poets. He
read aloud the sonnets to the Nile by Keats, Shelley,

and Leigh Hunt, comparing them, telling us how correct they were and how incorrect were those of Shakspeare. To Leigh Hunt's sonnets he gave the preference, and seemed to enjoy all as if it were his first reading of them. So in every thing he read he found some new beauty, and spoke of it with almost boyish pleasure. We listened with delight to all: then he said, 'You will tire of me and my nonsense. Come and meet my daughters. I shall not let you go: you must drink a cup of tea with us.' Then we were led into the large, cheerful dining-room, where was spread a delicious luncheon. Miss Alice presided; Miss Annie being engaged in superintending the meal laid on a tiny table out on the broad porch, where two little children were being made happy. Mr. Longfellow was called, and we followed, to look upon the pretty scene; and when the children saw him they dropped their 'goodies,' and ran to climb up and receive his kiss and beg him to play with them. Then we gathered around the table, spread with delicate china, the copper kettle singing merrily; and Mr. Longfellow made the tea with his own hands, and poured it from the antique silver teapot for our enjoyment. While many dishes were offered us, the poet took simply his tea and Graham biscuit: there was no ostentatious ceremony, but all was served with quiet ease, as if only the family circle were gathered there. After lunch Mr. Longfellow led us through the house, pointing out his favorite pictures and treasures, relating interesting incidents as we passed from room to room. He said he first took up his residence in the historical house as a bachelor, with several bachelor friends, each renting rooms therein; then he took half the house, a friend the other half, and set up housekeeping; finally his means enabled him to purchase the house and grounds, and there had been his home ever since. Nothing had been changed in the arrangements of the house since the days when it had served as the headquarters of Gen. Washington. Much of the paint and paper looked as though it, too, had stood the wear and tear of time since those old days. All was scrupulously clean, but so different from the house decoration of to-day. Then we nestled upon the broad south porch, while the poet smoked a cigarette and chatted the while of many books and authors, and I was closely questioned about our little city of Pullman, in which he expressed great interest, saying that it seemed impossible that such a work could be done in so short a time. He said that he more than ever wanted to visit the great West, where we must have won the assistance of Eastern genii in our magical growth. When the hour arrived for our departure, the venerable poet walked with us to the gate; and, under the beautiful lilac hedge which surrounds the place, we said good-by, and promised to make another visit soon. A few days later, on opening the door of our little hotel parlor, we beheld the friend, who had come to return our visit. He apologized for not sending a card, and we pardoned him on condition that he would write his name in our birthday books. To this he cheerfully assented, and now we value those autographs beyond price."

A neighbor of Mr. Longfellow writes to The New York Independent as follows : —

"The poet was never more attractive than in these unexpected interviews with absolute strangers. He received them with gentle courtesy, glided readily into common topics, but carefully warded off all compli-

LONGFELLOW'S HOME.

MALL ON THE WEST SIDE OF THE CRAIGIE HOUSE, CAMBRIDGE.

mentary references to his works. This was his invariable custom in general conversation. I was present when a distinguished party from Canada was introduced, and remember, when a charming lady of the party gracefully repeated a message of high compliment from the Princess Louise, how courteously he received it, and how instantly he turned the conversation in another direction. I remember, at another of these introductions, a stranger lady distrustfully asked Mr. Longfellow for his autograph. He assured her by at once assenting, while he remarked, 'I know some persons object to giving their autographs; but if so little a thing will give pleasure, how can one refuse?'

"Mr. Longfellow often amused his friends with humorous accounts of some of these visits. I recall his account of one which seemed to delight him hugely. An English gentleman thus abruptly introduced himself without letters: 'Is this Mr. Longfellow? Well, sir, as you have no ruins in your country, I thought,' growing embarrassed, 'I thought I would call and see you.'

"I suspect that even very distinguished visitors sometimes bored him. I recollect his telling me that the Duke of Argyll, a persistent ornithologist, troubled him considerably by asking him names of birds whose notes they heard while sitting on his veranda. Mr. Longfellow was no naturalist: he did not know our birds specifically, and flowers are sometimes found blooming at extraordinary seasons in his poetry. He remarked to me once upon the flaming splendor of the *Cydonia Japonica* (red-flowering quince), and asked the name of that familiar shrub, saying, 'I know nothing about flowers.' Yet he saw in Nature what no mere naturalist could ever hope to see."

Another says, " I was in his library last fall with a young girl from California. She had been the wide world over, but stood shy and silent in his presence, moved to tears by his kindly welcome. It was touching to see the poet's appreciation of this, and his quick glance over his table, that he might find something to interest her and make her forget her embarrassment. Taking up a little box covered with glass, he put it into her hand, and said, 'This is a mournful thing to put into the hands of a beautiful, bright girl; but think of it! six hundred years ago the bit of wood in that box touched Dante's bones.' And he related how this piece of Dante's coffin had come into his possession. He led her to his piano, and asked her to play for him. He told her anecdotes of Coleridge and Moore, as he showed her their inkstands. He touched upon the fascinating life of Cellini as he pointed out a bit of his marvellous work, and concisely showed the difference between the Italian and French schools of art, illustrated by Cellini's Tintoretto and David. Soon his young visitor was chatting with him as freely as if she had not entered his door with a timidity amounting almost to fear. After that, he turned to us. I hope he understood how this act had been silently appreciated by us; yet I think he was all-unconscious of the picture he created, — a picture never to be forgotten by those of us who witnessed it."

An anonymous newspaper contributor says : —

" Neilson, the beautiful English actress, Miss Genevieve Ward, Blanche Roosevelt, Miss Sarah Jewett, — whose poems he thoroughly appreciated, and whom he encouraged with his advice both as an actress and a poet, — and many others, have a charming recollection of their reception at the Craigie House. When Mlle. Rhea was here during the last winter of his life, she expressed an earnest desire to visit Cambridge and be introduced to the great poet. Mr. Longfellow was unwell at the time, and there was some doubt as to whether he would be able to see her. She was driven out by Capt. Nathan Appleton, however; and to her great joy the poet was able to receive her in his customary gracious manner. The short call was highly enjoyed both by the poet and the actress. Mlle. Rhea recited to the author in English the little poem, ' The Maiden and the Weathercock,' then recently written, a graceful compliment, which gave great pleasure to the venerable poet.

" At Nahant he was constantly receiving visitors, some of whom came from distant countries across the ocean. Often they would drive with him at the early hour of three, and return to Boston on the afternoon boat.

VISITS FROM YOUNG LADIES.

" Two young ladies from Iowa, visiting in Boston, wrote a note to him, telling how much they loved his poems, and what a wish they had to see him. In the next mail came a most cordial reply, appointing a time when he would be at liberty to meet them ; and since then they have loved the man even more than his poetry. This is but one instance of his universal kindness. His neighbors and friends in his own city will feel his loss far more than his world-wide circle of admirers. Said a gentleman who had known him long, ' I shall miss his familiar form, which I used to see so often on our street; I shall miss the cheery voice and gracious wave of the hand with which he always greeted me.

I don't believe he had an enemy in the world, and I am sure that every person who ever knew him feels that he has lost a friend.' "

THE ORIGIN OF SOME OF HIS POEMS.

The late James T. Fields, writing about Longfellow, said : —

" You must look to Shakspeare for a larger stock of the currency of thought than Longfellow's ; for he is quoted in Westminster Palace, in the British Parliament, and in all the pulpits of England. It is because he humanizes whatever he touches, that his lyre has nothing alien to any soil. I have heard him quoted by an Armenian monk with a cowl, and sung at camp-meetings on the hills of New Hampshire.

" As I happen to know of the birth of many of Longfellow's poems, let me divulge to you a few of their secrets. The 'Psalm of Life' came into existence on a bright summer morning in July, 1838, in Cambridge, as the poet sat between two windows at a small table in the corner of his chamber. It was a verse from his inmost heart, and he kept it unpublished for a long time. It expressed his own feelings at that time, when recovering from a deep affliction, and he had it in his own heart for many months. The poem of 'The Reaper and the Flowers' came without effort, crystallized into his mind. 'The Light of the Stars' was composed on a serene and beautiful summer evening, exactly suggestive of the poem. 'The Wreck of the Hesperus' was written the night after a violent storm had occurred ; and, as the poet sat smoking his pipe, the Hesperus came sailing into his mind. He went to bed, but could not sleep, and wrote the celebrated verses. It hardly caused him

an effort, but flowed on without let or hindrance. On
a summer afternoon in 1840, as he was riding on the
beach, ' The Skeleton in Armor ' rose as out of the deep
before him, and would not be laid.

"One of the best known of all of Longfellow's shorter
poems is ' Excelsior.' That one word happened to catch
his eye one autumn eve in 1841 on a torn piece of newspaper; and straightway his imagination took fire at it.
Taking up a piece of paper, which happened to be the
back of a letter received that day from Charles Sumner,
he crowded it with verses. As first written down,
' Excelsior ' differs from the perfected and published
version; but it shows a rush and glow worthy of its
author."

LONGFELLOW ABROAD.

Cardinal Wiseman, in an enthusiastic eulogy of Mr.
Longfellow, says, " He was a true philosopher who said,
' Let me make the songs of a nation, and I care not who
makes its laws.' There is one writer who approaches
nearer than any other to this standard, and he has already gained such a hold on our hearts that it is almost
unnecessary for me to mention his name. Our hemisphere cannot claim the honor of having brought him
forth; but still he belongs to us, for his works have
become as household words wherever the English language is spoken. And whether we are charmed by
his imagery, or soothed by his melodious versification,
or elevated by the high moral teachings of his pure
muse, or follow with sympathizing hearts the wanderings
of Evangeline, I am sure that all who hear my voice
will join me in the tribute I desire to pay to the genius
of Longfellow."

At a dinner given in London in 1877, to Chief Justice Shea of the Marine Court, Sir (then Mr.) Theodore Martin, the biographer of Prince Albert, related to the judge that the queen once told him, when he called at Windsor Castle, "I wished for you this morning, for you would have seen something that would have delighted you as a man of letters. The American poet Longfellow has been here. I noticed an unusual interest among the attendants and servants. I could scarcely credit that they so generally understood who he was. When he took leave, they concealed themselves in places from which they could get a good look at him as he passed. I have since inquired among them, and am surprised and pleased to find that many of his poems are familiar to them. No other distinguished person has come here that has excited so peculiar an interest. Such poets wear a crown that is imperishable."

DOM PEDRO II. OF BRAZIL.

Among the many opinions of the dead poet recorded in every tongue, there may be mentioned those of Dom Pedro II. of Brazil. In 1855 Rev. J. C. Fletcher took a number of specimens of American literature, art, and manufactures to the capital of Brazil, where he was permitted to exhibit them in the National Museum. They were first visited by Dom Pedro, who, after an examination of the various works, made remarks on Irving, Cooper, and Prescott, showing an intimate acquaintance with each. He then, with great earnestness of manner, said, "M. Fletcher, avez-vous les poëmes de M. Longfellow?" Mr. Fletcher replied in the negative, whereupon his Majesty said, "I am exceedingly sorry; for I have sought in every bookstore in Rio de Janeiro for Longfellow, and I cannot find it. I have a number of beautiful *morceaux* from him, but I wish the whole work. I admire him so much." Afterward, at the Palace of St. Christopher, when Mr. Fletcher took leave of the emperor, the latter said to him, "When you return to your country, have the kindness to say to Mr. Longfellow how much pleasure he has given me, and be pleased to tell him *combien je l'estime, combien je l'aime.*"

ONE OF THE POET'S LAST ACTS

was to sign a petition to the Legislature to remove the disability of atheists in the matter of testimony in courts.

THE SOUTH OF FRANCE.

Mr. Longfellow was an enthusiastic admirer of the climate and scenery of the South of France, and often expressed a desire to revisit the localities with which he was so charmed. He talked quite seriously of accompanying Mr. and Mrs. Dana in their proposed trip to Europe in the spring of 1882, but it is improbable that his health would have permitted him to leave home for such an extended journey.

THE POET AND THE COMPOSERS.

Mr. D. E. Hervey of New York has published in The Tribune of that city the following classified list of poems of Mr. Longfellow which have been set to music. He remarks that it is by no means a complete list, but embraces such cases only as have fallen under his notice.

" *Operas.*— 'The Masque of Pandora,' libretto arranged by Bolton Rowe, music by Alfred Cellier; 'Victorian, the Spanish Student,' libretto by Julian Edwards, music by J. Reynolds Anderson.

" *Cantatas.* — 'The Wreck of the Hesperus,' composed by T. Anderton; 'The Consecration of the Banner,' by J. F. H. Read; 'The Building of the Ship,' by J. F. Barnett, and another by Henry Lahee; 'The Golden Legend,' by Dudley Buck, and another by the Rev. H. E. Hodson; 'The Bells of Strasburg Cathedral' (from 'The Golden Legend'), by Franz Liszt; 'The Tale of a Viking' ('The Skeleton in Armor'), by George E. Whiting.

" *Two, Three, and Four Part Songs.* — 'Stars of the Summer Night,' by Henry Smart, Dr. E. G. Monk, J. L. Hatton; 'Good-Night, Beloved,' by Ciro Pinsuti, J. L. Hatton, Dr. E. G. Monk; 'Beware' ('I know a Maiden'), by J. L. Hatton, J. B. Boucher, H. De Burgh, Mrs. Mounsey Bartholomew, M. W. Balfe, H. M. Dow; 'The Reaper and the Flowers,' by J. B. Boucher, A. R. Gaul; 'Song of the Silent Land,' by A. R. Gaul, A. H. D. Prendergast; 'The Curfew,' by T. Anderton, P. H. Dremer, W. Macfaren, Henry Smart; 'The Day is Done,' by A. R. Gaul; 'The Hemlock Tree,' by J. L. Hatton; 'The Village Blacksmith,' by J. L. Hatton; 'King Witlaf's Drinking-Horn,' by J. L. Hatton; 'The Arrow and the Song,' by Walter Hay; 'The Wreck of the Hesperus,' by Dr. H. Hiles; 'A Voice came over the Sea' ('Daybreak'), by F. Quinn, J. C. D. Parker; 'A Psalm of Life,' by Henry Smart, Dr. Mainzer; 'The Rainy Day,' by A. S. Sullivan, J. Blockley; 'Woods in Winter,' by W. W. Pearson; 'Up and Doing,' by Dr. Mainzer; 'Heart within and God o'erhead,' by Rossini; 'The Nun of Nidaros,' and 'King Olaf's

Christmas,' from the 'Saga of King Olaf,' by Dudley
Buck; 'Brooklet,' by F. Booth; 'Excelsior,' by M. W.
Balfe; 'Hymn to the Night,' by S. Glover; 'Sea hath
its Pearls,' by Ciro Pinsuti. As for songs for a single
voice, they are very numerous."

The following are found, alphabetically arranged, in
the list published by Oliver Ditson & Co. of Boston: —

"*Songs for a Single Voice.* — 'Arrow and the Song,'
by M. W. Balfe; 'The Bells,' by J. L. Hatton; 'Be-
ware,' by B. F. Gilbert; 'Bridge.' by Lady Carew, A.
Landon, M. Lindsay; 'Brook and the Wave,' by J.
L. Molloy; 'Catawba Wine,' by W. R. Dempster;
'Changed' ('Aftermath'), by F. Boott; 'Children,'
by W. R. Dempster; 'The Curfew,' by T. Anderton;
'Daybreak' ('Wind came up out of the Sea'), by M.
W. Balfe; 'Day is Done,' by M. W. Balfe; 'Death of
Minnehaha,' by C. C. Converse; 'The Dead' by Y. Van
Antwerp; 'Excelsior,' by J. Blockley, S. Glover, M.
Lindsay; 'Footprints on the Sands of Time,' by A. W.
Titus; 'Footsteps of Angels,' by W. R. Dempster;
'Good-night, Beloved.' by M. W. Balfe; 'Green Trees
whispered Low,' by M. W. Balfe, J. Blockley; 'It is
not always May,' by C. Gounod; 'Kyrie Eleison,' by F.
Boott; 'My Lady sleeps, ' by G. W. Marston; 'Night
is Calm and Cloudless,' by J. L. Hatton; 'Old Clock
on the Stairs,' by Dolores; 'Old House by the Lindens'
('Open Window'), by J. Blockley; 'Psalm of Life,' by
J. Blockley, G. W. Hewitt; 'Rainy Day," by W. R.
Dempster; 'Reaper and the Flowers,' by M. W. Balfe,
J. R. Thomas; 'Resignation,' by J. E. Gould; 'Sad
Heart, O take thy Rest,' by V. Gabriel; 'Sea hath its
Pearls,' by F. Lichner, J. C. D. Parker, B. Tours; 'She
is fooling Thee,' by A. H. N. B.; 'Stars of the Summer

Night,' by F. Boott, C. H. Compton, II. Kleber, B. Tours; 'Suspiria,' by Y. Van Antwerp; 'Village Blacksmith,' by D. A. Warden, W. H. Weiss; 'Voice of Christ,' by D. A. Warden; 'Wreck of the Hesperus,' by J. Blockley."

In the catalogue of Ditson & Co., lists of other authors' poems that have been set to music are given. Longfellow heads the list with thirty-nine poems, next comes Tennyson with twenty-six, Byron has sixteen, Goethe eight, Holmes six, Whittier four, and Wordsworth one.

It may be mentioned here that Professor J. K. Paine of Harvard College has, since the death of Longfellow, expressed an intention of setting some of his poems to music.

A Scotch laborer in Cambridge told Mr. John Owen that very many of Longfellow's poems had been set to music in Scotland.

LETTER TO GEORGE W. CHILDS.

CAMBRIDGE, March 13, 1877.

MY DEAR MR. CHILDS, — You do not know yet what it is to be seventy years old. I will tell you, so that you may not be taken by surprise when your turn comes.

It is like climbing the Alps. You reach a snow-crowned summit, and see behind you the deep valley stretching miles and miles away, and before you other summits higher and whiter, which you may have strength to climb, or may not. Then you sit down and meditate, and wonder which it will be.

That is the whole story, amplify it as you may. All that one can say is, that life is opportunity.

With seventy good wishes to the dwellers in Walnut Street, corner of Twenty-second,

Yours very truly,
HENRY W. LONGFELLOW.

HERMES TRISMEGISTUS.

Hermes Trismegistus, his last published poem but
one, appeared in The Century (Scribner's) Magazine
for February, 1882.   It has all of its author's customary
grace, the opening and closing stanzas reading as follows : —

> Still through Egypt's desert places
>   Flows the lordly Nile,
> From its banks the great stone faces
>   Gaze with patient smile ;
> Still the Pyramids imperious
>   Pierce the cloudless skies,
> And the Sphinx stares with mysterious,
>   Solemn, stony eyes.
>
> But where are the old Egyptian
>   Demi-gods and kings?
> Nothing left but an inscription
>   Graven on stones and rings.
> Where are Helius and Hephæstus,
>   Gods of eldest eld?
> Where is Hermes Trismegistus,
>   Who their secrets held?
>   .   .   .   .   .
> Thine, O priest of Egypt, lately
>   Found I in the vast
> Weed-encumbered, sombre, stately
>   Graveyard of the Past;
> And a presence moved before me
>   On that gloomy shore,
> As a waft of wind, that o'er me
>   Breathed, and was no more.

ONE OF LONGFELLOW'S LAST LETTERS.

Mrs. Marie J. Pitman (*alias* Margery Deane), of Newport, sent Mr. Longfellow some spring flowers, among
which was a large number of tulips.   In a letter written

just two weeks before his death, and among the very last which he wrote, having employed an amanuensis for ten days previous to his death, he says, "I have been arranging these wonderful flowers under the lamp in my library. I can only think of the floral games of Toulouse in the times of the Troubadours: and, were I a good Troubadour, I would write you a letter in verse to-night; but I am worn and weary, so that I find it difficult to write even prose." The handwriting showed greatly increased feebleness. In this same letter he says, "Thanks is a little word; but it has much meaning when it has a heart behind it, and thus I send you mine for these Newport flowers." Mr. Longfellow loved Newport, and said not long ago to this lady: "I would choose Pelham Street, facing the town park and the Old Stone Mill, could I live in Newport. I like that street very much, but in the Newport air I should want no work to do. That is the climate to be idle in." Where stands the new Channing Memorial Church, Mr. Longfellow thought the most beautiful site for a home in all Newport.

REMINISCENCES OF A JOURNALIST.

A Boston journalist writes to The Boston Herald: "In the years 1870–71 I was employed by Fields, Osgood, & Co., and James R. Osgood & Co., in their old store at the corner of Tremont Street and Hamilton Place. Mr. Longfellow was a frequent visitor; and it was many a time my privilege to walk with him to Bowdoin Square, and carry a parcel too heavy for his own strength. I say privilege, for such indeed it was. On these occasions he invariably kept up a lively conversation, sometimes serious, and sometimes with a quaint strain of humor.   He had a keen sense of humor; and I recollect, that, as we were once walking through Court Street, he pointed to a huge Newfoundland dog that was wagging his tail vigorously, and said to me, ' Do you know why I am like that dog's tail?' and then, without waiting for me to answer, he replied, ' Because I am something of a wag.'

"I well recollect New Year's Day, 1871. On that day the late Mr. James T. Fields called me up to his little room, looking out on Tremont Street. Mr. Longfellow was there, with Oliver Wendell Holmes, and, I think, Mr. Whittier and Mr. Emerson. Mr. Fields said to me, ' After working for others for a great many years, I am now going to enjoy myself. I have to-day retired from active business life; and these gentlemen (calling them by name, and each of whom nodded as his name was called), Mr. Longfellow, Mr. Emerson, Mr. Whittier, and Mr. Holmes, have called on me to celebrate the happy event. Now, I want you to go to the peanut-stand on the corner, and get me a quart of peanuts. These gentlemen have called on me, and it is only right that I should treat them.'

" I brought in the peanuts; and Mr. Fields, after passing the bag to his guests — each of whom took a liberal handful — offered it to me, saying, ' You have been so good as to get these for us, you must eat some too.'

" So I sat down with these great and good men, and listened to a conversation, which, if I had been old enough to understand, I should have always treasured. This much I do remember: when I left Mr. Fields's room, the last peanut had been eaten.

" In May, 1871, just after recovering from a severe illness, I called in the store, and Mr. Benjamin H. Ticknor — widely known as one of the best and most kind-hearted of men — asked me if I would not like to ride out to Cambridge. Of course I was glad to go. He gave me a parcel to take to Mr. Longfellow. I rode out to the old mansion of the poet, and found him at home somewhat indisposed. He took me into his library, and bade me be seated. He would not allow me to remove the wrappers, but, with his own hands, carefully untied the strings, and took out the volumes, — some rare ones which had been hunted up for him, — and reverently wiped them with a silk handkerchief. Meanwhile I had not been idle. My eyes, in wandering around the room, lit on his waste-basket, and I asked permission to pick out a scrap of his writing. This was cheerfully granted; and, as a result of my search, I found a sheet on which was a draught, with many corrections, of the first verse of his poem 'Amalfi.' At last, having put away his books, he turned to me and said, ' Well, what have you found?'

" 'Something worth keeping,' said I, jealously putting it in my pocket.

" ' Let me see it,' said the poet.

" I gave it to him, and he laughed. Then he went to his desk, and wrote thereon, —

Rubbish, sacrificed to fame.

H. W. LONGFELLOW.

" This treasure I gave to a western library some years ago.

" I have, in connection with Longfellow, but one regret; that is, that in the time when I met him so frequently, I was but a mere boy, unable to appreciate the man's greatness, and garner up words which fell from his lips, and which I alone heard."

CRITICISED BY A BARBER.

It is related of Mr. Longfellow, that when his poem of The Village Blacksmith was going through the press, he read the first two stanzas to a hairdresser in Cambridge. The barber criticised the first line of the second stanza, "His hair is crisp and black and long," by saying that crisp black hair is never long. Mr. Longfellow was struck with the merit of this criticism, and instructed his publisher to substitute the word "strong" for "long" in that line. The next day, however, he reconsidered the matter, and sent his publisher the following note, now in the possession of a resident of Washington: —

CAMBRIDGE, Oct. 1, 1845.

DEAR SIR, — I wrote to you yesterday to have the word "long" changed to "strong," in The Village Blacksmith. The word "strong" occurs in the preceding line, and the repetition would be unpleasant. It had, therefore, better stand as it is, notwithstanding the hairdresser's criticism, which, after all, is only technical, for hair can be both crisp and long. Have you received any more numbers of The Mabinogion, a collection of Welsh stories? I have only five. Will you please furnish the remainder, if you have them, and, if not, import them for me?

I am glad to find that the "Poets of Europe" has been so well received. Do you mean to take out a copyright in England? If not, I shall, as it is best to keep the control of the book.

Yours very truly.

HENRY W. LONGFELLOW.

ORGAN-GRINDERS.

One of the duties of the policeman on guard at the Longfellow grounds on Friday, the day of the death of the poet, was to turn away the players on hand-organs. For years it has been the custom of the family to give six cents to each hand-organ man, the result being that few of the peripatetic musicians who come into the vicinity fail to take the house into their circuit. Three appeared on Friday afternoon.

VISITS TO PORTLAND.

It was Longfellow's custom always to visit Portland, his old home, for a week or so every year. He was always glad, however, to get back to Cambridge, which he regarded as his home, and from which he never liked to be absent. This reminds one of Carlyle's similar custom of annually visiting Scotland.

ANECDOTE OF THE SLIPPERS.

" Mr. Longfellow had a strong sense of the humorous, and many a witty impromptu resulted from the occurrence of some slight incident or accident. One summer, twenty years ago and more, when the Appletons were living in Lynn, the poet's son Charles Long-fellow, who was always very fond of sailing a boat, and who has since become known as a great yachtsman, came over in his boat one day to make a call. The surf was very high, the boat was capsized, and he was thrown into the water. He was wet to the skin, of course, and was compelled to make an entire change of clothing. Capt. Nathan Appleton, in place of his shoes, loaned him a pair of slippers which he wore home. A few days afterward his father, Mr. Long-fellow, returned the slippers in a neatly wrapped parcel, with the following lines written on the outside : —

> ' Slippers that perhaps another,
>   Sailing o'er the bay of Lynn,
> . A forlorn or shipwrecked nephew,
>   Seeing, may purloin again.' "

LONGFELLOW AND POLITICS.

'" Longfellow never took part in politics, and rarely expressed an opinion on this subject; yet he was well read in the current events of the time, and had a fair idea of the direction of events, and the movements of parties. I never heard him talk politics but once, and this was at his summer cottage at Nahant, I think in 1873. Charles Sumner was his guest. He had just got back from Europe. I called to see the distinguished senator about a certain political movement then on foot to give Gen. Butler the Republican nomination for governor. Longfellow was present, and, taking umbrage at Sumner's conservatism and reticence, launched out in a furious tirade against the men who were engineering the Butler movement, denouncing the whole scheme as a disgrace to Massachusetts. From this subject he drifted to the vote of censure passed by the Legislature on Sumner for his battle-flag resolution in the Senate, and said that Massachusetts had been falling pretty low of late years.[1] His blue eyes, usually so gentle, flashed fire as he alluded to these two incidents in the politics of the Commonwealth, which he was pleased to cite as an instance of the degeneracy of her statesmanship, and the lowering of the high standard she had always maintained in the sisterhood of States. It was a cold, misty morning, and

---

[1] It does not appear clearly from this language whether Mr. Longfellow sustained Sumner in his position. Such was, however, the fact, according to the testimony of Mr. Longfellow's friends in Cambridge.

the conversation was carried on in the poet's library,
where coffee was brought in as the proper beverage
with which to treat a visitor. As the poet drained his
cup of Mocha, he said, with more emphasis than he was
in the habit of using, " Put me down as an anti-Butler
man." — *New York Herald.*

THE WOLF BALLAD.

The history of the controversy about the plagiarism
or non-plagiarism by Longfellow of a certain ballad by
Wolf may be found in Graham's Magazine for 1845.

AN INCIDENT IN KANSAS.

In the summer of 1877, Acting Gov. Stanton of Kansas
paid a visit to the citizens of Lawrence, in that State.
After partaking of the hospitalities extended him by
Gov. Robinson, he addressed, by request, a crowd of
some five hundred Free-State men, who did not hesitate
to manifest their disapprobation at such portions of his
speech as did not accord with their peculiar political
views. At the close of his speech Mr. Stanton pictured in glowing language the Indian tradition of Hiawatha, of the " peace-pipe " shaped and fashioned by
Gitchie Manito, and by which he called tribes of men
together, and in his own language addressed them : —

> " I have given you lands to hunt in,
> I have given you streams to fish in,
> I have given you bear and bison,
> I have given you roe and reindeer,
> I have given you brant and beaver,
> Filled the marshes full of wild fowl,
> Filled the rivers full of fishes ;
> Why, then, are you not contented?
> Why, then, will you hunt each other?

> " I am weary of your quarrels,
> Weary of your wars and bloodshed,
> Weary of your prayers for vengeance,
> Of your wranglings and dissensions ;
> All your strength is in your union,
> All your danger is in discord ;
> Therefore be at peace henceforward,
> And as brothers live together."

The application of this quotation was felt by the excited crowd, and those who but a moment before had murmured the loudest joined heartily in the unanimous applause that followed the close of the speaker's remarks.

PAYMENT FOR HIS POEMS.

Mr. Francis H. Underwood writes thus of a visit he paid to the poet a few weeks before his death: "He told me of the early poems, and of the payments which he *did not* receive. The Psalm of Life and The Reaper appeared in the Knickerbocker, and were never paid for at all. The Voices of the Night were printed in the United States Literary Gazette, and the compensation was — dubious. Mr. Longfellow, having been informed on one occasion that the sum of thirteen dollars was subject to his order (for two prose articles and one poem), declined the so-called *honorarium*, and accepted a set of Chatterton's Works, which are still in his library. For his contributions to another periodical, covering some two or three years, he got — a receipted bill for the same period! We all know what magnificent appreciation came later." — *Boston Saturday Evening Gazette.*

LETTERS OF LONGFELLOW TO CHARLES LANMAN.

Charles Lanman, in a letter to The New York Tribune, gives some interesting reminiscences of Longfellow, with a number of his letters, together with an extract from his diary.   Mr. Lanman writes: —

"In 1871, while exhibiting a portfolio of my sketches in oil to a nephew of Mr. Longfellow, we stumbled upon a view of Norman's Woe, near Cape Ann, when he remarked, 'My uncle should see that picture, for I know it would greatly interest him.' On the next day, accordingly, I packed up the picture, and, with another, — a view on the coast of Nova Scotia, the home of Evangeline, — sent it off by express to Mr. Longfellow, accompanied by a note of explanation, in which I recalled the fact of our meeting many years before at the house of Park Benjamin in New York, who was the first to publish the poem about the Hesperus, and who paid for it the pittance of twenty-five dollars. The letter which Mr. Longfellow sent me in return, worth more than a thousand sketches, was as follows: —

'CAMBRIDGE, Nov. 24, 1871.

'MY DEAR SIR, — Last night I had the pleasure of receiving your friendly letter, and the beautiful pictures that came with it; and I thank you cordially for the welcome gift, and the kind remembrance that prompted it. They are both very interesting to me, particularly the Reef of Norman's Woe. What you say of the ballad is also very gratifying, and induces me to send you in return a bit of autobiography.

' Looking over a journal for 1839, a few days ago, I found the following entries : —

' "DEC. 17. News of shipwrecks, horrible, on the coast. Forty bodies washed ashore near Gloucester. One woman lashed to a piece of wreck. There is a reef called Norman's Woe, where many of these took place. Among others, the schooner Hesperus. Also the Seaflower, on Black Rock. I will write a ballad on this.

' " DEC. 30. Wrote last evening a notice of Allston's Poems; after which, sat till one o'clock by the fire, smoking, when suddenly it came into my head to write the Ballad of the Schooner Hesperus, which I accordingly did. Then went to bed, but could not sleep. New thoughts were running in my mind, and I got up to add them to the Ballad. It was three by the clock."

' All this is of no importance but to myself. However, I like sometimes to recall the circumstances under which a poem was written ; and as you express a liking for this one, it may perhaps interest you to know why and when and how it came into existence. I had quite forgotten about its first publication ; but I find a letter from Park Benjamin, dated Jan. 7. 1840, beginning (you will recognize his style) as follows : —

' " Your ballad, The Wreck of the Hesperus, is grand. Enclosed are twenty-five dollars (the sum you mentioned) for it, paid by the proprietors of The New World, in which glorious paper it will resplendently coruscate on Saturday next."

' Pardon this gossip, and believe me, with renewed thanks,

' Yours faithfully,

'HENRY W. LONGFELLOW.'

" During the summer of 1873, while spending a few weeks at Indian Hill, in Massachusetts, the delightful residence of Ben: Perley Poore, it was again my privilege to meet Mr. Longfellow. He had come down from Nahant, with his friend Charles Sumner, for the purpose of visiting, for the first time, the Longfellow homestead in Newbury. After that visit he came by invitation, with the Senator, to Indian Hill, where they enjoyed an early dinner and a bit of old wine ; after which Mr. Poore took us all in his carriage on a visit

to the poet John G. Whittier at Amesbury. The day
was charming; the route we followed was down the
Merrimac, and very lovely; and the conversation of
the lions was of course delightful. We found Mr. Whittier at home; and it was not only a great treat to see
him there, but a noted event to meet socially and under
one roof three such men as Whittier, Sumner, and Longfellow. The deportment of the two poets was to me
most captivating. The host, in his simple dress, was
as shy as a schoolboy; while Mr. Longfellow, with his
white and flowing hair and jolly laughter, reminded
me of one of his own vikings; and when Mr. Whittier
brought out and exhibited to us an anti-slavery document which he had signed forty years before, I could
not help recalling some of the splendid things which
that trio of great men had written on the subject of
slavery. The drive to Newburyport, whence Mr. Sumner and Mr. Longfellow were to return to Nahant, was
no less delightful than had been the preceding one;
and the kindly words which were spoken of Mr. Whittier proved that he was highly honored and loved by
his noted friends, as he is by the world at large. Before parting from Mr. Longfellow, he took me one side,
and spoke with great interest of the old homestead he
had that morning visited, and expressed a wish that I
should make a sketch of it for him, as it was then two
hundred years old, and rapidly going to decay. On
the following morning I went to the spot, and complied
with his request. A few weeks afterward I sent him
a finished picture of the house, not forgetting the well-
sweep and the old stone horse-block, in which he felt a
special interest; and he acknowledged the receipt of
the picture in these words: —

'CAMBRIDGE, Oct. 18, 1873.

'MY DEAR SIR, — I have had the pleasure of receiving your very friendly note, and the picture of the old homestead at Newbury; for both of which I pray you to accept my most cordial thanks. Be assured that I value your gift highly, and appreciate the kindness which prompted it, and the trouble you took in making the portraits of the old house and tree. They are very exact, and will always remind me of that pleasant summer day, and Mr. Poore's chateau and his charming family, and yours. If things could ever be done twice over in this world, — which they cannot, — I should like to live that day over again.

'With kind regards to Mrs. Lanman, not forgetting a word and a kiss to your little Japanese ward (Ume Tsuda), I am, my dear sir,

'Yours truly,

'HENRY W. LONGFELLOW.'

"When the poem of Kéramos was published, in November, 1877, I had a translation made into Japanese of that portion of it alluding to Japan, and forwarded it to the poet, with an explanation as to how the transformation had taken place; the young gentleman who made the translation having been Mr. Amano Koziro, then of the Japanese legation. The acknowledgment sent me by Mr. Longfellow was as follows: —

'CAMBRIDGE, Nov. 23, 1877.

'MY DEAR SIR, — I have this morning had the pleasure of receiving your letter, and the Japanese version of a portion of Kéramos, which you were kind enough to send me, and for which I beg you to accept my cordial thanks. I shall put it away with The Psalm of Life, written in Chinese on a fan. What I should like now is a literal retranslation of the Japanese into English.

' In the introduction there is a slight error, which is worth correcting. It is the Poet, not the Potter, who takes the aërial flight, and in imagination visits far-off lands; also, Kéramos is rather potter's earth than earthenware. But the difference is slight, and hardly worth noticing, unless one wishes to be very particular.

' You will rejoice, as I do, in the complete vindication of Sumner's memory from the imputations so recklessly cast upon it. With great regard.

' Yours very truly,
'HENRY W. LONGFELLOW.'

" In November, 1881, when my work entitled Curious Characters and Pleasant Places was published in Edinburgh, because of the fact that it contained a chapter on Anticosti, where Mr. Longfellow's first American ancestor lost his life (he who had built the Newbury homestead), I sent him a copy; and in my note I asked him for his views on the propriety of printing the private letters of living men without their consent. I had noticed in Barry Cornwall's autobiography several of Mr. Longfellow's own letters; and as I was then examining the very interesting correspondence of the late Professor Samuel Tyler, with a view to publication, I desired to be fortified with the poet's opinion; and the result of my application was as follows: —

' CAMBRIDGE, Dec. 3, 1881.

' DEAR MR. LANMAN, — I was very glad to get your letter, and the copy of your Recollections. It is a handsome volume, and most inviting in appearance. I shall read it with the greatest interest, as soon as I am able to read any thing; but at present I am confined to my room by illness, — a trouble in the head which prevents continuous attention to any thing.   I hope this will soon pass away, and all be right again.

' The publication of private letters of living persons is certainly a delicate question.   It is, however, universally practised in biographies.   One must be guided by the importance of the letters themselves.   I should omit every thing that could in any way compromise the writer, as I see by your letter you would.   There are letters that do honor to the writer and the receiver.   These certainly should not be omitted.

' Meanwhile, accept my sincere and cordial thanks for your kind remembrance, and believe me,

' Yours faithfully,

'HENRY W. LONGFELLOW.'

" The foregoing letter was among the last written by Mr. Longfellow; and the brief allusion to his illness, as we read it to-day, has a pathos allied to some of his saddest poems.

"CHARLES LANMAN.

"WASHINGTON, D. C., April 13, 1882."

THE POET'S EXPLANATION OF EXCELSIOR.

Mr. Longfellow wrote the following letter to Henry T. Tuckerman many years ago, and it has just found its way into print in The London Telegraph: —

I have had the pleasure of receiving your note in regard to the poem Excelsior, and very willingly give you my intention in writing it.   This was no more than to display, in a series of pictures, the life of a man of genius, resisting all temptations, laying aside all fears, heedless of all warnings, and pressing right on to accomplish his purpose.   His motto is Excelsior,—"higher."   He passes through the Alpine village,—through the rough, cold paths of the world, —where the peasants cannot understand him, and where his watchword is "an unknown tongue." He disregards the happiness of domestic peace, and sees the glaciers — his fate — before him. He disregards the warnings of the old man's wisdom and the fascinations of woman's love. He answers to all, "Higher yet!" The monks of St. Bernard are the representatives of religious forms and ceremonies, and with their oft-repeated prayer mingles the sound of his voice, telling them there is something higher than forms or ceremonies. Filled with these aspirations he perishes without having reached the perfection he longed for; and the voice heard in the air is the promise of immortality and progress ever upward. You will perceive that "excelsior," an adjective of the comparative degree, is used adverbially; a use justified by the best Latin writers. I remain,

Very truly yours,

HENRY W. LONGFELLOW.

AN APT QUOTATION.

It is said, that, when Mr. Longfellow was introduced to the late Nicholas Longworth of Cincinnati, reference was made to the similarity of the first syllables of their names, whereupon Mr. Longfellow immediately responded with the line from Pope, —

"Worth makes the man, and want of it the fellow."

The repartee, therefore, is one of the best on record.

CATAWBA WINE.

Speaking of Mr. Longworth, it is *apropos* to say that our poet's genial song, Catawba Wine, is understood to have been written on the receipt of a case of that delicate liquor from his Cincinnati friend. It was Mr. Longworth who first produced the Catawba grape by elaborate experiments in cross-fertilization. Let us hear a stanza or two : —

> For richest and best
> Is the wine of the West,
> That grows by the Beautiful River;
> Whose sweet perfume
> Fills all the room
> With a benison on the giver.
>
> .   .   .   .   .   .
>
> And this Song of the Vine,
> This greeting of mine,
> The winds and the birds shall deliver
> To the Queen of the West,
> In her garlands dressed,
> On the banks of the Beautiful River.

WASHINGTON AT CRAIGIE HOUSE.

At the close of the Revolutionary War, it was noticed that there was a large quantity of lead on the roof. Undoubtedly, if Washington had known this fact, he would have confiscated it for the purpose of having it cast into bullets,—lead being very scarce in those days. The fact that he did not discover it seems to indicate that he never visited the roof of the mansion which he was making his headquarters. The roof is four-sided, and has on its summit a flat area which is railed in, and forms a very pleasant place for lounging or star-gazing. But the Father of his Country had sterner business in hand than star-gazing, and looking at landscapes. His business was to think and plan wearily and anxiously in his own room below.

VIA SOLITARIA.

A curious bit of literary history is the following story of a poem published in The New York Independent shortly after Longfellow's death. It purported to be a posthumous production of the Cambridge poet, and to have been written by him in 1863, two years after the afflicting death of his second wife. It was nearly enough like Mr. Longfellow's other minor poems in style to pass unchallenged by anybody, yet doubtless many must have felt that somehow it had not the Longfellow stamp upon it. It is strange, too, that editors had not noticed the internal evidence against its authenticity. In the last stanza but one, the poet speaks of a "child and mother straying in robes of white." On the supposition that the poem was written by Mr. Longfellow, these lines are explicable only if referred to his first wife; but evidently only one person is referred to throughout the poem, and it is almost impossible that Mr. Longfellow would have referred to his first wife in a poem the subject of which is the death of his second wife. As a matter of fact, the poem was written by Mr. O. M. Conover of Madison, Wis., and was published in The New York Independent for July 2, 1863, p. 6, and signed "O. M. C., Madison, Wis." A Cambridge lady sent a copy of the poem to Mr. Conover, not long after it was published, and received a reply from him, with his corrections of certain errors that had crept into the piece during its wanderings.

The mistake probably arose in this way: The poem was sent in manuscript form to more than one friend in or near Boston. It is presumable that one of these manuscript copies was by some mistake sent to Professor H. M. Goodwin of Olivet College, Michigan, as a poem by Longfellow, after whose death Professor Goodwin sent it in good faith to The Independent.

It is here reproduced with its author's corrections (five in number) : —

VIA SOLITARIA.

Alone I walk the peopled city,
  Where each seems happy with his own;
O friends, I ask not for your pity, —
    I walk alone.

No more for me yon lake rejoices,
  Though wooed by loving airs of June;
O birds, your sweet and piping voices
    Are out of tune.

In vain for me the elm-tree arches
  Its plumes in many a feathery spray;
In vain the evening's starry marches
    And sunlit day.

In vain your beauty, summer flowers;
  Ye cannot greet those cordial eyes;
They gaze on other fields than ours, —
    On other skies.

The gold is rifled from the coffer,
  The blade is stolen from the sheath;
Life has but one more boon to offer,
    And that is — Death.

Yet well I know the voice of Duty,
  And therefore life and health must crave,
Though she who gave the world its beauty
    Is in her grave.

I live, O lost one! for the living
  Who drew their earliest life from thee,
And wait until, with glad thanksgiving,
    I shall be free.

For life to me is as a station
  Wherein apart a traveller stands —
One absent long from home and nation,
    In other lands;

And I, as he who stands and listens,
  Amid the twilight's chill and gloom,
To hear, approaching in the distance,
    The train for home.

For death shall bring another mating; —
  Beyond the shadows of the tomb,
On yonder shore a bride is waiting
    Until I come.

In yonder fields are children playing,
  And there — O vision of delight! —
I see a child and mother straying
    In robes of white.

Thou, then, the longing heart that breakest,
  Stealing its treasures one by one,
I'll call thee blessed when thou makest
    The parted — one.

LONGFELLOW'S LAST PUBLISHED POEM.

It was apppropriate, indeed, that Mr. Longfellow's last poem should appear posthumously in The Atlantic Monthly (May, 1882), a magazine to which, for nearly a quarter of a century, the world has turned with eager expectation for the first reading of so many poems from the pen of the most popular of living poets. It was fitting that his own eminent publishers, Messrs. Houghton, Mifflin, & Co., should publish his last poem. And that last manuscript, written in the old familiar hand, both publishers and printers might well have received with reverent hands, and with moistened eyes; for now the last string of the sweet instrument had snapped, and the music was forever ended.

But how delicate and melodious the last strain! How faithful to nature the imagery! The poem is entitled

MAD RIVER.

.Why dost thou wildly rush and roar,
  Mad River, O Mad River?
Wilt thou not pause, and cease to pour
Thy hurrying, headlong waters o'er
  This rocky shelf forever?

What secret trouble stirs thy breast?
  Why all this fret and flurry?
Dost thou not know that what is best
In this too restless world is rest
  From overwork and worry?

   .   .   .   .

A brooklet nameless and unknown
  Was I at first, resembling
A little child, that all alone
Comes venturing down the stairs of stone,
  Irresolute and trembling.

Later, by wayward fancies led,
  For the wide world I panted;
Out of the forest dark and dread
Across the open fields I fled,
  Like one pursued and haunted.

   .   .   .   .

Men call me Mad, and well they may,
  When, full of rage and trouble,
I burst my banks of sand and clay,
And sweep their wooden bridge away,
  Like withered reeds or stubble.

Now go and write thy little rhyme,
  As of thine own creating.
Thou seest the day is past its prime;
I can no longer waste my time;
  The mills are tired of waiting.

REMINISCENCES OF M. LOUIS DEPRET.

A valued friend and correspondent of Mr. Longfellow was M. Louis Depret of Paris. He says the poet "was wonderfully well acquainted with the capital of France; because he had lived in it a couple of years almost half a century ago when he was preparing himself, by conscientious study of the Old World, for the chair of professor of foreign literature in Harvard College. . . . Longfellow was, of all the great writers whom it has been my good fortune to approach, the one whose genial intercourse, without affectation, but still singularly authoritative, best exemplified what one ought to understand by a noble spirit."

M. Depret thinks that the conversation of Longfellow was "the original expression of a soul." He says he had a way of saying things as if he had found them out for himself. He continues, "I accompanied him all about Paris, — to the Sainte Chapelle, to the Hôtel Lambert, where the lamented M. Vautrain, the intimate friend of the Czartoriski princes, officiated as a guide; and we also visited numerous theatres. At the Comédie-Française, Longfellow made the curious remark that the French language was no longer pronounced by the actors of 1869 as it was by their elders of 1829. The apartment of the great American was in one of the pleasantest hotels in the Rue de Rivoli, and was visited by a very variegated collection of people daily. Among them was the Dominican, Hyacinthe. And in Longfellow's parlor we met for the first time the man whose name was famous, and whose personality was almost completely unknown, the old poet of the Iambics," namely, Auguste Barbier.

KÉRAMOS AND THE LONGFELLOW JUG.

Some one in The Literary World has written the following account of the Longfellow Jug: —

" It was certainly a bright and happy thought to enshrine ' Kéramos ' in a ' Longfellow Jug.' For many a day Mr. Richard Briggs, the Boston dealer in potter's wares, had been looking, as he tells us, for a fitting subject for such an achievement, and when ' Kéramos ' appeared he felt his opportunity had come. He undertook an expedition in person to the celebrated works of Josiah Wedgwood & Sons, at Etruria, Staffordshire, Eng., and gave an order for the execution of a ' Longfellow Jug ' in the well-known Wedgwood ware. The jug is now ready for the market, and is a beauty as well as a novelty, both intrinsically and in its suggestions.

" It is of a stout and useful-looking pattern, not very heavy in texture, but broad and capacious, standing about seven inches high, four inches and a half open at the top, and nearly seven inches wide at its greatest diameter. It is thus just about ' as broad as it is long ; ' proportions which give it a very solid, common-sensible, New-England aspect. It has an honest handle, and a nose which, as that on the human face may be, is a character in itself. It holds, when filled to the brim, two quarts and nearly a pint, and ' pours ' excellently well, which is no mean virtue in a pitcher. Its body color is, of course, the cream-white which the name of Wedgwood has made so familiar.

" The special charm of the jug, however, is in its decoration, which is appropriate, tasteful, and pleasing in almost every particular, while altogether simple and free from ostentation, as becomes the subject. Two panels occupy the sides, — one presenting a portrait of Mr. Longfellow, the other a verse of the potter's song. The verse is enclosed in a pretty border of antique design, the leading feature of which is a picture of the potter at his work. The border around the portrait might better have been a wreath of ivy or laurel than a girdle of stars and bars; but this is the single infelicity, in our judgment, in the whole work. The portrait, as a likeness, is simply admirable. No portrait of Mr. Longfellow which we have ever seen — in magazine, book, or even photograph — presents more accurately, not merely the general contour of his head and cast of countenance, but that peculiar expression, particularly of eyes and mouth, which cannot be described in words, but which is so marked and winning in the original. It is wonderful that such a likeness could have been secured on clay, and especially on a convex surface. The reader will be interested to know how it was done. A selected photograph of Mr. Longfellow was carried by Mr. Briggs to London, and a costly copper-plate engraving made from it by a very skilful artist for the foundation. From this copper-plate, impressions are taken on tissue paper, not in ordinary ink, but in the pigment used in ceramic work; and a paper print is then applied directly to every jug when yet in the unburnt clay. The jug then goes to the furnace; and the fires, consuming the paper, leave the print indelibly affixed."

MAIDENHOOD.

A minister once delivered a sermon which had a somewhat novel theme for the pulpit. He called it " Expounding Longfellow's Poem entitled Maiden-

hood." IIe read the poem through, and then read it
again in portions, enlarging on the thoughts in each part,
and drawing many useful life-lessons from the verses.
But the most noteworthy thing in the sermon was the
narration of the circumstance which gave rise to it.
The preacher told a story of a poor woman living in a
lonely cabin in a sterile portion of the Northwest, to
whom a friend of his had sent illustrated papers. From
these the woman had cut the pictures, and papered the
walls of her cabin with them; and an illustration of
Longfellow's 'Maidenhood,' with the poem underneath
it, she had placed directly over her work-table. There,
as she stood at her bread-making or ironing, day after
day, she gazed at the picture and read the poem, till, by
long brooding on it, she understood it, absorbed it,
as few people appropriate the things they read. When
the friend who had sent the papers visited her after a
time, he, himself a man of letters, stood amazed and
humbled while she talked to him artlessly about the
poem, expounded to him its interior meaning, and expressed the thoughts she had drawn from it. The
preacher said it was an instance of that benign compensation by which those who have little may draw the
more from that little, so that one cup deeply drained
may yield more of life's elixir than many that are
sipped. Altogether, it shows how a poet may be a
preacher, both from a pulpit and from a cabin-wall,
sweetening the lowliest life as well as enchanting the
highest.

"I KNEW BY THE BOOTS THAT SO TERRIBLY CREAKED."

The mother of Capt. Nathan Appleton was a Miss
Sumner, a cousin of Charles Sumner. She was of

about the same age as Longfellow, and the two were always intimate friends. Before she married Mr. Appleton, and before Mr. Longfellow was married, one day when the poet came from Portland to call upon her, he wore a pair of new boots, which were very noisy. When he went away the next day he left a little poem written on a card, which Capt. Appleton still has in his possession. It is as follows : —

> "I knew by the boots that so terribly creaked,
>   Along the front entry, a stranger was near:
>   I said, If there's grease to be found in the world,
>   My friend from the East stands in need of it here."

SALE OF HIS WORKS IN ENGLAND.

Amelia B. Edwards, of Westbury, Eng., gives in The Literary World some interesting data concerning the sale of Longfellow's works in England:—

"There cannot, I imagine, be any doubt that Professor Longfellow is in England the most widely read of living poets. Messrs. Routledge & Sons, who are his authorized publishers in this country, have on sale at the present moment eight different editions of his works, varying in price from one shilling to one guinea; while at least a dozen other houses — profiting by the absence of an international copyright law — publish unauthorized editions adapted in like manner to the tastes and purses of all classes. Thus it is that our English versions, answering to the demand created by an unbounded popularity, are as the leaves on the trees, or the pebbles on the shore. Thus it is that at every bookseller's shop in town or country 'Longfellow's Poems' are a staple of trade. As a prize-book for schools, as a gift-book, as a drawing-room table-book, as a pocket volume for the woods and fields, our familiar and beloved friend of something like forty years meets us at every turn.   Of new copies alone, it is calculated that not less than thirty thousand are annually sold in the United Kingdom ; and who shall estimate the average sale of copies in the second-hand market?   That it should repay his English publishers, in the face of unlimited competition, to purchase a few weeks' precedence at the high rate paid by Messrs. Routledge for Professor Longfellow's early sheets, is evidence enough of the eagerness with which we welcome every line that falls from his pen. For advance proofs of the ' New-England Tragedies ' — perhaps the poet's least successful volume — those eminent publishers gave no less a sum than one thousand pounds sterling."

A LETTER OF THE POET.

CAMBRIDGE, MASS., Nov. 29, 1852.

DEAR MISS COOK, — It gives me very sincere pleasure to add my name to the list of subscribers for Hood's monument, as you request in your friendly note ; and I will forward my contribution through Mr. Fields, who will have some others to send at the same time.

Do not weigh my admiration for Hood's genius by the amount of my subscription.   That must be estimated by a very different scale of weights and measures.   Dear Hood I should say instead of Poor Hood !   For he who wrote the " Song of the Shirt " and the " Bridge of Sighs " is very dear to every human heart.

Poor Mrs. Hood and the children, who have lost him ! They will have forgotten the stranger who called one October morning some years ago with Dickens, and was hospitably entertained by them.   But I remember the visit, and the pale face of the poet, and the house in St. John's Wood.

If the family is still there, may I beg you to present my regards and remembrances. With many thanks for your note and many expressions of friendly interest,

Yours faithfully,

HENRY W. LONGFELLOW.

Per Steam Packet.
Miss Eliza Cook, 54, Gt. Ormond St.,
Queen Square, London.

— The Athenæum.

GEN. JAMES GRANT WILSON'S REMINISCENCES.

From an article by Gen. James Grant Wilson, in The New York Independent, the following charming reminiscences are extracted: —

" The poet having told me that he had seen scores of parodies of 'Excelsior,' but had never met with one that my father had written, in which many dialects are introduced, I sent it to him; and when we met again he amused all present by repeating three or four of the twenty-five verses describing a singing hodman's ascent of a lofty ladder: —

'Mon ami I vill parley vous
Von leetle vord; 'tis mah you do!
Ver goot, sare; Chacun à son gout;
Excelsior!

'Brava! brava! bravissima!
Encore! excellentissima!
Primo tenor! dolcissima!
Excelsior!

'By coot Saint Tavit an' hur leek!
She'd rather fast for half ta week
Tan shuffle on tat shoggy stick!
Excelsior!

> ' Mein Cot! dot man vill break him pones,
> And knock him prain upon de stones;
> Der Teufel! did you heert vat tones!
> Excelsior!'

Longfellow imitating the French, Italian, Welsh, and German speakers in a most successful manner.

" Mr. Longfellow writes to me in 1870 saying: —

" ' I have read your privately printed volume with great pleasure. It is a most interesting life, and the sweet and dignified face of the Chief Justice gives an added grace to it. The powdered hair and white cravat remind me of the old judges and gentlemen of the bar that I used to see when I was a boy in Portland.'

" Writing in 1872, the poet says: —

" ' Your letter and the valuable present of Mr. S. C. Hall have reached me safely. Please accept my best thanks for the great kindness you have shown in taking charge of and bringing from the Old World a gift so precious as the inkstand of the poet who wrote the Rhyme of the Ancient Mariner. Will you be so good as to send me the present address of Mr. Hall? I wish, without delay, to acknowledge this mark of his remembrance and regard, and am not sure where a letter will find him.'

" Referring to this precious souvenir, the venerable Richard Henry Dana wrote to me soon after: —

" ' It greatly pleased me to receive a few lines from you, just returned from that glorious old city, London, which, it is sad to think, I shall never see. . . . And so you brought over Mr. Coleridge's inkstand for Mr. Longfellow. I am almost tempted to commit burglary, or even murder if necessary, to possess it. Mr. Longfellow must look out for himself.'

"This inkstand, I may mention, had been used for many years by Coleridge, and also for nine years by Longfellow, on the centre of whose library-table he pointed it out to my daughter, while showing her his most highly prized treasures. Said Mr. Longfellow, —

"'This memento of the poet recalls to my recollection that Theophilus Parsons, subsequently eminent in Massachusetts 'jurisprudence, paid me for a dozen of my early pieces, that appeared in his United-States Literary Gazette, with a copy of Coleridge's poems, which I still have in my possession. Mr. Bryant contributed the Forest Hymn, The Old Man's Funeral, and many other poems, to the same periodical, and thought he was well paid by receiving *two dollars* apiece, — a price, by the way, which he himself placed upon the poems, and at least double the amount of my *honorarium*. Truly, times have changed with us *littérateurs* during the last half-century.'

"The year following (1873) Mr. Longfellow writes: —

"'It was only a day or two ago, that, happening to be in the college library, I found the volume you were kind enough to send me. As Mr. Sibley does not undertake to distribute the parcels sent to his care, they being very numerous, one sometimes may wait for weeks before getting his own. This is my apology for not thanking you sooner for your most entertaining book; but it has come safe, at last, and I have read it with great interest. . . . I remember very well the poem of "Sukey," an imitation of Halleck's "Fanny." It was written by William Bicker Walter, a contemporary of mine at Bowdoin College, who died young. You will find an account of it and its author in the second volume of Duyckinck's American Cyclopædia.'

"Writing in April, 1875, the poet says, —

"'I shall be most happy to subscribe to the S. C. Hall testimonial. Please let me know the average amount of subscription, and I will immediately send you mine. Many thanks for the Gaelic versions of Suspiria and the Psalm of Life. They are indeed literary curiosities. . . . I send you a copy of the poem you mention for your daughter, which please present to her, with my kindest regards.'

"Mr. Longfellow, writing in 1876, remarks, —

"'I am much obliged to you for sending me the proof-sheets of Mr. Symington's article on Freiligrath. I return a portion of it, with a few corrections. He is wrong in attributing to me any translations of Freiligrath's poems. There are several in the Poets and Poetry of Europe, which probably led him astray. Had he, however, looked at the table of contents, he would have found the authors or sources of all the translations. If you are writing to Mr. Symington, please set this matter right. . . . In the volumes of my Poems of Places, devoted to Scotland, you will find several of your father's compositions.'

.   .   .   .

"At our last meeting, as I learn from a little memorandum-book, he alluded to the death of Bryant and Dana, and said, 'The years are thinning us out, and we old graybeards must close up our ranks.' Pointing out the portraits of Emerson, Hawthorne, and Sumner, which hung in his library, he said of them and of his own pictures, that some of the photographs were admired, and remarked that they 'rendered justice without mercy.' A fine oil portrait, which was painted long ago by Alexander, had been engraved for some magazine. He preferred it and some other early counterfeit presentments to the later ones, saying, ' We old gentlemen, like Irving, generally prefer to be remembered as we were, rather than as we are.' He dwelt at considerable length and with undisguised pleasure on his last sojourn in Italy, alluding to our meetings at Sorrento, Naples, and elsewhere, and concluded by saying, ' Alas! I shall never see that sunny land again.'

" Longfellow spoke of some mutual friends at Nahant, from which place he had recently returned, and said, ' Yes, I have had two months of delicious idleness at Nahant, and it is time that I put on the harness again.' Alluding to Bryant having taken up the translating of Homer at seventy-two, for occupation of mind, he remarked that he 'found that 'translating was like floating with the tide.' He agreed with what Bryant said to me, that old men should keep the mind occupied, to preserve it, and introduced the incident of the old horse who fell down the moment that he stopped! Showing some of his pictures, he particularly dwelt on Buchanan Read's famous group of his three daughters, and on one of Copley's, representing two of Sir William Pepperell's children, the style of which the poet thought strongly resembled some of Gainsborough's paintings. It occupied the place of honor in his reception-room.

" The poet mentioned an agreeable visit that he had received the previous summer from the Duke of Argyll, and expressed admiration for him as a man of ability and as a member of the literary guild. ' When I was in England the last time,' said Mr. Longfellow, ' I listened to an extremely interesting and able debate between the Duke and Bishop Wilberforce, sometimes

described as " Soapy Sam ; " and in the lower house I
heard a warm encounter between Disraeli and that truly
great man, Gladstone ; ' adding, in answer to my inquiry, ' Yes, it was my good fortune to have met these
political rivals.'

" Having been intrusted with a commission from an
English author, who wished to obtain data from the
poet with a view to writing his life for a series then in
course of publication,[1] Longfellow said, ' I have no possible objection to your friend's undertaking a memoir,
if he deems me worthy of being included among his
biographies ; but for me to sit down, and prepare material for Mr. Symington, would be like writing my autobiography.'   And in urging him to be present during
the unveiling, in the following month, of the Burns
statue in the Central Park, and to be our guest at that
time, he said, ' Unfortunately, I have too many friends
in New York, and, troubled as I am at present with
neuralgia, I fear the excitement and bustle would be
too much for me.   No : I could not keep quiet there,
and I trust that you will kindly excuse me to your
committee.   I feel sure that it will be a pleasant occasion ; and I promise myself much pleasure from reading
the address that Mr. Curtis is to deliver, for Burns is a
subject in which I am always interested.   Pray, do not
feel that it is necessary to send me a formal invitation,
as I cannot possibly come.'

" Before our departure we were invited to sit down
in the carved chair made from the ' spreading chestnut-
tree,' presented to the poet by the school-children of
Cambridge, and shown many other objects of interest,

----

[1] Biographies of Bryant, Lover, Moore, and Wordsworth. By Andrew J. Symington, F.R.S.

including the old clock on the stairs and the pen received from 'beautiful Helen of Maine,' with its 'iron link from the chain of Bonnivard,' 'its wood from the frigate's mast' that wrote on 'the sky the song of the sea and the blast,' and its three jewels from the sands of Ceylon, the mountains of Maine, and the snows of Siberia.

"We parted at the poet's gate on that sunny September morning, never to meet again; but I shall always retain the remembrance of his venerable appearance, his sweet old-school courtesy of manners, and of the many meetings that it was my privilege to have enjoyed with the best loved of American poets.

> 'Say not the poet dies!
> Though in the dust he lies,
> He cannot forfeit his melodious breath,
> Unsphered by envious Death!
> Life drops the voiceless myriads from its roll:
> Their fate he cannot share,
> Who, in the enchanted air,
> Sweet with the lingering strains that Echo stole,
> Has left his dearer self, the music of his soul!'"

ORIGIN OF ONE OF HIS SONNETS.

Apphia Howard, writing to The Providence Star, of how one of Mr. Longfellow's famous sonnets came to be written, says, —

"I found in 1864, on a torn scrap of The Boston Saturday Evening Gazette, a description of a burying-ground in Newport News, where on the headboard of a soldier might be read the words: 'A Union soldier mustered out,' and this was the only inscription. Knowing Mr. Longfellow's intense patriotism and devotion to the Union, I thought it would impress him greatly. After carefully pasting the broken pieces together on a bit of cardboard, I sent it to Mr. Longfellow by Mr. Greene, who did not think Longfellow would use it, for he declared 'a poet could not write to order.' In a few days Mr. Longfellow acknowledged it by a letter, which I did not at all expect, as follows: 'In the writing of letters more, perhaps, than in any thing else, Shakespeare's words are true; and

> "The flighty purpose never is o'ertook
> Unless the deed go with it."

For this reason, the touching incident you have sent me has not yet shaped itself poetically in my mind as I hope it some day will. Meanwhile I thank you most sincerely for bringing it to my notice, and I agree with you in thinking it very beautiful.' After a while it did shape itself in the poet's mind into the form of the exquisite sonnet beginning, —

> '"A soldier of the Union mustered out,"
> Is the inscription on an unknown grave
> At Newport News, beside the salt-sea wave,
> Nameless and dateless.'"

SMALL BOOKS.

Mr. Longfellow once said to J. J. Piatt, "People like books of poems which they can read through at a sitting. The publishers insist on quantity, but I have always aimed to have my books small."

QUID PRO QUO.

There was one matter in which Mr. Longfellow set a fine example to professional men. He was always extremely scrupulous not to receive something for nothing. That is, he always paid for books, papers, and other things which some authors and professional men are accustomed to get gratis.

HIS AUTOGRAPH.

As many persons know, he was perpetually besieged for his autograph. His patience never failed. He kept in advance of the demand a large number of his autographs written on little slips, storing them away in an envelope for future use. These slips he would paste on larger slips when needed.

RELATIONS TO PRINTERS AND PUBLISHERS.

Mr. Longfellow never exhibited any irritability in his relations with his printers. A gentleman connected with the University Press, where most of Mr. Longfellow's works were printed, has stated that in all the years of his business relations with the poet, as printer of his books and other work, he never heard him utter an impatient or irritable word.

AN APOCRYPHAL POEM.

The following story and poem carry within themselves their own refutation. They are admitted here only that the reader may enjoy a laugh over them. They have gone the rounds of American newspapers as though they were matters of fact; but Mr. Longfellow himself stated to the compiler of the Longfellow Birthday Book that the story and the poem were both unauthentic. The story runs as follows: —

"When our great poet was nine years old, his master wanted him to write a 'composition.' Little Henry, like all children, shrank from the undertaking. His master said, 'You can write words, can you not?'

"'Yes,' was the reply.

"'Then, you can put words together?'

"'Yes, sir.'

"'Then,' said the master, 'you may take your slate, and go out behind the schoolhouse, and there you can find something to write about, and then you can tell what it is, what it is for, and what is to be done with it; and that is a composition.'

"Henry took his slate, and went out. He went behind Mr. Finney's barn, which chanced to be near, and, seeing a fine turnip growing, he thought he knew what it was, what it was for, and what would be done with it.

"A half-hour had been allowed to him for his first undertaking in writing compositions. In a half-hour he carried in his work all accomplished."

MR. FINNEY'S TURNIP.

Mr. Finney had a turnip,
  And it grew, and it grew;
And it grew behind the barn,
  And the turnip did no harm.

And it grew, and it grew,
  Till it could grow no taller;
Then Mr. Finney took it up,
  And put it in the cellar.

There it lay, there it lay,
  Till it began to rot;
When his daughter Susie washed it,
  And put it in the pot.

Then she boiled it, and she boiled it,
  As long as she was able;
Then his daughter Lizzie took it,
  And she put it on the table.

> Mr. Finney and his wife
> Both sat down to sup;
> And they ate, and they ate,
> Until they ate the turnip up.

NAHANT.

Lady Duffus Hardy, in the last pages of her work, entitled Through Cities and Prairie Lands, gives a slight and airy, but pretty picture of the poet at his seaside cottage in Nahant (about 1881) : —

"After shaking hands, and exchanging the usual greetings, he presented us to his two brothers-in-law, who reside with him. The household was not entirely masculine, however : the poet's two daughters were out in their yacht enjoying a sail; the one is married, and, with her little child, is only on a visit; the other, a very charming young lady, lives at home with her father. We went through the house, and sat in the back veranda. A tempting-looking hammock swung there; and wild roses climbed up the lattice-work, and nodded their odorous heads at us, and showered their pink petals at our feet. The poet gathered us a bunch of the fairest blossoms: they lie faded and scentless in my album to-day, but the memory of that July afternoon at Nahant is fresh and green still. . . . We sat there chatting in a pleasant way of the Old World and the New. . . . Mr. Longfellow is no egotist: he evidently does not care to talk of himself or his work. He is full of that modesty which generally characterizes great genius. . . . The meal, gastronomically considered, was on strictly gastronomical principles : we sipped the vintage of Champagne while we enjoyed the pork and beans of Boston, and washed down corn-cobs and hominy with mineral waters of Germany." Probably very few of Lady Hardy's British readers understand that in speaking here of corn-cobs, she refers to that strictly aboriginal prandial custom, so rife amongst us, of eating green Indian corn from the cob.

LONGFELLOW AT VESUVIUS.

A correspondent of The London Times for March 28, 1882, gives some crude although interesting impressions derived from a single day's intercourse with our American Chaucer at Naples and Vesuvius. They struck up an acquaintanceship at a *table-d'hôte*, and agreed to ascend Vesuvius together, in company with three vivacious young ladies from Boston. The vehicles were open carriages. Mr. Longfellow was in his happiest vein, and talked incessantly. Our somewhat pert tourist may now speak for himself: —

"In Mr. Longfellow I could see no difference between the poet and the pleasant elderly gentleman who was discoursing gayly on all things in heaven and earth; and, as I listened, a sufficiently obvious reflection was forced upon me. What was this most perfect product of American civilization but a serious, severe — I had almost said bigoted — conservative, and a most fervent Christian? Longfellow's talk was his poetry rendered into flowing prose. I conjured up Paul Flemming in 'Hyperion,' and at length mustered courage to ask, 'Was Paul Flemming a character drawn from life?' He paused a full half-minute, then answered exactly in the following words: 'He was what I thought I might have been; but I never' — He shaded his face with one hand, and did not complete the sentence. From the sadness of the poet's tone I conjectured that there was some implied confession of failure in his reticence. I guessed that he was struggling between the natural humility of a religious man and the unwillingness of a well-bred man to intrude the sorrows of his mind upon others. Mr. Longfellow was right: he never attained to those cold heights on which he had placed the creation of his fancy; he found a better resting-place.

"All three persons in the carriage, the Englishman and the two ladies, almost simultaneously, now besought the poet to recite some of his poetry, which he did. The gentleman then asked him how long he had taken to compose The Golden Legend. He replied, 'It seems easy, doesn't it?' The friend replied, that he supposed that, after he had thoroughly saturated his mind with mediæval lore, the composition of the poem would have been a comparatively easy matter. 'Well,' he rejoined, 'you are about right. The first draught I did in four weeks, not counting the Sundays — I don't like to work on Sundays — not even to write a hymn. But I spent about six months correcting — and cutting down.' The dashes in this little speech stand for the pauses so frequent in Mr. Longfellow's utterances, — pauses which were the result of constant introspection. One fancied the poet had been asking his conscience whether he had been telling the truth, the whole truth, and nothing but the truth. A terribly exact man in moral dealings with himself, — afraid even of an inaccuracy which might possibly cause a fellow-man to make a mistake twenty years after.

. . . .

"We lunched at a small inn on the side of Vesuvius, where the wine, by the way, was not of a kind to fire

a poet's fancy; after this we went to sniff and sneeze,
in the usual way of tourists, over the sulphurous gases
of the water, suggesting a poem on Empedocles, and
wondering what rhymes Longfellow could hammer out
for the name of this 'young man with the indestructi-
ble boots,' as the poet called him [because his sandal
was thrown up undestroyed from the crater]. Our
French companion was busy with a paradox of his own
as to Empedocles having been a young shoemaker
nobly desirous of advertising his father's shop *à l'Amé-
ricaine*, — i.e., regardless of cost, — and we were about
to descend the steeps laughing over this fancy, when,
to our considerable dismay, Mr. Longfellow expressed
his intention of spending the night upon the mountain.
Within a short distance of the crater, then only
smouldering with occasional unsavory whiffs and puffs,
stood a ruined plank shed, used in fine weather by a
screaming old woman who sold ornaments made of
lava; and this place it was that the poet chose for his
vigil. Without a smile on his face he said, 'I want to
gather poetic impressions.' We looked becomingly
serious, and only begged to be permitted to keep watch
with him. 'No,' with two or three shakes of the
head; 'I must be alone.'

"A whispered consultation between some members of
the party followed. 'He is quite in earnest, and must
do as he pleases,' said a brother of the fair Bostonians;
and he added that there was no danger just then of
the greatest of American poets meeting with the same
fate as the younger Pliny. 'But the brigands?' suggested the Frenchman. 'Dear me! he will catch such
a dreadful cold,' chimed in one of the ladies. Finally
we decided to leave the poet to his reveries, after order-

ing a Maltese courier to stand sentinel, unobserved, within hailing distance. It is probable that this courier fulfilled at least the half of his duties faithfully, for his presence was certainly never noticed by Mr. Longfellow. The author of Excelsior turned up in the morning, looking none the worse for his night's frolic with the ghosts of Herculaneum and Pompeii; but he persistently parried every question put to him as to whether he had found 'inspiration.' All he would say was, that, on coming down from the mountain, he had been requested by a gendarme to exhibit his passport, and, being unable to produce this document, had been nearly marched off to the police-station. 'I purchased my liberty for two *lire*,' he remarked smiling: 'the price of that commodity has decreased since Cœur de Lion's time.'"

BASS'S PALE ALE.

At a dinner-party in London, some one asked Mr. Longfellow what he had been most impressed with in England. "Bass's pale ale," he replied. Thereupon some one at the lower end of the table perpetrated an execrable pun by saying in a deep *bass* voice, "A good joke, that!"

A RURAL PARTY VISIT CRAIGIE HOUSE.

One day some people from way down in Maine called at Mr. Longfellow's, and said they would like to see "Washington's house." The host good-naturedly acted as their *cicerone*, showing them over the various rooms, and explaining matters as he went along. When they reached the dining-room, one of them said, "And so Washington sot in this room, did he?" — "Yes." — "And who lives here now?" — "I do, and my name is Longfellow." — "Longfeller! Longfeller! Air you any relation of the Wiscasset Longfellers?"

BYFIELD.

Mr. Longfellow had never seen the old family homestead at Byfield, Mass., until about the year 1876, when he visited it in company with Charles Sumner. They drove to Amesbury, and called on the poet Whittier; thence to Newburyport, where they took the cars for Nahant. While visiting Indian Hill, near Byfield, they planted an oak-tree.

An exquisite story is told of this visit to Byfield. The Longfellows there are long-fellows indeed, and heavily-built into the bargain. Mr. Longfellow felt the difference between his size and theirs, and remarked to one of them, with a twinkle in his eye, "It seems to me that our branch of the family is sadly degenerating."

THE POET'S VIGOROUS OLD AGE.

Mr. Longfellow in his seventy-sixth year was said to be the only poet whose productions, in his old age, were fully equal to those written in the days of his prime.

THOROUGHNESS OF PREPARATION.

"I had the fever a long time burning in my own brain," said Mr. Longfellow, "before I let my hero take it. 'Evangeline' is so easy for you to read, because it was so hard for me to write."

LONGFELLOW'S BIRTHPLACE.

The house in which Longfellow was born in Portland is now used as a tenement-house. One day a schoolmistress in one of the schools in Portland asked the scholars if any one of them could tell her where the poet Longfellow was born. After considerable cogitation, a little boy shouted out, "I know, — in Patsy Connor's bedroom!"

PORTRAITS BY THOMAS BUCHANAN READ.

One of the best likenesses of Mr. Longfellow was painted by Read, and now hangs in the poet's library. The famous group of the three daughters of Longfellow was also painted by Read. One of the daughters was so depicted that she seemed to be without arms. It is well known that there was a widely spread belief among people that the daughter was actually born without arms. The poet Lowell was one day riding up Brattle Street, Cambridge, in a horse-car, when he overheard one woman telling another, with an air of the most solemn conviction, the story of the armless child. Mr. Lowell was unable to refrain from the attempt to undeceive her, and said, "My dear madam, I assure you that you are mistaken. I am an intimate friend of the family, and I know that the facts are not as you say." The woman drew herself up with an injured look, and replied, "I have it, sir, from a lady who got it from a member of the family!" When the picture of the children was engraved, Mr. Longfellow received many letters asking if it were true that one of his daughters had been born without arms.

PORTRAIT BY WYATT EATON.

In the November (1878) number of Scribner's Monthly was published Wyatt Eaton's portrait of Longfellow engraved on wood for that magazine.

Opposite to the portrait is the following verse, in *fac-simile* of the poet's handwriting : —

> All are architects of Fate
> Working in these walls of Time,
> Some with massive deeds and great,
> Some with ornaments of rhyme.

The handwriting of this stanza, written Sept. 20, 1878, is as clear and firm as if it had been written by a youth of twenty.

ANECDOTE OF LORD HOUGHTON.

" Lord Houghton, when in this country, was delighted, but somewhat surprised, to hear a gentleman at a social gathering quoting something from his own favorite Keats; but no American would be surprised to hear Longfellow quoted anywhere in the world," says a writer in The Philadelphia Ledger and Transcript.

HIS WALKS.

One who knew Longfellow says that in the early days of his Cambridge life it was "a pleasant sight to see Longfellow out walking with his children, always with his stately, calm, and noble bearing, though bending to their slightest word, and seeming to take great delight in their company. Before the country west of his mansion was cut up by cross-streets and built upon, it was customary to see him, on pleasant days, in the winding lanes leading to Fresh Pond, or strolling over the hills."

When Professor Longfellow came into possession of Craigie House, there were scarcely any houses on the south side of Brattle Street, and what is now Sparks Street was then a winding grassy way, called Vassal Lane.

INCIDENT IN ENGLAND.

In a letter by Hon. Robert C. Winthrop, read before the Massachusetts Historical Society, after the death of Longfellow, the following pleasant little incident was mentioned: "The last time he was in Europe I was there with him, and I was a witness to not a few of the honors which he received from high and low. I remember particularly that when we were coming away from the House of Lords together, where we had been hearing a fine speech from his friend the Duke of Argyll, a group of the common people gathered around our carriage, calling him by name, begging to touch his hand, and at least one of them reciting aloud one of his most familiar poems."

HIS LATER YEARS.

Professor Charles Eliot Norton, in his remarks at the meeting of the Massachusetts Historical Society, has spoken feelingly of the last years of Longfellow:—

"Life was fair to him almost to its end. On his seventy-fourth birthday, a little more than a year ago, with his family and a few friends round his dinner-table, he said, 'There seems to me a mistake in the order of the years: I can hardly believe that the four should not precede the seven.' But in the year that followed he experienced the pains and languor and weariness of age. There was no complaint: the sweetness of his nature was invincible.

"On one of the last times that I saw him, as I entered his familiar study on a beautiful afternoon of this past winter (1881–82), I said to him, 'I hope this is a good day for you.' He replied, with a pleasant smile, 'Ah, there are no good days now!'"

STATUE TO LONGFELLOW IN CAMBRIDGE.

A few days after Mr. Longfellow's death, Mr. Francis Brown Gilman, in conversation with his kinsman, Mr. Arthur Gilman of Cambridge, suggested the propriety of purchasing the open ground in front of the Longfellow mansion, on the opposite side of the street, and erecting on it a statue to the "First Citizen" of Cambridge. Mr. Arthur Gilman thereupon brought the matter before the public in a communication to The Boston Daily Advertiser, and also called at his house a meeting of friends and neighbors of the poet. At this meeting a committee was appointed, which drew up a constitution for the "Longfellow Memorial Association." The constitution was adopted at a meeting held Thursday, April 13, 1882.

The object of the Association, as set forth in the constitution, is to provide "suitable memorials to the late HENRY WADSWORTH LONGFELLOW, and to arrange for their care and preservation." The immediate object is to purchase of the Longfellow heirs the lot that has been mentioned, and erect on it the statue of Longfellow. The owners have already signified their willingness to part with the land. As soon as the officers of the Association have been elected, subscription-books will be opened. "All persons who contribute to the funds of the Association the sum of one dollar or more at one time shall become honorary members." The annual meeting for the election of officers is to be held on Longfellow's birthday, the 27th of February. The active members are all either prominent in the municipal and social life of the city, or are eminent in some department of art or science. It is intended to raise a hundred thousand dollars in subscriptions of any amount, no matter how small, from any person in the Old World or the New, who may wish to contribute, as it is intended that the movement shall be strictly popular. James Russell Lowell was chosen first president of the Association, and Dr. Oliver Wendell Holmes, President Charles William Eliot, John G. Whittier, Charles Deane, and Alexander Agassiz, vice-presidents.

SAMUEL WARD'S REMINISCENCES.

Mr. Samuel Ward first became acquainted with Longfellow in Europe. Their friendship was very intimate. He relates that the poet on Thanksgiving Day in 1881 expressed to him great admiration for George Cable's "Grandissimes," and hoped that it would be the type of a new style of American novels. It was due to Mr. Ward that the translation of " The Children of the Lord's Supper " was made. Baron Nordin, Swedish Minister to Washington, gave him the poem, and he took it to the poet in Cambridge.

SALE OF A POEM.

There was some doubt in the minds of the poet's Boston friends as to the value of " The Skeleton in Armor." Mr. Ward says, " I took the poem, and read it aloud with a certain fervor inspired by its heroic measure, and I think that his own opinion was confirmed by my enthusiastic rendering of the part. I carried it to New York, where, having shown it to the poet Halleck, and obtained a certificate from him of its surpassing lyric excellence, I sold it to Lewis Gaylord Clarke of the Knickerbocker Magazine, for fifty dollars, a large price in those days for any poetical production."

THE HANGING OF THE CRANE.

Mr. Ward says, "About ten years ago, when paying my usual Christmas visit, he read to me 'The Hanging of the Crane,' two hundred lines, for which Robert Bonner of 'The New York Ledger' paid me four thousand dollars, having offered one thousand when I mentioned the existence of the poem. Mr. Longfellow declined that price, when the owner of 'Dexter'— whom the poet, in his letters to me, called 'Diomed, the tamer of horses'—quadrupled his bid, and obtained the prize."

LONGFELLOW IN HEIDELBERG.

Mr. Ward tells of calls he made upon Longfellow in Heidelberg in the spring of 1836. "Longfellow had led a secluded life since the death of his young wife, in Holland, the previous summer. My budget of rattling talk was, therefore, a cheering and interesting peep into the social world from which his mourning had so long excluded him. . . . The following day I visited him at his rooms, which were strewn with books, in a house on the main street, embracing a view of the castle. He was ready for another of my Sindbad narratives ; and in later years more than once recalled, with a smile, the fact of my taking off my coat, as his room was warmed by a German stove, to talk more freely in my shirt-sleeves. With me it was a case of love at first sight, which has burned with the steady light of a Jewish tabernacle ever since."

The following letter, addressed to Mr. Ward, is one of the last Mr. Longfellow ever wrote. It appeared in The North American Review for May, 1882.

CAMBRIDGE, Jan. 23, 1882.

MY DEAR UNCLE SAM, — "Whom the gods love die young," because they never grow old, though they may live to fourscore years and upward.

So say I, whenever I read your graceful and sportive fancies in the papers you send me, or in those I send you.

I am now waiting for the last, announced in your letter of yesterday, not yet arrived.

Pardon my not writing sooner and oftener. My day is very short; as I get up late, and go to bed early, — a kind of Arctic winter's day, when the sun is above the horizon for a few hours only.

Yes, the " Hermes " went into The Century.

I come back to where I began, the perpetual youth of some people. You remember the anecdote of Ducis. When somebody said of him, " *Il est tombé en enfance,*" a friend replied, " *Non, il est rentré en jeunesse.*" That is the polite way of putting things. But, old or young,

Always yours,

H. W. L.

THE SKELETON IN ARMOR.

Of " The Skeleton in Armor " Mr. Longfellow says, " This ballad was suggested to me while riding on the seashore at Newport. A year or two previous, a skeleton had been dug up at Fall River, clad in broken and 'corroded armor; and the idea occurred to me of connecting it with the Round Tower at Newport, generally known hitherto as the Old Windmill, though now claimed by the Danes as a work of their early ancestors." Mr. Longfellow rode to see the exhumed skeleton, accompanied by Mrs. Julia Ward Howe and others. The poet urged Mrs. Howe to write a poem on the subject, but fate ordered it that the honor should fall to him. The ballad has been set to very spirited music, and has also furnished themes for the pencil of the artist, the Old Round Tower proving especially attractive to the artistic eye.

TAX-BILL OF WILLIAM LONGFELLOW.

The following note, received from Mr. H. F. Longfellow, explains itself: —

APRIL 18, 1882.

MR. W. S. KENNEDY.

My dear Sir, — I have in my possession a tax-bill of William Longfellow (the emigrant ancestor), and send you the following copy: —

Mr. WILLIAM LONGFELOW
> his rates in the year 1686.
>
>   1 — 2 — 9
>   Credit   .   0 — 15 — 0

> JOSEPH ILSLEY [then Constable for Newbury].

> Yours very truly,
>   HORACE FAIRBANKS LONGFELLOW.

BYFIELD, MASS.

SOUVENIR OF LONGFELLOW.

A most valuable and interesting memento of the dead poet, which we have been permitted to examine, is owned by a gentleman of Boston. It consists of the poem of Excelsior, in the poet's own handwriting, and signed by him. This is preceded by a two-page autographic letter from Mr. Longfellow, explaining how

OLD ROUND TOWER, NEWPORT.

he came to select the title for the poem; another autograph letter is to the present owner, forwarding the lines to him. A series of twenty-five illustrations by various artists, which are inlaid to quarto size, illustrate the poem. This is followed by a curious parody in Chinese "pigeon English," with four illustrations.

In addition to this, in the same volume, is an extract from The Bridge: —

"I stood on the bridge at midnight,"

also verses in the poet's handwriting, and signed by him in 1845, with a proof illustration of the same; then comes an autographic letter of Jared Sparks to a friend, announcing that Mr. Longfellow is preparing another poem. "It relates," says the writer, "to the Plymouth Pilgrims; and it contains a romantic story about Miles Standish, the military champion of the Pilgrim band." This is followed by an autographic letter of Longfellow's respecting the writing and publishing of Miles Standish, and proof illustrations of the poem. A notable autographic memento in this unique volume is a letter from Charles Dickens to Moxon, the London publisher, which runs as follows: —

DEVONSHIRE TERRACE,
Tuesday, Oct. 17, 1842.

MY DEAR SIR, — Mr. Longfellow, the best of American poets (as I have no doubt you know), is staying with me, and wishes to see you on the subject of republishing his verses.

We breakfast with Mr. Rogers to-morrow morning, and will call upon you, if convenient, when we leave his house.

Faithfully yours,

CHARLES DICKENS.

EDWARD MOXON, Esq.

Fourteen different portraits of the poet, from the earliest to the latest taken, principally proof impressions of the engravings, are contained in the work, which is further illustrated by fine engravings of the poet's residence in Cambridge, both exterior and interior views, and also of the Longfellow mansion at Portland, Maine. Other engravings referring directly to the poet and his career, and others of his letters, — one referring to the Wadsworth coat-of-arms, — are contained in this collection, which the owner proposes to have placed in a sumptuous binding, and which, as a whole, is certainly a unique as well as an exceedingly valuable memento. — *Boston Advertiser.*

POETIC INSPIRATION.

" Mr. Longfellow had a peculiar gift for ingratiating himself into the good-will of children, and always showed a keen appreciation of their bright speeches. He was one day walking in the garden with a little maiden of five years who was fond of poetry, and occasionally "made up some " herself. " I, too, am fond of poetry," he said to her. " Suppose you give me a little of yours this beautiful morning ? " — " Think," cried he afterward to a friend, who tells the story in The Boston Courier, throwing up his hands, his eyes sparkling with merriment, " think what her answer was. She said, ·O Mr. Longfellow, it doesn't always come when you want it ! ' Ah me ! how true, how true ! " Several months later the friend and the little girl called at the poet's home. After showing his little friend many things of interest in his study, and especially delighting himself at her amazement on telling her he "supposed the Ancient Mariner came out of the inkstand upon his table " (it once belonged to Coleridge), he said in a low tone, as if thinking aloud, " It doesn't always come when you want it ! " — *New York Tribune.*

HIS AUTOGRAPH.

A friend of Mr. Longfellow writes : —

" It is the penalty of famous men to be pestered for autographs. Mr. Longfellow was not chary of his, when properly asked for, but rather took it as an evidence of good-will, and complied with pleasure. But knowing how annoyed noted men are by the professional autograph-seekers, who make a business of begging their names to sell for a consideration, I disliked very much to ask the poet for a bit of his writing, even to gratify a friend who I knew would value it. I noticed that he would take the book home I wished him to write in. I disliked to give him this trouble, and told him so : but he said it was no trouble at all; and in the morning he would come down with it as cheery and pleasant as if I had done him a favor instead of having received one.

" This habit of writing at home may account for the uniform appearance of his autograph : at least it shows the deliberate care with which he did every thing, even to writing his name. Sometimes he would give a stanza from the poem most admired in the book, or in some way show his genuine good feeling. I once expressed my delight with a poem he had written about a locality I was familiar with, and wished he could give me a few lines of it. He brought me the whole poem carefully written out on the broad sheet he was accustomed to use for his writing (for he had one kind of paper for his pencil, and another for his pen, and both were of the usual letter size).

" But even he sometimes rebelled at the demand for his name. People would apply by postal-card for his autograph, not reflecting, that, in order to send it, he would have to furnish an envelope and pay postage. There may be some who will say he never replied to them ; but I believe it will be those who would impose upon him in this way, or who, at least, were very thoughtless and inconsiderate, and those whose letters may have never been received by him."

LONGFELLOW AT HOME.

A neighbor of the poet writes to The New York Independent as follows : —

" While all the English-speaking world mourns the departed poet, Cambridge, the community in which Mr. Longfellow lived, groans at the loss of the man, the friend, the neighbor, the most honored, and the most beloved. I will respond to your request to speak of Mr. Longfellow in his ordinary relations as a member of a New England community. I speak from no greater intimacy, perhaps, than hundreds of his neighbors enjoyed ; but thus, it may be. being without the partiality of special friendship, I can better express the general sentiment with which he was regarded.

" That the kind of appreciation in which Mr. Longfellow was held here may be better understood, it may be well to mention some of the social characteristics of ' Old Cambridge,' as it is familiarly called, or rather that portion of it in which Mr. Longfellow lived. Whether from Puritan inheritance, or the happy influence of letters, or the simple tastes and modest means of the scholars who have given tone to its society, or the semi-rural habits encouraged by the possession of broad grounds and extensive gardens, there is a simplicity, almost homeliness, in the social life of Cambridge, not ordinarily attributed to the New England metropolis of letters. There is not only a pervading kindliness within what might be esteemed the more select circles, but a freedom and friendliness of intercourse among all classes of the community seldom seen elsewhere. To this excellent social spirit Mr. Longfellow greatly contributed; certainly he largely partook of it. And this may explain how he became so closely identified with all classes of the community in which he lived, and how he gained the privilege of that general appreciation which he enjoyed.

" Hundreds of men honored him who knew nothing of him as a poet. The first notice I had of the impending calamity was from an Irish porter in an office in Boston, who rushed into my room with this exclamation: ' It is on the bulletin-boards that our dear good friend Mr. Longfellow is dying. I have worked at his house, repairing his furnace, many a day. There was nobody like him in all Cambridge.' On the way home in the horse-cars, the fatal end being then publicly known, men and women talked about it to their fellow-passengers, though strangers, as they are wont to do in some great public calamity. And in his own town I believe that on that night there was scarcely a home which was not pervaded by the common sorrow. On the next morning the sentiment, if not the words, was uttered from every lip: ' The sun of Cambridge is extinguished.'

  .   .   .   .

" The sturdy and practical men of Cambridge liked Mr. Longfellow for his methodical business habits, his punctuality in his engagements, his good sense in his affairs, his interest in the concerns of the town, and his soundness on public questions. Though he rarely attended political meetings, he was a pronounced Republican, and always contributed to the funds required for political exigencies. Though never engaging in controversy, he took care that his political sympathies should be known; and while the people of his town are somewhat conspicuous for their erratic, or, as they would call them, independent views in politics, Mr. Longfellow, with his practical good sense, recognized the necessity of parties in politics, and was accustomed to say, 'I vote with my party.'

"The people of Cambridge delighted in Mr. Longfellow's loyalty to the town of his residence and its society. They could not fail to be gratified that he and his family did not seek the society of the neighboring metropolis, or rather usually declined its solicitations, and preferred the simple and familiar ways and old friends of the less pretentious suburban community. Nothing could be more charming than the apparently absolute unconsciousness of distinction which pervaded the intercourse of Mr. Longfellow and his family with Cambridge society.

"The people of Cambridge are quite justly proud of their historic monuments, which, with the growing greatness of the West, will soon be nearly all left us of the East to boast of. Under any circumstances, they would be chiefly proud of the Craigie mansion, the headquarters of Washington during the siege of Boston. They were doubly proud that this mansion should receive a new glory from the world's poet and *their* friend. They became accustomed to associate him with

Washington: at least, they regarded him as the only one worthy of being Washington's successor in that residence.

.   .   .   .

"I know the peculiar charm of his language in talking of the commonest things; how, in speaking of the trees, the clouds, or the weather, he would express some delicate thought or quaint conceit, as agreeable as unexpected. But I can recall but a few of these expressions, and these too trivial to be preserved, if they had not fallen from him.

"My first impression of his sweetness I gathered some years ago, when I accidentally overheard him in conversation with Mr. James Russell Lowell, as I walked behind them on Brattle Street. A sweet little girl came running by them; and I heard Mr. Longfellow say to Mr. Lowell, 'I like little girls the best,' and he continued: —

> 'What are little girls made of?
> Sugar and spice
> And all things nice, —
> That's what little girls are made of.'

We can see how by a sort of instinct all the little girls in the land are repeating the verses of the poet who loved them so well.

"Of late years Mr. Longfellow has gone very little into general society: but the archery-parties recently given in his neighborhood seemed to afford him especial pleasure; and we have several beautiful afternoons to remember when he honored the Elmwood Archery Grounds, and gazed upon the sport. 'How they come like a band of young braves!' I remember hearing him say, as the young men returned with arrows from the targets. In the most ordinary conversation he was forever dropping pearls; and I recall a walk on the Charles-river Bridge, when, as the breeze from the river swept through the commonplace telegraph-wires, he called them 'an æolian harp hung in the sky.'

"We felt the loss of our beloved friend the more because it was so unexpected; for although his health had been delicate for some months, there was no serious apprehension of fatal results. His bearing was so erect, and his gait so light and springing, he was so genial, so cheerful, so beautiful, and apparently so untouched by old age, that when I last saw him and talked with him, not three weeks ago, it seemed as though he would live many years longer, the most cherished possession of the old town he loved so well. The legacy he has left is not merely his divine poems: it is also the memory of the benign presence which almost consecrated the scenes among which he dwelt."

THE OLD CHESTNUT-TREE.

Some years ago the "village smithy" on Brattle Street was removed, and a dwelling-house erected in its place. To make room for the house, it became necessary to lop the branches of the famous old horse-chestnut. The tree was also trimmed from the street side, and had become so unsightly an object, that, when the order came from the City Council that it must be cut down, Mr. Longfellow, although loath to have it fall, yet said to a Cambridge citizen, that it might as well come down now, for its beauty was forever gone. A friend who was in Cambridge at the time writes: —

"Early in the morning the choppers were at it. Like burning sparks from the anvil the chips flew in every direction ; and soon a crash was heard, and the cry went up, ' The old chestnut is down!' The word ran from lip to lip ; and a crowd was quickly collected, — all rushing out from house and shop, just as they were, without coat or hat, and bearing off some fragment as a souvenir. They looked like ants bearing a burden bigger than themselves. But some city officer interfered, and the work of plunder ceased.

" From this destruction sprung the arm-chair which the children of Cambridge presented to Longfellow, — if not to appease the manes of the old tree which had been so abused, certainly to show their love for the good old poet who had immortalized it by his verse. How busy the children were making their little collections for this object ! It was the talk in the school and in the street, and was in the heart and mind of everybody. But when the gift came it was a genuine surprise to Longfellow, — not that he had not heard of what was doing, but it came with such an enthusiastic outburst of feeling, and was so fine a piece of work, that he was fairly overcome, and conquered in the ' round tower of his heart.' He seemed to have written the poem to the children, in acknowledgment of their gift, with great spontaneity, and scarcely a change was made in the proof of it. It came from the heart, and went to the heart ; and he took delight in having it printed to distribute among the school-children."

A PITEOUS INCIDENT.

Mr. George W. Childs of Philadelphia, who several years ago entertained the poet at dinner in Rome, relates, that, while they were walking to the dining-room, on the way through the corridor of the hotel, they passed a series of lighted wax candles placed in candelabra surrounded by flowers ; and Longfellow immediately shaded his face with his hand, and begged his companion to hasten his footsteps. He had probably been reminded of the death of his wife by burning.

LONGFELLOW'S GENTLENESS AND GRACE.

Sydney Chase contributes to The Washington Post the following story of a visit to the poet : —

"Provided with a letter of introduction, I entered the gate of the grounds, which is ever hospitably open ; and standing on the piazza was the gray-haired poet himself. He advanced, and saluted his visitor with a gracious courtesy that would have put the most timid at their ease, and kept the most presumptuous in check. He has an artful kindliness and a beautiful simplicity in manner, — that which the French have aptly called the politeness of the heart.

> ' His eyes diffuse a venerable grace,
> And charity itself was in his face.'

There is something about him, in his nice observance of the small, sweet courtesies of life, that carries one back to the bygone days when good-breeding was a study and politeness an art. He is so natural and unassuming that he is of necessity elegant in deportment, — as simplicity is the last form of elegance to be attained. A young enthusiast exclaimed, after seeing him, 'All the vulgar and pretentious people in the world ought to be sent to see Mr. Longfellow, to learn how to behave.' Mr. Longfellow himself thus defined the law of politeness: 'The consciousness of being assured of one's position is the great promoter of good manners; and this explains the utter absence of pretension in English people of rank, — there is, for them, no need of assertion. They can afford to be polite.' He led the way to his library, a sunny corner room, and, wheeling up a comfortable chair for his visitor, seated himself in his own especial chair.

" ' Now,' said he in his kindest voice, ' tell me what you have written.'

" He listened with an admirable attention to the story, old, but always interesting to a veteran, of the struggles of a literary beginner. Then he said impressively, ' Always write your best,' — repeating it with his hand upraised. ' Remember, *your best*. Keep a scrap-book, and put in it every thing you write. It will be of great service to you.'

" His visitor mentioned to him the pleasant lines in which his lot was cast, in comparison with other literary men, noticeably Sir Walter Scott, — that he had all

> That which should accompany old age,
> As honor, love, obedience, troops of friends.'

" ' Yes,' he said, ' I feel it, — I feel it daily.' When he was asked as to the number of visitors who came to pay him their respects, he said, ' They come every day from all parts of the country.' He might have added from all parts of the world.

" He spoke of Thackeray with admiration. ' He was so great, — so honest a writer.' In speaking of the saints whom the Roman Catholics revere, he said, ' I, too, have a favorite saint, — St. Francis of Assisi.'

" I told him of having been forced in childish days to learn the Psalm of Life. He laughed heartily at the

A CORNER IN LONGFELLOW'S STUDY

IN THE POET'S HOME, CAMBRIDGE.

description of the profound distaste and complete mystification of a miss of eight years at this, his immortal poem; but he asked, 'You came at last to understand it, did you not?'

"He agreed with his visitor in a dislike for the modern verse that makes sense subservient to sound, and turns poetry into an elaborate arrangement of ornate phrases. In response to a quotation on the question, from Macaulay, to the effect that literary style should not only be so clear that it can be understood, but so clear that it cannot be misunderstood, he said, 'I like simplicity in all things, but above all in poetry.'

"He spoke with strong aversion of the crude scepticism of the day, explaining that the term 'sceptic' was habitually misapplied, as it meant not necessarily an unbeliever, but a seeker after truth. I remarked that the first order of mind was not sceptical, — Shakspeare, Dante, Milton, Bacon, Pascal, as compared with minds of the caliber of Voltaire and Gibbon; following with a quotation of Thackeray's noble lines, 'O awful, awful Name of God! Light unbearable! Mystery unfathomable! Vastness immeasurable! O Name that God's people did fear to utter! O Light that God's prophet would have perished had he seen! Who are they who now are so familiar with it!' He seemed much struck. 'That,' he said, 'is a very grand sentence.'

He took down his magnificent volumes of Dante. 'This is my latest present,' said he. I opened it, and exclaimed, 'Why, this is Dutch!'—'Yes, it is—high Dutch,' said Mr. Longfellow, smiling; 'and do you know there is no language in the world in which Dante can be so successfully translated as in Dutch, owing to the formation of the participle;' and he gave a short explanation of the differences and difficulties of translating Dante into English verse."

THE POET'S VILLA IN OCTOBER.

"October is the best month for seeing the place in all its beauty," says a writer in The Boston Book Bulletin. "Then the clustering lilacs, still green with summer freshness, are overrun with the wild, red beauty of riotous woodbine, dying in a glow of defiance. Then from the trees fluttering leaves of welcome float into the outstretched hand, or fall gently before the advancing feet.

"The old elm at the door is stripped of its leaves, and you wonder at the fine network of interlacing boughs. Charles River, now clearly seen, winds along like an S of running silver. October, too, is the time to walk in the old-fashioned garden, — a garden such as Andrew Marvell's must have been : —

> 'I have a garden of my own,
>   But so with roses overgrown,
>   And lilies, that you would it guess
>   To be a little wilderness.'

"This 'little wilderness' is shut out from inharmonious sights and sounds. To come from the noisy world into its cool retreat, is from Avernus to the Happy Valley.

"One can imagine fairies in the flower-cups, and spirits gliding down the shaded walks, — spirits of stately dames in embroidered petticoats and high-heeled slippers, and gallant courtiers with sheathed swords and powdered cues; and, with these majestic ghosts, the fair young Muse of poetry, gazing at them with clear eyes unabashed, knowing that at her hands they lose not one grace or remembered glory.

"Sitting in the half-ruined summer-house, I sometimes almost wished the doctrine of Pythagoras were reversed, and that my soul might pass into the flower growing beside me, or the bird singing overhead. I envied the little golden lady-bugs that sunned their magnificence in the poet's garden, and wondered if the lazy caterpillars knew what good fortune awaited them as butterflies in this earthly paradise."

JOHN T. TROWBRIDGE'S REMINISCENCES.

John T. Trowbridge, in an entertaining biographical sketch in The Youth's Companion, says: —

"A little more than sixty-five years ago, in the city of Portland, Me., — which, by the way, was not a city then, — an important literary event took place ; though surely nobody was aware of its importance at the time (with the exception, perhaps, of one small boy), and the world has not rung with it since.

"The said small boy, aged ten, stole out of his father's house one evening, with an agitating secret in his breast and something precious in his breast-pocket. That something was a copy of verses, — a little, a very little poem, — which he had written by stealth, and which he was now going to drop into the letter-box of the newspaper-office on the corner.

"More than once he walked by the door, fearing to be seen doing so audacious a deed. But hope inspired him; and, running to the editor's box when nobody was near to observe him, he stood on his toes, and, reaching up, dropped the poem in.

"He hurried home with a fluttering heart. But the next evening he walked by the office again, and from the opposite side of the street looked up at the printers at their work.

"It was summer-time, and the windows were open; and seeing the compositors in their shirt-sleeves, each with a shaded lamp over his case, making a little halo of hope and romance to the boy's eyes, he said to himself, 'Maybe they are printing my poem!'

"When the family newspaper came, and he carried it to a secret corner, and opened it with hope and fear — sure enough, heading the Poet's Corner, and looking strange, but oh, so beautiful in print, there were his precious verses!

"Many years after, he told me the story of this first literary venture, much as I have told it here. That earliest poem had been followed by works which had become familiar as household words in the mouths of English-speaking people all over the world. Honor and fame were his in full measure. But he said, with a smile, 'I don't think any other literary success in my life has made me quite so happy since!' . . .

"He became a contributor to the best periodicals of those days. But the pay he received was ridiculously small. In later years, when editors were glad to get a contribution from him on any terms, he once spoke of having just received for a poem a price which seemed to him very large. I replied, that it did not seem to me excessive, considering the name and fame that went with it. 'Ah,' said he, 'you young fellows [to be called by him a *young fellow* was delightfully flattering to my gray hairs!] have had the luck to come along at a time when good prices prevail. You would think differently if you had written as many poems for five dollars apiece as I have.' . . .

"He was of medium height, with strong, symmetrical features, mild blue eyes under fine brows, and hair and beard of patriarchal whiteness in his later years. Charles Kingsley said of him in 1868, 'Longfellow is far handsomer and nobler than his portraits make him: I do not think I ever saw a finer human face.' This might have been truly said of him to the last.

"The same gentle and humane spirit which characterized his writings showed itself also in the manners of the man. He had the simplicity which belongs to strong and true natures. He never remembered, and his affability made you forget, that you were in the presence of one of the most eminent of living men.

"His fine sympathy prompted him to meet people on their own ground of thought and interest, and to anticipate their wishes. His ways with children were delightful. I well remember his setting the musical clock in his hall to playing its tunes for a little girl while he was occupied with her elders, because he could not bear that she should not also be entertained.

"On another occasion, when the same little girl and her younger sister, in their own home, approached with bashful pleasure as he held out his arms to them, he broke down all barriers at once by saying, 'Where are your dolls? I want you to show me your dolls. Not the fine ones which you keep for company, but those you love best and play with every day.'

"Before the mother could interfere, they had taken him at his word, and brought the shabby little favorites with battered noses, and were eagerly telling Mr. Longfellow their names and histories, while he questioned them with an interest which wholly won their childish hearts.

"It was some time before this that he brought a friend to the house, and our W——, then a boy of thirteen, took us out on the lake in his boat. The friend, who was in feeble health, wished to pull one oar. W——, full of health and spirits, pulled the other, and pulled too hard for him. He continued to do so, in spite of my remonstrance, when Mr. Longfellow said, —

"'Let him row in his own way. He enjoys it, and we mustn't interfere with a boy's happiness. It makes no difference to us whether we go forward, or only around and around.'

"He seemed to consider the happiness of the young as something sacred.

"He was hospitable and helpful to other and younger writers. How many are indebted to him for words of encouragement and cheer! The last letter I ever received from him was written during his illness in the winter, when he took the trouble to send me an exceedingly kind word regarding something of mine he had just seen in a magazine, and which had chanced to please him.

"He was tolerant to the last degree of other people's faults. I never heard him speak with any thing like impatience of anybody, except a certain class of critics who injure reputations by sitting in judgment upon works they have not the heart to feel or the sense to understand.

"Some kind friend once sent me a review in which a poor little volume of my own verses was scalped and tomahawked with savage glee. Turning the leaf, I was consoled to see a volume of Longfellow's treated in the same slashing style. For I reflected, 'The critic who strikes at him blunts the weapon with which he would wound others.'

"Meeting him in a day or. two, I found that some equally kind friend had sent a copy of the review to him. Seeing that he was annoyed by it, I said, 'I may well be disturbed when they try to blow out my small lantern, but why should you care when they puff away at your star?' He replied, 'The ill-will of anybody hurts me. Besides, there are some people who will believe what this man says. If he cannot speak well of a book, why speak of it at all? The best criticism of an unworthy book is silence.'

"He had suffered from abundant foolish and unjust criticism in earlier days; but his wise, calm spirit was never more than temporarily ruffled by it."

HIS RELIGION

At a Longfellow memorial service in the Unitarian Church at Newport, the pastor took occasion to remark that Longfellow, in his religious sympathies, was an earnest and life-long Unitarian, and, like his fellow-poets William Cullen Bryant, Bayard Taylor, John Greenleaf Whittier, Oliver Wendell Holmes, and James Russell Lowell, had given distinguished honor to the liberal faith to which he, as they, belonged.

GENERAL CRITICISM.

"POETRY," says Ruskin, "is the presentation to the imagination, in musical form, of noble grounds for the noble emotions;" and Goethe said that art is form alone (*Die Kunst ist nur Gestaltung*).

If these canons are applied to the poems of Longfellow, most of them will be found to stand the test. His poetry is musical, is imaginative, is noble. He is the moral poet, the children's poet, the people's poet. He is "everybody's poet." His poetical productions are monochromatic, monotonic; the range of their rhythms and rhymes is narrow; but the diction is so felicitous, the sentiment so artless, the thought so pure, and the melody so perfectly sweet, that we not only do not miss the intricate harmonies and winding *rhythmus* of Swinburne and Tennyson, but are well pleased that the poet of the fireside should sing in his own simple way. We like to remember him as one

> "Whose songs gushed from his heart,
> As showers from the clouds of summer,
> Or tears from the eyelids start."

The man who could write Sandalphon, The Ladder of St. Augustine, Snow-Flakes, Daybreak, The Children's Hour, Suspiria, Seaweed, The Day is Done, The Wreck of the Hesperus, The Skeleton in Armor, Excelsior, A Psalm of Life, The Old Clock on the Stairs,

Paul Revere's Ride, Noël, and Morituri Salutamus, — the man who can write such poems as these, is immortal.

In accordance with the plan pursued throughout this work, the writer will give in this part the thought and criticism of various minds, thus bestowing upon the reader some portion of the pleasure experienced in a social or literary conversation. Detailed criticisms on the poet's separate volumes have already been given.

INFLUENCE ON AMERICAN LITERATURE.

An anonymous critic says, " To appreciate aright Mr. Longfellow's literary service to this country, it is necessary to go back in imagination to the epoch when he began his literary career, — 1825. American literature was not then born. The very appetite for it had to be evoked; the very means of giving it to the public, to be created. The only great publishing house of the day was almost wholly devoted to furnishing readers with English reprints. Not one of our present magazines or literary periodicals existed. A few religious weeklies were narrow, intolerant, and controversial: the dailies were intensely partisan and bitterly personal. Charles Dickens's caricatures in Martin Chuzzlewit, published in 1843, would not have been so hateful if they had not been so true. Companionship in letters hardly existed for the Americans. Bryant . had indeed published his Thanatopsis, and Washington Irving his Knickerbocker's History of New York, a few years previous. But Poe had not yet issued his first book. Motley was trying his pen unsuccessfully at fiction, and was yet to learn that he was an historian. Whittier was just leaving the farm and the shoemaker's bench, to become editor of a short-lived tariff news-

paper. Cooper had yet in the crucible his unformed
stories of Indian and pioneer life. Hawthorne had
hardly touched pen to paper, except in college exercises; and Prescott was unknown, save as a brilliant
essayist, and only to the limited circle of readers of The
North American Review. American life was prosaic;
and, before it could feel the glow of its own poetry, it
must know something of the poetry of the past. This
was Mr. Longfellow's first service to his countrymen:
he was a mediator between the old and the new; he
translated the romance of the past into the language of
universal life. Out of the closed volume he gathered
the flowers that lay there pressed and dead and odor-
less. He breathed into them the breath of life; and
they bloomed, and were fragrant again. He came to
the past as the south winds come to the woods in
spring; and the trees put out their leaves, and the
earth its mosses, and the dell its wild-flowers, to greet
him. Each of his larger poems is thus a revivification of
a buried past. For each he made patient preparation
in most careful and pains-taking study."

LONGFELLOW A PURITAN.

Another has said : —

" The Puritan in some directions was strong in him.
It made him manful, and it kept him cleanly. It made
him deplore the misused talents of a De Musset, and
sorrow with real sorrow over the grand genius of Swinburne grovelling in the mire of sense. The women he
has given us — Evangeline, Minnehaha, Priscilla — are
pure creations. They are not void of emotion, though
they may not thrill with passion. As he was a Puritan,
he made them live with a full consciousness of life in its

duties and affections.   As he was a Puritan, he turned away from the wilder tumults of their hearts.   His, in fine, was a Puritanism which had lost its rancor, its narrowness, and its bigotry, and displayed only its vigor, its virtues, and, if not its overshadowing God-fearing, at least that simple reverence for the Godlike essence which tells its story more in the turn of thought to divine attributes than in the loud cry to the clouds. His passing away is the end of a beautiful song that has not had a single false note in it.   Such gentle voices as Whittier's and Holmes's remain behind him, but with him falls the lordly oak of American poetry; and, let his decline have been ever so gentle, the earth must resound as he touches the clay."

THE AMERICAN.

In an editorial The American thus spoke of his genius : —

"His is a book for a quiet hour, a sweet solace when the heart is weary (as whose is not?) with the cares and turmoils of the world.   In his pages we find home, friends, loving companionships, and the hopes and fears common to humanity, all transfigured and glorified by the touch of genius.   In the translucent mirror of his mind are reflected, not only the brightness of the sky and the brave splendors of the flowers, but the veiled beauty of the clouds that pass."

WILLIAM D. HOWELLS.

William Dean Howells in The Harvard Register for January, 1881, called Longfellow "a poet only less known than Shakspeare."   And of his art he says, "Never marred by eccentricity or extravagance, by fal-

tering good feeling or faltering good taste, it is still,
what it has always been, a humane and beneficent influence, as well as an exquisite science."

LITERARY STYLE.

Of his style some one has said : —

" The subtle analysis of a simple feeling follows the
simple musical statement of its cause, and is illustrated
by a figure growing directly from that statement, and
all combined in a manner that is masterly in its presentation."

THE NEW YORK TRIBUNE.

The New York Tribune said : —

" It has been his fortune to exemplify the value of
literature in the world's affairs. During an era spe-
cially marked by devotion to material advancement and
successes, he has maintained the dignity of literature.
It is unnecessary to inquire here whether he was a man
of great and original genius ; nor would he probably
have claimed to be, since his critical faculties were of
that kind which are proof against an over-estimate of
self : but he was a dexterous interpreter of the highest
genius of others, while his work was marked by that
talent which sometimes it is difficult to distinguish
from marked original faculty and indisputable creative
power. His taste was infallible. In all his numerous
volumes it would not be easy to find a single instance
of careless or slovenly work. In scholarly acquirements, in the almost universal knowledge which informs much of his poetry, in thorough acquaintance
with the books of all ages and of all peoples, among
American men of letters he stood almost alone, — at

least, was surpassed by none. As the memory recalls the variety of his productions, ranging as they do through ancient and modern themes, and the rare and unusual knowledge which informs them and lends to them perpetual illustration, we comprehend the difference between a mere lumber of learning which makes the pedant, and that universal research which richly furnishes the poet. He was eminently a gracious writer. Through all his pages one anxious to make such a quest would look in vain for any trace of irritability, of satirical impatience, of morbid feeling, of jealousy, or of vanity. There was in him a natural amiability which forbade the least thought of giving pain. He always sang with a kind of native politeness, and put into his poetry a sympathetic courtesy which won the hearts of his innumerable readers. To this more than to any other cause Mr. Longfellow owed his remarkable popularity. If his talents and acquirements had been less, he would still have been admired and beloved. The world yields its highest reverence to few; but it surrenders its heart and its grateful appreciation the more readily to those who make no inordinate demands upon its intellect, but keenly comprehend the vicissitudes of life, mourning with those who mourn, rejoicing with those who rejoice, and extending sympathy wherever and whenever the need of it is most keenly felt."

MARGARET FULLER'S CRITICISM.

A writer in The Nation has spoken of Margaret Fuller's criticism of the poet, and touched upon his general characteristics. He says: —

"It is nearly forty years since Margaret Fuller, writ-

ing in The New York Tribune, startled the proprieties
of Boston by some sharp criticisms on Longfellow and
Lowell, then in the first flush of their fame. She declared Lowell's early poems to be crude and imitative,
and those of Longfellow to be, in a great degree, 'ex-
otic.' Each poet met the charge in his own way, —
Lowell with brilliant sarcasm, and Longfellow with
good-natured indifference. Public sympathy went with
them; but we can now see, at this distance of scene,
how each profited by these criticisms. Lowell dropped
from his collected works the greater part of his early
poems, and Longfellow soon achieved his greatest successes by boldly drawing strength from his own soil.

"In justice to Margaret Fuller, it must be remembered that she was one of the first to recognize the pure
and elevating tone of Longfellow's verse, and to defend
him cordially from the charge of plagiarism as brought
in those days by Poe and others. But she pointed out
with some truth, that it was at first his tendency to
offer us, as she pointedly phrased it, 'flowers of all
climes, and wild flowers of none;'" that in the pretty
prelude to Voices of the Night, for instance, which
all schoolgirls were then reciting, he sought the woods
at 'Pentecost,' and found 'bishop's-caps,' when both
of these words came really out of books, and did not
habitually pass current on any New England hillside.
She also said, with perfect truth, that in The Spanish
Student — then his only long poem — the execution was
to a certain extent 'academical;' and she instanced
as works of far more promise on his part such short
poems as The Village Blacksmith and To the Driving Cloud, which she considered to be, so to speak,
indigenous. These criticisms were expressed somewhat

abruptly, no doubt, for tact, which has been called the virtue of cowards, certainly was not Miss Fuller's prime merit; but it will always remain doubtful whether, without them, we should have had Evangeline and Hiawatha.

" It is impossible to say, at this distance of time, how much of Longfellow's poetic change of base was due to criticism, and how much to inward development. It is to be noticed that he had already published a few other poems essentially American in *motif* besides those Miss Fuller mentioned; among which should especially be named The Skeleton in Armor and The Wreck of the Hesperus. It is at any rate certain that from this time he dwelt more and more upon these home themes which he had been accused of discarding, so that he soon became as essentially national in his poetic spirit as Emerson or Whittier. It is now clear that his great successes, his signal triumphs, were won by throwing himself wholly upon cis-Atlantic themes in Evangeline and Hiawatha.

.   .   .   .

" That tempting phrase of Coleridge's has much to answer for, — 'the kind of obscurity which is a compliment to the reader.' Coleridge himself certainly flattered his readers pretty profusely, if this be the standard; while Longfellow, though he wrote from Coleridge's own inkstand, drew from it no such ink. There is undoubtedly a profound delight in poems like many in Browning's 'Men and Women,' which seem to be inexhaustible in what they yield to you, because they yield very slowly. They are like the fountain called 'La Roche qui Pleure' at Fontainebleau, which gives the thirsty traveller only a drop at a time, but you can always go back to it, and be sure of another drop. Shall we, therefore, do injustice to Longfellow's ever-fresh and ever-living spring? As we turn the leaves of his books, each page tells an experience, utters an emotion, or affords a thought; each page, like each day in the life of his Village Blacksmith, offers 'something attempted, something done.' If you say, that, after all, the very ease of the execution shows that the work is not difficult to do, the answer is obvious: why does not some one else do it? After all, poetry has two factors, — the thought or emotion and the expression; and the success lies in the just combination of the two. Grant that we or our cousins and friends get up every morning with thoughts profounder than any of Longfellow's: it does the world no good unless we express them. Take the poets we proclaim as greater than Longfellow, — Browning, for instance, or Emerson, — and how often they fail to express their thoughts so that anybody can enjoy them without a course of lessons from an experienced professor! If we admit as true for poets what Ruskin says of painters, that 'it is in the perfection and precision of the instantaneous line that the claim to immortality is made,' we must say that no American up to this time has built his fame on surer grounds than Longfellow."

LE TEMPS.

In Le Temps of Paris (Jan. 13, 1879), almost a whole *feuilleton* was given up to a review of Kéramos and its author. The writer of the article thought that "the French translations of Longfellow surpass all the rest, and seem to have been produced by magic." He further said, "Is it not strange to see one of the most illustrious and most popular citizens (a representative man, according to the expression of Emerson) of this great, go-ahead nation, taking delight in these visions of Europe, and the evocation of the past? An explanation of this contrast, after all very reasonable, will be given to us some day.

"In America, by the side of intrepid explorers, undaunted miners and colonists, by the side of engineers with vertiginous conceptions, bankers or silk-merchants whose millions or failures seem to come to us from fabulous countries, there is a people who live in the past. Their minds dwell on the places consecrated by history, for which they feel a kind of nostalgia; places where ruins testify that man has loved and suffered: they dream with passion of Europe, — its legendary personages; the monuments of Rome, of Paris, of London, and of Vienna; the paintings of Florence; the marble palaces of Genoa, of Venice; the 'burgs' of Germany. Their minds constantly commune with the soul of the past.

"Besides other very great merits, we cannot deny to Longfellow that of having been and of still being the most learned and most eloquent interpreter of that class (numerous, we are informed) of his valiant fellow-countrymen."

THE BOSTON EVENING TRANSCRIPT.

A contributor to The Boston Evening Transcript has some words on the poet as a translator of German verse: —

"Mr. Longfellow has been said to have borrowed largely from German sources; and, indeed, his more popular lyrics are filled with the spirit, and often with the melody, of German poetry. He has, as it were, acclimatized a foreign flower, and made its fragrance our own; though all that he has given us is sweet, too, with the natural aroma of his own gracious personality. It is a true service he has rendered his countrymen, and a good they may well be grateful for. Not all of us may leave our cares, and wander at will beside the Rhine, or float upon lakes that mirror the snow-wreathed summits of Switzerland: shall we not, then, thank the friend who brings us home the forget-me-not and the mountain-violet to plant beside our doorways? This is what Longfellow has done for us in much of his own song, and still more in his translations, which have become a part of our household words. Has he not made Uhland's delightful ballad, 'The Castle by the Sea,' as dear a possession to the English as it ever was to the German heart? The student of German literature misses, perhaps, the indescribable harmony of Uhland's melodious verse; but the main current of feeling and remarkable simplicity of the original are given us with a faithfulness that is almost as rare in works of this kind as it is altogether admirable.

"Indeed, it is one of the pleasantest glimpses we get of the charming simplicity of Mr. Longfellow's character, — this faithful following of the author he would introduce to his countrymen. He never adds any thing for effect, but simply repeats the words they have given him as they were uttered; and the result is, we get the flavor of the German vintage, not some pleasant beverage of an entirely different growth. Most translations are too much like the delicate foreign wines, fortified with brandy for trans-shipment till all the 'bouquet' is lost in the fiery addition. Longfellow brings them

to us unchanged, except that in the transportation,
necessarily losing an evanescent something of their
distinctive character, they have imbibed a trace of his
own gracious and sunny nature. It would be pleasant
to recall them all, were there space to do so, — the
tender sadness of the Song of the Silent Land, a *word-
for-word* translation; the gushing brooklet of Müller's
‘ Whither ? ’ the many lovely voices he has made musical again in all our hearts.”

MERITS AS A TRANSLATOR.

In regard to his general merits as a translator, another critic thinks that “ some of his versions of German and Spanish poems are incomparable save with
Freiligrath's finest Germanizations of English verse,
and Fitzgerald's superb reproductions of Omar Khayyam. The plaintive minor of the ballads of Uhland,
Tiedge, Müller, Von Salis, the serene Catholic earnestness and virile feeling of Spanish devotional poets, and
the pastoral evangelic spirit of Tegnér, he has echoed
exactly. Even as a translator, it is true, he has his
limitations. His Jasmin is not the fiery loving Gascon
barber, last of the Troubadours. It is a Cambridge
version, gloved and cravatted for drawing-rooms, and
the society of young ladies, not perhaps ‘ of the period.’
His Dante, severely accurate as it is, is accurate only,
not adequate. This he felt himself, for no man had a
more truly delicate and sensitive literary perception.
He used to say, and say truly, that there was ‘more
of Dante in Thomas William Parsons's noble lines on
a bust of the great Florentine, than in all his versions.’
He never attempted to recast the matchless yet cynic
grace of Heine's bitterest verse; and he quite failed to

interpret the lyric rush of Johannes Ewald's 'King Christ,' the high national hymn of Denmark. In his own walk he is without an equal. The grace, the purity, the sweetness, the unaffected dignity, the rhythmic felicity in the form of his work, are his alone. . . . Longfellow has done more than any other American writer to dignify the literary character in America. Often assailed, and often with virulence and brutality, he kept his pen free from controversy, eschewing bitterness, and adorned his art by steadfast devotion. Posterity will honor in him an artist, who, in an eminently sensational and heady and uproarious age, never wrote a sensational nor a heady line ; and never printed a poem till he had brought it by repeated polishings as near perfection as he could."

PROFESSOR J. A. HARRISON.

The sonnets of Longfellow are exquisite productions, faultless and lucid. Mr. Charles D. Deshler thinks that the finest are those entitled 'Three Friends of Mine' (Agassiz, Sumner, Felton), and the ones on Dante, Chaucer, Keats, Shakspeare, and Milton. Professor J. A. Harrison of the University of Virginia has, in The Literary World for Feb. 26, 1881, a most dainty and poetical paper on Longfellow's sonnets. Happy the poet who falls into the hands of such a critic as this !

Professor Harrison says : —

"English is full of beautiful sonnets. Sidney, Shakspeare, Wordsworth, Keats, Browning, — it needs not the mention of these names to call up troops of beautiful things that have taken this subtile form, and tremble before us like dewdrops in amber, — immortal loves,

shining eulogies, contemplations that sing themselves
into poems, passion

> 'That eagle-like doth with her starry wings
> Beat,' —

as old Chapman sings; but few of them are subtler or
tenderer than these airy filaments of Longfellow, woven
of his memories and his tears,

> 'Like his desire, lift upward and divine.'

"How free Longfellow is from those 'jigging veins
of rhyming mother-wit' from which Marlowe called his
audience! how natural and spontaneous his utterances
are! *Quocumque adspicias, nihil nisi pontus et aer*, might
well in Ovid's tongue typify the large features of his
art — its breadth, ambience, and simplicity. Howells
delicately caught the tone of these sonnets when he
said of one of them 'that the effect in the sonnet on
Chaucer is of a rich translucence, like that of precious
stones.' In them the poet is the prey of memories and
whisperings. 'The Old Bridge at Florence' stirs him
to quaint monosyllables as of 'an old man babbling of
green fields;' 'Milton' is a far and mysterious music
on his spirit, like the wooings of some Vita Nuova; in
'Keats' there is pity as for some glorious chrysalis that
never found the way out of its own beauteous laby-
rinth into the yellow light of day; in 'Shakspeare'
alone is full fruition of memory and hope. Changing a
word in Habington's lines, we might read, —

> 'while our famous *Charles*
> Doth whisper Sidney's Stella to her streams,' —

so full of pleasant rememberings is the poet of the
winding river at his feet. There are few more touch-

ing lines in all literature than those that close the sonnet to Charles Sumner, —

> 'Thou hast but taken thy lamp and gone to bed;
>   I stay a little longer, as one stays
>   To cover up the embers that still burn.'

"Longfellow is wonderful in these homely felici-
ties. Reproach him as you please for excessive har-
moniousness, — a swan overladen with song, — there is
a spiritual sweetness that penetrates like the odor of
aloe-wood, a richness as of ambergris, a reverence for
things holy and absent that is not so much unction as
awe. With all his comprehensive learning, he is as
plain and pure as an ascetic; the dust of libraries has
become an illumined dust, which flickers in his sunny
fantasy, and moulds itself into all imaginable gracious
forms. He exhales his poems as a flower does its perfume; he never writes good poetry and then spoils it
by keeping it by him till old age, as Davenant said of
Lord Brooke. The beauty of his youth is with us no
less than the wisdom and pathos of his age, — a circle
in which the two edges of the golden ring are but a
span apart.

"A friend finely said that the Greek worship of ideas
was the least gross of all idolatries. This ethereal pagan-
ism is not an obvious part of Longfellow's poetry: he is
no would-be psychologist, though he is so full of the first
part of that compound. An overshadowing tenderness,
regret, longing, is the burden of much of his poetry and
many of these sonnets. He touches the spirit with an
infinite softness, like a hand from the other world: he
breathes upon the clear mirror of the soul, and for a
moment it is clouded with tears. He is a voice like

those beautiful muezzin voices of the East, that are chosen for their harmony and depth, rather than a trumpet. Could the liquid intonations of Voices of the Night break into the discords of a war-song? Could a violet burst into a tiger-lily? The gentle philosophies of the past are more to him than the *criard* speculations of the present, — a mellow drop out of the cellars of the monks, than all the fuming vintages of the morrow. Essentially a romanticist, a deep drinker of German mysticism, a sonneteer devoted to the forms in which Dante and Petrarch breathed their early and their late effulgence, a delightful traveller lingering in his wayside inns to tell us some musical story, a swallow that has built under the roof of Legend, a scholar that has the instinct of picking out the precious things from an ancient or dilapidated literature, like the diamond eye of the Delhi idol, and transforming them into palpitating lines, — how many things does the poet suggest!

"If there is one quality in him, however, which pleases the writer beyond all others, it is his lovely tranquillity, — that dew of Hermon which he sprinkles on his readers with a gesture of such benignity. In an age so full of storm as ours, — of dissolving beliefs, and groaning theologies, and metaphysical phantasmagoria, — the spell of his serene and potent verse is what the Orientals call *kief*, a state which Bayard Taylor describes in a chapter on pipes and tobacco. Anxiety, disease, impatience, are remote from this delicate indolence in which, as Longfellow says in one of his sonnets, our thoughts

'Slowly upon the amber air unroll,'

and one's whole physiology and psychology become

pure vision. Do not these visualized memories and foreshadowings come to us more richly in Longfellow than in any other? Quaint Thomas Carew must have been writing of him, two hundred and fifty years ago, when he said, —

> ' Ask me no more where those stars lighte
> That downwards fall in dead of nighte,
> For in your eyes they sit, and there
> Fixèd become as in their sphere.' "

THE LONDON TIMES.

The London Times of March 25, 1882, contained a long editorial on Longfellow, from which the following is extracted: —

" Those who hereafter may read the poems of Bryant, Whittier, Mrs. Sigourney, or Longfellow, will find it difficult to understand that they wrote just while the development of the United States was most striking; and that they penned their finished lines in the vicinity of mighty rivers, pathless forests, and untrodden prairies. In the well-turned classic allusions, and in the ample knowledge of European models, they will find much for admiration. They will miss — and the omission may affect the durability of the reputation of this school — native savor and that true local color which atone for much uncouthness and lack of skill in versification. . . . We are not forgetting his Hiawatha, when we say that he might have written his best poems with as much local fitness in our own Cambridge as in its namesake across the Atlantic. . . .

" There will be no disposition at this season to speak a harsh word of a poet who had in a remarkable degree the gift of inspiring his readers with affection for him;

and, in fact, there are few points at which criticism can find an opening. His dulcet verses, or some specimens of them, — for posterity is pitilessly fastidious to all but a few singers, — are likely long to be attractive to the multitude of those who do not care to analyze their pleasures too minutely, or to sift the ethical beauty of their moral or sentiments from the elements of imagination. Some of his touching and simple ballads are pretty sure to be familiar to generations yet to come. The purity of his thoughts, his affinity to all that is noblest in human nature, and his unfailing command of refined, harmonious language, may continue to draw to him readers who will not be deterred by the judgment of critics that he was not a great poet. He himself well knew that he was not in the first rank. He had in the youth of both countries ardent admirers; and there was a time when men their elders used to say that he was to prove another Tennyson. But poetry at its best is a fabric spun only by the strongest brains. Force of will and strength of mind — qualities akin to the gifts of the successful general or the great mathematician — go to the making of a poem which the world cares to read. The elegance and refinement and ingenuity of The Golden Legend are far away from mediocrity, and are worth more than the affectation of vigor and profuse inspiration in more pretentious writers. But the author of that poem does not belong to the same strong, swift-souled race as Byron or Shelley, and has little affinity to it.

.   .   .   .

"One cannot readily point to worthy successors to the brilliant Boston group. We are told that in Walt Whitman's rough, barbaric, untoned lines, full of ques-

tionable morality, and unfettered by rhyme, is the
nucleus of the literature of the future. That may be
so, and the Leaves of Grass may prove, as is pre-
dicted, the foundation of a real American literature,
which will mirror the peculiarities of the life of that
continent, and which will attempt to present no false
ideal. Yet we shall be surprised if the new school,
with its dead set towards ugliness, and its morbid turn
for the bad sides of nature, will draw people wholly
away from the stainless pages, rich in garnered wealth
of fancy and allusions, and the sunny pictures, which
are to be found in the books of the poet who has just
died. Mr. Longfellow has left no enemies behind him;
he had many warm friends and admirers; and his reputation as a poet may survive much longer than those
who vaunt the ' poetry of realism ' care to admit."

R. H. STODDARD.

Richard Henry Stoddard has said of the poet: " He
has more than held his own against all English-writing
poets, and in no walk of poetry so positively as that of
telling a story. In an age of story-tellers, he stands at
their head. . . . Mr. Longfellow's method of telling a
story will compare favorably with any of the recognized masters of English narrative verse from Chaucer
down."

THE SPRINGFIELD REPUBLICAN.

" He never lacked," says The Springfield Republican,
" the essential moral sympathy with America, yet that
sympathy never became with him a flaming fire, as with
Whittier, or a rapier edge, as with Lowell; nor did he
have that grand sweep of external nature which set
aside Bryant as the embodiment of the American

scene; or the inimitable brilliancy that marks Holmes so far in advance of contemporary England; or the shrewd uniŏn of Yankee and Orient genius that revealed a gospel in Emerson. The scarcity of Longfellow's anti-slavery and patriotic poems proves this lack of absolute Americanism in the humanitarian aspect of his verse."

THE LONDON DAILY NEWS.

The London Daily News thinks that "Perhaps one secret of Longfellow's being a favorite with us is, that he is apt to be one of the first poets who are read at all. He is an author fit in every sense for boys and girls, and especially congenial to the more healthy minds among the young. He thus acquires a hold upon the imagination at a time when it is 'wax to receive, and marble to retain;' and much that he wrote is seen through the delusive vista of early charm and old association."

GEORGE STEWART.

Of the influence of Longfellow upon Canadian thought, George Stewart writes thus in The Literary World: —

"In Lower Canada, where the highest mental development is exemplified by French writers, who do their work with singular grace and expression, and whose muse takes the *spirituelle* form, Longfellow's influence may be perceived to a very great extent. His suggestiveness and harmony can frequently be seen in the poetry of such men as Fréchette, Sulté, and Le May; and it is worth noting the controlling tendency which such minds as Longfellow's and De Musset's and Béranger's have on the intellectual action of these young poets. The blending of American and French thought forms a striking combination, and its charming outcome may be readily enough detected in many of the really delightful things which these clever young singers have sent out. Pamphile Le May, a tender poet himself, and a man of exquisite taste, has done much to encourage a love of Longfellow among his compatriots. We are told, that, by reading Le May's Evangeline, many persons were induced to learn English, that they might get the gentle story at first hand, and in the exact words of its creator. Some, too, learned English from the book itself and a dictionary; but a very great deal of the poem's present popularity among the French is due to Le May's efforts to crystallize it in the susceptible hearts of his countrymen. For many years the Longfellow version of the story has been implicitly regarded as historically correct, even among the English, who cared to accept no other authority. Among the French, of course, no other account of the expulsion will ever be looked upon as true. This one poem, because of the sympathy of the author, as well as his treatment of the incident, has wound itself around the hearts of the people of French Canada; and Longfellow's name is as reverently treasured and respected and loved by them as any of their own writers, ecclesiastical, historical, or poetical."

REV. GEORGE E. ELLIS, D.D.

At a meeting of the Massachusetts Historical Society held soon after the poet's death, the Rev. Dr. George E. Ellis thus characterized his writings: —

" But few of our associates in its nearly a century of

years can have studied our local and even national history more sedulously than did Mr. Longfellow. And but fewer still among us can have found in its stern and rugged and homely actors and annals so much that could be graced and softened by rich and delicate fancies, by refining sentiments, and the hues and fragrance of simple poetry. He took the saddest of our New England tragedies and the sweetest of its rural home scenes, the wayside inn, the alarum of war, the Indian legend, and the hanging of the crane in the modest household, which his genius has invested with enduring charms and morals. Wise and gentle was the heart which could thus find melodies for the harp, the lute, the lyre, and the plectrum in our fields and wildernesses, wreathing them as nature does the thickets and stumps of the forest with flowers and mosses. While all his utterances came from a pure, a tender, and a devout heart, addressing themselves to what is of like in other hearts, there is not in them a line of morbidness, of depression or melancholy, but only that which quickens and cheers with robust resolve and courage, with peace and aspiring trust. He has, indeed, used freely the poet's license in playful freedom with dates and facts. But the scenes and incidents and personages which most need a softening and refining touch receive it from him without prejudice to the service of sober history."

REV. T. T. MUNGER, D.D.

In an article in The New York Independent entitled " The Influence of Longfellow on American Life," the Rev. T. T. Munger, D.D., said : —

" In a restless age he has given us an example of quiet, and breathed not a little of it into our lives. No one ever reads a line of this poet without feeling rested. He never lacks spirit. The thought is up to the theme; there is no indolence, no Oriental, will-less dreaming; there is nothing that enervates or unfits for action. Still the feeling inserted into the reader is that of repose. This is not so in the greatest poets, but it may be so in a great poet. Milton and Shelley and Tennyson and Browning summon you to the intensest activity, and leave you in a stress of tumultuous thought; but Longfellow both feeds and refreshes the mind. He takes off your burden, instead of adding to it: he does not withdraw the lesson he sets before you, but he soothes you while you fulfil it. He is pre-eminently the poet of peace and repose. In Whittier we feel the pressure of an over-acute moral nature: his lash of duty drives us to our tasks again (a very useful thing to do), but at the same time we need a little rest in a less rasping air. It is a marvel, when we think of it, that this restless age, this age of the superlative, this driving, crowding, loud-mouthed age, that is nothing if not extreme, should produce a poet utterly without these characteristics. I think this is a main reason why we love him. We need him, as a tired child needs a soothing nurse. This influence is not fanciful. I do not mean that busy merchants and harassed lawyers and perplexed railroad managers go to the pages of Longfellow for rest; but many a scholar, many a preacher and editor and teacher, reads these pages, and turns to his work with a calmer spirit, that shows itself in other printed pages, in sermons and editorials of a better temper, and in patience and cheer in the school-room.

"He has made a fine example of the value and power

of simplicity in thought and feeling.   Hardly any thing
in him is so conspicuous.   Read any poem of his, and
you say: How simple!   There is nothing startling in
the thought.   It may or may not be new; it is certainly
true; but it comes to you in so natural a way that it
does not surprise you.   It is the same in his language.
There are no contortions demanding your wonder, nothing of what is sometimes called *style*, except transpar-
ency.   No surging and pounding and piling on and
extravagance, or striving for effect; but only a clear,
simple reflection of clear and beautiful thought.   It is
not a slight thing that a million or more of children
are daily drilled in this utter truthfulness of speech."

THE SOUTHERN LITERARY MESSENGER.

A writer in The Southern Literary Messenger as long
ago as March, 1840, in reviewing Voices of the Night,
thus characterized Mr. Longfellow's poetry in general : —

"Professor Longfellow ranks among the first of our
American poets.   There may be those who excel him
in profundity and grasp of thought, in beauty of language, and smoothness of versification; but there is no
one to whose vision the 'land of song' opens fairer and
brighter.   His are

'The lids of Fancy's sleepless eyes;'

and when he touches the chords of his lute, — that has
been charmed, perchance, by the spell of some gay
troubadour, and awakened from its silence of ages, —
when he touches the chords of his lute, his thoughts
drop in music from its golden wires, and thrill us with
a pleasant melody and a wizard power.   His poetry is

quaint, sweet, and beautiful. While we read it, we are surrounded with visions, forms, and images — fancy-summoned, thought-created. We read his rhymes, where the sun streams through stained windows and Gothic arches upon curious carvings of oak, and storied monuments, and illuminated volume, or by the side of streams that glide along under green and drooping leaves, and flow with sweet murmurings over silver sands; or we look out ever and anon, and catch the glimpses of the watching heavens and the solemn stars, and hear

> 'the trailing garments of the Night,
> Sweep through her marble halls.'

Or, in perusing his earlier poetry, our brows are fanned by the breezes that come from the hills and the living streams, and we behold the sunshine, and the freshness and the gladness of nature."

The following estimate of our poet is found in vol. viii. (1842) of the journal just quoted : —

"Nor is it on paper alone that Longfellow is a poet. Poetry enters into the very nature of the man, and forms a portion of his being. Unlike those 'who coin their brain for daily bread,' and whose inspiration only lasts with the occasion which calls it forth, Longfellow is a poet by nature, to whose gifted eye the humble clod of the valley bears the impress of its great Creator. His melodious words, gushing forth full of tenderness and melody, are but the outpourings of a soul as responsive to each touch of human sympathy, as the fabled lyre of Memnon to the rays of the morning sun. The selfish man cannot be a poet. To charm the eye and fascinate the ear of those who know him not; to cause the selfish and indifferent to forget the reality, and to regard the phantoms of his imagination as living and breathing beings; to touch the hearts of the cold, the callous, and the vain, and to transfer to them the light of that inspiration which kindled his own soul, — this is the province of the poet. And, to do this, it requires that he should himself possess the most boundless sympathy with human weakness and human suffering. Some few matchless spirits there have been, who seem to soar above human weakness and human folly; who, enthroned in a majestic serenity of soul, sit like monarchs of the intellectual world. But these, though they command our admiration, cannot win our sympathy and love.

.   .   .   .

" Professor Longfellow has written more prose than poetry. Outre-Mer and Hyperion are, however, steeped in the poetry of the writer's thoughts: and the latter may well be regarded as a poem in every thing except the metre; for it bears about the same analogy to the ordinary novel, that Spenser's ' Faerie Queene' does to the ' Columbiad ' of Dwight. In these volumes much of the inner life of the student is unconsciously revealed, embodying, as they do, the thoughts and feelings of the scholar who visits for the first time the land so rich in historic recollections, and who wanders with rapt enthusiasm among the castled ruins of the glorious Rhine. An abler hand than ours has already done justice to the merits of Hyperion. But there is one thought which struck us as peculiarly true and beautiful, and which seems to have escaped the notice of the reviewer. It is this: speaking of the troubles which beset the path of life, the author thus concludes: ' The shadows of the mind arc like those of the body : in the morning of life they all lie behind us ; at noon we trample them under foot ; and in the evening they stretch long, broad, and deepening before us. But the morning shadows soon fade away ; while those of evening stretch forward into night, and mingle with the coming darkness.' The depth and beauty of this thought must strike the most careless observer.'

THE ECLECTIC MAGAZINE.

In The Eclectic Magazine for February, 1862, the following is found : —

" As a truly popular poet, — the man of the million, — no American songster has obtained such a favorable hearing as Henry Wadsworth Longfellow. How it may be in his own hemisphere we know not, but certainly in this part of the world Mr. Longfellow's poems have had a greater circulation than those of all the other American poets together. Possibly it might be no great disgrace even to be ignorant that Bryant and others had written poetry at all; but it would argue a strange isolation from the world of letters to know nothing of Excelsior and the Psalm of Life. These, and other lyrics from the same pen, have been promoted to the rank of household words. Young ladies everywhere sing Excelsior to the accompaniment of the piano; and promising lads, just gliding out of their teens, are imbued by thousands with the stirring sentiments of the Psalm of Life, — resolved, at all hazards, not to quit the world without leaving some 'footprints on the sands of time.' Nay, we have heard of a certain minister, better known as a popular lecturer, who frequently commences his Sabbath worship with 'Tell me not in mournful numbers,' etc. This somewhat strange effusion, while in many quarters regarded almost with a veneration due to inspired words, has not always been spared from running the gauntlet of adverse criticism. There is no mystery about the success it has obtained. It has a certain number of pithy aphoristic utterances on the value of time and the greatness of men's destinies; and these, given in the full flow of poetic grandiloquence, produce their effect. There is genuine poetry in the composition; though some of the lines are exceedingly uncouth, and the figures such as will not bear much handling. To many a reader, who refuses to sacrifice logic for sound, the following lines are still a stumbling-block: —

> Lives of great men all remind us
>   We can make our lives sublime,
> And, departing, leave behind us
>   Footprints on the sands of time; —
>
> Footprints that perhaps another,
>   Sailing o'er life's solemn main,
> A forlorn and shipwrecked brother,
>   Seeing, shall take heart again.

" How it is that these footprints can make any permanent impression on the 'sands' of time, how it is that this forlorn brother sailing o'er the solemn main can manage to see these prints on the shore, or what is the particular connection between seeing them and taking heart again, are, we confess, things not easily understood. It is useless, however, to quarrel with them now: the world has consented to receive them. A more important question, we think, remains. What is to be understood by the lives of great men reminding us that we may make our own lives 'sublime'? Sentiments like this have occasioned a deal of castle-building. The sophistry that identifies a sublime life with a life that makes a great figure in the world is a very common snare and delusion. The true sublime of life is to turn to the best account the means which Providence has actually placed at men's disposal; and were this actually done, all the world over, the number would be very small of those who were sublime enough to have books written about them. As a rule, the lives of great men cannot do much by way of example, whatever they may suggest in the way of instruction; for that which has made them great in the world is not imitable by the generality of mankind. It is all very well that examples should be given of those who, through difficulties mostly regarded as insurmountable, have made their way to eminence of whatever kind; but that is a false and pernicious teaching which leaves the impression that, where what the world calls 'greatness' is wanting, — the sublime of life is wanting. No more important lesson can be learned than that the ordinary, the un-poetical business and duties of every-day life are enough to stamp that life with its true greatness; that

> ' The simple round, the daily task,
> Will furnish all we want or ask ; '

for those ordinary duties are very often neglected by many a precocious aspirant after greatness, whose life in consequence exhibits a sad predominance of the sublime over the beautiful. It would be captious thus to dwell on an occasional poetical extravagance, were it not that sentiments of a false or doubtful character are, when embodied in popular poetry, mischievous in the extreme. In Excelsior the leading idea — that

progress must be resolutely maintained, come what
will — is unexceptionable; and this moral, conveyed
as it is in words of much force and beauty, makes us
comparatively indifferent to the circumstantials of the
tale, which have in some quarters been mercilessly
ridiculed. 'We have no very bright example,' it is
said, 'of the true spirit of progress, in the career of
a hasty and inconsiderate youth, who, at a very un-
seasonable time of the night, hurries through an Alpine
village with his Excelsior banner in his hand; and,
disregarding all manner of peril from torrent, preci-
pice, and avalanche, treads his way upward, eventually
perishing in the snow, where the monks of St. Bernard
find him on the following morning.' This statement
cannot be gainsaid. The jury at the coroner's inquest
would, doubtless, express their opinion that deceased
met his death from causes too clearly attributable to
want of proper caution. But when the voice comes
'like a falling star,' answering to the watchword of
the noble victim, we must have done with these matter-
of-fact objections, or take them elsewhere. No greater
injustice, however, could be done to Mr. Longfellow
than that of testing his merits as a poet by the verses
which have found most favor in the drawing-room. He
is confessedly at the head of all the American bards.
No other has written so much and so well in the main,
although we can easily point out in the other collections some single poems which please us better than
any thing this author has produced. His longer pieces,
— Evangeline, Hiawatha, and Miles Standish, — his
many and varied lyrical effusions, and his translations
from the German, Spanish, and other languages, are
scarcely ever below mediocrity, and are generally of

great excellence. True, his flights are never of the highest character: he never rises to those altitudes upon the mount of song where the great poets of the world have 'based the pillars of their imperishable thrones.' On the other hand, it must be remembered that the men to whom the genius of poesy has distributed its noblest of gifts have mostly written for a limited class of readers. Paradise Lost has never been a popular poem; Hamlet, Macbeth, and The Tempest can hardly yet be said 'to take' with the people. Tennyson's poetry is not for the million; and Wordsworth is still 'like a star, dwelling apart.' It may be said, in reply to this, that poets of less caliber are not much complimented by being told that their popularity is mainly owing to the fact that the best poetry is not the most highly appreciated; and this may be granted. But there is another side to the story.

"To gain the ear, to stir the pulses, to delight the imagination, of the thousands and tens of thousands on whom the highest efforts of poetic genius are comparatively lost, is no mean triumph. Mr. Longfellow has done this. His pages are everywhere instinct with life, beauty, and grace. Seldom very sublime, seldom very pathetic, — for the cast of his mind is, on the whole, gleesome and joyous, — no writer exhibits a better combination of those general qualities which make poetry pleasant and lovable. The healthful and breezy freshness of nature is on all his productions; and in the rich and teeming variety of his muse we have the results of that passion for the fair and bright things of the present and the past, so well described in his own Prelude."

PRESIDENT C. C. FELTON.

President Cornelius Conway Felton of Harvard University, in reviewing Ballads and Other Poems in The North-American Review for July, 1842, said, —

" Mr. Longfellow's profound knowledge of German literature has given a very perceptible tincture to his poetical style. It bears the romantic impress, as distinguished from the classical, though at the same time it is marked by a classical severity of taste. Nothing can exceed the exquisite finish of some of his smaller pieces, while they also abound in that richness of expression and imagery which the romantic muse is supposed to claim as her more especial attribute. The melody of his versification is very remarkable : some of his stanzas sound with the richest and sweetest music of which language is capable. It is unnecessary to illustrate this remark by quotations: the memories of all readers of poetry involuntarily retain them. In the range of American poetry, it would not be easy to find any that is so readily remembered, that has sunk so deeply into the hearts of the people, and that so spontaneously rises to the speaker's tongue in the pulpit and the lecture-room."

THE PENN MONTHLY.

The Penn Monthly for February, 1874, said, in speaking of Aftermath, " It is a common fault among writers of a certain order, that when they have attained to a recognized excellence in their art, they are willing, under cover of their reputation, to produce works that are unworthy of it. . . .

" Without supposing for a moment that Mr. Longfellow has any thing in common with this set, we wish

that he would not act so much like them. In other
words, we would be glad to have him explain the
raison d'être of this last volume of poems. It cannot be
that he thinks that he had any thing new to say, for he
has not said it; and it is hardly possible that he believes
that the tones of his 'one clear harp,' which have
echoed so long in our ears, will bear continual rever-
beration. Mr. Longfellow must compose with the as-
surance that whatever he writes will be eagerly read by
the people of both hemispheres, in whose hearts he is
so safely enthroned that no one but himself can dethrone
him; and the consciousness of this fact should make
him very critical. We, for our part, have so often seen
his kindly face in his charming poems, and, we may add,
his poetry in his kindly face, that the associations there-
with are among the last that we should part with.
Indeed, there is no poet of the day so popular. He is
translated into as many languages as he has translated.
He is the most frequently read of foreign verse-writers
in Germany, for his lines are brimming with the simplicity and sentiment that the Germans have learned to
love in their own poets. His charms have long since
broken down the stiff barriers of English prejudice,
and in the first cheap edition of standard poets published in England (the Chandos Classics) he comes
second in order after their own Shakspeare. He is
described in the preface as 'the American writer, whose
poems are as household words in English homes, and
whose genius has naturalized him in our land;' and his
poetical works may be bought to-day in London, and
are bought, in good clear type, for the small sum of
ninepence. Our chiefest dread, then, in reading Aftermath, is that the position which he has acquired among

us, and which we would protect from even his own
assaults, may .be thus by himself materially affected.
For if it be shown that the secret which produced the
many beautiful poems that gush from his heart with
the freshness of sunshiny April showers from the sky,
and whose power over us we ever love to acknowledge,
is indeed no secret, but a 'knack,' and that the sympathy and comfort in the gentle rhythmical flow of his
verses may be served up to order in lines of seven and
six, — if such a dreadful revelation is in store for us,
then, as Tiny Tim says, 'God bless us every one!'"

DR. O. W. HOLMES.

Dr. Oliver Wendell Holmes, in a masterly address
before the Massachusetts Historical Society, of which
Longfellow was a member, spoke with keen and delicate discrimination of the writings of his brother-poet
and friend : —

"From the first notes of his fluent and harmonious
song to the last, which comes to us as the 'voice fell
like a falling star,' there has never been a discord. The
music of the mountain-stream in the poem which
reaches us from the other shore of life is as clear and
sweet as the melodies of the youthful and middle
periods of his minstrelsy. It has been a fully rounded
life ; beginning early with large promise, equalling every
anticipation in its maturity, fertile and beautiful to its
close in the ripeness of its well-filled years."

Speaking of the simplicity of Longfellow's style, he
continued : —

"In respect of this simplicity and naturalness, his
style is in strong contrast to that of many writers of
our time. There is no straining for effect, there is no

torturing of rhythm for novel patterns, no wearisome iteration of petted words, no inelegant clipping of syllables to meet the exigencies of a verse, no affected archaism, rarely any liberty taken with language, unless it may be in the form of a few words in the translation of Dante.

.   .   .   .

" Although Longfellow was not fond of metrical contortions and acrobatic achievements, he well knew the effects of skilful variation in the forms of verse and well-managed refrains or repetitions. In one of his earlier poems ('Pleasant it was when woods were green'), the dropping a syllable from the last line is an agreeable surprise to the ear, expecting only the common monotony of scrupulously balanced lines. In Excelsior, the repetition of the aspiring exclamation which gives its name to the poem lifts every stanza a step higher than the one which preceded it. In The Old Clock on the Stairs, the solemn words, ' Forever — never, Never — forever,' give wonderful effectiveness to that most impressive poem.

.   .   .   .

" I suppose if the great multitude of readers were to render a decision as to which of Longfellow's poems they most valued, the Psalm of Life would command the largest number. This is a brief homily, enforcing the great truths of duty, and of our relation to the Eternal and Invisible. Next in order would very probably come Excelsior, a poem that springs upward like a flame, and carries the soul up with it in its aspiration for the unattainable ideal. If this sounds like a trumpet-call to the fiery energies of youth, not less does the still, small voice of that most sweet and tender poem,

Resignation, appeal to the sensibilities of those who have lived long enough to have known the bitterness of such a bereavement as that out of which grew the poem. Or take a poem before referred to, The Old Clock on the Stairs; and in it we find the history of innumerable households told in relating the history of one, and the solemn burden of the song repeats itself to thousands of listening readers as if the beat of the pendulum were throbbing at the head of every staircase. Such poems as these — and there are many more of not unlike character — are the foundation of that universal acceptance his writings obtain among all classes. But for these appeals to universal sentiment, his readers would have been confined to a comparatively small circle of educated and refined readers. There are thousands and tens of thousands who are familiar with what we might call his household poems, who have never read The Spanish Student, The Golden Legend, Hiawatha, or even Evangeline. Again, ask the first schoolboy you meet which of Longfellow's poems he likes best, and he will be very likely to answer, Paul Revere's Ride. When he is a few years older he might perhaps say, The Building of the Ship, that admirably constructed poem, beginning with the literal description, passing into the higher region of sentiment by the most natural of transitions, and ending with the noble climax,

> 'Thou, too, sail on, O Ship of State!'

which has become the classical expression of patriotic emotion.

" Nothing lasts like a coin and a lyric. Long after the dwellings of men have disappeared, when their temples are in ruins, and all their works of art are shattered, the ploughman strikes an earthen vessel holding the golden and silver disks on which the features of a dead monarch, with emblems, it may be, betraying the beliefs or the manners, the rudeness or the finish of art, and all which this implies, survive an extinct civilization. Pope has expressed this with his usual Horatian felicity in the letter to Addison on the publication of his little Treatise on Coins, —

> ' A small Euphrates through the piece is rolled,
> And little eagles wave their wings in gold.'

Conquerors and conquered sink in common oblivion ; triumphal arches, pageants the world wonders at, all that trumpeted itself as destined to an earthly immortality, pass away ; the victor of a hundred battles is dust, the parchments or papyrus on which his deeds were written are shrivelled and decayed and gone,

> ' And all his triumphs shrink into a coin.'

So it is with a lyric poem. One happy utterance of some emotion or expression which comes home to all may keep a name remembered when the race to which the singer belonged exists no longer. The cradle-song of Danaë to her infant as they tossed on the waves in the imprisoning chest has made the name of Simonides immortal. Our own English literature abounds with instances which illustrate the same fact so far as the experience of a few generations extends. And I think we may venture to say that some of the shorter poems of Longfellow must surely reach a remote posterity, and be considered then, as now, ornaments to English literature. We may compare them with the best short poems of the language without fearing that they will suffer. Scott, cheerful, wholesome, unreflective, should be read in the open air; Byron, the poet of malecontents and cynics, in a prison-cell; Burns, generous, impassioned, manly, social, in the tavern-hall; Moore, elegant, fastidious, full of melody, scented with the volatile perfume of the Eastern gardens in which his fancy revelled, is pre-eminently the poet of the drawing-room and the piano; Longfellow, thoughtful, musical, home-loving, busy with the lessons of life, which he was ever studying, and loved to teach others, finds his charmed circle of listeners by the fireside. His songs, which we might almost call sacred ones, rarely, if ever, get into the hymn-books. They are too broadly human to suit the specialized tastes of the sects, which often think more of their differences from each other than of the common ground on which they can agree.

" Shall we think less of our poet because he aimed in his verse not simply to please, but also to impress some elevating thought on the minds of his readers? The Psalms of King David are burning with religious devotion and full of weighty counsel; but they are not less valued, certainly, than the poems of Omar Khayyam, which cannot be accused of too great a tendency to find a useful lesson in their subject. Dennis, the famous critic, found fault with The Rape of the Lock because it had no moral. It is not *necessary* that a poem should carry a moral, any more than that a picture of a Madonna should always be an altar-piece. The poet himself is the best judge of that in each particular case. In that charming little poem of Wordsworth's ending,

> ' And then my heart with rapture thrills,
> And dances with the daffodils,'

we do not ask for any thing more than the record of the impression which is told so simply, and which justifies itself by the way in which it is told. But who does not feel with the poet that the touching story, Hart-leap Well, must have its lesson brought out distinctly to give a fitting close to the narrative? Who would omit those two lines —

> ' Never to blend our pleasure or our pride
> With sorrow of the meanest thing that lives ' ?

No poet knows better than Longfellow how to impress a moral without seeming to preach. Didactic verse, as such, is no doubt a formidable visitation; but a cathedral has its lesson to teach, as well as a schoolhouse. These beautiful medallions of verse which Longfellow has left us might possibly be found fault with as conveying too much useful and elevating truth in their legends; having the unartistic aim of being serviceable as well as delighting by their beauty. Let us leave such comment to the critics who cannot handle a golden coin fresh from the royal mint without clipping its edges, and stamping their own initials on its face."

FRANCIS H. UNDERWOOD.

Mr. Francis H. Underwood has thus spoken of several of Longfellow's poems: " The poems, Voices of the Night, about the earliest of his writings, though not the first printed, really formed the turning-point of his career. He has written greater poems, and had afterward a wider education; but he never wrote any thing more characteristic of his genius and of his judgment than those early poems. They have become current as proverbs; the lines are interchangeable, like fragments of Shakspeare; they are current as coin in conversation; they are, and they will remain, a gospel of goodwill and good music; they were written, not for admiration, but for the hearts of the people, and have become heart treasures." Referring to Longfellow's participation in public affairs, Mr. Underwood said the poet was probably never seen on the platform at any anti-slavery meeting, yet his anti-slavery poems gave all the influence of his mind and character on that subject. The Arsenal at Springfield was written very shortly after Mr. Sumner had delivered his oration on The True Grandeur of Nations; and Paul Revere's Ride was written in January, 1861, three months before the attack on Fort Sumter; and both of these were written to have an influence upon the public mind in regard to slavery and the impending war.

EDITH M. THOMAS.

In The Critic for April 22, 1882, Edith M. Thomas said: "Have not astronomers told us that certain remote stars are already stricken from the firmament? And yet, because their light is still coming, their lamps nightly re-appearing in the roof of heaven, we will not believe in their annihilation. How can we credit the cold fact of mortality while the poet's starlight still reaches us? It seems to us that never, in all his long ministry of song, has Longfellow been so clearly present, so vividly alive, to the eyes of the heart and the imagination, as in the few days since his death. In many and diverse circles his verse has been re-read, and found to be wondrously eloquent of the author himself, — authentic spiritual autobiography, not before revealed, and not to be revealed except under the light of the inverted torch. New pathos and beauty are discovered in such lyrics as The Bridge; an added delicacy and grace in such poems as Endymion; and the chords struck in The Ladder of St. Augustine vibrate with more resonance and sweetness when we accept them as the embodied music of a life so fair, high-purposed, and trustful as Longfellow's. Remembering his parable of The Singers, could it not be said that he united in himself the several missions of that God-sent triad, ' to charm, to strengthen, and to teach '? for his voice had been heard in youth, in his strong prime, and in his harmonious old age. . . .

" The 'slender reeds of song' have always bent with love and reverence in the direction of this strong pillar in the temple of American literature. If the truth were told, doubtless every one of the younger brood of poets would confess that he had long anticipated the deserved red-letter day when he should be permitted to touch the old poet's kindly hand, to gaze in that face,

> ' Whose looks increased
> The silvery setting of his mortal star.'

Where this privilege has been granted, 'what Longfellow said' has been passed on from one custodian to another as a sort of sacred oral tradition, just as in old time the oracle may have been forwarded from Delphi to some far outpost of Thule."

THE BOSTON BOOK BULLETIN.

Says a contributor to The Boston Book Bulletin, "In his home his hospitality was proverbial. Bret Harte has called him the ideal poet, and he was ideal host as well. His gentle tact and exquisite courtesy remind one of that fine compliment paid to Villemand, — which is a fine definition of politeness, — 'When he spoke to a lady, one would think he had offered her a bouquet.'

" He was emphatically the poet of the beautiful, and his life was as rounded and complete as one of his own sonnets, or a Beethoven symphony. He was not one of those great men who must be seen like an oil-painting, at a distance; but the nearer one approached, the finer showed the outlines and shadings of his character. Success did not make him indifferent to the aspirations of the unknown. The young poet who went to Longfellow with his verses needed not to fear a cold reception nor an indifferent listener. Sympathy he would surely find; and also, did his verses contain one glimmer of the sacred fire, that encouragement for want of which many a young genius has been stifled.

" He was to the last an earnest worker, composing with great care. Time took from him only the gold of his hair and the smoothness of his brow, and gave him year by year added grace and sweetness and strength. Wide-spread as his influence was, yet his mission is but begun; for, as long as the heart of humanity shall beat, his voice will be heard in tones of music, singing words of consolation and hope."

PROFESSOR C. E. NORTON.

In his address before the Massachusetts Historical Society, Professor Charles Eliot Norton said, " The accord between the character and life of Mr. Longfellow and his poems was complete. His poetry touched the hearts of his readers because it was the sincere expression of his own. The sweetness, the gentleness, the grace, the purity, the humanity, of his verse, were the image of his own soul. But, beautiful and ample as this expression of himself was, it fell short of the truth. The man was more and better than the poet. . . .

"Intimate, however, as was the concord between the poet and his poetry, there was much in him to which he never gave utterance in words. He was a man of deep reserves. He kept the holy of holies within himself, sacred and secluded. Seldom does he admit his readers to even its outward precincts. The deepest experiences of life are too sacred to be shared with any one whatsoever. 'There are things of which I may not speak,' he says in one of the most personal of his poems.

> ' Whose hand shall dare to open and explore
> Those volumes closed and clasped forevermore?
> Not mine. With reverential feet I pass.'

"It was the felicity of Mr. Longfellow to share the sentiment and emotion of his coevals, and to succeed in giving to them their apt poetic expression. It was not by depth of thought, or by original views of nature, that he won his place in the world's regard; but it was by sympathy with the feelings common to good men and women everywhere, and by the simple, direct, sincere, and delicate expression of them, that he gained the affection of mankind.

"He was fortunate in the time of his birth. He grew up in the morning of our Republic. He shared in the cheerfulness of the early hour, in its hopefulness, its confidence. The years of his youth and early manhood coincided with an exceptional moment of national life, in which a prosperous and unembarrassed democracy was learning its own capacities, and was beginning to realize its large and novel resources, — in which the order of society was still simple and humane. He became, more than any one else, the voice of this epoch of national progress, an epoch of unexampled prosperity for the masses of mankind in our new world, — prosperity from which sprang a sense, more general and deeper than had ever before been felt, of human kindliness and brotherhood. But, even to the prosperous, life brings its inevitable burden. Trial, sorrow, misfortune, are not to be escaped by the happiest of men. The deepest experiences of each individual are the experiences common to the whole race. And it is this double aspect of American life, — its novel and happy conditions, with the genial spirit resulting from them, and, at the same time, its subjection to the old, absolute, universal laws of existence, — that finds its mirror and manifestation in Longfellow's poetry. . . .

" No one can read his poetry without a conviction of the simplicity, tenderness, gentleness, and humanity of the poet. And we who were his friends know how these qualities shone in his daily conversation. Praise, applause, flattery, — and no man ever was exposed to more of them, — never touched him to harm him. He walked through their flames unscathed, as Dante through the fires of purgatory. His modesty was perfect. He accepted the praise as he would have accepted any other pleasant gift, — glad of it as an expression of good-will, but without personal elation. Indeed, he had too much of it, and often in an absurd and trying form, not to become at times weary of what his own fame and virtues brought upon him. But his kindliness did not permit him to show his weariness to those who did but burden him with their admiration.

It was the penalty of his genius, and he accepted it with the pleasantest temper and a humorous resignation. Bores of all nations, especially of our own, persecuted him. His long-suffering patience was a wonder to his friends. It was, in truth, the sweetest charity. No man was ever before so kind to these moral mendicants."

THE LONDON ECHO.

Longfellow's patriotism was commented on by The London Echo, March 25, 1882, as follows: "Perhaps one of the chief reasons of Longfellow's fame on this side the ocean is that he was less national than some of his distinguished compeers, such as Whittier and Lowell. And yet he was no lukewarm patriot. While as yet it was regarded as almost treason to the Commonwealth to denounce the sum of all villanies, as far back as 1843, he published his Poems on Slavery, in one of which, with almost prophetic foresight, he compared the African race in America to 'that poor blind slave of Gaza, the scoff and jest of all, in whose fall thousands perished. The great civil war did not kindle in him the passionate enthusiasm that inspired the chief anti-slavery poets; but he took occasion, on the destruction of the Cumberland, to pay a tribute to the brave men who died in her, and to predict, in the dark hours of Northern defeat, that the old flag should yet once more float 'without a seam.' It seems strange that American poets should revert so sparingly to the Revolutionary period of which they are so proud. Longfellow has done so only once, in the spirited story of Paul Revere's Ride; but even here he avoids the blood and smoke of battle, and the fury of national passion. It was not in him to hate. He could not hate even the Evil One.

In The Golden Legend he has created the least devilish
devil that ever the heart of man conceived, and then
closes the book with the eminently optimist and charita-
ble conclusion, that, 'since God suffers him to be, he, too,
is God's minister, and labors for some good by us not
understood."

RELIGIOUS ATTITUDE.

At the close of the biographical portion of this volume were quoted opinions of various persons upon the
religious attitude of Mr. Longfellow. The great humanitarian poets are always broader than all sects:
they include such sects in the scope and range of their
sympathies. Hence they are claimed by the most radi-
cally antagonistic thinkers. It is known to the writer
that Mr. Longfellow expressed to an eminent Harvard
instructor his strong disapproval of the invitation extended to the Rev. Phillips Brooks, D.D., to become
preacher at the Harvard-College Chapel, on the ground
that he was not a Unitarian.

The Rev. George Zabriskie Gray, D.D., dean of the
Episcopal Theological School in Cambridge, said in a
recent sermon: "He was a Christian poet. Though
not of our particular fold, yet his influence was cast,
through all his long career, on the side of our precious
faith. . . . Some years ago he met Dr. Stone in front
of St. John's Memorial Chapel, and said, 'I never pass
your grounds, and this chapel, without thinking of the
words of the benediction in the prayer-book, "The
peace of God which passeth all understanding." ' "

Mr. Longfellow's residence almost adjoined St. John's
Chapel; and in it were baptized his two grandchildren,
on which occasion he was present, the Rev. Dr. Phillips

ST. JOHN'S MEMORIAL CHAPEL, ADJACENT TO LONGFELLOW'S HOME, CAMBRIDGE.

Brooks standing as their godfather. He has made the chapel famous by a beautiful sonnet beginning, —

> " I stand beneath the tree whose branches shade
>   Thy western window, Chapel of St. John,
>   And hear its leaves repeat their benison
> On him whose hands thy stones memorial laid."

POETS' TRIBUTES.

" Garlands upon his grave,
And flowers upon his hearse,
And to the tender heart and true
The tribute of this verse." — LONGFELLOW.

TO H. W. L.

(On his birthday, 27th February, 1867.)

I NEED not praise the sweetness of his song,
  Where limpid verse to limpid verse succeeds
Smooth as our Charles, when, fearing lest he wrong
The new moon's mirrored skiff, he slides along,
  Full without noise, and whispers in his reeds.

With loving breath of all the winds his name
  Is blown about the world; but to his friends
A sweeter secret hides behind his fame,
And Love steals shyly through the loud acclaim
  To murmur a *God bless you!* and there ends.

As I muse backward up the checkered years
  Wherein so much was given, so much was lost,
Blessings in both kinds, such as cheapen tears, —
But hush! this is not for profaner ears:
  Let them drink molten pearls nor dream the cost.

Some suck up poison from a sorrow's core,
  As nought but nightshade grew upon earth's ground:
Love turned all his to heart's-ease; and the more
Fate tried his bastions, she but forced a door
  Leading to sweeter manhood and more sound.

307

Even as a wind-waved fountain's swaying shade
  Seems of mixed race, a gray wraith shot with sun,
So through his trial faith translucent rayed
Till darkness, half disnatured so, betrayed
  A heart of sunshine that would fain o'errun.

Surely if skill in song the shears may stay,
  And of its purpose cheat the charmed abyss,
If our poor life be lengthened by a lay,
He shall not go, although his presence may,
  And the next age in praise shall double this.
.   .   .   .

JAMES RUSSELL LOWELL.[1]

LONGFELLOW.

(Dead March 24, 1882.)

ALONE, at night, he heard them sigh, —
  These wild March winds that beat his tomb, —
Alone, at night, from those that die
  He sought one ray to light his gloom.

And still he heard the night winds moan,
  And still the mystery closed him round,
And still the darkness cold and lone
  Sent forth no ray, returned no sound.

But Time at last the answer brings;
  And he, past all our suns and snows,
At rest with peasants and with kings,
  Like them the wondrous secret knows.

Alone, at night, we hear them sigh, —
  These wild March winds that stir his pall;
And helpless, wandering, lost, we cry
  To his dim ghost, to tell us all.

He loved us while he lingered here:
  We loved him — never love more true!
He will not leave, in doubt and fear,
  The human grief that once he knew.

[1] Printed with permission of Houghton, Mifflin, & Co.

For never yet was born the day
  When, faint of heart and weak of limb,
One suffering creature turned away,
  Unhelped, unsoothed, uncheered by him!

But still through darkness, dense and bleak,
  The winds of March moan wildly round;
And still we feel that all we seek
  Ends in that sigh of vacant sound.

He cannot tell us — none can tell
  What waits behind the mystic veil!
Yet he who lived and died so well,
  In that, perchance, has told the tale.

Not to the wastes of Nature drift —
  Else were this world an evil dream —
The crown and soul of Nature's gift,
  By Avon or by Charles's stream.

His heart was pure, his purpose high,
  His thought serene, his patience vast:
He put all strifes of passion by,
  And lived to God from first to last.

His song was like the pine-tree's sigh
  At midnight o'er a poet's grave,
Or like the sea-bird's distant cry,
  Borne far across the twilight wave.

There is no flower of meek delight,
  There is no star of heavenly pride,
That shines not sweeter and more bright
  Because he lived, loved, sang, and died.

Wild winds of March, his requiem sing!
  Weep o'er him, April's sorrowing skies!
Till come the tender flowers of Spring,
  To deck the pillow where he lies;

Till violets pour their purple flood,
  That wandering myrtle shall not lack,
And, royal with the Summer's blood,
  The roses that he loved come back:

Till all that Nature gives of light,
  To rift the gloom and point the way,
Shall sweetly pierce our mortal night,
  And symbol his immortal day!

WILLIAM WINTER, *in The New York Tribune.*

THE POET AND THE CHILDREN.

WITH a glory of winter sunshine
  Over his locks of gray,
In the old historic mansion
  He sat on his last birthday,

With his books and his pleasant pictures,
  And his household and his kin,
While a sound as of myriads singing
  From far and near stole in.

It came from his own fair city,
  From the prairie's boundless plain,
From the Golden Gate of sunset,
  And the cedarn woods of Maine.

And his heart grew warm within him,
  And his moistening eyes grew dim;
For he knew that his country's children
  Were singing the songs of him:

The lays of his life's glad morning,
  The psalms of his evening time,
Whose echoes shall float forever
  On the winds of every clime.

All their beautiful consolations,
  Sent forth like birds of cheer,
Came flocking back to his windows,
  And sang in the poet's ear.

Grateful, but solemn and tender,
  The music rose and fell
With a joy akin to sadness
  And a greeting like farewell.

With a sense of awe he listened
  To the voices sweet and young:
The last of earth and the first of heaven
  Seemed in the songs they sung.

And waiting a little longer
  For the wonderful change to come,
He heard the summoning angel
  Who calls God's children home!

And to him, in a holier welcome,
  Was the mystical meaning given
Of the words of the blessed Master:
  "Of such is the kingdom of heaven!"

    John Greenleaf Whittier, *in The Wide Awake.*

On the occasion of the poet's seventy-fourth birthday, The Literary World published the following poetical tributes: —

Not yet! "O loved historian of hearts!"
"Ultima Thule" draweth not in sight;
For Love's own angel in her raiment white
Stands at the prow, and as the bright foam parts
She gives her mandate: "Helmsman, bear away
From rocky coast where hidden dangers throng:
Rich freight we bear, the crownèd king of song, —
A king to whom the nations homage pay!"
Not yet! for great "Sandalphon" waiting stands,
And gathers prayers and wishes one by one,
To bear to that far clime beyond the sun,
All changed to flowers in his immortal hands.
Ah, royal friend! Love would detain thee long
From that far distant "Utmost Isle" of song.

    Mrs. J. Oliver Smith.

Throned in thine ebon chair, O Poet! may
We bring thy brow a wreath? 'Tis twined with more
Than the Ravenna myrtle Dante wore,
Or than Petrarca's crown of Roman bay,

Or sad Torquato's, which he could not stay
From heaven to await.   For if thy deathless store
Of song were lost to us, with all its lore,
How poorer were the whole world's heart to-day!

Therefore, among the laurel leaves we bind
Rose, heather, shamrock, olive, fleur-de-lys,
And Alpine edelweiss, with aster blue,
And Mayflower, and magnolia; and close-twined
Among them, breathing grateful odor, see
A shy Virginia violet wet with dew!

MARGARET J. PRESTON.

SOME souls are vernal — thine is young to-day,
   As sun-dawn melting in the eyes of May;
Age a mist-woven, futile mask wherethrough
   Shines thy brave Life, still touched by morning dew!

No sin-begotten wrinkles mar the grace,
   The fair, frank lustre of thy spirit's face:
Time's snows on thee have brought no saddening blight,
   But crowned thy heart as head with radiant white!

PAUL HAMILTON HAYNE.

WHEN thou didst hymn the "Voices of the Night,"
   While youth's fresh flowers were still thy path adorning,
Their deep-toned music thrilled the advancing light,
   And they were thy true Voices of the Morning.

Thy latest lays, that, echoing from afar,
   Reach us as on thou sail'st toward Ultima Thule,
Thy Vespers — Voices of the Evening — are:
   The sun sinks low — the stars will shine forth duly.

The world's great heart, between thy morn and eve,
   Thy verse has charmed, as manifold as glorious;
Nor need'st thou dread the night, for thou wilt leave
   A light that through the dark will stream victorious.

But may the twilight of thy day be long;
   May day so blessed have e'en as blessed an ending,
And soft reverberations of thy song
   Lull thee to sleep, with psalms celestial blending !

W. L. SHOEMAKER.

I.

To the land of granite and ice,
  In the month of frost and snow,
A strain of music from Paradise
  Came seeking a home below.
It entered a child's white heart;
  And the little human tent
Grew to a shrine for its guest divine,
  The poem the gods had sent.

II.

Now the rocky hills are crossed
  By snatches of happy tune:
The month of darkness and frost
  We honor above the June.
For thou, O Poet we love!
  Art the bloom of our northern clime;
And we know that song, through the ages long,
  Is the sweetest fruit of time.

CATHERINE E. BATES.

GREAT souls there are like mountain heights,
  Which through the mists uprear
Their stately heads in shining light,
  And know no stain nor peer.

And souls there are which shine like stars,
  Far off in evening skies,
And ever move, unchanged, undimmed,
  Before our wondering eyes.

Like mount and star to future years,
  Wise singer, thou wilt seem;
But more to us thy gracious life
  Is like a noble stream,

Whose course through all the meadow-lands
  Is marked by trees and flowers,
And whose broad breast, unvexed by storms,
  Reflects our sunniest hours.

ANNIE SAWYER DOWNS.

Not seldom genius bids us call men great
    Who are ignoble in their deeds or soul;
    Not seldom genius, with supreme control,
    Makes us unmindful of the body's trait
That ill befits the royal dweller's state.
    But with thy genius is the liberal dole
    Of gifts that make it shine unmarred and whole,
    And that the years augment and not abate.
As though unconscious of the laurelled name, —
    Its heavy honors on thy temples bound, —
    Thou treadest life's familiar, simple way;
And thy whole self accords so with thy fame,
    That with consummate fitness, thou art crowned.
    Joy to this sabbath of thy fame and day!

CHARLOTTE FISKE BATES.

WHOSE SHALL THE WELCOME BE?

The wave goes down, the wind goes down,
    The gray tide glitters on the sea,
The moon seems praying in the sky.
    Gates of the New Jerusalem
    (A perfect pearl each gate of them)
Wide as all heaven swing on high:
    Whose shall the welcome be?

The wave went down, the wind went down,
    The tide of life turned out to sea;
Patience of pain, and grace of deed,
    The glories of the heart and brain,
    Treasure that shall not come again;
The human singing that we need,
    Set to a heavenly key.

The wave goes down, the wind goes down,
    All tides at last turn to the sea.
We learn to take the thing we have.
    Thou who hast taught us strength in grief,
    As moon to shadow, high and chief,
Shine out, white soul, beyond the grave,
    And light our loss of thee!

ELIZABETH STUART PHELPS, in N. Y. Independent.

LAUS LAUREATI.

HENRY WADSWORTH LONGFELLOW.

FEB. 27, 1807-1882.

(Read before the Maine Historical Society at their celebration of the poet's seventy-
fifth birthday.)

I SING no common theme, but of a man, —
One who, full-voiced, the highway of the King
Gladdens with song; inspiring lives which span
A fruitless field where little joy may spring,
And which, from birth, may win no better thing
Than paltry bread, and shelter from the blast,
Till unto Death's low house they come at last.

It needs more fluent tongue than mine to sing,
In fitting measure, of a poet born —
Greater than crosiered priest or sceptred king,
Since such are made, and may by chance be shorn
Of all their glory by to-morrow morn;
But born a poet, he shall surely be
Ever a poet to eternity.

Of such I strive to sing: one who shall live
In Fame's high house while stars make glad the sky, —
That happy house which many hapless give
Life's choicest pearls to gain, since none may die
Who come within its halls so fair and high.
Would I might win it, with no thought but this,
That I might others bring soul-health and bliss.

But, Master, one who is about to die
Brings thee a crown, which, though not one of bay,
May haply mind thee of some things gone by
Pleasant to think of, — matters put away
In rooms forgot, where truant memories play
At hide and seek; for, beareth it, forsooth,
Savor of things well loved by thee in youth.

Of Deering's Woods, which whisper softly, still,
A boy's will is the wind's will, as of yore
They lisped to thee, where sweet-voiced birds would trill,
In haunts wherein thou soughtest tuneful lore.
Of bluff and beach along our rugged shore,

Girting the bay, whose isles enchanted drew
Thy venturous thoughts to havens ever new.

Dear Master, let me take thy hand a space,
And lead thee gently wheresoe'er I may;
With the salt sea's cool breath upon thy face,
And in thine ears the music of the spray,
Which rapt in days agone thy soul away,
Where hung full low the golden fruit of truth,
Within the reach of thy aspiring youth.

Thou knowest well the place : here built George Cleeves
Almost two centuries before thy birth;
Here was his cornfield; here his lowly eaves
Sheltered the swallows, and around his hearth
The red men crouched, — poor souls of little worth:
Thou with clear vision seest them, I know,
As they were in the flesh long years ago.

Surely the shrewd, persistent pioneer
Built better than he knew: he thought to build
A shelter for himself, his kith and gear;
But felled the trees, and grubbed and ploughed and tilled,
That in the course of time might be fulfilled
A wondrous purpose, being no less than this,
That here a poet might be born to bliss.

Ah! could he but have tracked adown the dim
Long, weary path of years, and stood to-day
With thee and me, how would the eyes of him
Have flashed with pride and joy to hear men say,
Here Cleeves built the first house in Casco Bay;
Here, too, was our Longfellow's place of birth,
And sooth, God sent his singers upon earth.

Thou canst not find Clay Cove ?   'Twas here, wilt say,
When thou didst listen to the runnet's song,
Leaping to meet the full lips of the bay.
Well, let us climb Munjoy; lo! good and strong,
In the same coat of red it hath so long
Disported bravely, spite of flood and flame,
The old Observatory, still the same.

And there the forts; and, farther seaward yet,
A pillar of fire by night, of cloud by day,
The lighthouse standeth still, as firmly set
Upon its flinty throne amidst the spray,
As erst when thou didst dream thy soul away
To the hoarse Hebrides, or bright Azore,
Or flashing surges of San Salvador.

And, ere we leave, look, where still sleep the two
Brave captains, who in bloody shrouds were brought
From the great sea-fight whilst the bugles blew,
And drums rolled, and gaunt cannon terror wrought
In childish hearts: the place thou oft hast sought
To dream the fight o'er, while the busy hum
Of toil from wharf and street would strangely come.

But now along the teeming thoroughfare
Thread we our way. Strange faces, sayest thou?
Yet names well known to thee, some haply bear,
And, shouldst thou scan more closely face and brow,
Old looks would come well known to thee enow,
Which shone on faces of the girls and boys
Who shared with thee the sweets of youthful joys.

And now we come where, rough with rent and scar,
The ancient ropewalk stood, low-roofed and gray,
Embalmed with scent of oakum, flax, and tar,
Cobwebbed and dim, and crammed with strange array
Of things which lure the thoughts of youth away
To wondrous climes, where never ship hath been,
Nor foot hath trod, nor curious eye hath seen.

Gone! — why, I dreamt! A moment since 'twas there,
Or seemed to be. Their lives' frail thread, 'tis true,
The spinners long since spun; the maidens fair,
Swinging and laughing as their shadows flew
Along the grass, have swung from earthly view,
And the gay mountebanks have vaulted quite
Into oblivion's eternal night.

And they are gone. The woman at the well;
The old man ringing in the noontide heat;
The shameless convicts with their faces fell;
The boy and kite, and steeds with flying feet,
And sportsmen ambushed midst of leafage sweet;

Ay, and the ships rejoicing in the breeze
Are rotting on the shores of unknown seas.

But, Master, let us fare to old Bramhall,
Up Free and Main Streets — this is State, full well
The house where Mellen lived you must recall,
Seeing a poet once therein might dwell;
Though short of Fame's fair house he hapless fell,
Tracing his name, half listless, in the reach
Of every tide which sweeps Time's treacherous beach.

And here is cool Bramhall; and there still stands
The Deering house, as thou hast known it long;
Where Brackett's house stood, ere with murderous hands
The Indians thronged around it — witched of wrong —
One August day, with torch and savage song,
And swept it from the earth.   Ah! void of hope,
Might feeble Falmouth then midst ruin grope.

But time hath made all right now.   Lo! a-west,
Whither the red man gazed with fervid eyes,
The mountains in eternal whiteness drest,
He called the crystal hills, and, childishwise,
Did fondly deem, that way lay Paradise;
Whither each evening went the chief of day,
Bedecked with painted robes and feathers gay.

   'Twas not so far amiss, for type more grand
Of the celestial hills no eye may see;
Towering in splendid majesty, they stand
Like the fixed portals of eternity,
Curtained with shining clouds tumultuously,
Which rise and fall, yet ever seem to hold
A mystery bosomed in each shadowy fold.

Pile upon pile they rise; and meet the sky,
Blue, overarching, like a mighty dome.
Even such a temple doth my spirit's eye
Limn for those souls who through achievement come
To well-won fame.   Lo! in this glorious home
I see them sit august, and, crowned with bays,
Across the silent centuries calmly gaze.

Homer unkempt, with close, sagacious look;
Plato, in whose calm face pale mysteries bide;
Virgil, smooth-cheeked, with oaten pipe and crook;
Grave Sophocles, with eyes unsatisfied,
Where riddles all unread in ambush hide;
Keen-eyed Euripides, whose books were men,
And jovial Horace with satiric pen;

And dear old Chaucer, loved of gods and men,
Benign, keen-witted, childlike, quaint, and wise;
Spenser, pure knight, whose lance was his good pen,
The praise of ladyes fayre his loved emprise;
Great Shakspeare, with a seer's unhindered eyes;
Blind Milton, listening for a seraph's wings;
And Burns, in whose blithe face a skylark sings;

Wordsworth, so simple; and poor, fragile Keats,
Who poured his heart out like a nightingale,
Whose affluent verse half cloys with wealth of sweets;
A master, spite of faulty work and frail,
Whose luckless loss the world full long shall wail:
And here, placed fairly in this hall of Fame,
A glorious seat with newly-carven name.

'Tis plain, dear Master, 'tis thy name forsooth
Deep graven in the everlasting stone.
There shall it be untouched of Time's sharp tooth,
While sunshine kisses bud to bloom, and zone
Answers to zone with fruitage all its own;
And quiring stars with universal song
The boundless arch of heaven majestic throng.

Here will I bid thee, Master, fond good-by,
Wishing thee soul-health and full many a day
Of blissful living, ere thou mayest try
The scope of other joys. And now I may
This wreath from Deering's Woods, O Master! lay
Upon thy brow. God speed thee while the sun
Shines on the faithful work which thou hast done!

JAMES P. BAXTER, in the Portland Advertiser.

HENRY WADSWORTH LONGFELLOW.

Seventy-five bright golden years,
  Journeying toward an all-wise Giver;
Seventy-five! — yet scarce he hears
  The rippling sob of Time's great river!

Still is the Minstrel's music heard,
  Strong and clear are his notes of warning;
Still are his lute-strings sweetly stirred,
  Warm is his heart as in life's morning.

Turn, O Muse! to that wondrous page,
  Glowing for aye with song and story;
Brush with thy wing the mists of Age,
  Sing of the Minstrel's youthful glory.

His was a triumph brave and grand,
  Worthy the laurel's fond caressing;
His the touch of a master-hand,
  Ever the notes of Hate suppressing.

Turn, O Potter! thy magic wheels, —
  Ixion-like, turn on forever;
While at thy shrine *Kéramos* kneels,
  Nought from his song thy name can sever.

Here the scenes of his boyhood's hours,
  And here old ocean's blue is gleaming;
Yonder the oaks' primeval bowers,
  Where infant Fancy fell a-dreaming.

Low the sun on the western wave,
  Slowly the night apace is creeping;
Strong is the Minstrel's heart and brave,
  Ever is Faith her vigils keeping.

Fancy leans from her casement-bar,
  Lists to the song that's upward pealing;
Into the Isle of Dreams afar,
  Lo! a shadowy bark is stealing!

Only the gleam of silver sails,
  Under the even's purple glowing;
Only a glimpse of distant vales,
  Where the fountains of Youth are flowing.

Yet still for thee, O Minstrel! beam
  Twinkling lights from Memory's portal;
Dancing away on life's dark stream,
  Into the realms of blest Immortal!

ROBERT REXDALE, in The Portland Transcript.

FEB. 27, 1882.

TO H. W. L.

ON HIS SEVENTY-FIFTH BIRTHDAY.

(Suggested by the poem, My Lost Youth.)

THEY err who say the poet dies,
  Or suffers foul eclipse:
Old age is never in his eyes,
  Nor palsy on his lips.

Nature and love and truth and faith
  Know no black, biting frost.
The poet feels no bated breath,
  His youth is never lost.

ISRAEL WASHBURN, JUN., in The Portland Transcript.

THE NESTOR-POET.

His day is spent, and he is dead:
The Nestor-poet's silvered head
Is lying low, as, sad and slow,
They bear him to his hollow bed.

His lips a voiceless silence keep;
He sleeps, alas! a mortal sleep;
His rayless eye cannot reply
To other eyes that vainly weep.

No more, through sinuous tones, his song,
In fresh-drawn notes, shall move along;
No magic theme through him shall dream
In rhythmic music to the throng.

We call it Death : it cannot be!
From land to land, from sea to sea,
A winged fame has borne his name:
No Death can still his minstrelsy.

O poet of the golden lyre!
O glory of our western choir!
Thy living page, from age to age
Shall light with an immortal fire.

S. II. THAYER in Christian at Work.

LONGFELLOW.

'TWAS but a few brief days ago, so proud
　We were of thy long life and what it bore:
And now, for all that wealth of praise, the shroud,
　And hearts all hushed, since they thy loss deplore;
For swift as glowing sunset dies in gloom,
Thy flashing brightness darkens in the tomb,
And we that gazed with rapture and delight
Now stand bereft of that inspiring sight!
Yet no! thy years were long, thy song was sweet,
　And welcome won from all who heard its strain;
As birds our own New-England woodlands greet,
　So came to us thy pleasant, glad refrain.
And, while the seasons come with flowers and song,
Our Minstrel shall their happiness prolong.

WILLIAM BRUNTON in The Christian Register.

A LAUREL-LEAF.

How sweet he sung!   The laborer heard
His carol, like a cheering bird,
Till labor grew a noble thing,
With music in the anvil's ring.

How sweet he sung 'midst dying men,
The song that souls will meet again;
Till mourners rolled doubt's stone away,
And through the tomb saw breaking day!

Eternal life is in his song,
Forever lifting souls from wrong:
If thus the earthly, what must be
His song of immortality?

FLETCHER BATES, *in The Cambridge Tribune.*

LONGFELLOW.

HE who would wield the glorious power of song,
  Who in the immortal choir would take his stand,
  Must win his birthright in that sacred band
By suffering and by strivings stern and long;
And at the best oft bear this cruel wrong, —
  To feel the lyre torn from his stricken hand
  Ere its sweet chords have waked the unheeding land
To fame's responsive anthem full and strong.
Not so with thee, great master whom we love,
  Harsh Fate herself has helpless passed thee by;
  No room was there for envy, malice, hate,
So laurels thicken still thy brows above,
  And still the world beholds, with well-pleased eye,
  Thy peace-crowned life whereon all blessings wait.

CHARLES TURNER DAZEY, *in The Harvard Register.*

LONGFELLOW.

IN MEMORIAM.

ALAS, our harp of harps! the instrument,
On whose fine strings the nymph Parnassus-bred
Played ever most melodiously, is rent,
  And all its music fled.

Alas, our torch of truth! the lofty light,
That yet a tender household radiance cast,
And made the cottage as the palace bright,
  Is blotted out at last.

Alas! the sweet pure life, that ripened still
To holier thought and more benignant grace,
Hath spread its wings, and who is left to fill
  The dear and empty place?

How poor thou art, O bleak Atlantic coast!
How barren all thy hills, my mother-land!
Where now amid the nations is thy boast,
   And where thy Delphic band ?

Of that bright group who sang among thy wheat,
And cheered thy reapers lest their brown arms tire,
Whom ermined Europe raised a hand to greet,
   As princes of the lyre,

The first have fallen, and the others wait,
The snow of years on each belovèd head,
With weary feet before the sunset gate
   That opens toward the Dead.

And who abides to sing away our pain,
As these our bards we carry to their rest ?
We need thy comfort for the tears that rain,
   O poet! on thy breast.

It is our earth, where prophet steps grow few,
For which we weep, and not, O harper gray!
For thee, who carolled from the morning dew
   To noontide of the day,

Nor left thy task when twilight down the wall
Stole silently in shadowy flakes and bars,
And whose clear tones, while night enfolded all,
   Sang on beneath the stars.

The knights and dames had bent their heads to list,
The serving-maids were hearkening from the stair,
And little childish faces, mother-kissed,
   Had flocked about thy chair,

When ceased thy fingers in the strings to weave,
O'er thine anointed sight the eyelids fell;
And thou wert sleeping, who from dawn to eve
   Hadst wrought so wondrous well.

O gentle minstrel, may thy rest be deep
And tranquil, as thy working-day was long!
Our lonely hearts will grudge thee not thy sleep,
   Who grudged us not thy song.

        KATHARINE LEE BATES, *in The Literary World.*
WELLESLEY, MASS.

"ULTIMA THULE."

H. W. L.

WRAP the broad canvas close; furl the last sail;
　Let go the anchor; for the utmost shore
　Is reached at length, from which, ah! nevermore,
Shall the brave bark ride forth to meet the gale,
Or skim the calm with phosphorescent trail,
　Or guide lost mariners amid the roar
　Of hurricanes, or send, far echoing o'er
Some shipwrecked craft, the music of his "Hail."

And he has laid aside his travel gear;
　And forth to meet him come the mystic band
Whom he has dreamed of, worshipped, loved so long, —
The veiled Immortals, who, with lofty cheer
　Of exultation, take him by the hand,
And lead him to the inner shrine of Song !

　　　　MARGARET J. PRESTON, *in The Literary World.*
LEXINGTON, VA.

DEATH OF THE POET LONGFELLOW.

DEPARTED! and no "prophet's son" to say,
　As all unseen along its star-path came
　The God-sent chariot with its steeds of flame, -
"Behold, thy Master shall be called to-day!"
If some far gleam of radiance we had caught,
How mute a throng those parted waves had sought!

Less than six moons have waned since one sad morn,
Our royal bard so felt a nation's pain,
That, born of tears, fell his melodious strain
On weary hearts by tooth of anguish torn.
Then Death, that marksman all too sure of aim,
Had ruthless borne away our nation's head.
Again our heart he rends : but "deathless fame"
Above his range shall proudly be upborne.

And still Columbia mourns — by Sorrow led,
She stands like Niobe beside her dead!

　　　　Mrs. J. OLIVER SMITH, *in The Literary World.*
JOHNSTOWN, N.Y.

HENRY WADSWORTH LONGFELLOW.

(Born Feb. 27, 1807.   Died March 24, 1882.)

A Life Psalm, staidly sweet and simply strong
As any the dead Singer gave the throng,
Sinks to its close.   But Fame will yet prolong,

In echoes clear, across two worlds wide winging,
And in all English hearts like home bells ringing,
Glad memory of the Singer and his singing.

From London " Punch."

LONGFELLOW.

Poet whose sunny span of fruitful years
Outreaches earth, whose voice within our ears
Grows silent, shall we mourn for thee ?   Our sigh
Is April's breath, our grief is April's tears.

If this be dying, fair it is to die:
Even as a garment weariness lays by,
Thou layest down life to pass, as Time hath passed .
From wintry rigors to a springtime sky.

Are there tears left to give thee at the last,
Poet of spirits crushed and hearts downcast,
Loved of worn women who when work is done
Weep o'er thy page in twilights fading fast ?

Oh, tender-toned and tender-hearted one!
We yield thee to the season new begun,
Lay thy white head within the arms of Spring:
Thy song had all her shower and her sun.

Nay, let us not such sorrowful tribute bring
Now that thy lark-like soul hath taken wing:
A grateful memory fills and more endears
The silence when a bird hath ceased to sing.

H. C. Bunner, *in Puck.*

THE DEAD POET.

SINGER serene! in whose calm compass lay
  The mellowed richness of deep sunset glows,
The unclouded freshness of clear, opening day,
  The stately sombre shade of night's repose,

Long hast thou stood, and in unbroken strain
  Poured forth the plenitude of thy pure art:
Now that thy voice hath ceased we pause in vain,
  Loath from the sacred stillness to depart.

Mute are those lips which once with music flowed;
  Mute to all life, to beauty and to fame:
Yet may we marvel if some rare abode
  Of death hath grown melodious through thy name.

Or do we only in time's chalice hold,
  Imperishable still, the fragrance of thy years?
God knows alone, whose hands alike unfold
  Life, giving song, and death, dispensing tears.

> EMILY B. ELLIS, *in The Christian Union.*

H. W. LONGFELLOW.

SWEETLY as sinks the sun
  In golden west,
So sank our honored one
  Calmly to rest.

Home of the poet-soul
  Tenantless now:
Still we, in reverence,
  O'er thy dust bow.

Like sweetest melody
  His songs linger yet.
Words so familiar grown
  Who can forget?

Poet no more than friend,
  Teacher of life sublime,
Thy name be honored still
  Through coming time.

> ELIZA M. HICKOK, *in The Christian Register.*

H. W. LONGFELLOW: IN MEMORIAM.

Nec turpem senectam
Degere, nec cithara carentem.

"Not to be tuneless in old age!"
Ah! surely blest his pilgrimage,
  Who, in his winter's snow,
Still sings with note as sweet and clear
As in the morning of the year
  When the first violets blow!

Blest!—but more blest, whom summer's heat,
Whom spring's impulsive stir and beat,
  Have taught no feverish lure;
Whose muse, benignant and serene,
Still keeps his autumn chaplet green
  Because his verse is pure!

Lie calm, O white and laureate head!
Lie calm, O Dead, that art not dead,
  Since from the voiceless grave
Thy voice shall speak to old and young
While song yet speaks an English tongue
  By Charles' or Thamis' wave!

Austin Dobson, *in The London Athenæum.*

HENRY WADSWORTH LONGFELLOW.

Sweet Poesy, most shy and gentle maid,
  Hiding alone, far off, by English rills,
  How didst thou flee our wind-swept, sunny hills,
Till he, pursuing long in bosky glade,
His gentle spell on thy sweet wildness laid!
  Now, by our rivers, how thy wood-note thrills,
  How the far echo each deep valley fills,
Since thy dear feet came hither unafraid!
  Mourn for him now,—our eldest son of song,—
Eldest but one,—and dearest in thy sight,
  That made the New World echo of thee long,—
Mourn with those thousand voices of the night
  That rose and fell along that rocky shore
  Whose solemn music he shall hear no more.

James Herbert Morse, *in The Critic.*

LONGFELLOW.

GONE to his rest, — such rest as they must find
Who leave but sweetness with their fellow-kind.

How flowed his life one silver song of praise,
How beautiful his crown of many days!

Age seemed not age, so fresh the spirit grew,
Such broadened love to God and man he knew.

His sympathies went out to lonely lives,
And breathed that hope which every grief survives.

At last hath come his goodly recompense,
Above the cold, dim world of mortal sense.

" The faces of the children " shall be there,
And all pure things that claimed his tender care.

Gone to his rest: oh, be our own as sweet,
When fail like his our weary pilgrim feet!

   GEORGE H. COOMER, *in The Youth's Companion.*

LONGFELLOW.

(On his seventy-fifth birthday, Feb. 27, 1882.)

I COME as one who feels how near thou art,
 And yet how far — how near in thy sweet song,
 That wafts us like the breath of heaven along,
And breathes its blessing into every heart:
And yet how far — as if from all apart
 Thou wert uplifted from the minstrel throng,
 To bear the sceptre as becomes the strong
Who learn by suffering how to heal its smart.

Oh, may the years touch lightly as they fall,
 And leave thee long to sing as thou hast sung,
The friend, companion, and delight of all
 Who love the pure and good in every tongue —
The grand ideal of the world's best thought,
Teaching by truth as thou by truth art taught.

(March 24, 1882.)

But late the land was ringing with his fame,
  And city vied with city to express
  The nation's and the world's indebtedness
To the enduring works that bear his name;
And the whole people with their tributes came
  As round the Patriarch of Song to press,
  Leading the children in their loveliness
To crown him master, with the world's acclaim.

But now the universal voice of praise
  Is saddened by the muffled cry of pain
That bursts from every heart in blind amaze,
  And bows the nation in deep grief again;
But in the love that triumphs o'er the grave
He lives immortal with the good and brave.

HENRY H. CLARK, *in The Boston Transcript.*

LONGFELLOW.

I.

Poet of simple folk, thou art so wise,
And from such wisdom-deeps hast drawn thy song,
Thy page is magical to children's eyes,
And still to thee the old and learned throng.
Not thine tempestuous verse of writhing thought
That tosses frothing words against bleak skies,
Or from black bottoms in a whirlpool caught,
Stirs up a gleaming slime of passion-dyes.
These are hot shallows: where the sea is deep,
The mightiest storm leaves the cool waters clean.
So doth thy verse blow fervently, but sweep
No foulness up from the heart-deeps serene.
  Where in sweet visions child and man unite,
  Appear the heights and depths of human sight.

II.

Reading a while, I said — This poet's verse,
Whereunto shall I liken it? A brook
That in the valley doth the songs rehearse
Of mountain-tops, that is this poet's book;

And children wade in it from side to side,
And toss its sparkling drops from face to face.
Reading again, I said, 'Tis a river wide,
A stately stream that flows by towns apace,
And gathers in its breast toil-songs of men.
Reading once more, I cried, I sail a sea,
A deep where storms and calms of joy and pain
Mingle in harmony with heaven and me.
  I ceased: yet not opprest with thoughts in strife
  How this could be.   I had been reading LIFE.

J. VILA BLAKE, in The Literary World.

IN MEMORIAM.

HENRY WADSWORTH LONGFELLOW.

IT flashed through the sea, — that message;
  And the heart of England again
To the brief, sad words responded
  With the thrill of a sudden pain.

For next to his own great country
  She cherished the poet's name,
Rejoiced in his song, and crowned him
  With the laurel-wreath of fame.

And wherever her tongue is spoken,
  Wherever her children tread,
Will be heard with a throb of sorrow
  That Longfellow is dead.

For in spirit he dwelt amongst us;
  His name is a "household word:"
Where liveth the Anglo-Saxon
  Whose feeling he hath not stirred?

And in spirit we stand beside you,
  O brothers beyond the wave!
As with sorrowful hearts ye bear him,
  Love-crowned, to his honored grave.

Lay him to rest in "God's Acre;"
  But in earth's remotest lands
Will be seen through the coming ages
  His "footprints on the sands."

MRS. E. B. PRIDEAUX.

MODBURY, ENGLAND, March 27, 1882.

SONNET TO H. W. LONGFELLOW.

A REMINISCENCE.

A LITTLE onward tend thy feet, sweet friend:
  How brief the space since, side by side, were we,
  Weird children, in that "city by the sea," —
Each golden-haired, — whose mystic visions tend
To nobler heights than youthful fancy kenned!
  Then Cushman's[1] classic mind enthusèd thee,
  And Martin's[2] stately grace coercèd me.
Thy retrospective eye a moment bend:
  I was thy Dian then, Endymion thou, —
  A timid boy, a thoughtful girl, — nor knew
The bond that linked, and yet estranged, us two.
  I see the glory of thy youth but now,
  As, rolling back, the golden gateway threw
  Its flash of light athwart thy entering brow.

ELIZABETH OAKES SMITH, *in Baldwin's Monthly.*

BLUE POINT, L. I., April 2.

LONGFELLOW DEAD!

I.

AYE, it is well! . . . Crush back your selfish tears;
For from the half-veiled face of earthly Spring
Hath he not risen on heaven-aspiring wing
To reach the spring-tide of the eternal years?

[1] Bezaleel Cushman, who kept the Portland Academy when I was a child, was a most accomplished educator for perhaps half a century. He was an enthusiast for literature and scholarship, and formed the minds of William Pitt Fessenden, Seba Smith, Henry W. Longfellow, and others who made their mark in the world.

[2] The Martins were three English sisters, who, for the same length of time, educated the girls of Maine. They were conscientious, thorough teachers, and accomplished women. They used to boast that "all their pupils turned out well."

The young gentlemen of the Academy were assiduous in their respectful attentions to Miss Penelope Martin's scholars, which amounted to little more than lifting the hat as they passed. There was an old post at the corner of Middle and King Streets into which time had deftly wrought a pigeon-hole, which served us as a post-office; and into this aperture the young gentlemen of the Academy deposited harmless missives addressed to heathen deities of the feminine order. Once upon a time the boys of the public school detected the treasures thus hidden, and with irreverent curiosity sought to identify the designated deities by peering impudently under the school-bonnets that shielded our divinities; but the girls of that day were somewhat dignified, and, being above all giggle, the annoyance did not last long.

With life full-orbed, he stands amid his peers,
The grand Immortals! . . . a fair, mild-eyed king,
Flushing to hear their potent welcomes ring
Round the far circle of those luminous spheres.

Mock not his heavenly cheer with mortal wail.
Unless some human-hearted nightingale,
Pierced by Grief's thorn, shall give such music birth
That he, the new-winged soul, the crowned and shriven,
May lean beyond the effulgent verge of heaven,
To catch his own sweet requiem, borne from earth!

II.

Such marvellous requiem were a pæan too —
(Woe, touched and quivering with triumphant fire); —
For him whose course flashed always high and higher,
Hath passed beyond the strange, mysterious blue:
Ah! yet, we murmur, *can* this loss be true?
Forever silent here, that tender lyre,
Tuned to all gracious themes, all pure desire,
Whose notes dropped sweet as honey, soft as dew?

No tears! you say — since rounded, brave, complete,
The poet's work lies radiant at God's feet.
Nay! nay! . . . our hearts with grief *must* hold their tryst:
How dim grows all about us and above!
Vainly we grope through death's bewildering mist,
To feel once more his clasp of *human* love!

PAUL HAMILTON HAYNE, *in Baldwin's Monthly.*
"COPSE HILL," GEORGIA, March 27, 1882.

VALE ET SALVE.

WHAT greeting reached our poet from the skies,
  Just when the farewells, lowly uttered here,
  Past echo died in spaces fair and clear?
What rumors on his starward progress rise?
What glad salutes the entering guest surprise?
  And who — what sweet-lipped bard, or ancient seer —
  Is first to render him large heaven-cheer,
And break the light to unaccustomed eyes?

Farewell, — and hail!   Oh, doubt not he renews
  The interrupted measure of his song,
The gyves of age undone that weighed him long:
  Shall poets folded in Elysium lose
Their native fire, the theme each here pursues?
  'Tis there the same, but soars more rapt and strong.

Edith M. Thomas, in The Critic.

EARLY POEMS.

THE twelve poems which appear below are reprinted
directly from the United States Literary Gazette,
where they appeared during the years 1824–26. They
were written by Longfellow when he was between the
ages of eighteen and twenty, and were not thought by
him to be worthy of a place among his later poems.
Five others, however, which appeared in the same periodical, he has included in his complete works. Yet
many which he saw fit to reject are characterized by so
quiet and pensive a beauty, that they will be eagerly
perused by all admirers of his poetry.

In 1831 George B. Cheever, in his American Commonplace Book of Poetry, said of these earlier poems: —

"Most of Mr. Longfellow's poetry, indeed, we believe
nearly all that has been published, appeared, during
his college life, in The United-States Literary Gazette.
It displays a very refined taste and a very pure vein of
poetical feeling. It possesses what has been a rare
quality in the American poets, — simplicity of expression, without any attempt to startle the reader, or to produce an effect by far-sought epithets. There is much
sweetness in his imagery and language; and sometimes
he is hardly excelled by any one for the quiet accuracy

exhibited in his pictures of natural objects. His poetry will not easily be forgotten."

The dates of the appearance of the poems are here given : —

Thanksgiving. — 'When first in ancient time, from Jubal's tongue.' Nov. 15, 1824.

Autumnal Nightfall. — 'Round Autumn's mouldering urn.' Dec. 1, 1824.

Italian Scenery. — 'Night rests in beauty on Mont Alto.' Dec. 15, 1824.

The Lunatic Girl. — 'Most beautiful, most gentle!' Jan. 1, 1825.

The Venetian Gondolier. — 'Here rest the weary oar!' Jan. 15, 1825.

Dirge over a Nameless Grave. — 'By yon still river, where the wave.' March 15, 1825.

A Song of Savoy. — 'As the dim twilight shrouds.' March 15, 1825.

The Indian Hunter. — ' When the summer harvest was gathered in.' May 15, 1825.

Jeckoyva. — 'They made the warrior's grave beside.' Aug. 1, 1825.

The Sea Diver. — 'My way is on the bright blue sea.' Aug. 15, 1825.

Musings. — 'I sat by my window one night.' Nov. 15, 1825.

Song. — 'Where, from the eye of day.' April 1, 1826.

THANKSGIVING.

WHEN first in ancient time, from Jubal's tongue
The tuneful anthem filled the morning air,
To sacred hymnings and elysian song
His music-breathing shell the minstrel woke.
Devotion breathed aloud from every chord: —
The voice of praise was heard in every tone,
And prayer, and thanks to Him the eternal one,
To Him, that with bright inspiration touched
The high and gifted lyre of heavenly song,

And warmed the soul with new vitality.
A stirring energy through nature breathed: —
The voice of adoration from her broke,
Swelling aloud in every breeze, and heard
Long in the sullen waterfall, — what time
Soft Spring or hoary Autumn threw on earth
Its bloom or blighting, — when the Summer smiled,
Or Winter o'er the year's sepulchre mourned.
The Deity was there! — a nameless spirit
Moved in the breasts of men to do him homage;
And when the morning smiled, or evening pale
Hung weeping o'er the melancholy urn,
They came beneath the broad o'erarching trees,
And in their tremulous shadow worshipped oft,
Where pale the vine clung round their simple altars,
And gray moss mantling hung.   Above was heard
The melody of winds, breathed out as the green trees
Bowed to their quivering touch in living beauty,
And birds sang forth their cheerful hymns.   Below,
The bright and widely wandering rivulet
Struggled and gushed amongst the tangled roots,
That choked its reedy fountain — and dark rocks
Worn smooth by the constant current.   Even there
The listless wave, that stole with mellow voice
Where reeds grew rank on the rushy-fringed brink,
And the green sedge bent to the wandering wind,
Sang with a cheerful song of sweet tranquillity.
Men felt the heavenly influence — and it stole
Like balm into their hearts, till all was peace;
And even the air they breathed, — the light they saw, —
Became religion, — for the ethereal spirit
That to soft music wakes the chords of feeling,
And mellows every thing to beauty, — moved
With cheering energy within their breasts,
And made all holy there — for all was love.
The morning stars, that sweetly sang together —
The moon, that hung at night in the mid-sky —
Dayspring — and eventide — and all the fair
And beautiful forms of nature, had a voice
Of eloquent worship.   Ocean with its tides
Swelling and deep, where low the infant storm
Hung on his dun, dark cloud, and heavily beat

The pulses of the sea, — sent forth a voice
Of awful adoration to the spirit,
That, wrapt in darkness, moved upon its face.
And when the bow of evening arched the east,
Or, in the moonlight pale, the curling wave
Kissed with a sweet embrace the sea-worn beach,
And soft the song of winds came o'er the waters,
The mingled melody of wind and wave
Touched like a heavenly anthem on the ear;
For it arose a tuneful hymn of worship.
And have *our* hearts grown cold ?   Are there on earth
No pure reflections caught from heavenly light ? —
Have our mute lips no hymn — our souls no song ?—
Let him that in the summer-day of youth
Keeps pure the holy fount of youthful feeling, —
And him that in the nightfall of his years
Lies down in his last sleep, and shuts in peace
His dim pale eyes on life's short wayfaring,
Praise Him that rules the destiny of man.

H. W. L.

Sunday Evening, October, 1824.

AUTUMNAL NIGHTFALL.

Round Autumn's mouldering urn,
Loud mourns the chill and cheerless gale,
When nightfall shades the quiet vale,
    And stars in beauty burn.

'Tis the year's eventide.
The wind, — like one that sighs in pain
O'er joys that ne'er will bloom again,
    Mourns on the far hillside.

And yet my pensive eye
Rests on the faint blue mountain long,
And for the fairy-land of song,
    That lies beyond, I sigh,

The moon unveils her brow;
In the mid-sky her urn glows bright,
And in her sad and mellowing light
    The valley sleeps below.

Upon the hazel gray
The lyre of Autumn hangs unstrung,
And o'er its tremulous chords are flung
    The fringes of decay.

I stand deep musing here,
Beneath the dark and motionless beech,
Whilst wandering winds of nightfall reach
    My melancholy ear.

The air breathes chill and free;
A Spirit, in soft music calls
From Autumn's gray and moss-grown halls,
    And round her wither'd tree.

The hoar and mantled oak,
With moss and twisted ivy brown,
Bends in its lifeless beauty down
    Where weeds the fountain choke.

That fountain's hollow voice
Echoes the sound of precious things; —
Of early feeling's tuneful springs
    Choked with our blighted joys.

Leaves, that the night-wind bears
To earth's cold bosom with a sigh,
Are types of our mortality,
    And of our fading years.

The tree that shades the plain,
Wasting and hoar as time decays,
Spring shall renew with cheerful days, —
    But not my joys again.

ITALIAN SCENERY.

——NIGHT rests in beauty on Mont Alto.
Beneath its shade the beauteous Arno sleeps
In Vallombrosa's bosom, and dark trees
Bend with a calm and quiet shadow down
Upon the beauty of that silent river.
Still in the west, a melancholy smile

Mantles the lips of day, and twilight pale
Moves like a spectre in the dusky sky;
While eve's sweet star on the fast-fading year
Smiles calmly: — Music steals at intervals
Across the water, with a tremulous swell,
From out the upland dingle of tall firs,
And a faint foot-fall sounds, where dim and dark
Hangs the gray willow from the river's brink,
O'ershadowing its current.   Slowly there
The lover's gondola drops down the stream,
Silent, — save when its dipping oar is heard,
Or in its eddy sighs the rippling wave.
Mouldering and moss-grown, through the lapse of years,
In motionless beauty stands the giant oak,
Whilst those, that saw its green and flourishing youth,
Are gone and are forgotten.   Soft the fount,
Whose secret springs the star-light pale discloses,
Gushes in hollow music, and beyond
The broader river sweeps its silent way,
Mingling a silver current with that sea,
Whose waters have no tides, coming nor going.
On noiseless wing along that fair blue sea
The halcyon flits, — and where the wearied storm
Left a loud moaning, all is peace again.

   A calm is on the deep!   The winds that came
O'er the dark sea-surge with a tremulous breathing,
And mourned on the dark cliff where weeds grew rank,
And to the autumnal death-dirge the deep sea
Heaved its long billows, — with a cheerless song
Have pass'd away to the cold earth again,
Like a way-faring mourner.   Silently
Up from the calm sea's dim and distant verge,
Full and unveiled the moon's broad disk emerges.
On Tivoli, and where the fairy hues
Of autumn glow upon Abruzzi's woods,
The silver light is spreading.   Far above,
Encompassed with their thin, cold atmosphere,
The Apennines uplift their snowy brows,
Glowing with colder beauty, where unheard
The eagle screams in the fathomless ether,
And stays his wearied wing.   Here let us pause!
The spirit of these solitudes — the soul

That dwells within these steep and difficult places —
Speaks a mysterious language to mine own,
And brings unutterable musings.   Earth
Sleeps in the shades of nightfall, and the sea
Spreads like a thin blue haze beneath my feet,
Whilst the gray columns and the mouldering tombs
Of the Imperial City, hidden deep
Beneath the mantle of their shadows, rest.
My spirit looks on earth! — A heavenly voice
Comes silently: "Dreamer, is earth thy dwelling? —
Lo! nursed within that fair and fruitful bosom
Which has sustained thy being, and within
The colder breast of Ocean, lie the germs
Of thine own dissolution!   E'en the air,
That fans the clear blue sky and gives thee strength —
Up from the sullen lake of mouldering reeds,
And the wide waste of forest, where the osier
Thrives in the damp and motionless atmosphere, —
Shall bring the dire and wasting pestilence
And blight thy cheek.   Dream thou of higher things; —
This world is not thy home!"   And yet my eye
Rests upon earth again!   How beautiful,
Where wild Velino heaves its sullen waves
Down the high cliff of gray and shapeless granite, —
Hung on the curling mist, the moonlight bow
Arches the perilous river.   A soft light
Silvers the Albanian mountains, and the haze
That rests upon their summits, mellows down
The austerer features of their beauty.   Faint
And dim-discovered glow the Sabine hills,
And listening to the sea's monotonous shell,
High on the cliffs of Terracina stands
The castle of the royal Goth * in ruins.

But night is in her wane: — day's early flush
Glows like a hectic on her fading cheek,
Wasting its beauty.   And the opening dawn
With cheerful lustre lights the royal city,
Where with its proud tiara of dark towers,
It sleeps upon its own romantic bay.

* Theodoric.

THE LUNATIC GIRL.

Most beautiful, most gentle! Yet how lost
To all that gladdens the fair earth; the eye
That watched her being; the maternal care
That kept and nourished her; and the calm light
That steals from our own thoughts, and softly rests
On youth's green valleys and smooth-sliding waters.
Alas! few suns of life, and fewer winds,
Had withered or had wasted the fresh rose
That bloomed upon her cheek; but one chill frost
Came in that early Autumn, when ripe thought
Is rich and beautiful, —and blighted it;
And the fair stalk grew languid day by day,
And drooped, —and drooped, and shed its many leaves.
'Tis said that some have died of love, and some,
That once from beauty's high romance had caught
Love's passionate feelings and heart-wasting cares,
Have spurned life's threshold with a desperate foot:
And others have gone mad, —and she was one! —
Her lover died at sea; and they had felt
A coldness for each other when they parted;
But love returned again, and to her ear
Came tidings, that the ship which bore her lover
Had suddenly gone down at sea, and all were lost.
I saw her in her native vale, when high
The aspiring lark up from the reedy river
Mounted, on cheerful pinion; and she sat
Casting smooth pebbles into a clear fountain,
And marking how they sunk; and oft she sighed
For him that perished thus in the vast deep.
She had a sea-shell, that her lover brought
From the far-distant ocean, and she pressed
Its smooth cold lips unto her ear, and thought
It whispered tidings of the dark blue sea;
And sad, she cried: " The tides are out! —and now
I see his corse upon the stormy beach!"
Around her neck a string of rose-lipped shells,
And coral, and white pearl, was loosely hung,
And close beside her lay a delicate fan,
Made of the halcyon's blue wing; and when
She look'd upon it, it would calm her thoughts

As that bird calms the ocean, — for it gave
Mournful, yet pleasant memory.   Once I marked,
When through the mountain hollows and green woods,
That bent beneath its footsteps, the loud wind
Came with a voice as of the restless deep,
She raised her head, and on her pale cold cheek
A beauty of diviner seeming came:
And then she spread her hands, and smiled, as if
She welcomed a long-absent friend, — and then
Shrunk timorously back again, and wept.
I turned away: a multitude of thoughts,
Mournful and dark, were crowding on my mind;
And as I left that lost and ruined one,
A living monument that still on earth
There is warm love and deep sincerity, —
She gazed upon the west, where the blue sky
Held, like an ocean, in its wide embrace
Those fairy islands of bright cloud, that lay
So calm and quietly in the thin ether.
And then she pointed where, alone and high,
One little cloud sailed onward, like a lost
And wandering bark, and fainter grew, and fainter,
And soon was swallowed up in the blue depths.
And when it sunk away, she turned again
With sad despondency and tears to earth.

  Three long and weary months, — yet not a whisper
Of stern reproach for that cold parting!   Then
She sat no longer by her favorite fountain! —
She was at rest forever.

THE VENETIAN GONDOLIER.

Here rest the weary oar! — soft airs
  Breathe out in the o'erarching sky;
And Night! — sweet Night — serenely wears
  A smile of peace; — her noon is nigh.

Where the tall fir in quiet stands,
  And waves, embracing the chaste shores,
Move o'er sea-shells and bright sands, —
  Is heard the sound of dipping oars.

Swift o'er the wave the light bark springs,
　Love's midnight hour draws lingering near:
And list!—his tuneful viol strings
　The young Venetian Gondolier.

Lo! on the silver-mirrored deep,
　On earth, and her embosomed lakes,
And where the silent rivers sweep,—
　From the thin cloud fair moonlight breaks.

Soft music breathes around, and dies
　On the calm bosom of the sea;
Whilst in her cell the novice sighs
　Her vespers to her rosary.

At their dim altars bow fair forms,
　In tender charity for those,
That, helpless left to life's rude storms,
　Have never found this calm repose.

The bell swings to its midnight chime,
　Relieved against the deep blue sky!
Haste!—dip the oar again!—'tis time
　To seek Genevra's balcony.

DIRGE OVER A NAMELESS GRAVE.

By yon still river, where the wave
　Is winding slow at evening's close,
The beech, upon a nameless grave,
　Its sadly-moving shadow throws.

O'er the fair woods the sun looks down
　Upon the many-twinkling leaves,
And twilight's mellow shades are brown,
　Where darkly the green turf upheaves.

The river glides in silence there,
　And hardly waves the sapling tree:
Sweet flowers are springing, and the air
　Is full of balm,—but where is she!

They bade her wed a son of pride,
  And leave the hopes she cherish'd long:
She loved but one, — and would not hide
  A love which knew no wrong.

And months went sadly on, — and years: —
  And she was wasting day by day:
At length she died, — and many tears
  Were shed, that she should pass away.

Then came a gray old man, and knelt
  With bitter weeping by her tomb: —
And others mourned for him, who felt
  That he had sealed a daughter's doom.

The funeral train has long past on,
  And time wiped dry the father's tear!
Farewell, — lost maiden! — there is one
  That mourns thee yet, — and he is here.

A SONG OF SAVOY.

As the dim twilight shrouds
  The mountain's purple crest,
And summer's white and folded clouds
  Are glowing in the west,
Loud shouts come up the rocky dell,
And voices hail the evening-bell.

Faint is the goatherd's song,
  And sighing comes the breeze:
The silent river sweeps along
  Amid its bending trees, —
And the full moon shines faintly there,
And music fills the evening air.

Beneath the waving firs
  The tinkling cymbals sound ;
And as the wind the foliage stirs,
  I see the dancers bound
Where the green branches, arched above,
Bend over this fair scene of love.

And he is there, that sought
  My young heart long ago!
But he has left me, — though I thought
  He ne'er could leave me so.
Ah! lovers' vows, — how frail are they!
And his — were made but yesterday.

Why comes he not? I call
  In tears upon him yet; —
'Twere better ne'er to love at all,
  Than love, and then forget!
Why comes he not? Alas! I should
Reclaim him still, if weeping could.

But see, — he leaves the glade,
  And beckons me away:
He comes to seek his mountain maid! —
  I cannot chide his stay.
Glad sounds along the valley swell,
And voices hail the evening-bell

THE INDIAN HUNTER.

WHEN the summer harvest was gathered in,
And the sheaf of the gleaner grew white and thin,
And the ploughshare was in its furrow left,
Where the stubble land had been lately cleft,
An Indian hunter, with unstrung bow,
Looked down where the valley lay stretched below.

He was a stranger there, and all that day
Had been out on the hills, a perilous way,
But the foot of the deer was far and fleet,
And the wolf kept aloof from the hunter's feet,
And bitter feelings passed o'er him then,
As he stood by the populous haunts of men.

The winds of autumn came over the woods
As the sun stole out from their solitudes,
The moss was white on the maple's trunk,
And dead from its arms the pale vine shrunk,
And ripened the mellow fruit hung, and red
Were the tree's wither'd leaves round it shed.

The foot of the reaper moved slow on the lawn,
And the sickle cut down the yellow corn, —
The mower sung loud by the meadow-side,
Where the mists of evening were spreading wide,
And the voice of the herdsman came up the lea,
And the dance went round by the greenwood tree.

Then the hunter turned away from that scene,
Where the home of his fathers once had been,
And heard by the distant and measured stroke,
That the woodman hewed down the giant oak,
And burning thoughts flashed over his mind
Of the white man's faith, and love unkind.

The moon of the harvest grew high and bright,
As her golden horn pierced the cloud of white —
A footstep was heard in the rustling brake,
Where the beech overshadowed the misty lake,
And a mourning voice, and a plunge from shore; —
And the hunter was seen on the hills no more.

When years had passed on, by that still lakeside
The fisher looked down through the silver tide,
And there, on the smooth yellow sand displayed,
A skeleton wasted and white was laid,
And 'twas seen, as the waters moved deep and slow,
That the hand was still grasping a hunter's bow.

JECKOYVA.

The Indian chief, Jeckoyva, as tradition says, perished alone on the mountain which now bears his name. Night overtook him whilst hunting among the cliffs and he was not heard of till after a long time, when his half-decayed corpse was found at the foot of a high rock, over which he must have fallen. Mount Jeckoyva is near the White Hills.

THEY made the warrior's grave beside
The dashing of his native tide:
And there was mourning in the glen —
The strong wail of a thousand men —
    O'er him thus fallen in his pride,
Ere mist of age — or blight or blast
Had o'er his mighty spirit past.

They made the warrior's grave beneath
The bending of the wild elm's wreath,
Where the dark hunter's piercing eye
Had found that mountain rest on high,
  Where, scattered by the sharp wind's breath,
Beneath the rugged cliff were thrown
The strong belt and the mouldering bone.

Where was the warrior's foot, when first
The red sun on the mountain burst ? —
Where — when the sultry noon-time came
On the green vales with scorching flame,
  And made the woodlands faint with thirst ?
'Twas where the wind is keen and loud,
And the gray eagle breasts the cloud.

Where was the warrior's foot, when night
Veil'd in thick cloud the mountain-height ?
None heard the loud and sudden crash, —
None saw the fallen warrior dash
  Down the bare rock so high and white! —
But he that drooped not in the chase
Made on the hills his burial-place.

They found him there, when the long day
Of cold desertion passed away,
And traces on that barren cleft
Of struggling hard with death were left —
  Deep marks and foot-prints in the clay!
And they have laid this feathery helm
By the dark river and green elm.

THE SEA-DIVER.

My way is on the bright blue sea,
  My sleep upon its rocking tide;
And many an eye has followed me
  Where billows clasp the worn sea-side.

My plumage bears the crimson blush,
  When ocean by the sun is kissed!
When fades the evening's purple flush,
  My dark wing cleaves the silver mist.

Full many a fathom down beneath
  That bright arch of the splendid deep
My ear has heard the sea-shell breathe
  O'er living myriads in their sleep.

They rested by the coral throne,
  And by the pearly diadem;
Where the pale sea-grape had o'ergrown
  The glorious dwellings made for them.

At night upon my storm-drenched wing,
  I poised above a helmless bark,
And soon I saw the shattered thing
  Had pass'd away and left no mark.

And when the wind and storm were done,
  A ship, that had rode out the gale,
Sunk down — without a signal gun,
  And none was left to tell the tale.

I saw the pomp of day depart, —
  The cloud resign its golden crown,
When to the ocean's beating heart,
  The sailor's wasted corse went down.

Peace be to those whose graves are made
  Beneath the bright and silver sea! —
Peace — that their relics there were laid
  With no vain pride and pageantry.

MUSINGS.

I sat by my window one night,
  And watched how the stars grew high;
And the earth and skies were a splendid sight
  To a sober and musing eye.

From heaven the silver moon shone down
  With gentle and mellow ray,
And beneath the crowded roofs of the town
  In broad light and shadow lay.

A glory was on the silent sea,
  And mainland and island too,
Till a haze came over the lowland lea,
  And shrouded that beautiful blue.

Bright in the moon the autumn wood
  Its crimson scarf unrolled,
And the trees like a splendid army stood
  In a panoply of gold!

I saw them waving their banners high,
  As their crests to the night wind bowed,
And a distant sound on the air went by,
  Like the whispering of a crowd.

Then I watched from my window how fast
  The lights all around me fled,
As the wearied man to his slumber passed
  And the sick one to his bed.

All faded save one, that burned
  With distant and steady light;
But that, too, went out, — and I turned
  Where my own lamp within shone bright!

Thus, thought I, our joys must die,
  Yes — the brightest from earth we win:
Till each turns away, with a sigh,
  To the lamp that burns brightly within.

SONG.

Where, from the eye of day,
  The dark and silent river
Pursues through tangled woods a way
  O'er which the tall trees quiver;

The silver mist, that breaks
  From out that woodland cover,
Betrays the hidden path it takes
  And hangs the current over!

So oft the thoughts that burst
  From hidden springs of feeling,
Like silent streams, unseen at first,
  From our cold hearts are stealing:

But soon the clouds that veil
The eye of Love, when glowing,
Betray the long unwhispered tale
Of thoughts in darkness flowing!

TWO SONNETS FROM THE SPANISH OF FRANCISCO DE MEDRANO.[1]

I.

ART AND NATURE.

THE works of human artifice soon tire
The curious eye; the fountain's sparkling rill,
And gardens, when adorned by human skill,
Reproach the feeble hand, the vain desire.
But, O! the free and wild magnificence
Of Nature, in her lavish hours, doth steal,
In admiration silent and intense,
The soul of him, who hath a soul to feel.
The river moving on its ceaseless way,
The verdant reach of meadows fair and green,
And the blue hills, that bound the sylvan scene,
These speak of grandeur, that defies decay, —
Proclaim the Eternal Architect on high,
Who stamps on all his works his own eternity.

II.

THE TWO HARVESTS.

BUT yesterday these few and hoary sheaves
Waved in the golden harvest; from the plain
I saw the blade shoot upward, and the grain
Put forth the unripe ear and tender leaves.
Then the glad upland smiled upon the view,
And to the air the broad green leaves unrolled,
A peerless emerald in each silken fold,
And on each palm a pearl of morning dew.

---

[1] These Sonnets appeared in Mr. Longfellow's first volume, "Coplas de Don Jorge Manrique, translated from the Spanish, with an introductory essay on the Moral and Devotional Poetry of Spain. By Henry W. Longfellow, Professor of Mod. Lang. and Lit. in Bowdoin College." Boston: Allen & Ticknor, 1833. pp. 85–87. They were accompanied by the Spanish original on the opposite page.

And thus sprang up and ripened in brief space
All that beneath the reaper's sickle died,
All that smiled beauteous in the summer-tide.
    And what are we ? a copy of that race,
The later harvest of a longer year!
And, O! how many fall before the ripened ear!

BIBLIOGRAPHY.

[From The Literary World, Boston, with corrections and additions.]

I.

PUBLISHED WORKS TO DATE.

MANUEL DE PROVERBES DRAMATIQUES. [Portland, Me., S. Colman, 1830.]

[Editor.] MONTGOMERY, Jorge (Washington). Novelas Españolas. El Serrano de las Alpujarras; y El Cuadro misterioso. [Brunswick: Griffin, 1830.]

The Preface states that "Estas novelitas, sacadas de las tareas de un solitario, son imitaciones del Rip Van Winkle y del Joven Italiano . . . del celebre Washington Irving."

ELEMENTS OF FRENCH GRAMMAR. Translated from the French of C. F. L'Homond. [Boston: 1830.]

ORIGIN AND PROGRESS of the French Language. North Am. Rev., xxxii. 277. [April, 1831.]

DEFENCE OF POETRY. North Am. Rev., xxxiv. 56. [January, 1832.]

HISTORY OF THE ITALIAN LANGUAGE AND DIALECTS. North Am. Rev., xxxv. 283. [October, 1832.]

SYLLABUS DE LA GRAMMAIRE ITALIENNE. [Boston: 1832.]

COURS DE LANGUE FRANÇAISE. [Boston: 1832.]

    I. Le Ministre de Wakefield.

    II. Proverbes Dramatiques.

SAGGI DE' NOVELLIERI ITALIANI D'OGNI SECOLO: Tratti da' più celebri Scrittori, con brevi Notizie intorno alla Vita di ciascheduno. [Boston: 1832.]

SPANISH DEVOTIONAL AND MORAL POETRY. North Am. Rev., xxxiv. 277. [April, 1832.]

COPLAS DE MANRIQUE. A translation from the Spanish. [Boston: Allen & Ticknor. 1833.]

Jorge Manrique was a Spanish poet of the fifteenth century. His *Coplas* is a funeral poem on the death of his father, extending to five hundred lines. Mr. Longfellow's volume is prefaced with the above essay on the moral and devotional poetry of Spain, from the North Am. Rev., xxxiv. 277; and included in it are translations of sonnets by Lope de Vega and others.

SPANISH LANGUAGE AND LITERATURE. North Am. Rev., xxxvi. 316. [April, 1833.]

OLD ENGLISH ROMANCES. North Am. Rev., xxxvii. 374. [October, 1833.]

OUTRE-MER; a Pilgrimage beyond the Sea. 2 vols. [New York: Harpers, 1835.]

A series of prose descriptions of foreign travel; a sort of "sketch-book." Reviewed by O. W. B. Peabody in North Am. Rev., xxxix. 459–467; in Am. Month. Rev., iv. 157. Its publication was begun in numbers, by Hilliard, Gray, & Co. [Boston: 1833.]

THE GREAT METROPOLIS. North Am. Rev., xliv. 461. [April, 1837.]

A lively review of a new work on London.

HAWTHORNE'S TWICE-TOLD TALES. North Am. Rev., xlv. 59. [July, 1837.]

TEGNER'S FRITHIOFS SAGA. North Am. Rev., xlv. 149. [July, 1837.]

ANGLO-SAXON LITERATURE. North Am. Rev., xlvii. 90. [July, 1838.]

HYPERION, a Romance. 2 vols. [New York: S. Colman, 1839.]

This was the first of Mr. Longfellow's works written in his Cambridge home, — in the very Washington chamber, indeed, of Craigie House. Reviewed by C. C. Felton in North Am. Rev., li. 145–161; in So. Lit. Mess., v. 839.

VOICES OF THE NIGHT. [Cambridge: John Owen. 1839.]

Mr. Longfellow's first volume of poems, containing the "Psalm of Life," "The Reaper and the Flowers," and six other poems, some of which were originally published in The Knickerbocker Magazine; also seven "Earlier Poems," as follows, all of which were composed before the author was nineteen: "An April Day," "Autumn," "Woods in Winter," "Hymn of the Moravian Nuns at Bethlehem," "Sunrise on the Hills," "The Spirit of Poetry," "The Burial of the Minnisink."

Reviewed in North Am. Rev., l. 266–269; Christ. Ex., xxviii. 242.

THE FRENCH LANGUAGE IN ENGLAND. North Am. Rev., li. 285. [October, 1840.]

BALLADS AND OTHER POEMS. [Cambridge: 1841.]

Including "The Skeleton in Armor," "The Wreck of the Hesperus," "The Village Blacksmith," "God's Acre," "To the River Charles," and "Excelsior." Reviewed by C. C. Felton in North Am. Rev., lv. 114–144; by Poe in his Literati.

POEMS ON SLAVERY. [Cambridge: 1842.]

Composed during a return voyage from Europe, in 1842.

THE SPANISH STUDENT. A play in three acts. [Cambridge: 1843.]

In this dramatic poem may be found the song entitled "Serenade," beginning "Stars of the Summer Night." Reviewed in Lond. Ath., 1844, 8; in Irish Quart. Rev., June, 1855, 202; in Poe's Literati; in Whipple's Essays and Reviews, i., 66.

[Editor.] THE WAIF: a Collection of Poems. [Cambridge: 1844.]
[Editor.] THE POETS AND POETRY OF EUROPE. [Philadelphia: 1845.]

A collection of selections, translated from a large number of European poets, with introductions and biographical and critical sketches. Many of the translations are by Mr. Longfellow. A new edition, revised and enlarged, was published in 1871. Reviewed by Francis Bowen in North Am. Rev., lxi. 199.

THE BELFRY OF BRUGES, and Other Poems. [Cambridge: John Owen. 1845.]

[Editor.] THE ESTRAY: a Collection of Poems. [Boston: 1847.]

EVANGELINE: a Tale of Acadie. [Boston: 1847.]

KAVANAGH: a Tale. Prose. [Boston: 1849.]

THE SEASIDE AND THE FIRESIDE. [Boston: 1849.]

Contains "The Building of the Ship," "Resignation," and twenty-one other poems.

THE GOLDEN LEGEND. [Boston: 1851.]

Reviewed in Blackwood, v. 71; in Eclec., 4th s., xxxi. 455.

THE SONG OF HIAWATHA. [Boston: 1855.]

Reviewed by E. E. Hale in North Am. Rev., lxxxii. 272.

THE COURTSHIP OF MILES STANDISH. [Boston: 1858.]

With "Birds of Passage, Flight the First," twenty-two poems, including "In the Churchyard at Cambridge" and "The Fiftieth Birthday of Agassiz."

Reviewed by Rev. Dr. A. P. Peabody in North Am. Rev., lxxxviii. 275.

TALES OF A WAYSIDE INN. [Boston: 1863.]

"First Day," with "Birds of Passage, Flight the Second," seven poems, including "The Children's Hour" and "The Cumberland."

FLOWER-DE-LUCE. [Boston: 1866.]

Twelve poems.

NEW ENGLAND TRAGEDIES. [Boston: 1868.]

    I. John Endicott.
    II. Giles Corey of the Salem Farms.
       Reviewed by E. J. Cutler in North Am. Rev., cviii. 669.

DANTE'S DIVINE COMEDY. A Translation, with essay and notes. [Boston: 1865-1867.]

Three vols. I. — Inferno. II. — Purgatorio. III. — Paradiso. The same in one vol.

Reviewed by Charles Eliot Norton in North Am. Rev., cv. 125; by George W. Greene in Atlantic M., xx. 188.

THE DIVINE TRAGEDY. [Boston: 1872.]

CHRISTUS: A MYSTERY. [Boston: 1872.]

       Collecting, for the first time, into their consecutive unity:
    I. The Divine Tragedy.
    II. The Golden Legend.
    III. The New England Tragedies.

THREE BOOKS OF SONG. [Boston: 1872.]

Contents: "Tales of a Wayside Inn, Second Day;" "Judas Maccabæus" (a dramatic poem in five acts); and "A Handful of Translations," eleven in number.

AFTERMATH. [Boston: 1874.]

Contents: "Tales of a Wayside Inn, Third Day;" and "Birds of Passage, Flight the Third."

THE MASQUE OF PANDORA, and Other Poems. [Boston: 1875.]

Contents: "The Hanging of the Crane," "Morituri Salutamus," the Bowdoin College poem for the semi-centennial of the author's class of 1825; "Birds of Passage, Flight the Fourth;" and "A Book of Sonnets," fourteen in all. (An operatic version of "The Masque of Pandora" was produced on the Boston stage in January, 1881.)

[Editor.] **POEMS OF PLACES.** 31 vols. [Boston: 1876–1879.]

KÉRAMOS, and Other Poems. [Boston: 1878.]

Contents: A "Fifth Flight" of "Birds of Passage," sixteen in all, among which are the tribute to James Russell Lowell, entitled "The Herons of Elmwood," and "The White Czar;" a second "Book of Sonnets," nineteen of them, including "The Three Silences," the Literary World tribute to Whittier, "The Two Rivers," and "St. John's, Cambridge," and fifteen translations, eight from Michael Angelo.

ULTIMA THULE. [Boston: 1880.]

II.

NOTICES OF MR. LONGFELLOW.

ARNAUD, SIMON. La Légende Dorée. [In Le Correspondant: 10 juillet, 1872.]

COBB, J. B. Miscellanies. [1858.] pp. 330–357.

CURTIS, GEORGE WILLIAM. Atlantic Monthly. xii. 760.

Mr. Curtis's "Easy Chair" in Harper's Monthly contains notices of Mr. Longfellow and his writings, as follows: "The Dante," xxxv. 257; "Reception in England," xxxvii. 561; "New England Tragedies," xxxviii. 271; "The Divine Tragedy," xliv. 616. There is also a general article on Longfellow in i. 74.

COCHIN, AUGUSTIN. La Poésie en Amérique. [In Le Correspondant: 10 juillet, 1872.]

DEPRET, LOUIS. Le Va-et-Vient. [Paris: n. d.]

THE SAME. La Poésie en Amérique. [Lille: 1876.]

DE PRINS, A. Études Américaines. [Louvain: 1877.]

FRISWELL, J. H. Modern Men of Letters. [1870.] pp. 285–299.

GILFILLAN, GEORGE. Literary Portraits. Second Series.

PALMER, RAY. Longfellow and his Works. Int. Rev. [Nov., 1875.]

PECK, G. W. Review of Mr. Longfellow's Evangeline. [New York: 1848.]

P. T. C. Kalevala and Hiawatha. A review. [185-.] pp. 21.

WHIPPLE, E. P. Essays and Reviews. i. 60–63.

NOTE.—In Poole's forthcoming Index to Periodical Literature there will be found a very full set of references to notices and reviews of Longfellow's works.

III.

TRANSLATIONS OF MR. LONGFELLOW'S WORKS.

ENGLISH.

NoËL. [A French poem by Longfellow in Flower-de-Luce.] Tr. by J. E. Norcross. Philadelphia: 1867. Large paper. Fifty copies printed.]

GERMAN.

Englische Gedichte aus Neuerer Zeit. Freiligrath, Ferdinand. . . . H. W. Longfellow . . . [Stuttgardt und Tübingen: 1846.]

Longfellow's Gedichte. Übersetzt von Carl Böttger. [Dessau: 1856.]

Balladen und Lieder von H. W. Longfellow. Deutsch von A. R. Nielo. [Münster: 1857.]

Longfellow's Gedichte. Von Friedrich Marx. [Hamburg and Leipzig: 1868.]

Longfellow's aeltere und neuere Gedichte in Auswald. Deutsch von Adolf Laun. [Oldenburg: 1879.]

Der Spanische Student. Übersetzt von Karl Böttger. [Dessau: 1854.]

The Same. Von Maria Helène Le Maistre. [Dresden: n. d.]

The Same. Übersetzt von Häfeli. [Leipzig: n. d.]

Evangeline. Aus dem Englischen. [Hamburg: 1857.]

The Same. Aus dem Englischen, von P. J. Belke. [Leipzig: 1854.]

The Same. Eine Erzählung aus Acadien. Von Eduard Nickles. [Karlsruhe: 1862.]

The Same. Übersetzt von Frank Siller. [Milwaukee: 1879.]

The Same. Übersetzt von Karl Knortz. [Leipzig: n. d.]

Longfellow's Evangeline. Deutsch von Heinrich Viehoff. [Trier: 1869.]

Die Goldene Legende. Deutsch von Karl Keck. [Wien: 1859.]

The Same. Übersetzt von Elise Freifrau von Hohenhausen. [Leipzig: 1880.]

Das Lied von Hiawatha. Deutsch von Adolph Böttger. [Leipzig: 1856.]

Der Sang von Hiawatha. Übersetzt von Ferdinand Freiligrath. [Stuttgart und Augsburg: 1857.]

Hiawatha. Übertragen von Hermann Simon. [Leipzig: n. d.]

Der Sang von Hiawatha. Übersetzt, eingeleitet und erklärt von Karl Knortz. [Jena: 1872.]

Miles Standish's Brautwerbung. Aus dem Englischen von F. E. Baumgarten. [St. Louis: 1859.]

Die Brautwerbung des Miles Standish. Übersetzt von Karl Knortz. [Leipzig: 18–.]

Miles Standish's Brautwerbung. Übersetzt von F. Manefeld. [1867.]

Die Sage von König Olaf. Übersetzt von Ernst Rauscher.

The Same. Übersetzt von W. Hertzberg.

Dorfschmid. Die Alte Uhr auf der Treppe. Des Schlaven Traum. Tr. by H. Schmick. Archiv. f. d. Stud. d. n. Spr. 1858. xxiv. 214-217.

Gedichte von H. W. L. Deutsch von Alexander Neidhardt. [Darmstadt: 1856.]

Der Bau des Schiffes. Tr. by Th. Zermelo. Archiv. f. d. Stud. d. n. Spr. 1861. xxx. 293-304.

Hyperion. Deutsch von Adolph Böttger. [Leipzig: 1856.]

Ein Psalm des Lebens, etc. Deutsch von Alexander Neidhardt. Archiv. f. d. Stud. d. n. Spr. 1856. xxix. 205-208.

Die Gottliche Tragödie. Übersetzt von Karl Keck. [MS.]

The Same. Übersetzt von Hermann Simon. [MS.]

Pandora. Übersetzt von Isabella Schuchardt. [Hamburg: 1878.]

Morituri Salutamus. Übersetzt von Dr. Ernst Schmidt. [Chicago: 1878.]

Das Kesselhangen. Übersetzt von G. A. Zündt. [n. d.]

The Same. Das Einhängen des Kesselhakens, frei gearbeitet von Joh. Henry Becker. [n. d.]

DUTCH.

Het Lied van Hiawatha. In het Nederdeutsch overgebragt door L. S. P. Meijboom. [Amsterdam: 1862.]

Miles Standish. Nagezongen door S. I. Van den Berg. [Haarlem: 1861.]

SWEDISH.

Hyperion. På Svenska, af Grönlund. [1853.]

Evangeline. På Svenska, af Alb. Lysander. [1854.]

The Same. Öfversatt af Hjalmar Erdgren. [Göteborg: 1875.]

The Same. Öfversatt af Philip Svenson. [Chicago: 1875.]

Hiawatha. På Svenska af Westberg. [1856.]

DANISH.

Evangeline. Paa Norsk ved Sd. C. Knutsen. [Christiania: 1874.]

BIBLIOGRAPHY.

SANGEN OM HIAWATHA. Oversat af G. Bern. [Kjöbenhavn: 1860.]

FRENCH.

EVANGELINE; suivie des Voix de la Nuit. Par le Chevalier de Chatelain. [Jersey, London, Paris, New York: 1856.]

THE SAME. Conte d'Acadie. Traduit par Charles Brunel. Prose. [Paris: 1864.]

THE SAME. Par Léon Pamphile Le May. [Quebec: 1865.]

LA LEGENDE DORÉE, et Poëmes sur l'Esclavage. Traduits par Paul Blier et Edward MacDonnel. Prose. [Paris et Valenciennes: 1854.]

HIAWATHA. Traduit de l'Anglais par M. H. Gomont. [Nancy, Paris: 1860.]

DRAMES ET POÉSIES. Traduits par X. Marmier. The New England Tragedies. [Paris: 1872.]

HYPERION ET KAVANAGH. Traduit de l'Anglais, et précedé d'une Notice sur l'Auteur. 2 vols. [Paris et Bruxelles: 1860.]

THE PSALM OF LIFE, AND OTHER POEMS. Tr. by Lucien de la Rive in his Essais de Traduction Poétique. [Paris: 1870.]

ITALIAN.

ALCUNE POESIE DI ENRICO W. LONGFELLOW. Traduzione dall' Inglese di Angelo Messedaglia. [Padova: 1866.]

LO STUDENTE SPAGNUOLO. Prima Versione Metrica di Messandro Bazzini. [Milano: 1871.]

THE SAME. Traduzione di Nazzareno Trovanelli. [Firenze: 1876.]

POESIE SULLA SCHIAVITÙ. Tr. in Versi Italiani da Louisa Grace Bartolini. [Firenze: 1860.]

EVANGELINA. Tradotta da Pietro Rotondi. [Firenze: 1857.]

THE SAME. Traduzione di Carlo Faccioli. [Verona: 1873.]

LA LEGGENDA D' ORO. Tradotta da Ada Corbellini Martini. [Parma: 1867.]

IL CANTO D' HIAWATHA. Tr. da L. G. Bartolini. Frammenti. [Firenze: 1867.]

MILES STANDISH. Traduzione dall' Inglese di Caterino Frattini. [Padova: 1868.]

PORTUGUESE.

EL REI ROBERTO DE SICILIA. Tr. by Dom Pedro II., Emperor of Brazil. [Autograph MS.]

EVANGELINA. Traducida por Franklin Doria. [Rio de Janeiro: 1874.]

The Same. Poema de Henrique Longfellow. Traducido por Miguel
Street de Arriaga. |Lisbon: n. d.|
The Same. By Flavio Reimar, in the Aurora Brasileira, 1874; and
by José de Goes Filho, in the Municipio, 1874.

SPANISH.

Evangelina. Romance de la Acadia. Traducido del Ingles por
Carlos Mórla Vicuña. |Nueva York: 1871.|

POLISH.

Zlota Legenda. The Golden Legend. Tr. into Polish by F.
Jerzierski. |Warszawa: 1857.|
Evangelina. Tr. into Polish by F. Jerzierski. |Warszawa: 1857.|
Duma o Hiawacie. The Song of Hiawatha. Tr. into Polish by
Feliksa Jerzierskiego. |Warszawa: 1860.|

RUSSIAN AND OTHER LANGUAGES.

Excelsior, and Other Poems, in Russian. |St. Petersburg: n. d.|
Hiawatha, rendered into Latin, with abridgment. By Francis
William Newman. |London: 1862.|
Excelsior. Tr. into Hebrew by Henry Gersoni. |n. d.|
A Psalm of Life. In Marathi. By Mrs. H. I. Bruce. ·|Satara:
1878.|
The Same. In Chinese. By Jung Tagen. |Written on a fan.|
The Same. In Sanscrit. By Elihu Burritt and his pupils.

IV.

MISCELLANEOUS.

The sales of Longfellow's works up to 1857 are thus given by
Alliboue in his Dictionary of Authors: —

TITLE.	DATE OF PUBLICATION.	COPIES.
Voices of the Night	1839	43,000
Ballads and other Poems	1841	40,000
The Spanish Student	1843	38,000
The Belfry of Bruges	1846	38,000
Evangeline	1847	37,000
The Seaside and the Fireside	1850	30,000
The Golden Legend	1851	17,000
Hiawatha	1855	50,000
Outre-Mer	1835	7,500
Hyperion	1839	14,550
Kavanagh	1849	10,500
Total		325,550

Of Longfellow's collected works, in four of the leading editions, there were printed up to February, 1881, as follows: —

EDITION.	DATE OF PUBLICATION.	COPIES.
"Diamond"	1867	110,000
"Red Line"	1869	20,500
"Household"	1873	57,500
"Library"	1876	6,000
Total		194,000

"Longfellow Leaflets" is the title of a collection of short poems and prose passages from the poet's writings, selected for school use. [Boston: Houghton, Mifflin, & Co., 1881.]

The first work in the series entitled "American Classics for Schools" is a selection of Longfellow's poems, edited by Horace E. Scudder. [Boston: Houghton, Mifflin, & Co., 1882.]

A very pretty "Longfellow Birthday Book" was compiled by Miss Charlotte Fiske Bates, and published by Houghton, Mifflin, & Co., in 1881. It is described on p. 126 of this volume.

A volume of selections from the prose and poetry of Longfellow has also been edited by Miss Bates. It is entitled "Seven Voices of Sympathy," and is published by the firm mentioned above.

After the publication of "Ultima Thule," Mr. Longfellow published in The New York Independent a poem on Garfield; and in The Century for February, 1882, "Hermes Trismegistus." A posthumous poem entitled "Mad River" was published in The Atlantic Monthly for May, 1882. It is probable that the "Mad River" was not the last written poem; but it is the last one which has as yet been published.

At the close of 1880 Houghton, Mifflin, & Co. published in two quarto volumes a superb *edition de luxe* of the complete poetical works of Henry Wadsworth Longfellow. It contains about six hundred illustrations on wood, and a steel portrait engraved by Marshall. Among the artists who helped to make the work are F. O. C. Darley, George H. Boughton, F. S. Church, Mary Hallock Foote, John La Farge, and others. Few poets have ever been so lavishly illustrated. One feature of the work is the faithfulness of the pictures to actual local scenery. For instance, the designs illustrating Evangeline represent actual scenes in Grand Pré and other localities mentioned in the poem, and the costumes are those of Acadie one hundred and fifty years ago. The numerous half-titles and the vignette head-pieces and tail-pieces are of most delicate and intricate workmanship. The books are printed on thick, toned paper, made, like the type itself, especially for this edition. It is known that these superb volumes gave great pleasure to the poet. Had their contents no literary merit, they would command high praise as works of fine art; for almost all of the six hundred engravings are gems executed in every detail with the utmost skill: and, combined as they are with the purest poetic productions of the English language, the volumes become unsurpassed representatives of American literature and of the typographical and artistic skill of the nineteenth century.

In 1845 Huntington of Philadelphia published a costly illustrated edition of Longfellow's Poems.

In 1846 the Harpers of New York published a collection of Longfellow's Poems in cheap form.

Bogue of London published elegant editions of Evangeline, the Poems, The Golden Legend, and Hyperion. To prepare original designs for these London books, the artist, Birket Foster, made a special tour on the Continent. Cassell, Petter, Galpin, & Co., of London, have also published an *edition de luxe* of Evangeline, concerning which Mr. Longfellow wrote: "It is a very handsome book, and the paper and print remind me of the publications of Bodoni, the famous printer of Parma, who gloried in his art. The illustrations by Mr. Dicksee are very beautiful; particularly the face of Evangeline, so characteristic and expressive, pleases and touches me. I beg you to convey to him my thanks and my congratulations on his successful work."

In 1882 the John W. Lovell Co., of New York, taking advantage of the expiration of the copyright of the original edition of Outre-Mer and Hyperion, issued both these works in pamphlet form at twenty cents each. Immediately Houghton, Mifflin, & Co., of Boston, Longfellow's own publishers, issued the same works in equally attractive form at fifteen cents each, at the same time announcing the Lovell edition as an infringement of copyright; Mr. Lovell, it being said, having used a revised recopyrighted edition instead of the original, in making his reprint. Whatever may be the result to the publishers, the sale of the two books received a great impetus, and many thousand copies were sold in a few weeks.

INDEX.